"You were ashamed of me, Leigh,"

Wade said, his words clipped and filled with anger.

"It was never that," Leigh told him, and the tears spilled down her cheeks. "I was never ashamed of you. I was a scared, foolish teenager—I was so confused—"

"So confused that you were ready to let the man you supposedly loved take the blame for a crime he didn't commit?" Wade was determined to ignore her tears. He was the one who'd been wronged, not her.

"I know you won't believe this, either, Wade, but if the police chief had arrested you, I wouldn't have let you go to jail. I would have told him everything about that night. But he never arrested you—"

"Didn't you ever wonder *why* I wasn't arrested, Leigh? You'll feel even guiltier when you find out the answer."

Wade Conner's Revenge

JULIA QUINN

First published in Great Britain in 1995
by Silhouette Books, Eton House, 18-24 Paradise Road,
Richmond, Surrey TW9 1SR

© Darlene Hrobak Gardner 1992

Silhouette, Silhouette Sensation and Colophon are
Trade Marks of Harlequin Enterprises B.V.

ISBN 0 373 59608 1

18-9504

Made and printed in Great Britain

For my mother, who has always believed in me.

Chapter 1

A warm breeze swept over the small crowd of mourners gathered at Ena Conner's grave site and sent a chill through her only child. He raised his sorrow-filled eyes to the preacher at the head of the open grave and tried to focus on the holy man's words as his mother's coffin was lowered into the earth.

Somewhere in the background, a bird sang a happy tune and Wade absently noticed that the grass in the graveyard was lush and green from the spring rainstorms. Why was it that signs of life always surrounded the dead? The preacher's voice droned and then dimmed as Wade tried and failed to turn his thoughts from the hopelessness of the past to the reality of the present.

Ena Conner hadn't wanted her son to stay away from Kinley for twelve years, but the thought of coming back to South Carolina and facing the ugly suspicion again had kept Wade rooted in Manhattan. He mailed his mother a round-trip ticket to New York at least twice a year, but she only used it half the time. There must have been some sort of message in that, Wade thought sadly. He hadn't harbored any love for Kinley in years, but he regretted that Ena wasn't there to see her prodigal son return and that the only thing that had brought him back to town was her death.

Wade lifted the ends of his jet-black hair from the collar of his elegant navy blue suit and was surprised to find that his neck was damp with sweat. He raised his eyes briefly and saw that the sun shone brightly in a cloudless sky, a sign that signaled the stifling Carolina heat. He'd barely been aware of the warm sun until that moment. All he'd felt since arriving at the grave site was a numbing cold.

The preacher concluded his prayer and gently closed the Bible in his hands, prompting Wade into action. Anyone who looked at him would have seen a handsome man in his early thirties whose dark looks hinted at a touch of Indian blood. He had high, arching cheekbones, olive skin and a tall, proud carriage. Wade bent over the grave and lightly tossed a single long-stemmed yellow rose into the gaping hole, watching it flutter and then settle on his Texas-born mother's coffin. The yellow rose of Texas had always been her favorite flower.

Tears welled in Wade's eyes, and one of them trickled a salty stream down his cheek until it dropped from his face and followed the path of the yellow rose. Wade blinked determinedly, and the rest of the tears were gone as if they had never been. Ena Conner had been a tough, proud woman who had borne a child out of wedlock, raised him single-handedly and imparted her strength to him. Only her heart, which simply gave out three days before, had been weak. Wade didn't think his mother would want him to cry at her grave.

He turned from the burial site and silently accepted the condolences of the small group of townspeople who had come to the ceremony. For the hundredth time, he wondered why his mother hadn't left Kinley when he had. Although Ena wasn't ostracized as he had been, the people with long family ties to Kinley had never truly accepted her. She had taught their children at Kinley's high school and cared about their problems, but still they looked down their long noses at her because she hadn't been born one of them. There couldn't have been more than fifteen or twenty people at her burial; if one of their own had died, everyone in town would have shown up.

Wade swallowed his bitterness and started the long, lonely walk toward his rental car. He couldn't bear to turn back and see his mother's coffin covered with dirt. Now that Ena was dead, he'd probably always feel alone in Kinley. Although the people seemed to accept him for the moment, he sensed that they hadn't forgiven him the sins, real and imagined, of his past. He sure as hell hadn't forgiven them.

The sun's reflection off a woman's long, silken strands of hair caught Wade's attention, and he closed his eyes against another kind of torment. The yellow glow turned the dark hair golden brown and brought back twelve-year-old memories Wade wasn't ready to relive. He knew exactly how it felt to weave his fingers through the silky tangle of waist-length hair while gazing into eyes that were an unusual shade of blue-violet.

Those eyes, twelve years older but no less arresting, turned toward him now and filled with something he thought must be compassion. Wade stopped in his tracks and watched with a mixture of fascination and wariness as the woman with the violet eyes walked from his past into his present.

Her figure, although still slim, had lost its coltish look and had developed more womanly curves. She walked as though she was used to being stared at, and he supposed she was. Leigh Hampton didn't possess the obvious type of beauty that graced the pages of fashion magazines, but as a younger man, Wade had been instantly drawn to her subtle good looks. He would have been drawn to her now if he hadn't known that in her petite, perfect body beat a treacherous heart.

She had a small, straight nose and wide-set eyes, but the feature that commanded the most attention was her mouth. It was a hair too large for the rest of her face, and it had always reminded Wade of a luscious strawberry. Of all the things about her, he had liked her mouth best, especially when it smiled at him.

She wasn't smiling now, and he wondered what she would say. Some of her last words to him, spoken hastily in the darkness in front of her home twelve years ago and sealed with a kiss, had been that she would see him soon. It was a lie made uglier by all that had happened in the ensuing days.

He'd known that the bastard son of a Kinley newcomer wasn't supposed to keep company with the daughter of one of the community's established families, but he'd expected more from her than silence. He wondered if she looked at him now and saw the outcast he had been or the successful novelist he had become. But of course her opinion no longer mattered, just as years ago she had made it clear that he no longer mattered.

Leigh stopped a few feet short of him and tilted her head back slightly to meet his gaze. He'd forgotten how small she was. Wade was six feet tall, and the top of her head barely reached his chin. She was tougher than she looked, he remembered wryly, and felt a stab in the region of his heart.

He didn't want to feel anything when he looked at her, but his emotions were already raw, and she reminded him of a time in his life when he believed in love and happily ever after. He wasn't sure if the pain that seemed to be gripping his heart was due to his mother's death or to Leigh's reappearance in his life, but his expression revealed nothing. She had crushed his dreams as surely as a smoker crushes his cigarette with the heel of his foot, and Wade had lived with so much hurt, that concealing his emotions had become as much a part of him as his skin.

"Hello, Wade," she said in a voice so soft she could have been whispering.

"Hello, Leigh." Her name felt strange as it rolled off his tongue, and he knew it was because he hadn't spoken it even once in all those years they'd been apart. At first, it would have hurt too much. Later, after he had time to reflect on what she had done, he had preferred not to waste his time mooning over a woman he had every right to hate.

The other mourners had already reached their cars and were driving off, leaving them standing alone at the edge of the cemetery. Wade wondered why he hadn't noticed her at the grave or earlier at the church service and then reasoned that his mind had been on other things. Or maybe he had shut her out just as he had shut out the memories of what she had been to him.

"I'm sorry about Ena," she said in the same quiet voice, and he imagined he heard something that could have been fear. Was it possible that she could actually be afraid of him? The thought was oddly pleasing; he wanted her to suffer for what she had put him through.

"Me, too," he said tonelessly, watching her closely and schooling his expression to remain neutral. Her hair was still long and straight, but she had feathered her bangs and they fell in wispy strands on her forehead. If anything, he admitted grudgingly, she looked even better than she had at seventeen.

Leigh shifted uncomfortably under his gaze and raised the silken mass of hair from her neck, letting the breeze touch her exposed skin and reminding Wade of the sensitive spot she had just below her hairline. She pressed her lips together in the way Wade remembered signified that she was nervous. Beads of sweat had formed on her forehead, and there was a thin veil of perspiration above her lip.

She looked away from him and out toward Ena's grave. When her eyes returned to his face, they were sad. "When I said I was sorry, I meant it as much for me as for you. Ena and I were friends, did you know that? No, of course you didn't. I guess I just wanted you to know you weren't the only one who loved her."

He wanted to ask how she could love the mother of a man she had tossed aside like spare change, but he didn't. This wasn't the time or the place to bring up their relationship, especially when it had died long before Ena.

"She always told me that she didn't want any long faces at her funeral. She said she lived a good life, so someone should play some loud Texas music when she died," Wade said after a moment, his eyes still fixed on her face. "Somehow, I don't feel much like dancing to Cotton-eyed Joe."

Leigh nodded and tried to smile, but she didn't even come close. She reached across the chasm that separated them and squeezed his hand, a gesture so sudden, it had to be born of impulse. Wade let his hand lie limp at his side, neither responding to her overture nor withdrawing from it.

"I'm sorry it had to be this way, Wade," she said earnestly and broke off the momentary contact. Wade couldn't help but wonder if she were talking about his mother or their meeting.

She turned from him without another word, as though there were nothing more to say. Wade stood and watched her go, and the sense of loss he'd felt since he arrived in Kinley seemed more profound.

Leigh picked up a box filled with jars of pickles and lugged it to the front of her family's general store, stopping every few feet to catch her breath. By the time she had unloaded the jars and placed them onto the shelf, her breaths were coming in short, shallow gasps. She stood up and wiped at her jeans, which were dusty from rubbing against the box. Leigh ran a hand over her damp forehead, unwittingly leaving a smudge, and looked down at her dirty attire. She was twenty-nine and doubted she'd ever have a job that would require her to wear anything more businesslike than jeans and a T-shirt. The thought made her frown.

The bells on the front door jingled, letting her know that someone had just walked into the store. She peered around the counter to greet her customer and was met with a rumble of good-natured laughter. Drew Hampton, her younger brother by two years, sauntered over to her and playfully tweaked her chin.

"What's funny, Drew?" Leigh asked testily. Her brother's dark eyes sparkled with mirth. He reached into the back pocket of his jeans and withdrew a handkerchief. While he steadied her chin with one hand, he dabbed at the smear of dirt with his handkerchief.

"You, Leigh," he said, laughing. "I can hardly believe you're older than me. With your hair tied back in a ponytail like that and dirt all over your face, you look about seventeen years old."

Seventeen. That's how old she'd been when she made the mistake of thinking she could handle Wade Conner. She'd been a naive fool to think that a young, silly girl could keep a man's passion at bay, and she had paid dearly for that error.

"Hey, why the frown, Leigh?" Drew still held her chin, and she lifted her eyes to his. He was ridiculously tall compared to her, towering at least a foot above her five foot three. Otherwise, he looked like the male version of herself. Brown hair, wide-set eyes, straight nose, too-full mouth.

Leigh deliberately thrust her ill humor aside and gave her brother a quick hug. She and Drew worked in the family store together, and there wasn't a face she'd rather see first thing in the morning. Still, she wasn't going to miss an opportunity to narrow the thick streak of irresponsibility that ran through him. She lifted her wrist and pointed to her watch.

"Maybe I'm frowning because you're late, Drew. You were the one who was supposed to open the store this morning. It's a good thing I got here early." Drew winced, and Leigh felt a little guilty for having scolded him. She wasn't really mad, because she never expected Drew to show up on time. He was lovable, but he certainly wasn't punctual.

"Sorry, Leigh." He took a quick look around the store and saw that the neat rows of groceries and drugstore supplies seemed to be in order. Leigh had inherited the store's operation after their father died ten years ago, and she had done wonders with it. With the elder Drew Hampton in charge, the place had been such a hodgepodge that their customers couldn't find anything without help. "You didn't need me for anything, did you?"

"Just to carry the box of pickles I had to lug from the supply room," Leigh answered, but she couldn't sound angry when she wasn't.

She wore sneakers, so she didn't make a sound as she moved across the wooden floor to the old-fashioned cash register behind the front desk. It was black and unwieldy, but Leigh resisted replacing it with a modern machine because preservation was a way of life in Kinley. The older things were, the more valuable they seemed to be to town residents. A pot of coffee was brewing alongside the cash register, and Leigh poured Drew a cup before filling one for herself.

"So where were you last night?" Leigh asked as she handed her brother the mug.

He nodded his thanks. "Where else? I was at the bar." Drew put emphasis on the word *the,* because Kinley had only one bar. He liked to say a solitary night spot was one of the drawbacks of living in a small town that was miles away from a city of any real size. About forty miles to the south was Charleston, a growing city that still retained a beautifully preserved downtown historic district and made visitors feel as though they had stepped back in time. Georgetown, a less prosperous city tainted by the acrid smell of its paper mill, was twenty miles to the north.

"I knew it," Leigh said and started to laugh, but her brother's next words effectively silenced her.

"Wade Conner was there, too." He watched her, waiting for a reaction. Leigh swallowed and tried to keep the rising panic out of her voice.

"Oh, I thought he'd be gone by now. Ena's funeral was four days ago," she said evenly.

"I may be wrong, but I got the impression he wasn't going anywhere real soon. He was askin' about you, Leigh." Drew sounded worried. Her brother didn't know the whole story of what transpired between her and Wade all those years ago, but he knew she'd been hurt by it.

Leigh opened the cash register and took out a roll of quarters. She rapped it sharply against the hard edge of the desk until the paper tore, and then she emptied the coins into the cash register.

"It's been a long time since he's been home, Drew. I guess he's just curious about what's been happening with all of us," she said flatly.

"I didn't say that, Leigh. I said he was curious about you," Drew said slowly. "He wanted to know where you worked, where you lived, whether you'd been married—the works."

"And you told him?" Leigh asked sharply. Too sharply.

Drew shook his head and frowned. "Not me. Wade Conner's too smooth to question me about you. He was askin' the other guys."

Leigh bit her lip, and drew her eyebrows together. Once upon a time, Wade would have gone straight to the source for information about her. He had been her friend, her confidant, her lover. But then the fairy tale ended, and the nightmare began.

"I was sittin' at the bar talking to Everett Kelly, and I could tell he was getting steamed at Conner for askin' all those questions," Drew continued. "You know, I don't think you've ever gotten through to Everett, Leigh. I think Everett fancies you as his girl."

She raised her eyes skyward in exasperation, because Everett viewed their relationship with blindness. She had known him since childhood and was fond of him, but any romance was strictly in his imagination.

"But it's not Everett I'm worried about, Leigh. It's Conner." Drew stared at her intently, and she couldn't remember when she had seen him more serious.

"Lighten up, Drew," she said, trying to keep the hurt out of her voice. But the way Wade had treated her at the grave site had hurt. "I saw Wade at Ena's funeral, and he looked right through me as though I didn't exist. I hardly believe he's thinking about rekindling a romance.''

Drew drained his coffee with a large swig and set the cup down on the counter. He looked as if he was about to say something more, but he thought better of it and lifted a corner of his mouth in a half smile. "I'm tryin' to believe you, sis. Well, I guess I'd better get to work. It seems to me I promised to clean out the supply room.''

Drew groaned dramatically and headed for the back of the store, walking so solemnly, he could have been headed for the electric chair. Leigh laughed at his antics, but her amusement was short-lived. As soon as Drew was out of sight, Leigh sank into the chair behind the counter. She tapped her foot and bit her thumb, trying to make sense of Wade Conner's prolonged visit to Kinley.

He should be long gone by now, she reasoned. Now that Ena was buried, there was no need for him to stay. He'd already had time to put his mother's house up for sale. He could deal with everything else by telephone from New York. It wasn't as though he'd want to stay in Kinley longer than necessary. The town held ghosts for him she didn't think would ever be exorcised. So why was he still here?

Leigh shut her eyes and saw him as he was at the graveyard, a stranger who barely reminded her of the youth he'd been a dozen years ago. At twenty, Wade had been reckless and non-conformist. He was the only boy in town with a motorcycle, the only one who dropped out of high school to hitchhike across the country, the only one who said exactly what was on his mind. He was also the only boy who had the power to make Leigh's breath catch in her throat and her heart feel as though it had stopped beating.

He'd looked different at the cemetery, more mature. The years added character to his face and robbed it of the quality she'd liked the best: his quick, open smile. If he hadn't been so cheery and blithe, Leigh would never have gotten involved with him. Her body's instinctive, intense reaction to his would have frightened her far, far away. Instead, she'd been drawn to him because he was so darn likable.

Wade still had jet-black hair, worn slightly too long for to-day's standards, and the olive complexion that hinted at In-

dian heritage. But his slate-gray eyes were no longer filled with
trust when he looked at her, and she couldn't really blame him
for that. She didn't trust him, either. Leigh wished fervently
that he hadn't come back, but it was hopeless. She'd always
known that he'd return to town someday. Ena Conner's death
had only hastened the inevitable.

"Oh, Ena," she said softly. "Why did you have to die?"

The small bell on the front door sounded once more, and
Leigh scrambled to her feet, the beginnings of a smile on her
face. She liked to greet her customers by name, not only because it was good for business but also because she knew everybody in town.

The smile froze when Wade Conner walked into her store,
and she had the unshakable feeling that her life wouldn't return to normal until he left town. He looked less formal than
he had at the cemetery. A pair of running shorts and a T-shirt
inadequately covered the lines of his physique, and she could
see that his body had filled out since she'd known him. He had
grown from a good-looking boy into a handsome man, and he
was more muscular and more threatening looking. Leigh's
heart thudded so loudly against her chest that she wouldn't
have been surprised if he heard it.

The wind had mussed his dark hair, and stray locks of it fell
across his forehead. He was unsmiling, and it occurred to Leigh
that she hadn't seen him smile in twelve years. Wade closed the
gap until all that separated them was the front counter, a hundred unspoken questions and all those years.

"Hello, Wade," Leigh said to break the silence, aware that
she'd been staring. She'd imagined him coming through her
door a dozen times since the funeral, but she wasn't prepared
for the bolt of pure panic that shot through her when he did.

"Leigh." He nodded in greeting, but continued to stare at
her. Stop it, she wanted to scream. Where is the old Wade
Conner? The one who always had mirth in his eyes and a smile
on his lips? Even his voice had changed. Once, he'd had a slight
Southern drawl like her own, but all traces of the South seemed
to have been wiped out of his life. Instead of voicing her
thoughts, she shifted nervously behind the counter and indicated the store.

"Um, can I help you find something? I'm sure the store looks a lot different than it used to. When I took over after Daddy died, I went to this seminar about how to arrange things so customers would be able to find them easily and I—" Leigh stopped abruptly when she realized she was babbling. "What can I help you find?"

"I didn't come in here to buy anything." Wade spied the coffeepot behind her and nodded in its direction. "Is coffee still on the house at Hampton's General Store?"

She nodded, turned to retrieve a plastic cup and filled it with coffee. What had he meant when he said he didn't come into the store to buy anything? Why did she wish he'd go away without telling her? She handed him the cup and willed herself not to snatch her hand away when his warm fingers brushed hers.

He took a sip of the coffee and surveyed the store, taking in the neat aisles and the logical way in which the goods were arranged. "It looks more businesslike than when Mayor Hampton ran the place," he said reflectively. "Have you made it profitable, too?"

Coming from anyone else, the question would have seemed innocent. It was common knowledge that Drew Hampton III was such a hopeless businessman, the store was on the brink of bankruptcy when Leigh was saddled with it. Her father had extended too much credit, purchased too many different kinds of goods and kept too poorly abreast of what sold and what didn't. He was much too busy acting as the town's opinionated, involved mayor to make a go of the store.

Leigh had pinpointed the problems immediately and had gone to work whipping the store into shape. Within a few years, she was turning a profit. Leigh didn't want to let Wade know the extent of her father's incompetence, because he would have enjoyed hearing about it. After all, her father had once threatened to harm Wade if he touched his daughter again.

"We do okay," Leigh said. She took a deep breath. "If you're not here to buy anything, why are you here?"

Wade laughed shortly, but the sound held no mirth. "That's not a very neighborly thing to ask." His eyes were on her again, making Leigh feel helpless and trapped.

"We haven't been neighbors for a very long time," Leigh said, pursing her lips together.

One of the corners of Wade's mouth lifted, but the result still didn't equal a smile. He took another swig of coffee, watching her over the top of the plastic cup. "You're right, but I do have a neighborly proposition to make."

Leigh was silent, waiting for him to continue and trying not to dwell on his choice of words. The last time he had propositioned her, she had cast away all vestiges of modesty and given herself to him on the grass beneath the magnolia trees. If she wanted to keep her sanity, she couldn't think about that.

"Will you have dinner with me tonight?" The question was so unexpected and so ludicrous that Leigh's mouth actually dropped open. Her brain wouldn't accept the words, so she half convinced herself she hadn't heard him correctly.

"What?"

"I just asked you to have dinner with me. Surely you've done it before. You know the routine. Food. Plates. Utensils." The words were teasing, but his voice was not. He sounded miffed, but surely that wasn't possible. Wade Conner couldn't want to have dinner with her any more than she wanted to have dinner with him.

"You actually want to have dinner with me?" Leigh knew her comments bordered on rudeness, but she couldn't help it.

"Yes." The word was clipped, and she had the impression that he would withdraw the invitation at any moment. There were only two restaurants in town, and Leigh couldn't picture her and Wade dining at either one. She knew both of the proprietors and envisioned them watching her squirm uncomfortably as she tried to relax in Wade's company.

"I don't know whether going out to dinner would be such a good idea," Leigh said finally. "There are only a couple of places in town and—"

"I didn't mean out to dinner," he interrupted, and he still sounded sore. "I can cook, you know. I'm asking you to come over to my mother's house—I mean, my house."

Leigh gulped and thought that his invitation sounded worse by the moment. He couldn't actually expect her to deliberately plan to be alone with him. There was too much between them, too many memories that left a bad aftertaste, too much guilt.

"Why would you want to have dinner with me?" Leigh asked when she found her voice.

Wade shook his head and looked at the floor. When he spoke, she had the funny feeling he was trying to control his temper. "I was going through my mother's belongings, and I found a letter addressed to me. It's the closest she came to writing a will, and your name was in it. She wants you to have some of her things, and I thought tonight would be a good time to give them to you. But if you don't—"

"Of course I do," Leigh interrupted while a wave of embarrassment washed over her. Had she actually thought, even for a minute, that he'd asked her to dinner because of some renewed passion? "But you don't have to fix me dinner. I'll just come over after work, and you can show me what she wanted."

"I have to eat," he said stoically. "It won't be any trouble to make enough for two. How does seven o'clock sound?"

"Hey, Leigh. How 'bout showing me where you keep the broom. That place sure is dusty." Two heads snapped around at the interruption, and Drew Hampton emerged from one of the store's long aisles. If he were surprised to see Wade, he hid it well.

"How's it goin', Wade?" Drew asked with a semblance of a smile.

"Hello, Drew. Don't let me keep you from anything. I was just on my way out. I'll see you at seven then, Leigh." He gave her a measured look that dared her to dispute him, but she merely nodded.

"Seven," she said weakly. Wade finished his coffee and set the disposable cup on the counter.

"Thanks for the coffee," he said and then he was gone.

Brother and sister stared after him.

"What was that all about, Leigh? What did he mean he'd see you at seven?" Drew asked sharply after the door closed behind Wade.

"He asked me to come over to his house for dinner."

"And you said yes?" Drew asked incredulously.

"Well, not really. But he didn't give me a chance to say no," Leigh said defensively. "Ena willed me some of her belongings, and he wants to give them to me."

Drew's eyes narrowed, as though he suspected Wade's reason for asking her to dinner was a ruse. "I'll come with you, Leigh. I don't think it's a good idea for you to be alone with him. He could be dangerous."

"Don't be silly, Drew." She vetoed his suggestion impatiently, because her brother obviously believed some of the nasty rumors that had plagued Wade and caused him to leave Kinley. She, too, thought Wade was dangerous, but not in the same way that Drew believed. "Wade and I used to be friends. I'm not afraid to have dinner with him."

"I don't like this one bit, Leigh," Drew said, running a hand through his hair and shaking his head. "You shouldn't be having dinner with an accused criminal."

Wade picked up his pace and weaved through the streets of downtown Kinley, his running shoes making the slightest of sounds as they hit the pavement. There was little activity on the street and no traffic, a welcome change from the bustling Manhattan neighborhood where he lived. Kinley was the quintessential small town, a place so quiet you could hear the wind rustling through the trees in the middle of the afternoon. But he was no longer so naive that he didn't know that appearances could be deceiving.

Kinley's quiet, although seemingly serene, was pregnant with ugly, unvoiced suspicion where he was concerned. He had seen that suspicion in the eyes of the townspeople since he had returned. It was only a matter of time before he heard the words that would surely accompany their silent condemnation. He was sure they were already talking behind his back; after all, hadn't that always been part of living in small-minded Kinley?

Hampton's General Store was on Main Street, located just a few blocks from Mason Creek. When the breeze blew just right, as it blew today, it carried the smells of the town's seafood industry. Twelve years ago, Wade had toiled on a shrimp boat and the scent now made him recall the hard work of hauling in the catch and separating the shrimp from the other small fish and crustaceans that got tangled in the net. It was one of the few memories he associated with Kinley that wasn't unpleasant; he had liked having the smell of the sea on his hands.

He ran away from the water, passing bulletin boards plastered with notices and a huge oak resembling a buck's head that children had played under for more than one hundred years. A lone boy swung from a tire suspended on the tree and reminded Wade of his young self. He had skipped school many times and done just that. He certainly hadn't been a runner. In those days, he was too undisciplined to do anything as self-serving as jogging.

Wade started to jog after he moved to Manhattan because he didn't want his body to fall victim to the perils of too much food, too much drink and too little exercise. In the career he had built for himself, the temptation to pay more attention to the mind than the body was always present. Now, as he ran from Kinley's center to one of the long, winding roads leading out of town, Wade was thankful he had developed a passion for running, more for the exercise it provided his mind than his body.

The patrons at the bar last night had treated him warily, suspicion lurking behind their every word. He could almost hear the accusing whispers when he turned his back. He shouldn't have let it bother him, but it had. No matter how successful he became, in the eyes of his hometown he'd always be little more than the criminal they believed him to be. A restless night had convinced him that he should sell Ena's house and let the past die with her, but one more look at Leigh had squashed his intentions.

He hadn't meant to ask her to dinner. He was going to tell her that Ena had willed her some of her possessions. And he was going to say goodbye, knowing that this time their parting would be forever.

But when he saw her with her face scrubbed clean of makeup and her hair tied back in that childish ponytail, he hadn't been able to do it. A part of his childhood had come rushing back, and Leigh was an intrinsic part of it. He'd loved her once with a passion stronger than his common sense, and he hadn't felt quite that way about anything since he'd left Kinley.

He remembered the passion and the love when he looked at her in the general store, and the dinner invitation had sprung unbidden from his lips while a crazy notion formed. Wade craved peace and quiet while he wrote, and his hometown would be the perfect refuge while he worked on his next novel, a soul-searching journey into the past. The lead character could be a man suspected of kidnapping and murder, and the heroine could be a young girl who had the power to clear his name. The twist was that she was too afraid of small-town gossip to admit she had been with him when the crime was committed.

Wade pumped his arms harder and lengthened his stride, running so hard that he was drenched in sweat by the time he circled back and reached his mother's house. He stood on the sidewalk in front of the house, his body bent at the waist and his head down, gasping for breath. He'd have to come up with another idea for his next book. The one he had was too close to the cruel facts of his own life, and he wasn't yet ready to face them.

For a moment, he had allowed himself to forget Leigh's betrayal and what it had cost him, but he wouldn't make that mistake again. The next time he looked at her, he vowed not to see the sweet-faced, dulcet-voiced girl he had thought she was, but the traitor she had revealed herself to be. He would never forget that the words she whispered on those long-ago nights were lies, that she'd trampled on his heart without so much as a look backward. His heart had healed years ago, and he wasn't about to expose it to her again.

Chapter 2

The phone was ringing when Leigh unlocked the front door of her large antebellum house. When she bought the pale yellow structure with the wraparound porch and tall white columns, her family had insisted it was much too large for one person. As Leigh moved hurriedly over the hardwood floors in her living room, she had to concede that they'd been right. They'd also been wrong. She was constantly struggling to keep up with the large, rambling home, but she luxuriated in its open spaces and airy feel.

"Hello," Leigh said, grabbing up the receiver.

"God, Leigh, what took you so long? I was just fixin' to hang up," drawled a familiar voice. Her sister, Ashley Hampton Tucker, didn't mince words. "You really should keep more than two phones in that big, ole house."

"What do you want, Ashley?" Leigh asked wearily and kicked off her tennis shoes. She sat down on one of her Queen Anne chairs and rubbed her tired feet.

"Why, Leigh, is that any way to greet your only sister?" Ashley sounded dismayed, and it only served to make her Southern accent seem even broader. Leigh had never been able to figure out why she and Drew spoke with slight accents while

Ashley's voice was as rich as a slice of pecan pie. "If you had a hard day at the store, you shouldn't take it out on me."

"It wasn't a hard day, just a long one," Leigh countered, visualizing the pout on Ashley's pretty face. She took a deep breath, trying to dredge up some patience. "Are you calling for any special reason, Ashley?"

"Well, actually I am. I saw Drew today and he happened to mention that you were going to have dinner with Wade Conner." She paused dramatically. "Do you really think that's wise, dear?"

Leigh put the receiver in her lap and swallowed her annoyance. Ashley's tactless brand of meddling was one reason why the sisters had never been close, but it was far from the only cause. Leigh placed the receiver to her ear once more.

"I'm past the age where I need hand-holding from my big sister," Leigh said, avoiding the question. *Wise* was not the word she'd use to describe her agreement to have dinner with Wade, but she wasn't going to admit that to Ashley.

"I'm awful worried about you, honey," Ashley said, ignoring her sister's comment. "Wade Conner's been gone for a long time, but that doesn't change anything. People still think that poor, little Sarah Culpepper would still be around if it wasn't for him."

Trust Ashley to skip the preliminaries and get right to the point, Leigh thought wryly. "Well, I don't believe that, Ashley," she said firmly. "And, as I remember, you didn't used to think anything was wrong with Wade."

There was a pregnant pause at the other end of the line, and Leigh wished she could take back her comment. Ashley was married to the town's police chief and had two children, but years ago she had been a teenager who thought her blond hair and cornflower-blue eyes could charm any male. Her considerable graces had fallen short with Wade, and it was obvious that his rejection still smarted.

"That was uncalled for, Leigh," Ashley said finally, managing to sound hurt. "I just meant that you shouldn't be keeping company with a man like that. You don't know the first thing about him."

I know that he used to look at me with his heart in his eyes, Leigh thought. I know that a laugh was never far from his lips.

"Don't worry, Ashley," Leigh said aloud. "I'm just going over there because Ena willed me some of her things. I'm not going to get involved with Wade Conner."

"Were you involved with Wade Conner?" Ashley asked suddenly. "I always suspected something, but I was never sure."

"You tell me, Ashley. I thought you knew everything that went on in Kinley," Leigh said shortly, unwilling to admit anything to Ashley. Her sister had a way of storing bits of information and using them whenever it suited her purpose.

"You're obviously not in a confiding mood, but I'll be here if you want to talk to somebody later," Ashley said, Leigh's implied insult spilling off her like water.

"Don't wait up for a call, Ashley. I'm a big girl now. I can handle myself. And Wade Conner."

"Just watch him close, now. I think he has a little bit of the devil in him."

"I think we all do, Ashley," Leigh said before she rung off.

After she hung up the phone, Leigh slowly climbed the stairs to her second-floor bedroom. Her cherry bedroom set was beautifully complemented by a dusky rose carpet and walls that were a slightly lighter shade of pink, but the room didn't brighten Leigh's mood as it usually did.

She headed directly for one of her cedar-lined closets and yanked open the door to a jumble of clothes, boxes and shoes. Although she was an adequate housekeeper and kept the general store in good order, Leigh had never been meticulous about minor details. Her closet reflected that facet of her personality.

She raised her eyes to the shelf at the top of the closet and spied the item she coveted. Leigh dragged one of the heavy boxes from the closet floor and stepped on it, precariously balancing while she stood on tiptoe to retrieve her prize.

Moments later, she sat cross-legged in the middle of her queen-size bed and quickly flipped the pages of an old Kinley High yearbook. She didn't stop until she reached the photos of that year's senior class. Leigh ran her finger down the columns of names and stopped at Conner, Wade.

Above the name was a photo of a good-looking boy with twinkling eyes and an infectious grin, the way she remembered

him. She was surprised his senior picture was even in the yearbook, because Wade had dropped out of school midway
through the year to either join up with a shrimp boat or ride his
motorcycle cross-country, she couldn't remember which.

Leigh picked up the book and lay back against the bed, staring at the picture of Wade as he had looked more than a decade ago. He had been a reckless, devil-may-care young man
while she had been a straight arrow, always fully aware of her
responsibilities and the consequences of her actions—until she
started to sneak out of her house in the middle of the night to
be with him.

Leigh had always known who he was, of course. In a town as
small as Kinley, everybody knew everybody. She knew that
when he was twelve, he had moved to town with his mother,
whom everyone assumed was widowed. Later, the gossip
started and some unkind classmates pinned the word *illegitimate* on Wade. Since neither Ena nor Wade bothered to deny
or confirm the accusation, the gossip eventually became accepted as fact.

In a town like Kinley, where ancestry was paramount, that
had been a killing blow. Kinley was a place so antiquated that
whom you were related to was more important than how much
money you made or how successful you were. One of Leigh's
ancestors had been a founding father of nearby Charleston in
1670 and other relatives had lived in Kinley for more than a
hundred years, so her "pedigree" had never been in doubt. It
had long bothered her, and not just for Wade's sake, that she
lived in such a class-conscious society.

Wade was three years older than Leigh and three classes
ahead of her in school. Since senior high school students tended
to have little to do with junior high kids, Leigh and Wade seldom crossed paths. When they did, she'd sometimes catch him
staring at her and a little thrill of delight would pass through
Leigh.

Wade Conner wasn't like the other boys in town, and that
had fascinated her. His hair and complexion were darker and
she heard loud whispers that Wade had Indian blood. She knew
that Wade and school didn't mix any better than the Carolina
heat and humidity, and that he skipped town whenever he felt
the urge.

Ena probably hadn't been able to discipline him, especially since he could be delightful and witty and charming. He charmed his mother into letting him buy a motorcycle when he was only sixteen, and he charmed Leigh into taking a ride on it four years later. Leigh sighed and closed the yearbook, staring at the ceiling while she drifted into the past.

Seventeen-year-old Leigh lengthened her gait and tried to make up the ground she'd lost by oversleeping, but she fought a hopeless battle. A stiff breeze rustled the moss hanging from the tall oak trees that lined the path leading to school, and Leigh clutched at her books and papers too late. The wind took hold of her loose sheets of homework and carried them in the same direction from which she had come.

"I don't believe this," Leigh exclaimed, chasing her wind-blown homework at a dead run while she grabbed at air. Her legs weren't long, but they were lithe and slim and suited for running. Soon her homework papers were within reach, and Leigh clutched at the air one more time and hauled in her prey. She stared at the booty in her hands, but the grin of success faded on her face. The papers were crumpled and smeared with dirt.

The roar of a motorcycle filled the empty highway, and Leigh turned to see Wade Conner approaching. Even if he had been wearing a helmet, she would have known it was him because no one else in town drove a motorcycle.

He brought the big machine to a stop a few feet from her, and Leigh stared at him in surprise. Her hair was windblown, her cheeks were red from exertion and her clothes, a tailored white blouse and a plaid skirt that ended at midthigh, were disheveled. She couldn't imagine why Wade Conner, a twenty-year-old who was worldly and traveled, had stopped beside a high school student. She looked around, but no one else was in sight.

"Leigh Hampton, isn't it?" he asked, and she nodded mutely. "I'm Wade Conner."

It was an unnecessary introduction, because she had made it her business to know who he was from the moment he turned up in town. Besides, Kinley was so small that everyone knew everyone. Most of the girls in Kinley were fascinated by him, although it wouldn't be fashionable to admit it. Wade was a rogue who didn't obey the rules of a polite society, and he didn't number among the community's "fine young men." He certainly wasn't suitable company for the daughter of Kinley's long-time mayor. Still, she was curious.

He stared at her for a long moment, and she returned the look. He wore a black leather jacket to guard against the slight nip in the October air, and he appeared dangerous and exciting. Leigh's pulse quickened, and the corner of Wade's mouth lifted in a smile. "Wanna go for a ride, Leigh Hampton?"

The logical response would have been to tell him she was headed for school and then to politely refuse. But she was already late, and she held the crumpled, dirty remains of her homework in her hands. She looked down at the papers and back up at the raven-haired man, and a tremor ran through her. It could have been fear, but it felt more like unleashed excitement.

"Sure, Wade Conner," she said in a voice that didn't sound quite like her own and swung a slim leg over the back of the motorcycle. She handed him her books and he deposited them in a receptacle on the side of the bike.

Leigh hugged Wade's midsection just below his jacket and felt the heat of his skin through his thin shirt. She had never been more aware of a man's body and had an inexplicable urge to caress the hard planes of his stomach. But then he revved the bike and they were off, traveling with abandon over the empty highway in the opposite direction of Kinley High.

Wade inched the speedometer upward until they moved at breakneck speed, but the ride invigorated Leigh instead of frightening her. Wade had a daredevil's reputation, but he maneuvered the bike expertly and she didn't think he would let anything bad happen to her. Strangely, unexpectedly, she trusted him.

When Wade turned off the main highway onto a bumpy dirt road, Leigh hugged him tighter but still felt no fear. Today was special, like a piece of chocolate-fudge cake a dieter sneaks when no one is watching. She wasn't going to spoil it by regretting her impulsiveness or worrying that she would tumble off the bike onto her unprotected head.

The road gradually narrowed until it was little more than a path, and Wade compensated by slowing down the machine considerably. The path ended so suddenly that Leigh thought they would plow into the brush and trees that signified the end of the line, but Wade braked easily and she knew he had been there before.

She alighted from the motorcycle, and Wade did the same, watching her with an intensity that exhilarated her. All of her senses were heightened, and she was immediately aware of the babbling sound of water. Surprised, Leigh stepped through the brush until she entered a place that counted among nature's treasures. It was an inlet with gently rolling blue-green water that lapped at a grassy bank dotted with moss-covered oak trees.

"It's beautiful," she breathed and let her eyes shift from the beauty of the scene to the beauty of the man beside her. He smiled, and she immediately understood the gravity of him bringing her here. This was his secret place, and he wanted to share it with her.

Leigh smoothed her skirt and sat down on the grassy bank, folding her legs beneath her while she drank in the scene. A white egret stepped daintily in the shallow water near the bank, and the sight of it made her smile. Beauty surrounded her, and she was happy. Wade sank down next to her, near enough for Leigh to hear his even breathing but not close enough to touch. And she wanted to touch him.

"So how come you're here with me instead of at school?" he asked and leaned back against the grass, hooking his hands under his head and regarding her with lazy indulgence.

"How come you're not off shrimping?" Leigh challenged back and stared at him through her lashes, knowing she was flirting but not being able to stop herself. His dark hair was mussed from the motorcycle ride, and she had a sudden urge to smooth it.

He laughed, and the noise seemed to erupt from him in a burst of joy. While he laughed, Leigh took the opportunity to study him. Up close, he was even more arresting than from a distance. He had high, arching cheekbones, an olive complexion and hair as black as the night. She'd heard that he was a hellion, a black sheep and a troublemaker. But when she looked into his laughing gray eyes, she discounted all of it. For some reason that she couldn't finger, she trusted him.

"The shrimp boat's in, Leigh. I've been out on the water for almost a week hauling in catches. Don't you think I deserve some time off?" he asked, and plucked a strand of grass, twirling it around his finger. "So how come you're here?"

Leigh sat forward and hugged her bent knees, surveying the rippling water and the white egrets flying above it. "I don't know. I've never skipped school like this before," she said truthfully. "I was having a terrible morning. I slept in, missed breakfast and soiled my homework papers. When you asked me to come for a ride, I couldn't think of a reason not to."

"I thought you'd say no," he said. He picked up a pebble and threw it into the inlet. "No, I was sure you'd say no."

"Why?" Leigh asked but knew the reason.

"Come off it, Leigh. Girls like you don't hang out with guys like me." He tossed another pebble into the inlet. "Haven't you heard? I'm a high school dropout, a troublemaker, a ne'er do well. And you're the mayor's daughter."

"Are you trying to scare me?" she probed, never taking her eyes off his face, which had suddenly become lined and serious.

"Hell, no." He shook his head. A breeze suddenly kicked up and blew his slightly long, dark hair around his face. "If you knew how long I've wanted to sit down and talk to you like this, you wouldn't say that."

"How long?" she asked, mesmerized by his revelation.

"Since you were in about the seventh grade, although I don't know why I'm admitting it." He laughed again, and his eyes crinkled. "You should see your face, Leigh. You look like you can't decide whether I'm lying. Believe me, it's true."

"Why are you telling me this?" She was captivated by his honesty, because she felt sure he was being straight with her. Wade Conner seemed to speak every word from the heart.

"Because I want to kiss you," he said unexpectedly, and the smile faded. Leigh stared at him for a moment, and recognized the emotions that flitted across his face. Undisguised passion. Wry humor. Self-derision.

"Then do it," she invited softly. Wade's eyes widened, but then the smile crept back onto his face. He inched closer and tentatively placed his work-roughened hands on her shoulders before he touched his mouth to hers. The contact was soft, sweet and over before it began. Wade drew back slowly and put one hand on each side of her face, smiling at her sweetly.

"Wade Conner, surely you can kiss better than that," she teased him gently, not even pausing to wonder where she got the nerve. Leigh was seventeen, but her experience with the opposite sex was limited. She had kissed a few high school boys and found the sensation pleasant but hardly earth-shattering. But somehow she already knew that Wade wasn't like those other boys.

At her pronouncement, Wade's eyes darkened and he again claimed her lips. She gasped involuntarily at the profound pleasure that shot through her when his tongue slid inside the soft folds of her mouth to erotically circle her tongue. His hands left her face and moved caressingly up and down her back, and a liquid fire ignited and burned in her chest.

Leigh's arms crept around Wade and she kissed him back, reveling in the new sensations swimming within her. She traced the outline of his lips with her tongue, and he groaned. He gently caught her tongue with his teeth, and then released it while he deepened the kiss.

The world spun crazily out of control and Leigh didn't want it to stop, but Wade was the first to break the contact. He drew back slightly and they smiled at each other with their eyes, as though something incredibly special had just happened.

That was how it began. And for a while, it had been incredibly special. Leigh was much too straitlaced to skip school again, but she and Wade managed to steal a few hours together almost every afternoon. They filled the time with kisses, laughter and conversation.

"So tell me what your plans are after high school," Wade said one afternoon after he had plucked a daisy from the grassy bank and presented it to her with a flourish.

Leigh held the daisy up to her nose and sniffed the sweet scent. "Promise you won't laugh," she ordered, and Wade held up his right hand solemnly.

"I want to be an artist," she whispered as though the words were too precious to be said too loud. "Oh, I know it sounds silly. I'm just a small-town girl who doesn't know anything about what good art really is. But I have bunches of sketches and paintings tucked away in my bedroom, and more than anything I want to go away to college and major in art.''

"I don't think it sounds silly," Wade said, and she imagined for just a second that he sounded hurt. Could it be because she hadn't mentioned him in her plans? "I'd like to see your stuff sometime."

Wade smiled, and the hurt she thought she'd seen was gone. Impulsively she threw her arms around him and hugged him. "I never told anyone that before," she confessed. "What did I ever do without you?"

She brought him a few of her sketches the next time they met and blushed while he enthused over her talent. Wade was enthusiastic about a lot of things, and Leigh was one of them. His kisses became more ardent as they came to know one another better, but he never pressured her to make love.

For Leigh, each day with Wade was a glorious treasure to be tucked away in her memory and taken out to be relived. She refused to dwell on anything that threatened to tear the gentle fabric of their budding relationship, but it nagged at her that Wade seemed to live only in the present.

"You can't work on the shrimp boat forever," she ventured one evening as they watched the sun set. Wade's arm was around her shoulders, and she felt him stiffen.

"I never said I would," he answered woodenly.

"You never say anything about your future," Leigh continued, sensing that he wanted to avoid the subject but ignoring his wishes.

"If I did, it would scare the living daylights out of you." He effectively put an end to the conversation by starting a line of talk Leigh wasn't ready to finish. He was alluding to their future, and Leigh didn't want to think beyond the moment.

She always avoided the reason they couldn't have a future, the same reason they always met in secret, away from the prying eyes of the townspeople. Privately, Leigh acknowledged the ugly truth. Gossip would put a quick end to their clandestine meetings if her father, the third in a long line of Drew Michael Hamptons, caught wind of it.

The Hamptons had been one of the first families to settle in Kinley after the Civil War, and Leigh's father thought they were atop the town's social scale. Leigh loved him, but knew the idea of his daughter dating an outcast like Wade would throw him into a rage. Eventually, that's exactly what happened.

"Leigh," her father said sharply one evening while she was bent over her history book reading the pages the teacher had assigned. "Where do you disappear to in the afternoons?"

"What do you mean, Daddy?" Leigh looked up from her book, trying to mask her alarm. In her heart, she knew it was too late. She could tell by his voice that he had discovered her secret.

"You used to drop by the store after school. You don't do that anymore. Your mother says you don't come home until a few hours after school lets out." Drew Hampton III stood erect with his arms crossed over his chest. A tall man with a full head of prematurely white hair and a booming voice, he commanded respect and obedience. Leigh closed her book and gave her father her full attention.

"I go off and sit by the water," she said truthfully, not daring to lie to her father. He obviously had a reason for questioning her, and she didn't want to aggravate the situation by telling untruths. He wouldn't stand for that.

"I hear you go off with Ena Conner's boy." He delivered the words so coolly, they could have been chipped from a block of ice. At his pronouncement, Leigh's hands began to shake. When Leigh had been younger, he had punished her by swatting the palms of her hands with a ruler before sending her to her room. Her palms smarted at the memory.

"Where'd you hear that?" Leigh asked after a long pause, trying to avoid the inevitable for as long as possible.

"It doesn't matter where I heard it. What matters is if it's true. Are you seeing that Conner boy?" he asked stonily.

Leigh gulped, knowing that her day of reckoning had arrived, and willed herself to be brave. She lifted her chin a notch, unconsciously mimicking an action she had seen her father use when he was in a jam. "Yes," she said clearly.

She expected an explosion, and her father didn't disappoint her. He uttered an epithet she had never heard from him, and his booming voice raised a few notches. "Good God in heaven, girl, don't you know better than to run around with some no-account loser? You're a Hampton, the daughter of the town's mayor. I expect more from you than this."

"Wade isn't a loser," she objected, her feelings for Wade overriding her fear of her father. "And you don't have to get so upset. I said I was seeing him. I didn't say I was sleeping with him."

Hampton took a few threatening steps forward and then stopped, as though struggling to gain control of his temper. The veins in his neck stuck out and his temple throbbed. "You sure as hell better not be," he growled. "He's not good enough for any daughter of mine. He's a bastard, Leigh. He has Indian blood, and my daughter is not going to marry an Indian."

"We never talked about marriage," Leigh said, and she was angry now. "I'm only seventeen years old."

"That's right," he shouted at her. "You're seventeen and living under my roof, so you'll do as I say. And I forbid you to see Conner again."

He pivoted sharply and stomped out of the room. Leigh, fury coloring her face, looked after him in silence. Drew Hampton III had spoken, and he expected her to meekly obey as she always had. The Hampton children had been taught from an early age that their father's word was law, no matter how irrational and bigoted it was. She pounded her fist on the desk in frustration and made a decision that would come back to haunt her. Leigh Hampton, the model daughter and honor student, deliberately decided to defy her father.

During the following weeks, Leigh sneaked out of the Hampton house after midnight to see Wade. He greeted her by a cluster of bushes near her house with a hug and a kiss and, sometimes, a bouquet of wildflowers. They would then walk hand in hand to the spot a few blocks away where he had parked his motorcycle.

The lateness of the hour and the darkness of the night added an intimacy their meetings had previously lacked, and Leigh and Wade sank deeper into an abyss of passion. Only supreme acts of willpower on his part prevented them from learning each other's most intimate secrets. Leigh sneaked back into her house in the wee hours of the morning filled with the afterglow of their love and the fear of being caught.

She knew their stolen meetings couldn't last indefinitely, but she never expected them to end with shattering, irrevocable finality.

Leigh's parents were off on one of their rare overnight forays into Charleston, so she arranged to meet Wade just after dusk. She didn't have any fear of being discovered, since Drew wouldn't betray her even if he found out, and Ashley was already married and living out of the house.

The night was especially dark and oddly chilly, and Leigh had an eerie premonition that it belonged to the devil. She shook off the feeling the moment she was in Wade's arms. He had taken her to the grassy bank bordering the inlet they had visited on their first ride together, and Leigh smiled at the memory.

"Did I ever tell you that I love you, Wade Conner?" she asked impulsively. It was the first time she had said the words, and her voice was deep with feeling. She leaned her head against his shoulder and was surprised when she felt tension radiating from him. Leigh pulled away slightly so she could look at him and discern the reason for his discomfort.

She read uncertainty in his face and smiled reassuringly. "I just said that I love you, Wade. Is there anything wrong with that?"

"Not a thing," he said tightly. "Except that I don't believe it. If you loved me, you wouldn't care if the whole town saw us together. We wouldn't have to sneak around."

Leigh sighed heavily. She didn't want to spoil their night, but she knew they could no longer avoid the subject.

"Oh, Wade. You know how I feel. I'm not ashamed of you, but I don't want to upset my father," she said beseechingly.

"I see. You don't want to upset pompous, old Drew Hampton III, but you don't give a damn about upsetting me," he said bitterly.

"There's no need to talk about my father that way," Leigh said sharply.

"What about the way he talks about me, Leigh? Did you know that he stopped me on the street yesterday and threatened to see that I was fired down at the dock if I didn't leave you alone?" Leigh's eyes widened in shock, and Wade continued. "I didn't think so. He called me a no-good Indian bastard, Leigh. If he wasn't your father, I would have slugged him."

"He had no right—" Leigh began.

"He sure as hell didn't," Wade interrupted. "I don't care about bloodlines, Leigh. I don't care that you're a Hampton or that your father is mayor. I wouldn't care if your family was dirt-poor and lived in a one-room shack. That's what love's all about. It isn't about sneaking off in the middle of the night to be with someone you don't want to be seen with in the daylight."

Leigh parted her lips to speak. In the background, frogs ribbeted, crickets sang and the water lapped gently at the shoreline. No sound came from Leigh, because the truth echoed from every word Wade spoke. Her heart felt heavy, because the pain in her breast was visible on his face.

"You've gotta make some decisions, Leigh. You're going to have to choose between me and him," he said firmly. Leigh searched his face for some sign of compromise, but she couldn't see past his tight-lipped expression.

"But, Wade, I'm only seventeen," she protested. "I can't just cut all ties with my father. I want to go to college, Wade. I want to be an artist. I don't want to make this decision."

Wade cupped his chin in his hands and gazed at the water, which was only a few feet away but was barely visible because the night was so dark. "I know all that. And I know I shouldn't pressure you. But, God, Leigh, just once I'd like to take you on a real date. To go to the movies or drive into Charleston to have dinner at some restaurant. I'm sick of sneaking around."

Leigh heard the frustration in his voice and inched closer to him until their bodies touched. She tentatively put out one of her hands, and he took it and pressed it to his cheek.

"I never expected this to happen, but I love you, Leigh. I'm not asking you to marry me right now, because I don't have anything to offer. First I want to make a success of myself. I want to prove you don't have to be ashamed of me."

Leigh withdrew her hand and put her arms around him, pulling him down with her to the grassy bank. "I'm not ashamed of you," she whispered and then again spoke the words she had kept locked in her heart since he'd spoken to her from his motorcycle on that blustery day. "I love you, too."

The ground was hard and wet with dew, but they were so lost in each other that neither noticed the moisture. Their kiss was unlike any they'd ever shared, a mixture of passion and desperation and sweetness. Leigh threaded her fingers through his thick, dark hair, pressed her lower body closer to his and felt his obvious need through his jeans.

"Wade, Wade," she groaned when he moved his mouth to the open collar of her shirt. His trembling fingers undid the buttons impatiently, and he peeled the garment from her. He quickly unfastened her bra, and her full breasts, their nipples taut and rosy, were exposed to his eager mouth.

While he nibbled, she worked at the buttons on his shirt, hungry to feel his naked skin against hers at last. Wade lapped at her nipple with his tongue and pleasure rippled through her, centering in the core in the secret part of her. Leigh had never felt this way in her seventeen years, and she wanted to experience every corner of heaven she and Wade could give one another.

His fingers undid the button on her jeans and slipped into her panties and she pressed herself against his questing hand. Her own hands traversed the slightly furry expanse of his chest, caressing his taut stomach and outlining the proud tool of his passion through his clothing. Leigh and Wade didn't talk, but their murmurs and sighs told each other everything.

When Wade started to inch Leigh's jeans down over her rounded hips, she raised herself to make the task easier. Her underwear followed in short order, and Wade stared at her nude body for short, intense seconds before he crushed her to him. When Wade cut off his hot, searing kisses long enough to discard the rest of his clothing, Leigh quivered with unfulfilled, unfamiliar passion.

"Oh, baby. Oh, love," he said as he again covered her body with his and spread her willing legs with one of his knees. Leigh wouldn't have had a chance to quash the course of events even if she had wanted to, because Wade guided himself inside of her in the next instant.

She cried out involuntarily in pain, and he froze. He rose slightly to look at her, and the expression on his face was a mixture of passion and regret before he succumbed to an impulse stronger than both of them and started to move within her.

Leigh instinctively wrapped her legs around his upper thighs and moved with him as he established a tempo that made her forget her temporary discomfort. Her mouth turned to meet his, and their tongues mated as their bodies filled each other's emptiness. A ball of fire grew in Leigh until she thought it would singe her insides, and she clung to Wade with all her strength.

She realized vaguely that the whimpering sounds she heard came from her own throat, and she was so out of control, it seemed she would plunge to earth at any moment. Instead she soared, and Wade soared with her, higher and higher until they reached the heavens. Leigh clung to Wade as they returned to earth. For long moments, they lay immobile in each other's arms before Wade gently rolled off her.

Cuddled against his side, Leigh looked at Wade and waited for a rush of regret. Her mother had always told her to save herself for marriage, and she never thought she would lose her virginity at seventeen in the dead of night on the cold, hard earth. But Wade was looking at her as though she had just given him a precious gift, and there wasn't any room for shame in her heart.

But she shivered anyway, suddenly aware of the cold earth and the twigs and strands of grass flattened against her naked skin. Her body was still suffused with lethargy from their lovemaking, but she was cold. She started to reach for her clothes, but Wade caught one of her arms and turned her toward him.

"Leigh," he whispered, and she could barely make out the magnificent shape of his body in the weak glow of the moon. "Don't be ashamed. I never meant for that to happen, not now, not yet. You've got to believe that. But I'm glad I was your first."

Leigh smiled at him and touched his cheek, realizing that he had attributed her withdrawal to doubt rather than the chill in the air.

"I'm glad you were my first, too," Leigh said and kissed him softly on the lips. "But a woman cannot survive on love alone. I'm going to freeze if I don't put on some clothes."

She quickly reached for her discarded clothing, but not before she saw the relief that passed over Wade's face. She hurriedly tugged on her garments. Beside her, lost in thought, Wade did so more slowly. When they were both dressed, he took her hand and pulled her to within a few inches of his body. She looked up at him, expecting him to kiss her, but he was frowning.

"This was wonderful, Leigh, but it's not enough," Wade said, his voice low. "We haven't ironed anything out. I want more from you than sex."

"What exactly do you want?" Leigh asked, although she knew the answer. He wanted a future that included her, and she wanted that, too. It would be heavenly to marry him, bear his children, grow old with him. But not here. Not now. In another year she would go off to college, leaving Kinley behind. She didn't have to leave him, not if he came with her. But even if he didn't come, what they had could survive any obstacle, whether it be distance or time.

"I've already told you," Wade said, and the happiness she had glimpsed in his face after they had made love was gone. "I want a relationship. I want to walk down Kinley's main street with you and know you're not ashamed of me."

"Oh, Wade." Leigh sighed. "Don't you see that's not possible? Not now. Not yet."

"I thought you said you loved me. In my book, this isn't love," he said, and there was a catch in his voice. The flicker of pain caught at Leigh's heart. The overhanging trees cast shadows over his face and made him look vulnerable, a quality she had never before associated with him.

Tears filled her eyes and trickled down her cheeks, and she brushed them away. In minutes, her emotions had plunged from the ecstasy of lovemaking to despair. "It's not that simple. Love isn't enough, Wade. It doesn't change the fact that I'm only seventeen and that my father would kill you if he knew what happened."

Wade sniffed shortly. "Maybe I shouldn't have let this happen, but you wanted it every bit as much as I did."

Maybe more, Leigh added to herself. The hard planes and angles of his body had fascinated her ever since she hopped on the back of his motorcycle and rode blindly into the future.

Yes, she'd wanted him. And she loved him. But she wasn't ready to tell the world. She wasn't ready to tell her father.

"I don't deny that," Leigh said, trying to stop her tears. How had they gone from lovers to adversaries in such a short time? "But I'm not ready for this yet. You don't know my father, Wade. He's a very powerful man, and he knows how to get his way."

"I'm not afraid of your father," Wade snapped.

"But I am," Leigh said, crying freely now. "If he finds out about us, he won't let me go to college. And he'll follow through on his threat and get you fired. I've never defied him before this, Wade. I don't want to find out how bad the repercussions will be. But I don't want to lose what we have, either."

"Then stand up to him," Wade said, not yielding an inch.

"What if I can't?" Leigh asked, choking out the words. Didn't Wade understand how important it was for her to leave Kinley and make something of herself? Didn't he know how much she wanted to go to college and study art? "Are you saying that you don't want to see me anymore? Is that the bottom line?"

Her violet eyes stood out in her tear-streaked face, and she didn't look like a woman anymore. She looked small and vulnerable and not much different than the child she had been a few short years before. Wade covered the gap separating them and put his arm around her quivering shoulders. She leaned against him, and Wade brushed his lips against her silken hair.

"It's okay, sweetheart," he murmured. "I won't force you to make any decisions right now. No one has to know about us just yet. It's enough that we have this time together."

"Stolen moments," she said with a sigh when her tears had slowed to a trickle. "How long can we keep this up?"

"I don't know," Wade answered. "But I want to see you tomorrow night. And the next night. And the night after that. We don't have to make love or even kiss if you don't want to. I only want to be with you. Just say you'll see me."

Leigh turned in his arms and faced the sincerity shining in his gray eyes. She kissed her fingertips and touched them to his lips. "I'll see you tomorrow night," she promised.

* * *

The next morning was Saturday, and Leigh awakened late. She took a leisurely shower, dressed and peered at herself in the mirror. A friend had once told her that a girl changes into a woman after her first sexual experience, but Leigh detected nothing different about her appearance. She looked like she always looked, a pretty young girl with long, shining hair and unusual violet eyes.

Her parents were due back from Charleston later that day, and Leigh shuddered to think what would happen if Drew Hampton III looked at her and figured out what went on the night before. Her father would surely go into one of his patented rages, like the one he threw the night Drew took the family car without permission and wrapped it around a tree.

Leigh had been in bed, huddled under the covers, but she heard the elder Hampton's angry tirade through the house's thick, sturdy walls. She also heard the sickening thud when he threw Drew against the wall, but no one in the family had ever spoken of that. The next day, Drew sported a black eye and some cracked ribs and Leigh always suspected that he hadn't received all his injuries in the car wreck.

But it was silly to think that, after a single look, her father could guess what she had been up to. Besides, she didn't need his admonitions to feel guilty. She had spoken the truth when she'd told Wade that love wasn't enough. In the light of day, she knew she shouldn't have succumbed to temptation, and she felt a twinge of conscience that she hadn't held on to her virginity a little longer.

Leigh checked herself once more in the mirror, shrugged and walked down the stairs to face the day. The door banged open before she reached the bottom step, and Drew burst into the house. He was out of breath, and she guessed he'd been running.

"Leigh, somethin' awful's happened," he said breathlessly, and his thin chest heaved from exertion. "Somebody kidnapped Sarah Culpepper last night."

"What are you talking about, Drew?" Leigh asked skeptically. Her brother must have gotten the story wrong. People weren't kidnapped in small towns like Kinley, especially not sweet seven-year-old girls with long, golden hair. Things like that just didn't happen.

"Chief Cooper figures it happened around nine o'clock last night," Drew said breathlessly. "Mrs. Culpepper said Sarah went outside because her bicycle had a flat and she wanted to pump it with air. That's the last she saw of her. This mornin', the bike was still there but Sarah wasn't. Mrs. Culpepper didn't even realize she was missin' until midnight. You know that her sister lives next door? Well, she thought Sarah had gone over there and fallen asleep on the couch. But she didn't. She's gone and—"

"Wait a minute, Drew." Leigh halted her brother's rapid spate of words and tried to make sense of what he had said. "Are you saying that someone kidnapped Sarah Culpepper?"

"That's what I've been tryin' to tell you," he said in exasperation. "I've been out most of the morning looking for her with the rest of the town. No one can find a thing."

Leigh's eyes widened in horror. With angelic blue eyes and blond hair, Sarah Culpepper was her idea of the perfect child. The little girl's speech was peppered with thank you's, excuse me's and yes, ma'ams. "Oh, no," Leigh cried when the truth had sunk in.

"That's not all, Leigh. There's a suspect. About a half hour before she disappeared, Everett Kelly looked out his window and saw her talkin' to somebody." Drew's dark eyes widened and his voice lowered confidentially as he relayed the news.

"Who?" Leigh breathed without an inkling of what he would say. Who in Kinley could possibly do something so heinous?

"Wade Conner," came the reply. "The chief's questioning him now."

Wade Conner. A suspect. Questioning. The words raced through Leigh's mind, and she willed herself to make sense of them. Wade was a suspect in a kidnapping he couldn't possibly have committed, because she had been with him when Sarah Culpepper disappeared. Even if it hadn't been last night, it would have been a night that no woman could ever forget. She had lost her innocence, and he was being accused of a crime.

"Leigh? Are you okay? You look a little pale." The concerned voice of Drew IV penetrated her numbed senses, and Leigh swallowed the lump in her throat.

"Wade Conner didn't kidnap Sarah," Leigh whispered, her voice raw with choked panic. It was a statement of fact, but Drew mistook it for concern for the little girl.

"Of course, nothin's been proved yet, but it sure seems like he did," Drew said, shaking his head. "I know it's hard to believe, but who knows what goes on in someone else's head?"

Leigh knew, or at least she knew enough to be certain that Wade wouldn't do something so vile even if he hadn't been with her last night. But how would anyone else know? Wade hadn't been born into a family like hers, and that had worked against him ever since he and his mother had come to Kinley. By wearing his hair too long and rebelling against authority, he hadn't helped matters. If there weren't another suspect, it wouldn't be too hard for most of the townsfolk to pin the blame on Wade.

Face it, Leigh told herself. You're his alibi. But if she defended him, the entire town would figure out what had happened last night. It had been one thing to share her love with Wade on a dark night, but it was quite another to let everyone in town know that she wasn't as innocent as she seemed to be. They wouldn't understand what it was like to be seventeen and in love for the first time. Her father certainly wouldn't understand.

"You know what people say about Conner, Leigh," Drew continued, making it sound as though Wade had already been tried and found guilty. "He has a wild streak, and you can never tell what he'll do."

"But he didn't do it," Leigh said again, even more quietly than the first time. Drew searched her face, which was pinched and white.

"Do you know something you're not tellin' me?"

Leigh knew she should confess that she had been with Wade the night before, but she couldn't get the words past her dry lips. She loved Wade, but she didn't think it was fair to have to risk her friends, her family and her future to save him from something he might not even need saving from. After all, Sarah hadn't even been missing for twenty-four hours. She could be found at any time.

"No, Drew. I don't know anything," Leigh lied, and she hardly recognized the brittle voice as her own. Didn't Drew know that Wade was gentle and sensitive and passionate? At the memory of their passion, Leigh shuddered. It hurt to think that Sarah had been abducted while she and Wade made wild, frantic love. "It just doesn't make sense."

Not much made sense in the next few days. A frantic search for Sarah turned up nothing, and a town in mourning looked for someone to blame. Not everyone believed Wade was guilty, but that small group didn't include her father. "I told you he was trouble," he bellowed at Leigh. "I don't want to hear of you within a hundred yards of that boy."

Frightened and confused, Leigh deliberately missed her late-night assignation with Wade the night after Sarah's abduction. But Kinley was a small town, and it was virtually impossible to go more than a few days without running into the person you were trying to avoid. Leigh ran into Wade on her way to the general store the morning after she'd stood him up.

His eyes searched hers until she lowered them to her shuffling feet. "I missed you last night," he said, and Leigh heard the accusation in his voice.

"I couldn't get away," Leigh said inadequately after a moment. Why, oh why, did this have to be so hard? She'd taken one look at his sinewy body and remembered the way he'd made her feel on the grassy bank. She loved him and wanted to feel that way again, but she didn't want to face her father's anger or the town's scorn.

"You know they're saying I had something to do with Sarah Culpepper's disappearance," Wade said, and Leigh raised her eyes at the pain in his voice. He was holding his upper lip stiffly, but Leigh saw through his bravado to the hurt underneath.

"The chief hasn't charged you with anything," Leigh said when all she wanted was to take him into her arms and comfort him.

"No thanks to you," Wade muttered, and Leigh winced.

She started to say that she would tell her story if Chief Cooper threw him in jail, but then she glimpsed her father coming out of the general store.

"I'm sorry, but I've got to go," she said nervously, and Wade followed the path her eyes had just taken. When he spotted Drew Hampton III, the light of understanding filled his eyes.

"You were lying to me all along, weren't you?" he said bitterly, and every word was like a dagger through Leigh's heart. "You never loved me. I was just someone you used and tossed aside like yesterday's newspaper."

"You don't understand—" Leigh protested, but Wade interrupted.

"There's where you're wrong," he said, hurling the words at her. "I understand perfectly."

He turned and walked away, and even though her heart was breaking, Leigh didn't call him back. There was nothing she could say to improve the situation. Instead she just stood there, on the main street of Kinley in the middle of the morning, letting her tears flow.

Chapter 3

Leigh put down the yearbook and tried to bring herself back to the present, but the past still held her in its clutches. Sarah Culpepper had never been found, and neither had her kidnapper. As the weeks went by and the police chief came no closer to solving the crime, people stopped calling Wade a kidnapper and started calling him a murderer.

The only people in town who seemed to believe in Wade's innocence were Ena, the aunt and uncle who had raised Sarah Culpepper, and the police chief. Through it all, Leigh didn't breathe a word.

The grown-up Leigh squeezed her eyes tight, but she couldn't make the images of the past disappear. If she had acted differently, maybe she could have put the whole, ugly episode behind her.

She remembered the odd mix of love, regret and guilt that had plagued her during those days. She had been wrong to let the people of Kinley point their fingers at Wade, but she had been a scared kid with an overbearing father and a strong fear of him. And, as it happened, the need to tell Chief Cooper about Wade's whereabouts the night of Sarah's disappearance didn't arise. The chief never filed charges, and Wade moved out

of town two weeks after the kidnapping, strengthening specu-
lation that he was guilty. Leigh never saw him again. Until last
week.

When Leigh got to her feet, she was shaking. Their long-ago
relationship had run its course in only two months, but it had
burned bright and furious and changed her forever. She
wrapped her arms around her shoulders and willed herself to
calm down. She'd always known that she couldn't feel neutral
about Wade Conner. Once upon a time, he had inspired a passion greater than her common sense. Seeing him again had
summoned another emotion, and it flowed through Leigh until it filled every inch of her. It was guilt.

The slender, gold watch on Leigh's wrist showed that it was
half past seven when she approached the front door of Ena
Conner's home. She had been so lost in the past that time in the
present had gotten away from her. When Leigh finally realized
how late it was, she had hurriedly yanked on a clean pair of
jeans and T-shirt and ran a brush through her hair.

She paused at the door to catch her breath and take in her
surroundings. Although it wasn't yet summer, the grass was
lush and green and the temperature hovered near eighty de-
grees. Ena's house was a two-story structure that was probably
close to one hundred years old, and it was starting to show its
age. Some of the wood slats on the porch were cracked, the
screen door needed to be mended and the pale pink paint that
covered the house was old and faded. Leigh wrinkled her nose.
The color had suited Ena perfectly, but it was all wrong for her
son.

Before she could ring the doorbell, the door swung open and
Leigh stepped back as Wade filled the entrance. The last rays
of the sun cast a glow over him and outlined his hard, male
body, but she couldn't make out his features. He looked even
more like a stranger than he had at the graveyard in his expen-
sively tailored suit with his professionally cut hair.

"I thought I heard something out here. Come on in," Wade
said tonelessly, and stepped back to allow her entry. When the
sun's glare was neutralized, Leigh immediately saw that she had
underdressed. Wade wore a short-sleeved shirt in muted plaids
and pleated, off-white trousers. Stubble tended to appear on his

face as the day wore on, but his olive skin was smooth as though freshly shaved.

She looked down at her informal attire and tennis shoes, and bit her lip. She had barely been in the house for a minute, and she was already at a disadvantage.

"I'm sorry I'm so late. I, um, I kind of, um—" She stopped abruptly when she realized she couldn't admit that she'd spent the past few hours daydreaming about him. "Time just sort of got away from me."

"I thought you changed your mind again," he said flatly, deliberately giving his words a double meaning. Twelve years ago, she had changed her mind about keeping another date with him. Today, she showed up disheveled and a half hour late. That should tell him how much she thought of him, even though he had no intention of forgetting. "C'mon. Dinner's just about ready."

Wade strode in the direction of the outside patio, and Leigh followed at a slower pace. He was feeling irritable, at himself for the relief that had washed over him when he saw that she hadn't stood him up and at Leigh for not being the woman he had once thought she was. She hadn't even come close.

Wade weaved his way through his mother's home, where he had never felt comfortable, even as a boy. Ena's house was crammed with knickknacks and furniture, and it had always seemed too small to accommodate them. His mother had favored flowered wallpaper and frilly lace doilies, and the entire effect was feminine. *I really don't belong here*, he thought, and then wondered where he did belong. Although he had made a niche for himself in Manhattan, the city was too crowded and too ridden with crime. About the only thing he really liked about it was its impersonality. Nobody whispered about what their neighbors were up to; nobody cared.

Leigh followed him through the living room and dining room and came to a stop in the brightly colored breakfast nook adjacent to the kitchen while Wade went out the back door. It had always been her favorite corner of the house. Yellow-and-white wallpaper formed a perfect backdrop for the white booth situated under a bay window.

Wade had obviously gone to some trouble to make the table look attractive. A vase of freshly cut daffodils acted as a centerpiece and added another splash of yellow to the room. Tall, long-stemmed wineglasses complemented the ivory plates and matching salad bowls. The overhead ceiling fan effectively cooled the room, but Leigh's palms were suddenly damp. Why was Wade making an effort to impress her when her long-ago betrayal stood between them?

"I just put the steaks on the grill. They should be ready in a few minutes." Wade reentered the house, and there wasn't resentment or anything else in his eyes. His expression was as blank as an unused chalkboard. "It's still kind of hot outside, so I thought it would be better if we ate in here."

Leigh nodded and tried to swallow the nervousness that threatened to render her tongue-tied. It was all the more ironic because he had once teasingly referred to her as a magpie. She used to feel so comfortable with him that the words wouldn't stop coming. "Can I help you do anything?" she asked, hoping action would make her feel less awkward.

"No. There's nothing to do," Wade answered, and Leigh wondered when the enthusiasm had drained from his voice. The Wade she had known bubbled over with the joy of life. This Wade was almost lifeless.

"I've already mixed the salad and opened the wine," he continued. "Just have a seat, and I'll get everything together."

He turned abruptly and disappeared into the kitchen, feeling just as uncomfortable as Leigh. He knew that asking her to dinner was a bad idea almost before the invitation was out of his mouth. He didn't want to look at her and remember what had turned out to be the best and worst time of his life. But he had tried to make the best of it, buying some wine, grilling steaks and making the table look nice. He had tried to think of her as a casual dinner companion, but it wasn't working. And why should it? She wasn't a woman he had just met at the corner store; she was the woman who had taught him about deceit.

"Damn it all," he muttered and slammed his hand down on a countertop.

Leigh didn't think she could sit still while Wade prepared the meal, so she wandered into Ena's living room and ran her fingertips over the marble mantle above the fireplace. They came to a stop at a picture of Wade and Ena. She had seen it before, of course, but had never taken the opportunity to study it.

Mother and son stood in Manhattan atop one of the twin towers of the World Trade Center on a day so clear, the city was plainly visible in the background. Wade hugged Ena to him with one, long arm, and he was laughing. The old woman's eyes brimmed with love and laughter as she looked up at her tall, handsome son. It was a gem of a picture, and Leigh wondered who was on the other side of the lens.

She imagined the photographer was one of Wade's sophisticated New York lady friends, and for some reason that bothered her. A small-town girl like herself couldn't begin to compete with a New York sophisticate. But, of course, Leigh added sternly to herself, she didn't want to compete.

"Leigh. Dinner's ready," Wade called from the kitchen. She froze at the sound of her name on his lips. She'd always loved the way he said her name. He seemed to caress the syllable and draw it out, making it seem important. She took a deep breath, released it slowly and went to face what the evening had in store.

She looked nervous, Wade thought when Leigh walked into the kitchen, as though she were a little bit afraid of him. The observation made him feel better: he wanted her to look at him and remember the terrible thing she'd done. He wanted her to suffer the way he had suffered when he'd learned of her betrayal. Of course, he thought bleakly, wanting something and getting it were two different things. Leigh Hampton had taught him that when he was little more than a boy.

Leigh sat down, and Wade stood beside the table holding a platter with the two steaks. He gave her the smaller of the two.

"I cooked them medium-rare," he said. "That seemed like a safe guess."

"That's how I like them," Leigh said, while Wade settled into the opposite side of the booth. She chewed on a piece of succulent grilled steak and tried to stem the tide of uneasiness rising within her. Quite simply, she didn't know what to say. Leigh was by nature a quiet person, but she had never been subdued around Wade. Something about him used to make her open her mouth and reveal her soul, but those times were long gone.

"How's the steak? I can put it back on the grill if it's too rare," Wade said, and Leigh's violet eyes flew to his face. He didn't look nearly as uncomfortable as she felt.

She shook her head quickly. "No, the steak's good. Quite good. Delicious, actually," Leigh said and returned her attention to her plate.

She was still beautiful, Wade thought. He didn't want to think so, but he couldn't help it. Even in her casual attire with her hair slightly mussed, she was more appealing than any of the women he knew in New York. He had hoped she would have married, gained weight and lost her appeal, but none of those things had happened. If he had been seeing her for the first time, he would have been captivated in much the same way he had been twelve years ago. But he was older, wiser and determined to remain immune to her charms.

Leigh held the steak steady with her fork and cut another piece before she returned her attention to Wade. Her eyes collided with his and recognized the look of appreciation in their depths. Even when she had been a girl of seventeen, Wade had looked at her as though she were a woman. This look reminded her of the sensual, almost hungry way he used to regard her, but there was something different about it. It only took a moment to figure out what it was. His gray eyes were no longer laughing and open. Instead, they were steely and distrustful.

"I never would have guessed that you and my mother were friends," he said as he reached for a French roll fresh from the oven. He took a bite of it, and his teeth were very white and very straight. Ena Conner had been a good judge of character, but then so was he. If he had been wrong about Leigh, Ena could have been, too.

"Ena was a wonderful woman," Leigh said sincerely, glad that he had chosen a safe topic of conversation. "We became friends about five years ago, right after she fell and broke her leg. She had some trouble getting around, so I dropped by a couple of times a week to deliver whatever she needed from the store."

There was more to it than that, but Leigh didn't want to reveal all her secrets. She had been ripe for a friend after her closest schoolhood friend had moved to a larger city to improve her employment opportunities. It seemed that every other woman in town who was her age was married with children, and Leigh could take only so much of conversations about diapers and teething. It wasn't that she didn't want to have children someday; she did, but that seemed unlikely considering there was nobody she wanted to marry.

"That was nice of you," he commented between bites of salad, wondering what her motive had been. Ena hadn't been a wealthy woman, so Leigh couldn't have hoped for any monetary reward. Wade wasn't wealthy, either, but he had invested his money wisely and had been able to live fairly well while sending Ena a monthly check to make her life more comfortable.

Leigh held up a hand in protest. "It was no trouble, really. I always walk to the store, and Ena's house—your house—is on my way home. And I enjoyed the visits. After her leg healed, I stopped by two or three times a week just to talk."

Wade was silent as he digested the information, and Leigh wished she had the power to read his mind. She knew he didn't think much of her, but the news of her friendship with Ena seemed to give him pause. For some reason, it was important that he forgive her the sins of the past. The knowledge that she cared what he thought made her shift uncomfortably in her seat. She reached for her wineglass and took the smallest of sips, sensing the need to keep her wits about her.

"She never told me. But then I made it pretty clear after I left town that I didn't want to talk about you," he said and then could have bitten his tongue. He didn't want Leigh to know how deeply she had hurt him. He didn't want her to think her betrayal was still important when he had gotten over it, and her, years ago.

Wade took a healthy swallow of his wine, and Leigh drummed her fingers nervously on the table. They couldn't avoid the subject of her shoddy behavior indefinitely, but she wasn't ready to discuss it. He would want to delve into the reasons behind her betrayal, and a dozen years of second-guessing made them all seem inadequate.

"Why are you still here in Kinley working at the general store?" he said abruptly, changing the subject. Leigh's entire body stiffened. She had been prepared for a number of questions, but that hadn't been one of them. When he had known her, she wanted to become an artist more than she wanted to breathe. But she stopped painting shortly after Wade left town, and any hopes she might have had to resume her artistic aspirations died with her father. It still hurt to think about what might have been.

She folded her hands in her lap and stared at them for a moment while she composed her answer.

"Things just didn't work out like I thought they would. I went to college, but Daddy died in the middle of my sophomore year. Mother was too overwhelmed by everything to be much of a help at the store, so I came back to run it."

Wade's gray eyes narrowed in derision. "But what about Ashley and Drew? Why did you have to take over?"

"I was the logical choice. Ashley was already married and had a baby. And Drew was seventeen and had just been accepted into The Citadel," Leigh explained patiently, referring to the military college in Charleston. "Both Mother and Daddy had this dream of Drew becoming a serviceman and they wouldn't hear of him not going to college, so everything fell on me. I had to keep the business together for the family."

Wade mulled over what she had just told him, astute enough to realize she had left out large chunks of the story. Curiously, he didn't get any pleasure from the fact that she hadn't gotten what she wanted out of life. It sounded as though her parents had forced her to give up her future so her brother could have one. It figured that they were sexist as well as narrow-minded.

"Didn't you mind?" he asked, finding it hard to imagine that the Leigh he had known would have meekly returned to her hometown in what amounted to a prison sentence.

Leigh shrugged. When he had known her, she would have minded. She probably would have kicked and screamed and loudly proclaimed her independence from Kinley. But everything changed after Wade left town. With him went her love and, it turned out, her aspirations. She hated what she'd done to him, and that hate eroded her self-confidence. It followed that if she wasn't strong enough to stand up for the man she loved, she wasn't strong enough to make it on her own away from Kinley.

"Why should I have minded?" she said lightly, letting none of her feelings show. "I was needed at the store."

"Things didn't work out for Drew in the military?" he guessed.

Leigh shook her head. "He never even enlisted. Drew did go to The Citadel, but the strict regimen there turned him off the military and he came back home after he graduated."

Throughout the conversation, she had carefully avoided references to her painting, and she knew he picked up on it. How could he not remember the impassioned way she had talked about her art and the pride with which she had shown him her work?

"Do you still paint?" he asked, and knew the answer would be no even before she shook her head.

"No," she said shortly. She had shut away her paintings and her dreams in a back room of her house years ago, and she never discussed them. "Why don't we talk about you? Tell me how you became a novelist."

She could almost see the wheels spinning in his head at her sudden change of subject, and she chastised herself for being too blunt. He couldn't help but notice her sensitivity about her painting. Wade picked up the wine bottle and leaned across the table to refill her glass, but he didn't pursue the subject.

"There isn't much to tell. After I left town, I headed north and worked at a few construction sites. There wasn't much else I could do without a high school diploma." He laughed shortly, regretting even now the folly of not finishing school. "It was hard work physically, but my mind was bored as hell. So I started to read in my off-hours. I read so much, I went to sleep with red eyes every night. Then one night, I took out some paper and I started to write. Before long, I had papers all over my apartment with things I'd written."

"Then what happened?" Leigh prompted when he paused. She had once created beauty with a stroke of a paintbrush, and she was enthralled with the workings of another person's creative process.

Wade looked at her for a moment, wondering why he was revealing anything of himself. But her violet eyes were wide with interest, and her lips were slightly apart in anticipation of his next words. He remembered that her mouth was petal soft, and despite all that he knew about what kind of woman she was, he had an almost desperate urge to kiss her. Instead, he finished his story.

"I didn't think my stuff was publishable, but a friend was over one night and read something I'd written. She knew an agent, and she encouraged me to send it to him. The next thing I knew it was published by a small company."

It was the shorthand version of what had happened. His confidence had been shot after he left Kinley, and he might never have amounted to anything if it hadn't been for the woman he'd mentioned. He met Kim Dillinger while living in upstate New York, and she was everything another man might have dreamed of: smart, pretty, funny, loving.

But Wade hadn't been ready to love anyone but Leigh, and Kim realized she didn't have much of a chance almost from the start. That hadn't stopped her from encouraging him, pushing him and even talking him into moving to Manhattan for the career advantages it offered. The move had effectively ended their relationship, but they still exchanged letters once or twice a year.

"And you worked your way up to the big time?" Leigh asked, wondering what sort of relationship he'd had with the female friend who launched his career. Even after all that had come between them, it still pained her to think of him in another woman's arms.

"Almost," he corrected, feeling the familiar rush of pride that signified the hardest times were behind him. Novelists often had to struggle to make a living, and he wasn't an exception. It was only in the past few years, with the help of some successful books and a savvy investment planner, that he felt comfortable with his financial situation. "I've written a few books that turned out to be quite successful, and one of the top publishers is interested in whatever I come up with next. It's not a shoo-in or anything. I have to write it, and they have to like it."

He stopped suddenly, as though he had talked too much, and Leigh really looked at him for the first time since he returned to Kinley. Wade still had springy, dark hair and olive skin, but nothing else was the same. His chest was broader, his body was fuller and his jawline seemed more defined, more uncompromising. Wade looked like a man, not like the slender boy she had known, but the man was just as attractive as the boy.

"You've changed." She stated the obvious.

"You make it sound like a bad thing." Wade sat back against the breakfast bench, folding his arms in front of him. "As I remember, I was a hellion who only thought about having a good time. Now I'm a respected professional who doesn't do anything more risky than drive a little too fast or try to get by without putting enough coins in the parking meter."

Leigh almost protested that he had been much more than a hellion. She remembered him as a spitfire with a contagious zest for the moment, and she had never felt more alive than when she was with him. In the end, she merely shrugged.

"I didn't mean to sound negative. I only meant that I never had you pegged for a novelist."

"But it makes everything a little easier, doesn't it?" He let the bitterness that had been welling up inside of him since his return to Kinley seep into his voice. At that moment, he almost hated her.

"I don't understand," Leigh said, and she didn't like the hard glint in his eyes.

"You and me. Here. Now. Even your father couldn't have objected to you having dinner with a respectable novelist," he said harshly.

Leigh saw a glimmer of pain behind his rough demeanor, and her heart sank. After all this time, the rejection still stung. Oh, Wade, she wanted to say, I never was ashamed to be seen with you. I was just a silly, young girl who was scared to death of my father. Please understand. I was only seventeen.

"You've done well for yourself, Wade, and I'm happy for you," Leigh said when she had recovered her poise, and he frowned. The frown was so deep, she could make out the worry lines around his eyes and the muscle twitching in his jaw. Wade rubbed his chin thoughtfully while he reminded himself that he couldn't believe anything she said. He swallowed his bitterness, schooled his expression to go blank and got to his feet.

"I won't object if you want to help with the dishes," he said and walked into the kitchen, pulling a shutter on the past. Leigh sat at the table for a full minute before she followed.

A half hour later, Leigh fingered the lovely lace tablecloth that Ena had left her, and her eyes moistened with tears. Wade watched her quietly, not understanding her reaction. His mother had kept the lacy tablecloth beautifully preserved, but it was at least thirty years old. It was hardly the type of bequest most people would relish.

She brought the tablecloth to her face and held it against her cheek, drawing his attention to the curved softness of her face. She had a peaches-and-cream complexion, but he knew her skin took on a burnished glow in the summer. Leigh's hair still fell down her back in silky strands, but her bangs gave her a soft, vulnerable quality.

"Did she really want me to have this?" Her voice was filled with awe.

Wade nodded, mesmerized by her reaction despite himself. She was like a chameleon, changing from temptress to villainness to sentimentalist in the blink of an eye. "I don't understand," he said.

Her teary eyes became reflective. "This was one of her prized possessions. It's an heirloom that was handed down to Ena from her mother, your grandmother. When she put it on her table, she always thought of Texas and home."

"Why would she give it to you?" Wade asked thoughtfully, unable to take his eyes off the puzzling woman before him.

"Because I thought it was beautiful," she said matter-of-factly. "But that's not why I love it. It means so much to me because it meant so much to her."

They were sitting on the floor in Ena's bedroom amidst dozens of half-filled boxes. Wade knew he had to go through his mother's possessions, but he hadn't been able to finish the task. He studied Leigh, and didn't know what to think. His mother had cared enough for Leigh to leave her a sentimental gift, and she had seldom been wrong about people. Wade wanted to believe the worst of Leigh, but he couldn't dredge up the old resentment when she got teary over a tablecloth.

"Has anyone meant a lot to you, Leigh?" he asked, surprising himself with both the question and the gentle way he asked it. Leigh knew immediately that he was really asking if there had been other men in her life since him.

She could have told him about the fast-talking business student she'd dated in college or the traveling salesman who made an unsuccessful stab at settling down in Kinley, but she couldn't have said they mattered. The bald truth was that she hadn't even come close to feeling deeply about anyone since the forbidden nights of their youth.

She carefully folded Ena's tablecloth and placed it on her lap before answering. "You know what life is like in a small town, Wade. You either marry your next-door neighbor or you don't marry at all."

"Haven't you ever been tempted?" he prodded, and Leigh bit her lip. Why was he asking her these questions and staring at her as though the answers mattered? She lowered her eyes to hide her confusion and then raised them again. When she did, she saw the intensity burning in his gray eyes and remembered a long-ago night when a dark-haired man had said he wanted to marry her. She'd been tempted then, but she'd also been afraid.

"I don't believe in marriage just for marriage's sake," she said finally, and her voice was smooth. "I always told myself I would marry for love or I wouldn't marry at all, so I haven't married at all. Can we change the subject, please?"

She could have married him, Wade thought, and his lips set in a tight line. Even after all these years, it stung to hear her tell him why she hadn't. She'd just admitted that she'd never been in love with anyone, and that included him. He'd long suspected that her feelings for him had never run deep. It shouldn't matter after all this time, but it did. Somehow, it made the boy he'd been seem like even more of a fool.

"Does it make you uncomfortable to talk about love?" Wade shifted his weight so he was leaning against Ena's bed. His action brought Leigh's attention to the bed, which was stripped of its sheets and bedspread, and she thought it was a strange place to be having this conversation. "I can remember a time when you used the word freely."

He was referring to their last night together at the cove when she'd confessed her love for him, but his tone was sarcastic. Leigh winced. He'd told her he loved her, too, but it was obvious that love had died more than a decade ago.

"No, of course it doesn't make me uncomfortable," she said in denial, but the dampness of her palms and the way she pressed her lips together branded her a liar. She was so nervous that she had to do something to shift his attention from herself to him. She cleared her throat. "What about you? Have there been lots of women in your life? Have you ever been tempted to marry any of them?"

A hint of a grin stole over Wade's face, and he stroked his strong chin. He had the hands of an artist with long, graceful fingers. He considered how truthful he should be, then opted for evasiveness. "Those are very different questions. Yes, there have been lots of women in my life. But no, I haven't wanted to marry any of them. I don't think I'll ever want to marry anybody again."

The last sentence was laced with self-mockery and a trace of bitterness, and Leigh realized yet again that the youth she had loved was gone and in his place was a man she didn't know.

"I don't know you anymore, Wade." He didn't respond to her whispered assessment, so Leigh said what had been on her mind all day. "I don't even know why you wanted me to come to dinner."

He was silent for so long, she thought he wouldn't answer. The overhead light reflected off the brown sheen of her hair and the delicate smoothness of her face, highlighting her beauty. The truth was that he didn't know what he wanted from her, either. He only knew that his body wasn't listening to his mind. It had been over between them for a long time, but heat still spread through him when he looked at her. All he could think about was peeling off her T-shirt and jeans, and falling unclothed with her onto the unmade bed. He felt himself grow hard at the thought.

"Maybe I wanted to rehash old times." Wade broke the silence with a rough response. "Or maybe I wanted to give you the things from my mother. Or maybe I just couldn't help myself."

Leigh swallowed and tried to figure out which statement was true, but her brain was too muddled. Was it possible that some of the old desire still smoldered between them? Did he look at her and want to taste her lips and run his hands over the satin smoothness of her skin? Leigh closed her eyes briefly against the remembered passion, because she feared those were exactly the things that she wanted him to do.

"I can hardly believe that. You seem like a man who has his emotions well under control," Leigh said when she trusted herself to speak.

Less than a foot separated them, and Wade slowly closed the gap. He had never used cologne, and Leigh breathed in the clean, male scent that had always pleased her. He was so close, she could feel his breath fanning her cheeks. "Then why do I want to kiss you?" he asked, each word a puff of breath.

"For old times' sake?" Leigh asked just as softly and she unconsciously ran the tip of her tongue over her lips. Wade's eyes followed the action and then he pulled her unresisting body into his arms.

Their lips molded together as if they had never been apart, and Leigh closed her eyes to savor the sheer sweetness of his kiss. She had been kissed by other men since he'd gone, but their embraces had never made her feel as though she was being lifted off the earth and transported to a higher plateau. Wade's mouth moved roughly over hers, but he didn't have to coerce a response. Her heart and her very soul lifted within her. She opened her mouth in flagrant invitation, and Wade deepened the kiss by circling her inner softness with his tongue.

It had been so very long since he'd tasted her that Wade had almost forgotten how exquisite she was and how he loved listening to the tiny moans of pleasure that came from deep in her throat. Even when Leigh had been inexperienced, she'd never left him guessing as to how he made her feel. Even now her arms were snaking around his broad shoulders until her fingers rested on the warm, vulnerable column of his neck. She threaded her fingers into his thick hair, and he groaned.

The peaks of Leigh's breasts tautened and sought the warmth of his chest through the thin material of his shirt. She met his tongue with her own and engineered an erotic duel until she could feel his unmistakable hardness against her thigh. His hands moved up and down her back, almost as though he were trying to reassure himself that it really was Leigh he held. The Leigh he had loved with all his young heart. The Leigh who had betrayed him. Wade's mind reeled and then, as quickly as the kiss had begun, it was over.

He pushed roughly against her shoulders to extricate himself from the embrace, already hating himself for having yielded to her. Leigh stared at him with round, haunted eyes that revealed everything he made her feel.

Wade had already pulled a curtain over his emotions, and the mistrust she read in his slate-gray eyes caused her to hurtle back to earth. For a moment, she had actually believed that one kiss could erase everything that had gone wrong between them. She lowered her eyes, unwilling to reveal anything else through her naked gaze.

"Why did you kiss me?" she asked when she could no longer bear the silence. Her pulse had slowed and her face was no longer so open, so she fastened her violet eyes on his unreadable features.

"Why did you kiss me back?" he retorted, and Leigh scrambled to her feet. She bent to retrieve the tablecloth and retreated a few steps toward the bedroom door. Wade gazed at her from his position on the floor, and Leigh suddenly felt silly. She was no longer a schoolgirl, and she could handle Wade's verbal tosses. She just wasn't sure if she could handle the physical ones.

"Old habits die hard," she said cruelly, and Wade could have choked on his stupidity. For a crazy moment he had almost forgotten what stood between them, but now she was revealing her true colors. Oh, he knew that she still found him physically attractive. Maybe she'd be amenable to a romp in bed, but she didn't want the essence of who he was any more than she had twelve years ago. The difference was that he no longer wanted her in that happily-ever-after way, either.

He drew himself to his full six feet and smiled the half grin she was coming to hate. She viewed the pseudosmile as a mask he put on whenever the old Wade threatened to peek through.

"Then we'll have to see that those old habits don't get in the way of our new relationship, won't we?" he asked, and indicated with a flick of the wrist that she should precede him through the door.

Leigh didn't need to be prompted a second time. She gathered the tablecloth and gladly escaped the stifling confines of Ena's bedroom. It had been a bad, bad idea to accept his dinner invitation, and she was annoyed at herself because she had known it from the beginning. She walked swiftly into the living room, calling over her shoulder that she was leaving.

"I'll walk you home," Wade said.

Leigh whirled to face him. After what had happened in the bedroom, she didn't want to spend any more time with him than was absolutely necessary. As it was, her body was still trembling from the aftereffects of his kiss. "Oh, no, that's not necessary. I can walk myself home."

Wade's face was composed, as though he had already forgotten about the kiss, and he gave a negative shake of his head. He indicated the front door. "I'm trying to get used to living in the South again. And, here in the South, gentlemen walk ladies home. So I'll walk you home," Wade said again, this time with a firmness that brooked no argument.

The night was the kind of glorious darkness that descends on South Carolina in late spring. The temperature was in the low seventies, perfect for walking but not cool enough for a sweater. Leigh lifted her eyes to the sky and the legions of stars twinkling there. One of the advantages of living in a small town was that there were no big-city lights to obstruct the natural beauty of the sky's lights.

She and Wade walked about a foot apart, but their cadence was perfectly matched. Somehow, her long, quick steps made up for the discrepancy in the length of their limbs. The purr of a car's engine disrupted the stillness of the night, and Leigh and Wade waved when they noticed Everett Kelly behind the steering wheel. He raised a hand in greeting and pulled into the driveway across from Ena's house. Leigh mentally shook her head, because she supposed it was Wade's house now.

"Poor Everett Kelly," Wade drawled as they walked. It was the first thing he had said since they left his house.

"What do you mean by that?" Leigh gave him a sidelong glance.

Wade kicked a small rock and it careened into the distance. "Did you see the look the guy just gave me? He's still in love with you. After all these years."

Leigh laughed shortly. She supposed it was safer to talk about how Everett Kelly felt about her than how she and Wade felt about each other.

"You're imagining things. Everett has always had, well, a crush on me, but he knows how things stand. He's just a dear, old friend who thinks he knows what's best for me."

"You mean he doesn't think you should be out walking with me?" Wade said, and couldn't stop himself from sounding bitter. As a boy he had been unfairly labeled, and he'd suffer because of it as long as he stayed in Kinley.

"I don't care what he thinks," Leigh said and was surprised to realize she meant it. Maturity had finally given her the confidence to discount what other people thought in favor of what she thought.

"That's a change," Wade said, not really believing her. The essence of living in Kinley was caring about what was said and thought about you and yours. Anyone who didn't like living that way could simply leave, as he had done years ago. He turned in the direction of her parents' house but Leigh stalled him with her words.

"Wrong way. It's been a long time since I lived at my old home. Do you remember old Mrs. Lofton's house? I bought it after she died about five years ago."

"But that old house is huge," Wade exclaimed as he headed in the direction she'd indicated. Her parents' house was a ten-minute walk, but Leigh only lived three streets from Wade.

"That's why I like it. I have a lot of room to spread out in, and I never feel short of space when friends come to visit. Come to think of it, I'd have enough space if an army came to visit." Leigh laughed at her joke, and thought she saw Wade smile. They were walking under some tall magnolia trees that obscured the light from the moon and the stars, and Leigh couldn't be sure.

The pale yellow house was in darkness when Wade and Leigh approached, and she cursed herself for having forgotten to turn on the porch light. She hadn't left on a single light in the house, either.

Wade took her arm when she stumbled, and his touch sparked a sudden swell of desire that frightened her. She had been trying to arm her defenses against him since he broke off their kiss, but he had gotten through them with a single touch. She was rigid at his side until they reached her front porch.

Leigh extracted her arm from his hold and dug into the front pocket of her jeans for her house key. When she and Wade were growing up in Kinley, no one ever locked their doors. Even now, she sometimes forgot. But crime had made its mark, albeit a small one, on their town in recent years.

"Thanks for the dinner and for giving me Ena's tablecloth. It really means a lot to me," she said.

Wade stuck his hands into his pockets and shrugged. "Don't thank me. She wanted you to have it," he said shortly, needing to get away from her but not making any move to do so. How was it possible to hate her and to want to kiss her at the same time?

The moonlight illuminated Wade's face, and Leigh saw what was possibly a spark of desire in his eyes. She swallowed and turned to unlock the door. Leigh slipped into the house and gazed at him through the opening in the doorway. The light played tricks with his face, and highlighted his arching cheekbones and strong chin.

"I'll be seeing you around, Leigh," he said, and turned away from her with an effort. Leigh's words stopped him.

"When are you going back to New York?" She asked what was uppermost in her mind. She needed to know when he would disappear from her life again, so she could prepare for it.

When was he going back to New York? He hadn't come to any conclusion yet, but he supposed now was as good a time as any to decide. He didn't want to stay, but he didn't want to leave yet, either, and he didn't want to think about why. He wasn't sure what he was going to say until the words were out of his mouth.

"I'm not going anywhere anytime soon. I've decided to stay awhile," Wade said. "Good night, Leigh."

"Good night," Leigh managed to say before closing the door. She leaned against it to support a body that had suddenly gone weak, and her heart raced. Wade was going to stay in Kinley, and she wasn't sure she could deal with that after what had happened tonight.

Wade walked slowly back to his boyhood home, not quite enjoying the peaceful quiet that had settled over Kinley. It wasn't yet ten o'clock, but there was little activity on the streets. In Manhattan, it was as busy at ten o'clock as it was in the middle of the afternoon. But here the only signs of life were the subtle noises from nocturnal animals; he hadn't even seen a passing car since Everett Kelly pulled into his driveway. A black cat crossed the street fifty feet in front of him, and Wade shrugged in resignation; he didn't expect any good luck while he was in Kinley.

He'd thought he'd gotten this town, and Leigh Hampton, out of his system, but that wasn't the case. Coming here had been like hurtling back through time until all his insecurities and doubts were exposed. When Leigh didn't show up for dinner on time, he was sure she had broken another promise; he had had a hard time dealing with the disenchantment until she'd arrived. But why should he expect anything from her any more than he could expect anything from this town? Kinley and her people had never been good to him.

Maybe he should have stayed and fought to clear his name years ago, but it had been simpler to pack up and leave. He hadn't deserved to be treated like a criminal when all he'd done was fall in love with the wrong girl. He didn't deserve to be treated like a pariah now.

Wade kicked a stone and watched it skittle into the night. He'd made the decision to stay, but he didn't know how to handle his feelings toward both the town and Leigh. He knew she was like poison, but he hadn't wanted to let her go when he'd held her in his arms. It had only been a simple kiss, but his body responded with all the passion that she'd stirred twelve years earlier. Somewhere in the night, an owl hooted. It was a melancholy sound—as melancholy as Wade's mood.

Chapter 4

"Leigh. Wait up, Leigh." Everett Kelly's voice came from somewhere behind her, and Leigh stifled an urge to speed up and continue her walk to town alone. Instead, she affixed a smile to her face and turned to wait for him. Leigh had uncharacteristically decided against her usual jeans and T-shirt and wore khaki slacks and a red-and-beige short-sleeved shirt. She told herself her attention to her appearance wasn't because she might run into Wade, but she knew that was exactly why she'd dressed up.

Everett, briefcase in hand and glasses sliding down his nose, was almost running in his effort to join her. He was dressed in dark slacks, a short-sleeved white shirt and a dark tie that he wore a trifle too short. Leigh sometimes teased him about his drab attire, but Everett insisted the townspeople wanted their accountant to look businesslike. You don't want to talk about your money to someone who's dressed like a rainbow, he often said.

A bubble of amusement threatened to burst through Leigh's smiling lips as she watched Everett approach. It wasn't yet eight in the morning, and the tall, thin man already looked frazzled. His thinning blond hair was out of place, his white shirt was coming untucked and he was breathing hard from exertion. Leigh swallowed her laugh, because it would upset Everett, and she really was fond of him.

"Whew! I thought I'd never run you down. You really should let me stop by your place on the way to work, so we can walk together," he said while he pushed his wire-rimmed glasses back into position.

"'Morning, Everett," Leigh said and resumed her walk. "We've already settled that. I don't leave for work at the same time every morning, and my house is not on your way."

"I don't mind going a few blocks out of my way for you, Leigh," he said petulantly.

"I know, Everett. And it's very sweet of you, but walking to work together every morning just doesn't make sense. We should just enjoy the chance walks we do have," she said firmly, because that was the only way to deal with Everett. He was as sweet and as loyal as a puppy, but he'd follow her everywhere unless she asserted herself.

"It sure is a beautiful morning," he commented as they walked, and Leigh drank in the Carolina atmosphere. The sun was bright in the morning sky, but it hadn't yet heated the earth. Dew still glistened on the grass and hung in droplets on the magnolia trees lining the path to the town's center.

Until Everett mentioned it, Leigh hadn't noticed the beauty of the morning, because she had been trying to erase memories of the night before. A fitful sleep had left her face pale and had deposited dark circles under her eyes, and she had spent more time than usual with her makeup, trying to camouflage the ill effects.

"One of the bad things about living in the South is you become accustomed to days like this. It's so easy to take it all for granted, because we have so many beautiful mornings," Leigh said.

"It was a beautiful night last night, too. Didn't you think, Leigh?" Everett ventured, and Leigh knew he was trying to steer the conversation to Wade and their nocturnal walk. Leigh could have made it easy for him by bringing up Wade's name, but she didn't.

"Yes, I did," she answered simply, and Everett smoothed his hair nervously as he kept in step with her.

"I was, uh, sort of surprised to see you with Conner last night," he said after a long pause, presumably one in which he gathered his courage. "I thought that kidnapping business would have scared you off a long time ago."

Something snapped in Leigh, and she whirled on Everett with violet eyes blazing. "Wade Conner did not kidnap anyone. Do you hear me? It was all a pack of ugly lies. He's a decent man, and he doesn't deserve to have people talk about him that way."

Everett retreated a few steps and looked like a boy who just had his hand slapped for sticking it where it shouldn't have been. "Gosh, Leigh. I was just saying what everybody's been saying about Wade for years. I didn't mean to make you mad."

His meek, hurt demeanor penetrated Leigh's anger, and she struggled to control herself. "You did make me angry, Everett, but I shouldn't have snapped at you like that. It's just that Wade was never found guilty of anything, and the town still treats him like a criminal."

A muscle in Everett's jaw moved, and his mouth twitched. "You sound like you care a lot about Wade Conner," he observed shakily.

"Wade's a part of my past, Everett," Leigh said, reciting the speech she had been mentally giving herself all morning. "I don't know him anymore. I just went over to his house last night because Ena had left something for me. It didn't mean anything. But I guess I do care that he's been treated unfairly."

"Forgive me?" Everett asked after a moment, and Leigh smiled at him. She hooked an elbow through his and took a step toward town.

"C'mon, accountant," she said. "We're going to be late for work if we don't hurry."

The days passed slowly, in much the same way they always had. The only difference was that Leigh expected every customer who walked through the door of the general store to be Wade. None of them was. By the time Sunday and the traditional weekly dinner at Grace Hampton's table arrived, she was glad to be away from the store and thoughts of Wade. She had been thinking of him, and that sizzling kiss, far too often, and she needed a mental vacation. But Ashley made sure she wasn't going to get one.

"Aren't you going to tell us all about your dinner date with Wade Conner?" Ashley asked sweetly, turning a sugary smile to her sister while Grace Hampton let out an audible gasp. Leigh glared at Ashley, who set her elbows on the dinner table prettily while she regarded her younger sister.

Ashley couldn't have chosen a worse time to ask the question. The family gathered at Grace Hampton's table every Sunday afternoon for dinner and a chance to talk over the week's happenings. Ashley's husband and two children and Drew's steady girlfriend joined the gathering, and the eight of them engaged in spirited, lively discussions that went on simultaneously. Quiet moments were rare, but Ashley timed her bomb perfectly. The family had just finished eating and lapsed into a temporary, saturating silence. Everyone gave Leigh their undivided attention, but she couldn't take her eyes off her ashen-faced mother.

"You had dinner with Wade Conner?" Her mother gasped, and the years fell away until Leigh felt like a disobedient little girl again. Tall, regal Grace Hampton, with her flair for the dramatic, had a way of infusing Leigh with guilt with a mere look. It often served to make Leigh defensive, and this was one of those times.

"Yes, Mother," Leigh answered while she smoothed her hair. There was nothing to smooth. Leigh's long hair was caught in a French braid, a style that perfectly suited the red-and-white checked sundress she had whimsically put on that morning. "Ena left me an old, lace tablecloth I admired, and Wade wanted to give it to me."

"That hardly means you had to have dinner with him." Grace's voice contained all the snobbery and incredulity that had once laced Drew Hampton III's booming voice when he talked about Wade. A decade ago Grace had lived in her husband's shadow, but she had become a strong woman after his death.

"He asked, and it wouldn't have been polite to refuse," Leigh said, trying to squelch the anger that threatened to bubble to the surface. She reminded herself that, for the most part, Grace Hampton was a fine woman and a good mother. "Besides, it was nothing. I haven't even seen him since we had dinner."

"Your mother's right, Leigh. You shouldn't be having dinner with a man like Wade Conner." Burt Tucker, Kinley's police chief, added his unwelcome opinion, and Leigh scowled at him. Ashley's husband was a bruiser of a man who was about three inches over six feet tall and weighed thirty pounds more than he should, partly due to Grace's cooking. His brown hair had started to retreat, but he wasn't a bad-looking man. Leigh, however, had never liked the beefy type.

"C'mon, Leigh. Do tell," Ashley almost purred, and Leigh could have kicked her. She wondered how Burt, annoying though he could be, put up with her. "Do you really expect us to believe that dinner with the handsome, notorious Wade Conner was nothing? Surely you have some juicy tidbit you'd like to share?"

"Yeah, like did he tell you where he buried that little girl's body?" asked Michael Tucker breathlessly, his ten-year-old eyes wide with interest. Leigh closed hers briefly to blot out the sight of her freckle-faced nephew casting stones at an innocent man. An admonition didn't come from either of his parents, but from his twelve-year-old sister, Julie.

"You know we're not supposed to repeat rumors, Michael. Daddy always says you can't believe everything you hear." She sounded like a sophisticate and looked like a pigtailed preteen.

"What did you hear, Julie?" Leigh asked, not able to stop herself. She had to know what the town's younger generation whispered about Wade.

"Only that Wade Conner kidnapped a little girl a long time ago and killed her." Michael eagerly supplied the answer before Julie could. Leigh looked at Ashley and then Burt, expecting them to correct the misinterpretation, but neither said a word.

"Honey, your sister's right. You can't believe everything you hear," Leigh told Michael when she became convinced no one else was going to deny the rumor. "It's true that a little girl was kidnapped, but we don't know if she died, because she was never found. As for Mr. Conner . . . the police chief—the one before your daddy—never charged him with any crime. When you get a little older, you'll learn that even after someone's arrested you assume they're innocent until they're proven guilty. That's the way the law works in our country. Isn't that right, Burt?'' She cast an admonishing stare his way.

"Of course it is," he said, addressing his children. "But you'll also learn that the good guys don't always get their man."

The two Tucker children narrowed their eyes as though they were trying to piece together a difficult puzzle, and Grace fixed Leigh with a disapproving gaze.

"Don't worry yourselves, dears. That man only came to town for his mother's funeral. He'll be gone anyday." Grace spoke to her grandchildren, but her eyes were still on her younger daughter.

"Actually, that's not quite true," Leigh announced, because she knew her family would hear the news sooner or later. "Wade has decided to stay in Kinley indefinitely."

"What?" Grace and Ashley spoke in unison.

"He's going to stay," Leigh repeated steadily although she had yet to get used to the concept herself. "He told me so a few nights ago."

"What a fool thing to do. No one in town wants him here." Grace recovered from her shock before Ashley did. "I hope this doesn't have anything to do with you, Leigh."

"What could it possibly have to do with me?" Leigh exclaimed, quickly losing the thin hold she held on her temper. Grace started to answer when Drew cut in.

"Hey, that's enough 'bout Wade Conner. Why don't we all pitch in and clear off this table? Did you ever notice what a mess eight people can make? It's mind-bogglin'," he said lightly, and Leigh could have hugged him for sidestepping the argument. Drew's girlfriend, Amy, a quiet blonde who had looked decidedly uncomfortable throughout the exchange, quickly got to her feet. Leigh followed suit.

"The last one to clear off their place settin' does the dishes," Drew challenged, and Michael and Julie quickly reached for their plates and glasses.

"You can't avoid the subject forever, you know." Ashley sauntered up to Leigh after the dishes were washed and the family had spread out. Leigh stood at the edge of her mother's rose garden, ostensibly admiring the delicate beauty of the flowers while she simmered over her family's unfair treatment of Wade.

"That was a rotten thing to do and you know it, Ashley," she said tonelessly, keeping her eyes averted. They were still filled with anger, and she didn't want Ashley to see the smoldering flames.

"Why, honey—I just asked an innocent, little question. Now how could that be rotten?" Even though she wasn't looking at her, Leigh knew Ashley was fluttering her eyelashes. A mosquito landed on Leigh's arm and she slapped at it before composing herself and turning to Ashley. Her sister's startling blue eyes, set in a pretty face and framed by a crown of blond hair, made her look angelic. Leigh knew better.

"You were just trying to stir up trouble and make things unpleasant for me," Leigh accused.

"Oh, fiddle faddle. I was just trying to find out how every little thing went with Wade."

Leigh sighed audibly. "Why won't you believe that there's nothing to tell? We had dinner. He gave me Ena's tablecloth, and then he walked me home. Period. He hasn't even tried to get in touch with me since."

Ashley leaned closer and whispered. "Did he make a pass?"

"Maybe I made a pass at him," Leigh said just so she could see the shock on Ashley's face. She turned from her sister and walked swiftly toward the home in which she had grown up, but she wanted only to get away from her family's stifling presence.

A light sheen of perspiration dampened her brow and her long hair came loose from her ponytail as she ran, but Leigh didn't give a second thought to her appearance. Instead, she ran as though something were pursuing her, and for once it wasn't the past. The present had come into a grim, terrible focus earlier that morning when she'd heard that another little girl had disappeared. Her breath was coming in shallow gasps by the time she reached Wade's home. She pounded loudly on the front door.

"Open the door, Wade," she pleaded, and pounded again. She nervously looked around and noticed the group of people forming a few houses down the street. A couple of them were staring at her, and none was smiling. They were already casting blame, and Wade had to know that it was falling on him. The sun shone brightly and cast a bright glare over the morning, but it was a dark day. She drew back her fist to pound again but the door swung open.

"What the—" Wade stood in the doorway dressed in a pair of gym shorts and wearing a look of surprise, but Leigh was too agitated to be embarrassed by his long length of bare leg or the hair that lightly dusted his powerful chest. If she had been less frantic, she would have noticed that his dark hair was mussed from sleep and his eyes were bleary.

She pushed past him into the house without waiting for an invitation and shut the door behind them. It was an uncharacteristic gesture for a woman brought up on good manners and Southern charm.

"What is going on? It's nine in the morning, Leigh. Not everyone keeps general-store hours," Wade said roughly as he pushed a hand through his tousled hair and tried to overcome the effects of too-little sleep. He hadn't seen her since the night they'd had dinner, but that didn't mean he hadn't thought about her. Mostly he'd thought about her when the house was at its quietest and he was trying to drift off to sleep. That was when his defenses were at their lowest, and his lingering anger didn't distort visions of her sweet face and delectable body. That was when he imagined making love to her as he had on that long-ago night of their youth. And in the morning, he'd wake up hating himself, but hating her even more.

Instant irritation washed over him at the sight of her, but then he really saw her for the first time that morning, and the fright and helplessness he read in her face alarmed him. His hands gripped her shoulders in support.

"What's wrong, Leigh?" he asked, trying to stem the rising panic in his chest. Even she couldn't think they were on good terms, so something had to be dreadfully wrong for her to barge into his house like this. Suddenly, inexplicably, he wanted to help her. "Just calm down and tell me what's wrong."

Leigh bit her lip and stared up into his face, which didn't have any of the defiance or mistrust she was getting used to. He looked anxious and concerned and ready to help her. If only

Wade knew that it was he who needed her help. "A little girl has disappeared, Wade," she told him, and her lips trembled. It was so awful that she could hardly bear to repeat it.

The color drained from Wade's face, and his Adam's apple swelled as he swallowed. If she would have doubted him, even for a moment, that reaction would have convinced her of his innocence. "Who is it?" he asked.

"Her name's Lisa Farley, and she's eight years old. It happened last night around ten o'clock." Leigh related the facts as she'd heard them that morning at the general store. "She was supposed to spend the night at a friend's house, but apparently the girls had a fight and Lisa decided to walk home. She never got there."

Wade released her shoulders and only then did she realize he'd been squeezing them so hard he'd probably left red marks. She rubbed them unconsciously while trying to figure out how they should handle the inevitable accusations that would be hurled at Wade, but he wasn't thinking along the same lines.

It was unthinkable that a town as serene as Kinley could have two disappearances, even if they had come twelve years apart. It must be a misunderstanding, Wade thought. Lisa Farley had probably gotten to her house last night, and found everybody asleep and the door locked; she was probably safe at a neighbor's home. Evil didn't strike twice in small, southern towns that had charm oozing from the magnolia blossoms. But even as he rationalized away what Leigh had told him, he knew it was true. And he knew that he had to do whatever he could to help. He pivoted and took a few quick steps toward the stairway, but Leigh stopped him with her words.

"Where are you going?" she asked in confusion, biting her lip. Didn't Wade realize the significance of the second disappearance?

Wade looked at her blankly, wondering why his motives weren't obvious. Did she think he was the kind of man who would remain idle in a situation where every man, and every minute, counted? "To put on some clothes," he answered. "They must have organized a search party for the little girl. I want to help."

"You can't do that." Leigh hurried to his side, detaining him by taking his hands. They felt warm and strong, but hers were trembling. She searched his eyes and saw that he really didn't understand. "Don't you see, Wade? Half the people out there think you did it."

"Me?" Wade asked in surprise and then the mask Leigh hated fell over his face. So that was why she was here. He should have been more suspicious of her sudden appearance at his door, but he hadn't thought the situation through. Now it made perfect sense. Guilt over leaving him to languish alone a dozen years ago had driven her to his house that morning.

He pulled his hands from hers as though they'd been burned. His mouth curled downward in a bitter turn, and every part of his body seemed to sag. For a moment, he had forgotten where he was and what everybody thought he'd done. He'd even forgotten that Leigh was the person who'd enabled Kinley's population to think the worst of him. He wasn't foolish enough to think that her coming to him was anything more than an attempt to make amends. He'd never be that foolish again. Not for the first time, he wished that he'd never come back to Kinley, that he'd never again seen this woman before him.

"Why didn't I think of that?" Wade said bitterly. "God, some things never change. I was a fool to come back here and think the past would just stay in the past."

"Let the past go for a minute, Wade," Leigh said, trying to ignore the rejection emanating from him. He may not like her, but she was going to make sure he listened to her because it was imperative that he know the full story. "The Farleys moved to Kinley after you left," she said and then delivered the blow. "They live just five houses down the street from you."

Wade sank onto the bottom step of the mahogany staircase and rubbed his brow, feeling helpless and sad and angry. "So a little girl is missing and people assume I took her instead of trying to find out what really happened? The damnedest thing is I can't even help look for her."

"I heard that the police chief is coming over here this morning to talk to you," Leigh said. She ignored his dejection, knowing that any comfort she offered would be like applying a Band-Aid to a gaping wound. She didn't doubt that he'd reject her sympathy anyway.

"At least that's a small consolation," Wade said, but there wasn't any joy in his voice. "Chief Cooper likes me."

"Chief Cooper died of a heart attack a couple years ago," Leigh said bluntly. "It's Chief Tucker now."

"Burt Tucker?" he asked, and Leigh nodded. For an instant, Wade wished he had shown more interest in Kinley's affairs while his mother was alive, but he'd always changed the subject when she'd mentioned the personalities in Kinley. After a while, she stopped talking about them. It probably wouldn't have made any difference anyway.

Knowing Burt was police chief beforehand wouldn't have lessened the animosity between them. They had been in the same grade at school, and Burt had been insanely jealous because he thought there was something going on between Ashley and Wade. His jealousy wasn't entirely unjustified; Ashley had made it clear she'd welcome an advance from Wade. But he hadn't made one, because she wasn't the Hampton sister in whom he was interested.

"If it's the same Burt Tucker I remember," Wade said reflectively, "then I'm sure he'll be willing to believe the worst of me."

Leigh took a step closer to Wade and looked down at him, but all she saw was the top of his dark head. She wanted him to know that she was on his side, that she was sorry she'd ever left it. "Nobody has accused you of doing anything wrong," she said. *Yet.*

His gray eyes swung to hers and held them. It was a moment that she would remember clearly until she took her last breath, because everything was reduced to the simplest terms. They were a man and a woman who hadn't trusted each other for a very long time, and now the man wanted her honesty. "What about you, Leigh?" he said, and his next question was almost a whisper. "Do you think I did it?"

Leigh stared into his eyes and saw a blend of vulnerability and bravado. Her answer was more important than he'd ever admit, and it came swiftly and surely. "Of course you didn't do it. Do you think I'd be here if I thought you did?"

"Why are you here?" he asked roughly even while a thrill coursed through him at her defiant answer. She believed him; she really believed him. Leigh's violet-blue eyes widened as though she couldn't fathom why he had asked.

"I want to help you," she said.

He could have delved into the reasons behind her offer or told her that he didn't need her help, but he did neither. Something about this entire scenario still didn't make sense. "Why would I need help?"

"It's as obvious as the shrimp boats out there on Mason Creek," Leigh said, but he didn't think anything about this was obvious at all. "Think about it. A girl disappears, and you leave town. Nothing happens until twelve years later when you come back. Within a couple of weeks, another girl disappears."

She paused, and her face was flushed and her breasts were heaving. "It all makes sense now," she said, the passion rising in her voice.

"What are you trying to say, Leigh?" Wade asked, befuddled as much by her reaction to his predicament as by her pronouncement.

"Someone's trying to frame you. And we have to find out who it is," she said forcefully, determination shining in her eyes.

Wade ran a hand over his face. He was a man who wrote fiction for a living, and the past ten minutes had seemed like a scene from a novel. Real life didn't happen this way. "That sounds like a pretty crazy notion," he said and then paused to consider it. "I know that a lot of people in this town don't like me, but what would anyone gain by framing me? It doesn't make sense."

"I know it doesn't, but anything else makes even less sense." Leigh got down on her haunches so she was at eye level with Wade. "If Kinley has some crazy person running loose, why did he wait twelve years to strike again? And why did he wait until you were back in town?"

"Maybe it's a coincidence," Wade said, but she was causing the wheels of doubt to spin in his head.

"It's no coincidence. Someone's trying to set you up. I know it, Wade. I feel it." Her impassioned speech struck a vulnerable cord in Wade, and he momentarily shoved aside his distrust of her. He wanted to reach out to smooth the errant hairs from her damp brow. She looked as fierce as a lioness protecting her cubs, and it struck him that she was protecting him. He wanted to believe she was behind him, but he couldn't help

wondering what her motives were. Maybe she wasn't his enemy like many of the people in Kinley, but he wasn't ready to
count her as a friend. He'd done that once before, and paid too
steep a price.

A heavy pounding sounded on the door, and the invisible
bond that had formed between them snapped. Leigh sprang to
her feet. "That'll be Burt," she said unnecessarily.

Wade followed suit more slowly, once again erecting his defenses against Leigh and the rest of Kinley, and within moments opened the door to reveal Burt Tucker. Although Wade
wasn't small, Burt topped him by a few inches and outweighed
him by about fifty pounds. Burt had once been the type of boy
who got into playground fights, but the school bully had grown
into the town lawman. He smiled mirthlessly at Wade.

"I'll give you three guesses why I'm here, Wade, but I bet
you only need one," the police chief drawled. From the smirk
on his face, he looked as though he was almost enjoying himself.

"Nice to see you again, too, Burt. Come in." Wade stepped
back to admit the chief, struck by the irony that in the South it
was customary for antagonists to address each other by first
names. There had been animosity between them since high
school when Burt, consumed with jealousy after finding out
about Ashley's crush, challenged Wade to a fight. Wade, disinterested in both Burt and his girlfriend, walked away without raising a hand. Burt took it as an insult, believing Wade
thought Ashley wasn't worth fighting for.

Burt pulled back the screen door and stepped into the house.
It was then that Leigh, looking disheveled and defiant, came
into view. Burt muttered an epithet.

"What in God's name are you doing here, Leigh?" he asked,
scowling.

"Good morning, Burt," Leigh said, ignoring his displea-
sure and her instant irritation. Burt thought that being the law
in Kinley entitled him to voice his opinion on everybody's
business, including hers. She focused her attention on Wade.
"I was just filling Wade in on what happened to Lisa Farley."

Burt scowled again and cast a dubious look at Wade, as
though he suspected Wade already knew what had happened to
the little girl. "Now that you've told him, I want you to leave,"

Burt ordered. Just about every statement he made was an order.

Leigh's first reaction was to argue, but whether she stayed or left wasn't Burt's decision. She looked at Wade for guidance. "Would you like me to go, too?"

"That's up to you," Wade said, and Leigh wasn't sure by his expression if he wanted her to stay or not. But she had abandoned him once, and she didn't plan to do it again.

"Then I'll stay," she said firmly, but Wade's expression still didn't change.

"If you'll both excuse me for a minute, I'm going upstairs so I can wash my face and put on a shirt," Wade said, instead of responding to her declaration. "You can wait, can't you, Burt?"

Burt settled himself into one of the dining room chairs, looking as though he were getting ready for a long chat. "I got all day, Wade. Right at this moment, there's no one I'd rather talk to than you," Burt said.

Wade ignored the accusation in the chief's voice, and headed for his bathroom.

"What was that supposed to mean, Burt?" Leigh said the instant Wade was out of earshot. There was something about the way Burt Tucker went about his business that had agitated her since they were children. "You don't have all day. You have a little girl missing and some lunatic running loose."

"What's a smart girl like you doing in a place like this, Leigh? What would your mother say if she knew where you were right now?" Burt ignored her criticism and leaned back in the dining room chair until two of its legs were suspended from the floor. "Your mother's right. Wade Conner is bad news."

"Spare me the lecture, Burt," Leigh said, her hands on her hips. "I should be lecturing you. If you knew a thing about Wade, you wouldn't be wasting your time here. You'd be out there trying to figure out what really happened."

"I am tryin' to figure out what happened, Leigh. And right now I'm thinking Wade might help me with my figuring. What makes you so sure I'm not on the right track?" he drawled. "Are you forgettin' what happened all those years back to Sarah Culpepper?"

"I could never forget," Leigh said, and the secret she had kept for twelve years was out before she could give it another thought. "I know Wade didn't kidnap Sarah because I was with him that night. My parents were out of town, and I snuck away to meet him. Then I snuck back in at three or four o'clock in the morning. So, you see, he couldn't have done it."

There was a long pause before Burt spoke. Disbelief dripped from his voice. "I think Wade can take care of himself without you coming to the rescue."

"It's the truth, Burt," Leigh bit out, shocked that he didn't believe her. "I wouldn't make up something like that."

"The memory gets fuzzy as the years go by, Leigh," Burt said, just as Wade walked into the room.

"Gets fuzzy about what?" Wade asked, looking from one in-law to the other.

Burt snickered, as though her story barely merited retelling. "Leigh here says she was with you the night Sarah Culpepper was kidnapped."

Wade looked across the room at Leigh and saw that she looked almost desperate for Burt to believe her. Or maybe he was misreading her expression. Maybe she looked desperate for Wade to forgive her. Twelve years ago, the admission she'd just made would have meant the world. It would have meant that she wasn't ashamed of what they'd shared. Today, he told himself firmly, it meant nothing.

"I thought we were going to talk about Lisa Farley," Wade said, pulling his gaze from the desperation in Leigh's violet eyes before the past could come rushing back. He couldn't afford that. He would have wagered that the questioning was going to get nasty, and he wanted to have his wits about him.

On the way upstairs and back, he'd had time to reflect upon his predicament and had gotten angrier by the minute. What right did Burt have to walk into his home and imply that he'd kidnapped a young girl? What right did any of Kinley's people have to treat him like a criminal?

"You better get this over quick, Burt, because my patience is wearing thin," Wade said, sitting down in a chair opposite Burt's. "I'm not going to be a scapegoat this time."

Wade had barely glanced at Leigh since he came into the room, and she felt oddly disappointed. Didn't he realize that she was his ally, that this time she wasn't going to abandon him? Burt looked at her, though, and it wasn't hard to tell what he was thinking.

"Like I said before, it would be better if the lady left," Burt said, and Leigh's ire rose.

"I'm staying," she said, and sat down next to Wade. He looked at her then, but he didn't get any pleasure from her pronouncement. It was obvious that the in-laws didn't get along, and Wade suspected that part of her reason for staying was to provoke Burt. The chief scowled in resignation, cleared his voice and fixed Wade with the look he used whenever he wanted to be intimidating.

"We have a little girl missin', a little girl who happens to live on the same street as you do. I want to know exactly what you did last night. When you ate supper. When you went to bed. When you did anything."

Wade folded his arms across his chest, and his voice was filled with dislike and distrust. "That sounds like an accusation, Burt. Why do you want to know what I did last night?"

"You figure it out, Wade. I'm the police chief of a quiet town of law-abiding citizens, and all of a sudden I got a little girl missin'. The last time we had a little girl missin' was the last time you were in town. Even a stupid man could figure out why I'm asking you questions, and you're not stupid."

The two men glared at each other from across the dining room table, and their dislike was palpable. Leigh broke the spell of silence by striking the table with the palm of her hand, commanding the attention of both men. She focused her shining eyes on the chief. "That's sheer foolishness, Burt. Chief Cooper would have arrested Wade if there had been any evidence against him. Did it every occur to you that he didn't do that because Wade had nothing to do with Sarah's kidnapping?"

"We're not talking about Sarah Culpepper. We're talking about Lisa Farley. And if you continue to disrupt my investigation, Leigh, I'm going to insist that you leave and not take no for an answer. I have a little girl missin', and I aim to find out what happened to her." Burt had dropped his easy drawl, and his words sounded as though they'd been encased in flint.

"But Wade didn't have anything to do with it." Leigh ignored her brother-in-law's order that she keep quiet.

"If that's so, he shouldn't mind answering my questions," Burt retorted. "I'm just doin' my job—"

"Burt's right, Leigh," Wade broke in, irritated that she was taking on the role of his protector years too late. He was still angry about being interrogated, but the chief could turn his investigation elsewhere after Wade answered his questions. And then Wade could forget about his silly notion to stay in Kinley and get out of this godforsaken town. "I don't have anything to hide, and I want to find out what happened to Lisa Farley as much as anyone else. What do you want to know, Burt?"

Nearly an hour later, Wade showed Burt to the door. Leigh watched them from the dining room, reflecting on the performance each had given. It had been a strange, rambling sort of interview with distrust as the only common bond.

Burt had taken every opportunity to interject veiled accusations into his questions, and Wade had steadfastly ignored them. He'd given Burt his full cooperation, and his answers had made him sound as innocent as a baby. The only problem was his alibi, because he didn't have one. She was sure Burt had doubted him when he said he sat in front of a word processor for most of the night and didn't write a word.

"I hope you get your man, Burt," Wade said at the door, and Burt narrowed his eyes until it appeared as though he was squinting.

"You can count on it, Wade. You can count on it."

"I don't think he believed you," Leigh said the moment the door was closed. Wade leaned against it and chewed on his bottom lip. He was already rethinking his decision to cooperate; maybe he should have insisted on having a lawyer present. But this was crazy. He hadn't done anything except come back to town for his mother's funeral. He certainly hadn't kidnapped a little girl in the dark of night. But it was starting to dawn on him that he could be in serious trouble if Lisa Farley wasn't found soon.

Wade pinched the bridge of his nose; he was tired and angry, and he didn't want to rehash Burt's questions and his own responses with Leigh. He knew he couldn't trust her with his heart, and despite the fact that she seemed willing to support him through this second disappearance, he didn't think he should trust her at all.

She looked beautiful, dressed in a soft sundress of eggshell blue that made her eyes appear more blue than violet. She was biting her lip with what looked like concern, and absently twirling a piece of her hair around one of her long, slim fingers. It wasn't the time to think about how she might look in bed with her lips swollen from his kisses and her fingers entwined in his hair, but the image came anyway. She was so unconscious of her sex appeal that it would have been crazy for him not to want her. But he already knew that it was even crazier to want her.

He thought again of the way she'd stood up to Burt and had finally given him an alibi for that long-ago night, but it gave him no satisfaction. He turned and walked toward the staircase that led to the second floor. He paused halfway up the stairs and tried not to be swayed by the hurt he saw in her face.

"Go back to work, Leigh," he said harshly. "I needed your help twelve years ago. I don't need it now."

A stunned Leigh stood in the dining room for several minutes after his departure before she quietly exited his front door.

Chapter 5

It had been a miserable two days, Wade thought as he walked out the door of his mother's home into the bright Carolina sunshine. He had spent the morning staring at his word processor, unable to concentrate on writing fiction when his own life had taken such a strange turn.

The Culpeppers had moved from the house next door after Sarah's tragedy, and a lady Wade didn't recognize was tending her flower boxes. He lifted a hand in greeting when she turned at the sound of his front door thudding shut, but she hurriedly glanced away, keeping her eyes downcast. After two days of living in a town where people thought the worst of him, Wade was starting to expect such slights. But he'd never get used to them, and they'd never fail to anger him.

He turned his attention to the red Mustang convertible parked in his driveway. A few days ago, he had been renting a blue Chevrolet, but he'd driven into Charleston and told the rental company he wanted something less staid. Driving with the wind whipping through his hair had always helped clear his mind, and he was going to need some sort of relief as long as he lived in Kinley. It had been unwise for him to even consider staying, a fact he had realized soon after Lisa Farley had been kidnapped. But the choice about whether to stay or go, at least for now, had been taken out of his hands; Burt Tucker saw to that a couple of days ago.

Wade had been at the corner station filling the Chevy's tank with gasoline for his trip to Charleston when the police chief's black-and-white cruiser pulled alongside him. Since Wade had noticed the car moving slowly up and down his street on an inordinate number of occasions since Lisa's kidnapping, he hadn't been surprised, just annoyed.

Burt had rolled down his window and leaned forward until his head was slightly out of the car. "Goin' someplace, Wade?" he drawled.

Self-service gas stations hadn't yet come to Kinley, so the attendant had been pumping the gas into Wade's car while he waited. Wade leaned against the side of his vehicle and fixed Burt with a challenging look. He knew for certain at that moment that submitting to Burt's interrogation the other morning hadn't helped steer the investigation in the right direction; the police chief's finger was pointed squarely at him. "I don't see where that's any of your business, Burt."

The chief laughed one of those laughs meant to convey disbelief. "Oh, now, I don't know about that. Seems to me I have a right to keep all my eggs in a bushel where I can see 'em, if you know what I mean. If I was you, I wouldn't get any ideas about goin' anywhere."

"Seems to me I have rights, too," Wade shot back. "If you're telling me not to leave town, don't expect me to pay much attention. I'm not some country bumpkin who thinks what you say is gospel. The law's on my side, Burt. I can come and go as I wish, and you can't do a thing about it."

Burt's mocking laughter faded long before Wade finished his speech. The red flush of anger started at his collar and rose to infuse his face. "Don't be too sure about that. I can charge you with kidnapping, and if the charges don't stick, I can call the Manhattan police and tell them what I suspect. Somehow, I don't think a fancy novelist like you wants that kind of information getting around."

Burt's face was as bright as an overripe peach, and Wade knew he had a powerful enemy. At the moment, he was so angry, he didn't care. "You know what, Burt? I've been thinking too highly of you all these years. I always thought you had about as much intelligence as a nail, but I was wrong. You're even dumber.''

Wade peeled a few bills from his wallet and paid the stunned station attendant, who had overheard their exchange. He got into the car, started the ignition and drove straight out of town. Even after Burt had told him not to leave, Wade didn't expect the police chief to follow him. If he were leaving Kinley for good, Burt and everyone else in town would know about it. It was impossible to put a house up for sale or settle an estate without small-town tongues wagging, and he hadn't done those things yet. He'd hardly had time to grieve for his mother.

That had been Tuesday. Now it was Wednesday afternoon, and Wade needed to get away from Kinley if only for a while. He wished he were driving away forever, but it seemed wiser to stay until the mystery was solved; he didn't want anyone associated with his career to get wind of the ugly goings-on in Kinley. His professional reputation was at stake.

He slipped behind the wheel of the gleaming red Mustang and felt a little better. He knew his problems would be waiting when he returned, but there was time enough to face them. Because the more he thought about it, the more he suspected that Leigh had been right the other morning when he had brushed aside her offer to help. Considering that Burt didn't appear to have another suspect, it made even more sense. Someone in this godforsaken town was trying to frame him.

By the time Wednesday arrived, Leigh was even more ready for a break than usual. Leigh adored Wednesday afternoons and savored them like a dieter allowed only one piece of chocolate a day. Progress may have made its mark in Kinley, but the town still shut down most of its businesses at lunchtime and on Wednesday afternoons.

It had been a difficult couple of days, and Leigh thought she would surely scream if another customer mentioned Sarah Culpepper, Lisa Farley and Wade in the same breath. Even the long-unspoken alibi she'd given Wade for Sarah's kidnapping twelve years before didn't carry any weight. Nobody believed her, from the proprietor of the town's only gas station to her sister. She could still hear Ashley's reaction and the disbelief that had dripped from her voice.

"I don't remember you as the rebellious teen, dear," Ashley had said. "And now you want me to believe that you risked Daddy's wrath to sneak off in the middle of the night to be with Wade Conner?"

"It's true," Leigh had said, irritated that even Ashley didn't believe her. "A couple of days ago, you even said you'd always suspected I'd been involved with him twelve years ago. Why won't you believe me now?"

"You're sweet on Wade Conner, that's why. Maybe you always have been," Ashley had answered without a pause. "And it's blinding you to some hard facts, the simplest one being that you should just stay away from him."

Leigh had glared at Ashley, not even bothering to answer. What would be the point anyway? She couldn't say that she wasn't attracted to Wade all over again, because that would be a lie. And it seemed pointless to defend her right to see him when he'd made it perfectly clear that he didn't want her around.

The warm, afternoon sun felt so good that Leigh impulsively decided to take a long walk after closing her shop. She was dressed for walking anyway. Her hair was tied back in a ponytail and she wore old running shoes, blue jeans and a red T-shirt she had purchased in Charleston the year before during the city's annual arts festival.

Within minutes, she was walking out of town on the road that led to the old schoolhouse. The moss hanging from the giant oak trees rustled slightly in the breeze, and Leigh experienced a sense of déjà vu. Twelve years ago she had chased her homework down this very road when Wade Conner came into her life.

So much had changed since then, and so much hadn't. She was still residing in her hometown, still living the simple life and wondering why it wasn't enough. It never had been—not when she was a teenager and not now. She used to dream of herself in a metropolitan setting, hurrying to art classes, maybe even putting on an exhibition at a gallery.

Leigh sighed. She hadn't allowed herself to daydream like that in a very long time, but this walk on this road reminded her

of another time when a much-younger Leigh didn't know what
the future would bring. Would it all have been different if she
had had the courage to stick by Wade when he'd needed her?
Or was it her destiny to spend her life alone and childless in a
small corner of the world when she'd yearned for so much
more?

The hum of a sports car interrupted the afternoon quiet, and
Leigh looked over her shoulder to see a gleaming red Mustang. Even though she had never seen the car before, Leigh
knew instantly that it belonged to Wade. The townsfolk had a
saying that you had to be going to Kinley to get there, and no
one in town drove a red Mustang convertible. The car skidded
to a stop a few feet past her.

The car's top was down, and Wade turned completely around
in the seat. He lifted his sunglasses and peered at her with his
gray eyes. His hair was disheveled, and his bright yellow T-shirt
made his hair seem darker and his skin even more sun-kissed.
Leigh had been so deep in thoughts of the past and of destiny
that it almost seemed as though she had conjured him up. His
next words told her that maybe she had.

"Wanna go for a ride, Leigh Hampton?" he drawled,
speaking the same words he had used a dozen years ago.

"Sure, Wade Conner," she answered without pausing to
think. And then she knew that seeing Wade again had been inevitable. It had been inevitable ever since she spoke those words
of love in the darkness of their youth.

When Wade had seen the figure of a woman walking down
the lonely stretch of road, he knew instantly that it was Leigh.
He also knew instantly, despite his pronouncements to himself
that he didn't want or need her around, that he was going to
stop. He, too, recognized the echoes of the past and remembered how nervous he'd been the first time he'd approached
her. Wade hadn't been shy in his younger days, but his insides
had been quaking when he'd asked her to go for that motorcycle ride with him. He still had a touch of that boyhood fear
of rejection; he still wondered whether she would accept.

But she hadn't even hesitated, climbing into the Mustang and
sinking into the bucket seat. She'd even flashed him a smile
before she'd done so. And now here they were, a man and a

woman sitting in a car with the world, or at least a backwoods southern town, standing between them.

"Is this a new toy?" she asked, taking in the luxury around her.

"Let's just call it a rented toy," Wade said, and put the car in gear. The whoosh of wind freed tendrils of Leigh's long hair from their confines and sent them blowing about her face, and Wade couldn't help drinking in the sight through his peripheral vision. She suddenly looked very young, and it was as if all the years that stood between them had never passed.

"I don't remember seeing this car in your driveway last week," Leigh said, raising her voice to be heard above the wind. "It seems to me that I remember a gray Buick."

"It was a blue Chevy," Wade corrected just as loudly, cutting his eyes at her before returning his attention to the road. His hands were capable and strong on the steering wheel. "If I have to stay in Kinley, I figured I should at least have a little fun. I wanted to treat myself, and I've grown out of motorcycles."

A measure of sadness crept into his voice. "I know Mother wouldn't have minded. She always said the way to fight the blues was to buy something red."

Leigh laughed although he hadn't meant it to be funny. She couldn't help herself. Ena had been such a gem, so full of the love of life and of her son. Wade was still mourning, but he was right. Ena wouldn't have wanted him to lock himself away in her house and sulk. But would Ena have wanted him to stay in Kinley?

"Does getting this car mean you were serious?" Leigh asked as the sleek Mustang pulled to a halt at the stop sign leading to Highway 17, the roadway linking Charleston with Georgetown.

"About what?"

"About moving back to Kinley. I wasn't sure if you really meant it the other night." Leigh stared at him so intently that she missed the raccoon that crossed the road in front of Wade's car.

Something indefinable in her voice caught at Wade, and he turned to consider her. Should he admit that the decision to stay had been a rash one he'd reconsidered almost immediately? He didn't want to stay here, in this town where distrust was as palpable as the humidity in the air. Nobody trusted him, and he surely didn't trust the woman looking at him with her wide, violet eyes. But what he wanted didn't matter anyway. The town's lawman, her brother-in-law, had seen to that.

"I didn't buy the car, Leigh. I'm just renting it," Wade said finally, and his dark sunglasses shielded his eyes from the sun and from her. "And I don't have a choice about whether to stay or go. Burt ordered me not to leave town."

He stepped on the accelerator, and the roar of the wind prevented any more conversation. The main highway was long and desolate with mile after mile of bland scenery, and it always struck Leigh as ironic that a passerby would never guess that a jewel of a town lay just to the east. The car's speedometer inched past seventy, then eighty and neared ninety, and Leigh wondered how she would feel if she were leaving Kinley forever. Would it make a difference if this man were at her side?

But then reality stuck its cruel head into her daydream. Wade would leave town one day soon, and she couldn't abandon her responsibilities even if he did want her. And that was a very big *if*, because he hadn't shown any sign that he wanted to pick up where they'd left off. Besides, he was a man with a very big problem. Correction. They had a very big problem, because he needed her help whether he was willing to admit it or not.

The road was straight, flat and free of traffic, and Wade felt his worries fly away as the powerful machine sped over the concrete. Leigh looked at Wade and saw that his face was bathed in pleasure while the wind whipped through his hair. The devil in him hadn't really been exorcised, and that should have scared her.

About twenty miles down the highway, Wade slowed the car to make a U-turn and then quickly built up speed on the straightaway. It seemed as though only a few minutes passed before they were back at the welcoming sign that signaled the turn to Kinley and proclaimed it The Seafood Capital. Throughout the drive, neither Wade nor Leigh had said a word.

"You weren't kidding when you said one of your vices was speeding tickets." Leigh broke the silence as the Mustang headed toward town at a more leisurely pace. "You're lucky Burt didn't pull you over."

"It just goes to show that you should be more careful whom you accept a ride from," Wade teased, and Leigh thought that maybe he hadn't changed very much after all.

Leigh settled back against the comfort of the car's leather seats, breathed deeply of the fresh air and shut her eyes. For once, she felt at peace in Wade's company. She forgot everything until she felt the car slow and turn off the main artery onto a bumpy road. When she opened her eyes, she was in a place she hadn't been for more than a decade. Wade unfolded himself from the Mustang and Leigh followed him into the past as if pulled along by something stronger than herself.

The cove still looked the same: a bank covered with grass, an inlet with gently rolling water, a profusion of moss-draped trees. It brought back a thousand memories. She sat next to him on the grassy bank as she had years ago.

He didn't know why he'd brought her here any more than he'd known why he offered her a ride. Maybe it was because the past had a way of repeating itself. He'd brought her to the cove the night Sarah Culpepper was kidnapped: it was only fitting that they come here after Lisa Farley vanished. The crimes were linked in some irrational, bizarre manner in much the same way as his life was linked to Leigh's. The bond was there, but it didn't make a whit of sense.

"Are you going to listen to Burt?" Leigh asked, and it took a moment for Wade to realize she was talking about her brother-in-law's order that he remain in Kinley.

"I don't have much choice," Wade said, staring ahead at the water. For some reason, he had left his sunglasses in the car and felt exposed without them. "I know he doesn't have the right to order me around, but he could make trouble for me if I go back to New York. He's already threatened to call the New York authorities if I leave."

A gamut of emotions that started with relief and ended with outrage flowed through Leigh. She didn't want Wade to leave Kinley—not yet, not before they'd done what they should have done years ago—but she was appalled at the way Burt twisted the law to suit his purposes.

"That could hurt you professionally, couldn't it?" Leigh asked, and Wade nodded. He picked up a small rock and threw it into the water.

"I used to think all this was behind me," Wade said, and Leigh wondered if he included her in his sweeping reference. "But it's not. If anything, it's even worse than it was the last time. At least I had an alibi then. This time, all I have is my word."

"That's enough for me," Leigh said, but still he didn't look at her. He seemed absorbed in thought.

"In fact, the more I think about it, the more I think you were right the other morning," Wade said.

"Right about what?" Leigh said, finding it difficult to follow his train of thought. He was confiding in her, yet he was holding back something important. She had known that he wasn't telling her everything when he didn't respond to her murmured statement that she trusted his word. It was probably because he didn't trust her.

"It's too much of a coincidence. If the kidnapper is still in town—and it's obvious he is—why would he wait twelve years before striking again?"

"Because you're back," Leigh answered, and then paused. "Now the question is, what are we going to do about it?"

Wade shook his head helplessly, at a loss for an answer. A little girl was missing, and his reputation, maybe even his future, was on the line. The ironic thing was that he was discussing his problem with the woman who had a hand in ruining his past. He watched her and could see that she was formulating a plan. He noticed that she had asked what *they* were going to do about his dilemma rather than what he was going to do about it. For an instant, he thought about walking away, but he didn't; he needed all the help he could get and she owed him hers.

"I don't see how we can help find out what happened to Lisa Farley," Wade said reflectively. "Burt's already warned us to stay out of his way, and nobody in town would talk to me about it anyway."

"Maybe we won't be able to find out what happened to Lisa," Leigh said, her violet eyes shining, "but we can try to find out what happened to Sarah."

Wade's head snapped up. "What are you talking about?"

"It's a long shot, but I think it's our only shot," Leigh said, and the words and her idea flowed. "The crimes had to be related, right? If we find out who kidnapped Sarah, we'll know who kidnapped Lisa.''

Wade shook his head. "It won't work. The trail's cold. And besides, we can't be sure the same person took both girls. It's just a theory."

"Listen to me, Wade. It's the only theory we've got, and that's enough for now. I know the trail's cold, but we never tried to follow it. I hid my head in the sand, and you left town. Don't you think we owe it to ourselves, and to Sarah, to try?" Leigh was pleading, and she hardly understood why.

A muscle in Wade's jaw worked as he wrestled with what she had told him. He stared at her for long moments and noticed how her lush mouth was slightly parted in anticipation and how her eyes were wide and pleading. She had hurt him once, and he'd be a fool to believe in her again because the sun shone out of her eyes when she looked at him. But maybe it wasn't such a crazy idea, and maybe it was the only shot he had. She waited for his answer, and he sensed that she was holding her breath.

"What's our first move?" he asked levelly.

Leigh let out the breath she had been unconsciously holding. His agreement was more important than she had realized. "As soon as you're ready to go to Charleston, I think we should pay a visit to Martha Culpepper."

After a moment, Wade nodded in silent agreement and Leigh gave him a genuine smile. She needed to help him almost as much as he needed her help. For the first time since she'd seen Wade again, she felt a flash of hope. Maybe she could earn his trust again, maybe she could make things right. It was hot and sticky without the benefit of a manufactured breeze, and Leigh unconsciously lifted her ponytail to cool her skin.

"Why haven't you cut it?" Wade asked.

The answer came to her in a rush. A mane of hair that fell to the waist was highly impractical in hot, humid South Carolina, but she had never seriously considered another style. Years ago, a man had run his fingers through the silken mass and told her never to cut it. She never had.

Leigh dropped her eyes and lied. "I guess I'm too chicken to see what I'd look like without it," she said, letting her ponytail drop back against her neck.

He searched her face for tense seconds and then sighed, displeased with what he found there. She probably didn't even remember how much he had loved touching her hair; why should he expect her to have been unable to cut it because of him? After what had happened, why should he expect anything of her at all? He was probably crazy to let her help him try to find out what had happened to Sarah Culpepper. Wade lay back against the bank until the thick, dark strands of his hair mingled with the grass. Somewhere in the distance, a bird sang.

"I don't know why I brought you here," Wade admitted, his voice husky. "It brings back too many memories."

Leigh pressed her lips together as a vision of two young bodies entwined on the bank came into focus. She had told him that night that she loved him, and the next day their secret world of stolen moments had crumbled. That was the day that her life, the one that was full of hope and promise, had ended and another had taken its place. She hadn't only abandoned her lover, but herself, as well. But how could she tell him that?

"They weren't all bad memories, Wade," Leigh said instead.

"I wouldn't call a little girl vanishing into thin air a good memory," Wade said, deliberately misunderstanding. He didn't want to think about the good times. She was too much like the girl he remembered with the silken tresses and promise in her voice, the promise that had turned out to be a lie.

It was a warm afternoon, but she managed to look mesmerizing despite the wilting effects of the heat. He knew she must perspire, but he didn't see any trace of it. He also knew the years must have taken their toll, yet her face was as unlined as a teenager's. And that was what he couldn't forget: the teenager who had broken his heart. Before he could stop himself, the question he swore he'd never ask was on his lips.

"Why didn't you say anything, Leigh?" he asked, and he wanted an answer. He'd wanted an answer for twelve years.

Leigh's heart hammered against her ribs, because it was the question she'd been dreading. Even though she'd expected him to ask for an explanation, she hadn't prepared an answer. She turned to him slowly; his brows were knitted together, and she had too much respect for him to pretend she didn't know what he was talking about.

She bit her lip and shook her head. "You can't know how many times I've asked myself that. And I still can't be sure."

Wade pulled himself up into a sitting position and turned to face her, steeling himself against the way the sun illuminated the face he still found so compelling. "Why not?" he asked.

"Oh, I don't know," she said, lowering her eyes to the ground. "Everything back then seems so jumbled."

"Oh, come off it, Leigh," Wade bit out, surprising himself with the vehemence of his words. He'd told himself repeatedly during those twelve years that the past was gone and forgotten, but he hadn't meant it. The events of a dozen years ago were still as clear to him as the crystal in his mother's china cabinet. "You owed me an explanation a long time ago, and you've had twelve years to perfect it."

He was right, of course, but that didn't make the situation any easier. Leigh raised her face to the sky, because she couldn't talk about this and look at him at the same time. "Oh, I had my reasons," Leigh said sadly. "Back then, I used to think that living my life in Kinley would be like dying before my time. This place seemed so suffocating. I wanted to go to college and make something of myself. Then I fell for you, and I didn't know what I wanted anymore."

She paused, and she could almost feel his anger hanging between them in the moist Carolina air. He deserved an explanation, and she had just skirted around one.

"That's not entirely true," Leigh confessed, still not looking at him. "I knew I wanted you. But I didn't want to face my father's anger. I was so afraid of him. He seemed all-powerful back then. I even imagined he'd find a way to see that I never got out of Kinley."

Wade laughed shortly. Her story was preposterous, especially in light of the fact that her father was dead and she was living the kind of life she'd said she dreaded. "Do you expect me to believe that?"

"It's the truth," Leigh said, hurt by his mockery. "Why wouldn't you believe it?"

"Because look at you, Leigh," Wade said, and he was looking at her so bitterly that she flinched. "You're a small-town girl working in her dead father's general store. You never got away from Kinley. Maybe you never even wanted to."

"That's not true," Leigh protested, stung by his description of her. It wasn't entirely her fault that life had meted out blow after blow. First she'd lost Wade, then her father and finally her dreams.

"You could have left Kinley with me," Wade said, speaking aloud the dream he'd had in the days before he'd grown up and discovered that love was a lie. "You didn't have to wait around for your father's permission."

Leigh looked at him, shaking her head. Did he really think that had been a possibility? "Think about what you're saying," she pleaded. "I hadn't even finished high school. Remember, I wanted to go to college."

"You could have gotten your GED. We would have managed somehow," Wade said angrily. He wasn't even sure he believed what he was saying, but the words had been in his heart for so long that they had to be spoken.

"Without any money? Without our families? Without our friends? What would they have thought?"

"Ah, there's the rub," Wade said derisively. "You were always so concerned about what people thought. Why don't you just admit it, Leigh?"

"Admit what?" Leigh said, and there were tears in her eyes because he wasn't even giving her a chance. He was asking questions and she was answering them, but he was only hearing what he'd decided long ago to be true.

"That you were ashamed of me." The words were clipped and filled with what sounded like hate.

"It was never that," Leigh said, and the tears spilled down her cheeks. "You're right in that I didn't want people to gossip about me, but I was never ashamed of you. I was a kid who disobeyed her father and let a boy go all the way. I know I wanted to make love every bit as much as you did, but I wasn't ready to handle the consequences. I was confused, don't you see that?"

"So confused that you were ready to let me take the blame for a crime I didn't commit?" Wade spat out, determined to ignore her tears. He was the one who had been wronged, not her.

"I don't care if you don't believe anything else I say, but believe this, Wade," she beseeched. "If Chief Cooper had arrested you, I wouldn't have let you go to jail. I would have told him everything I knew. Only he didn't arrest you."

"Did you ever wonder why?" His lips barely moved when he phrased the question. Leigh nodded, trying to stop her flow of tears. She had wondered nothing else for months after Sarah Culpepper vanished.

"Chief Cooper knew about us," Wade said, and he wasn't surprised to see Leigh's mouth drop open. "He knew we met out here, and he saw us headed here the night Sarah disappeared. Mrs. Culpepper was quite sure it was a little after six o'clock when she saw me helping Sarah fix the flat on her bicycle. When Chief Cooper spotted us together that same evening on my motorcycle, for some reason he checked his watch. It was ten past six. So as far as he was concerned, I didn't need an alibi. He was my alibi."

"But . . . but," Leigh sputtered, barely able to make sense of it. Now that she knew the truth, she wasn't sure what she had believed. "Why didn't he tell anyone I was with you?"

Wade sat up and pushed his dark hair back from his face. There were beads of sweat on his forehead, and the sun suddenly seemed very hot. "It doesn't matter." He shook his head.

"Why?" Leigh asked again, and it was almost a minute before he replied.

"Because I asked him not to. I knew how you felt. I knew you didn't want anyone to know about you and me," Wade said, and his face was stony; he wouldn't have revealed what he was thinking for a lifelong contract with a prestigious publishing house. There was no reason why it should, but her rejection still hurt. After all this time and all the distance that had been between them, it still hurt. Wade had been stung by a bee before and had watched his foot swell to twice its normal size; this felt as though he had been stung on the heart.

Leigh stared at him and realized he didn't know anything at all. She hadn't told him how the seventeen-year-old Leigh had cried herself to sleep after he left town or how the grown-up Leigh was plagued with guilt over what she had done. Most of all, she hadn't told him that she meant what she said that long-ago night. She had loved him. If she had been older and more aware of what a rare treasure true love was, she would never have let him go.

"Let's just drop it," Wade said before Leigh could reply. What had he expected her to say anyway? That someone held a gun to her head and forced her to abandon him? That she hadn't been ashamed of him after all? He may not have been born into one of Kinley's great families, but he had as much pride as she did. And she was never going to know that she had mattered to him as much as she had. "It was all a long time ago, and it wasn't even that important back then."

Not important? It felt as though a dagger had pierced Leigh's heart. Is that really what he thought of their long-ago love affair? Had she really mattered so little that he could dismiss her greatest embarrassment, her greatest mistake, with a shrug of his shoulders?

"Do you really think that, Wade? That it wasn't important?" Leigh tried to hold them back, but the words still sprung from her lips.

He considered her for a long moment and then shook his head. Leigh could have wept with relief, but then she realized he was no longer talking about their relationship. "It was important that a little girl disappeared and was never heard from again. It is important that it's happened again. And it's important that we try to find out as much as we can."

"I was talking about us," Leigh said quietly, blinking a few times to try to stop her tears from flowing. Wade reached across the chasm separating them and gripped her shoulders, pulling her so close, she felt his breath on her face. It was an ignominious position, but her body leapt in response to his touch. She parted her lips, wanting his kiss as well as his forgiveness, but he didn't close the rest of the gap.

"There hasn't been an us for a long time," Wade shot back, shaking her. He released her abruptly, angry because his desire swelled at the contact. She let out a single sob, but he was determined to remain unmoved by her distress. It was too difficult to forgive what she had done, especially here in this cove where the past surrounded them. "You saw to that twelve years ago."

Wade rose abruptly and started walking toward the car. "Coming?"

Leigh stared after him, her face streaked with tears, and the flash of hope she'd experienced a few minutes ago was long extinguished. She didn't follow him to the car until she had dried her tears. She opened the door and hazarded a glance at Wade, but his attention was already on his driving. As far as he was concerned, there was nothing more to say.

"You're a fool, Conner," Wade said to himself a while later as he watched Leigh move down the sidewalk leading to her home. She paused after unlocking her front door and she took one more look at him before disappearing into the house. Wade was left with a vision of a long-haired, slim-hipped enchantress he couldn't exorcise.

"Fool," he repeated and noticed that his knuckles were white from the viselike hold he had on the steering wheel. He relaxed his grip, put the Mustang into gear and drove the few blocks to his boyhood home.

Since Leigh had appeared at his mother's burial with her sad eyes and her sympathy, Wade hadn't acted rationally. No, that wasn't accurate. He had acted like an infatuated idiot.

He cast his mind over the happenings of the past two weeks and knew his conclusion was on target. Leigh had wounded his heart with her betrayal a dozen years ago, and he vowed to have nothing more to do with her. But he had barely arrived in Kinley and already he had asked her to dinner, taken her into his arms, driven her to their secret cove and agreed to try to solve an ancient crime with her.

He'd also lost whatever grip he had on his temper and his mind. Despite his flare-up at the cove, he hadn't refused when, on the short drive to her house, she tentatively brought up the subject of their investigation. Instead, he made arrangements to pick her up at nine the next morning for the trip to Charleston to visit Martha Culpepper.

It was lunacy. Wade had made a life for himself in New York that didn't include the ugly suspicions of a small town or the damning silence from the woman he loved. He had become a success as a novelist through ambition and old-fashioned hard work. He had a niche in Manhattan, a circle of friends, female company whenever he wanted it and a measure of happiness. Why had he been willing to throw it all away after one more look at Leigh Hampton?

The early evening twilight cast Ena's home in shadows that suited his mood. It brought home the point that nothing was ever all black and all white, including Leigh's motives for not providing him with an alibi when tragedy struck. Anyway, what had he expected when he'd asked Leigh to explain? Wade hung his head, because he knew the answer.

He wanted her to say that she was sorry, that she'd regretted her action since that day because she'd always loved him. Hell, he wanted her to say that she loved him still. Instead, she dodged the question and murmured something about not wanting her father to know about them. "I never should have asked her," Wade said aloud. "I never should have let her back into my life."

He unfolded his long frame from the car and noticed that Everett was sitting on his porch across the street. Wade lifted a hand in greeting, but Everett didn't make any response. Instead, he vacated his chair and disappeared inside the house. When the town's accountant won't even acknowledge you, Wade thought, it's just one more indication that you're not wanted here.

Much later, Wade lay against the cool sheets in his bed and stared at the ceiling. He seldom doubted his course of action, but the decision to stay in Kinley even a minute more than necessary had been a bad one. Returning to the small town where he grew up was supposed to stimulate his writing, but thus far he had gotten himself accused of kidnapping and hadn't even come up with an idea for a new book.

Just days ago, he had actually thought he could start a new, simpler life in Kinley. But he'd been fooling himself even then. Hadn't he always had a daring streak that cut a wide swath through his body? How could he ever satisfy that part of himself in Kinley?

Wade locked his hands behind his neck and sighed. The more traditional part of him wanted a wife and a family, but he was thirty-two and no nearer to marriage than he had been at twenty. He was never short of dates, but his relationships seemed to fizzle after a few months. He thought of the last woman he'd taken out in New York, a slim blonde with delicate features and classic looks, but the image left him cold.

Thinking about Leigh would have a different effect on him, but he wouldn't let himself dwell on her; he had thought about her too much already. Wade closed his eyes and fell into a fitful sleep.

Chapter 6

White Point Garden, in the heart of Charleston's historic district, was a blend of yesterday's agony and today's promise. Cannons facing the Charleston Harbor lined the edges of the park, reminding visitors of the determined nation that had once fought for independence but had lost lives. The lush greenery and tall, shady oak trees surrounding the tools of death were alive with camera-toting tourists and children who giggled as they ran from one attraction to the other.

Wade drove his sleek Mustang down Murray Boulevard past the park, slowing to allow for the tourists who crossed the street without checking for cars. In the harbor, a powerboat skimmed the water no more than a hundred feet from the seawall. Leigh breathed the fresh sea air and was glad that Wade's car was a convertible.

Springtime in Charleston was a glorious mixture of pink and purple azaleas, fragrant scents, cleansing rains and near perfect weather. The only aspect of Charleston's spring that bothered Leigh were the hoards of tourists who descended on the city to sample its charms. She had been a small-town girl for too long to find comfort in a crowd, and White Point Garden was teeming with one.

The Mustang continued its path away from the park and Leigh was struck by the sudden transformation. The eastern end of Murray Boulevard was as quiet as the western end was noisy. A few Charlestonians, joggers and people walking their dogs, dotted the sidewalk by the seawall. On the other side of the street, majestic houses with wrap-around porches provided occupants with a stunning view of the sea.

The setting was made for a dark night, a sprinkling of stars and a pair of lovers. The image struck a painful chord that Leigh had replayed too many times, and she winced. On a long-ago night, she and Wade had driven to Charleston on impulse and strolled the boulevard with their arms wrapped around each other so securely, she thought they would never let go.

"It's still beautiful, isn't it, Leigh?" Wade asked, cutting his gray eyes at her to show that he remembered, too. Leigh winced again. Would it always be this way with them? Would they always share only the things that were too painful to remember?

Leigh merely nodded in response. Their conversation on the drive to Charleston had been impersonal, and Leigh was under the impression that Wade had called a truce. She had spent a miserable night dwelling on their disastrous confrontation at the cove, and she wasn't about to declare war again. Especially when she had been in the wrong.

Wade steered the Mustang around a slight bend in the road, and the dove-gray stucco house where Martha Culpepper lived came into view. Leigh pointed it out and they came to a stop in front of the large home. A brick sidewalk cut a straight path past flowering azalea bushes to the tall double doors that seemed more intimidating than welcoming. The house was the epitome of stately Southern charm with white pillars rising out of a generous wooden porch and shuttered windows facing the harbor.

Wade gave a low whistle as he surveyed the scene. "I never knew Mrs. Culpepper's family had money," he said.

Leigh shook her head as she alighted from the car. For the first time since they set out for Charleston that morning, her attention was focused on something other than Wade. She was looking beyond the beautiful facade of the old house and seeing its worn edges, such as a lawn that needed to be trimmed and a porch that could have used a coat of paint and repairs.

"They don't," she said. "Like a lot of fine old Southern families, the Culpeppers are cash poor. They have this house, but it takes just about every penny they have to keep it up."

"How do you know that?" Wade asked as he followed her up the sidewalk to the home. He took her arm, and the gesture caused the tiny hairs to stand up in an awareness that was out of proportion to the incidental contact.

"I work in a general store, Wade," Leigh said, trying to cover her reaction. "People talk. I bet I know a little bit about anyone who's ever lived in Kinley."

"Don't you ever get tired of living in a town where there's no such thing as a secret?" Wade asked under his breath as they climbed the steps to the porch. He sounded almost angry.

"You can look at that two ways. The town is either full of busybodies or of people who care a whole lot about you. I think it's a little bit of both." She paused and a cloud temporarily obscured the sun and cast a shadow over her face. "Besides, Kinley can keep a secret. We still don't know what happened to Sarah Culpepper."

Leigh's comments about the financial state of Martha Culpepper's family carried more weight now that they were nearer the house. Some of the wooden slats in the porch were cracked, and the paint on the house had started to chip. The house had no doorbell, so Leigh lifted the heavy brass knocker and let it fall against the door. Her heart, weighted with their improbable mission and the memory of the long-lost little girl, suddenly seemed as heavy as the knocker.

The air had already been warm when she awakened that morning, so she had donned a turquoise sundress. The garment had white embroidery on the bodice and a billowy skirt that drew attention to her shapely legs. Now, when she was standing at the doorstep of the home of a woman whose child had disappeared without a trace, the ensemble seemed frivolous.

"You did let her know we were coming?" Wade asked when Martha failed to appear at the door. He seemed so nonchalant that Leigh knew he didn't expect anything but a positive answer.

"Well, not really," Leigh confessed, and Wade's entire body tensed. She rushed to explain. "I was going to, but I was afraid she wouldn't want to see us."

The door swung open before Wade could reply and revealed a thin, tiny woman with deep wrinkles in her face and black hair liberally streaked with gray. Leigh knew the woman couldn't be anyone but Martha Culpepper, but her appearance had changed so drastically that Leigh might have passed her on the street without recognizing her. Martha had once been a small woman with generous curves and hair that had no trace of gray. Martha didn't have any similar difficulty in recognizing Leigh.

"Leigh Hampton. What a surprise. It's so good to see you," she began in a voice that sounded raspier than it used to. Martha's welcome came to an abrupt halt when she spotted Wade standing to one side of the door. Her complexion paled visibly. "Hello, Wade."

Concern ebbed into Wade's handsome face. "Hello, Mrs. Culpepper," he said, and he looked contrite. "We shouldn't have barged in on you like this. I can see now that it wasn't the right thing to do. If seeing me again upsets you, I'll just go."

Martha wasn't tall, but she stood very straight and seemed to pull herself together. At that moment, the strength that had weathered Sarah's disappearance and the fatal heart attack of her husband a year later was visible. Martha Culpepper was a survivor. "No, don't be silly. You don't upset me. It's just that seeing you again, well, it brings back a lot of memories."

Wade nodded, and Leigh felt a powerful empathy with the sad-eyed woman who had lost her niece so many years before. Seeing Wade again had also brought back poignant, painful memories for Leigh, and most of them were tied up with the mystery of Sarah Culpepper.

"I'd ask you in, but it's such a pretty afternoon I was fixing to sit outside. Won't you join me?"

The intricacies of Southern charm struck Leigh as she and Wade followed Martha's example and seated themselves in the wicker armchairs overlooking the harbor. Martha hadn't asked why they had reappeared into her life without warning, and Leigh doubted that she would. A polite Southern hostess waited for her guests to divulge their reasons for visiting, and Martha had lived in the South too long not to be schooled in its ways. She gave Wade her condolences on Ena's death and sat back and waited.

"I know you must be wondering why we're here," Leigh said without preamble and looked at Wade. He seemed uneasy and unwilling to hurt Martha any more than she'd already been hurt, and it occurred to Leigh that the mature Wade was at direct odds with the devil-may-care youth many had believed him to be. Leigh silently tried to reassure him that she'd be as gentle as possible. "Mrs. Culpepper, I know this is going to bring back things you'd rather not think about. But Wade and I need your help."

Martha sat forward in her chair, her eyes on the beauty in front of them. A boat cut through the harbor with its sails billowing gracefully while a duo of sea gulls circled overhead. The sky was as blue as a violet in bloom, and the entire scene could have been photographed and imprinted on a postcard to attract visitors to Charleston. They seemed far away from the horrible secrets buried in Kinley.

"How can an old lady like me possibly help you?" Martha asked, her gaze still on the sea.

"Mrs. Culpepper, a terrible thing has happened," Leigh said as gently as she could. "Another little girl has been kidnapped. Her name's Lisa Farley, and her family lives just a few houses from where you used to live. She was supposed to spend the night at a friend's house, but she changed her mind and started to walk home. It's only a couple of blocks, but she never made it."

Martha sat so still that Leigh thought at first she hadn't heard. But then the corners of Martha's mouth tilted downward, and she looked unutterably sad. "How old is she?" she asked.

"Eight," Wade answered, and he was as troubled as Martha. Golden-haired Sarah, who had adored Wade like the older brother she never had, was seven when she disappeared.

"Oh, mercy," Martha said and covered her mouth with wrinkled hands that again called to mind how much she had aged. Sarah was actually the daughter of Martha's older sister, but the Culpeppers had acted as her parents after Martha's sister and husband were killed in a car wreck when Sarah was a toddler. Martha had been nearly forty when she took over caring for Sarah, but she looked years older than Leigh knew her to be. She looked like she had been wrung through the grinder of an old washing machine.

"They think I did it, Mrs. Culpepper," Wade said. "People in Kinley still don't trust me. A lot of them still think I was responsible for Sarah's disappearance."

"Of course you weren't," Martha said with such conviction that her voice came alive. "Only a darned fool would believe such nonsense."

"Why do you believe that Wade didn't do it?" Leigh asked, and two sets of puzzled eyes fastened on her. Wade's were more piercing, because the question didn't make sense coming from the one woman who knew the truth.

"Because it's true, that's why," Martha said.

Leigh shook her head impatiently. "No, that's not what I meant. I know Wade didn't do it, but how do you know? Why are you so sure that he had nothing to do with Sarah's disappearance?"

"When you live to be my age, you get to know a couple of things about people. I know Wade didn't kidnap Sarah, because he's not the kind of man who goes around kidnapping people. Especially not Sarah, who I believed he had a soft spot for."

"You're right about that, Mrs. Culpepper," Wade said softly.

"Besides," Martha continued, looking at Leigh, "Ena and I knew that Wade went off just about every night to meet you. I would have bet my life he was with you the night Sarah disappeared."

Her eyes wide with surprise, Leigh turned to Wade. He tapped his index finger to the side of his mouth while he digested the information. *All those years,* he thought. *My mother knew the real reason I didn't want to come back to Kinley for all those years, and she never breathed a word.*

Martha was the first to break the silence. When she did, her voice wavered like a flutist who couldn't quite hit the note she wanted. "But I still don't understand why you need my help. I haven't even been back to Kinley in more than ten years."

"Mrs. Culpepper, I have a theory about Lisa Farley's kidnapping." Leigh sat forward in her chair, willing Martha to understand. "Before you say anything, just hear me out. I think Sarah and Lisa were abducted by the same person. Wade came to Kinley a few weeks ago for Ena's funeral. Before that, he hadn't been back since Sarah disappeared. Now another girl is missing, and fingers are pointing at Wade. I just can't buy that it's some kind of bizarre coincidence. I think someone is trying to frame Wade."

"I still don't understand why you're here," Martha said, and her voice was no louder than a whisper. "I don't even know the Farleys."

"We're not here to talk about Lisa Farley," Leigh said, and laughed nervously. "Chief Tucker has let us know he doesn't want our help. We're here to talk about Sarah...."

"We think the only way to find out what happened to Lisa is to find out what happened to Sarah first," Wade finished for her. His voice didn't carry the conviction that ran through Leigh's, because he was already doubting their strategy. If Martha Culpepper were an example, their investigation might bring only heartache.

"Don't you think we've already tried to do that?" Martha asked, the old pain marring her voice. She slumped in her chair and looked like a defeated, old woman. "My husband went over it so many times that his heart gave out. He couldn't find a clue. Why do you think you can after all these years?"

Because I have to, Leigh answered silently. Because I was a scared, selfish teenager when Sarah disappeared, and now I'm trying to make amends. Because I had something precious in my grasp, and I let it slip away. She glanced at Wade for support, but she could tell his thoughts were more in line with Martha's than her own. They both looked at her expectantly, and the irony of the situation struck her.

If she had been in New York a month ago and happened to catch a glimpse of Wade, she would have lowered her head and hoped he hadn't noticed her. And here she was sitting with him on a veranda overlooking the Charleston harbor talking to a woman whose niece had in a strange, sad way been the cause of their breakup.

Leigh's life had come around in a full circle to a spot that she left prematurely, and she knew it could never go forward again until she came to terms with that troubling time. She couldn't allow Wade to go on paying for her long-ago silence, and she couldn't be silent while she watched another tragedy unfold. Her eyes narrowed with new resolve.

"Mrs. Culpepper, I don't have a child so I can only imagine how terrible it would be to lose one." Leigh's voice was low, clear and strong. "I know it can't be easy for you to talk about this and I know that nothing may come of it, but we have to try. Another little girl is missing, and another mother is grieving. The police chief thinks Wade did it, and it's going to be a replay of what happened twelve years ago if we don't do something. Try with us. Please."

Martha sat sheathed in silence while Leigh begged for her help, but Wade couldn't take his eyes off Leigh. He'd told her yesterday at the cove that they'd been through for a long time, but even then he knew it wasn't true. They had a strange sort of connection he couldn't sever just by willing it to be so. The sun cast streaks of light in her dark hair, and he wanted to run a hand over the smooth curve of her cheek. Her violet eyes were so intense that Wade knew he couldn't refuse her anything if she looked at him that way. What was she? A traitor or a savior, an enemy or a friend, a lover or a user?

Martha was silent for so long, Wade was convinced Leigh's plea had fallen on deaf ears, but then she started to speak in a low, soft voice.

"It was such a dark night that you couldn't see the stars. I remember looking out my bedroom window and thinking it was a night made for secrets, a night where you shouldn't be anywhere except with someone who loved you," Martha said and paused, and Leigh kept her eyes studiously averted from Wade's. She remembered the night, too. She had spoken of love, but Wade hadn't believed her.

"I wasn't worried about my little Sarah, though," Martha continued, staring at the hands in her lap. "I thought she was safe and warm and loved. My husband, Frank, wasn't worried, either. We had been working in the yard all day planting flowers and pulling weeds, and we were so tired. Sarah had taken to spending the night with her cousin Joyce, my sister Mary's little girl, and we both thought she was there."

Martha cupped both sides of her face with her hands and shook her head. "I've thought about this so many times," she said, and her voice quavered. "I thought about calling Mary's to tell Sarah good-night and to say I loved her, but I was so tired. I ended up just going to bed."

"I don't understand," Wade broke in gently when Martha lapsed into silence. "Why were you so sure Sarah was at your sister's?"

Martha sighed as though she didn't want to remember, but she continued. "Mary only lived two doors down, and Sarah spent as much time there as she did at our house. She put her pajamas on early that night and told me she was going to fix her bicycle and go over to see Joyce. It was a chilly night, and I told her to put on a sweater.

"I looked out the window a few minutes later and saw Wade helping her with the bike. We had this old grandfather clock that chimed every hour, and I remember that it had just struck six. But since it was November, it was already dark. Sarah was wearing those kind of pajamas that had feet in them. They were white with tiny pink—or was it purple—hearts. And she had on this green sweater that was a size too big with her red blanket tucked in one of its pockets. She carried that blanket everywhere. She said it was her good luck charm."

Martha smiled sadly at the irony and seemed to have forgotten there was anyone with her. "I turned away from the window, and I never saw her again. She never did go to Mary's, and Mary just figured the girls had gotten tired of their sleepovers. But I didn't find that out until the next morning. Until it was too late."

When Martha finished her story, it was so quiet that Leigh could hear the water gently lapping at the seawall. The old woman stared unseeingly at the bay, as though something in the distance could give her the answers she had sought for so long.

Wade's eyes were lowered, and the sun cast a shadow over his long eyelashes that made it look as though there were streams of tears running down his face. He raised his eyes to Martha's, and they were dry but troubled.

"I'm sorry, Mrs. Culpepper," he said simply.

"It was a long, long time ago," Martha answered, but the pain in her voice made it seem like only yesterday. "I've tried telling myself that she's in Heaven with her parents, but it only helps some of the time. I still wish she was here with me."

Sensing that Martha wanted to be alone with her grief, Leigh stood up and Wade followed suit. She placed a hand on the old woman's shoulder and squeezed softly, surprised at how delicate Martha felt. "Thank you for talking to us, Mrs. Culpepper."

They left her sitting in the sun amid yesterday's shadows.

"Are you sure you want to fight this crowd and have lunch here?" Wade sounded dubious after he pulled his Mustang into what looked to be the only vacant parking spot in Charleston's Market area.

Leigh was out of the car before she turned to answer him, and a breeze played with her long hair. She normally avoided tourists and the manufactured cheeriness that surrounded them, but their visit with Martha Culpepper had been so depressing that she longed for some levity. There would be plenty of time later to think about what Martha had said. "Oh, come on. What kind of New Yorker are you? I can't believe this crowd has anything on the ones in Manhattan. Besides, how often do we get to Charleston?"

The last sentence was delivered on a pleading note, and Wade found that he couldn't disappoint her. She looked angelic with her windblown hair, bare legs and soft smile, and she seemed to be eager to spend some leisure time with him. God knew he needed to relax a little after the events of the past few weeks. He smiled back at her and got out of the car, for once forgetting to distrust her motives.

"I expect crowds in Manhattan," he said while pumping the parking meter full of quarters. "I don't expect them in South Carolina. But I never expected to be here with you either, so let's join the throng."

She impulsively reached for his hand, telling herself it was because she didn't want them to get separated, but knowing that she just wanted to touch him. They walked in silence, and Leigh felt like a schoolgirl again. Her heart raced, her skin tingled and it was all because she held hands with Wade Conner.

He wore khaki pants and a loose white short-sleeved shirt that underscored his darkness. In profile, his features were angular and strong, calling attention to his Indian heritage.

A display of paintings was just ahead, and they stopped to look at them. Most were pastel watercolors of the city painted with the tourist dollar in mind, and the artist had done a passable job. Leigh's sharp eye looked deeper and noted the lack of any emotion in the paintings. She had favored bright colors, and her own works had vibrated with life even when they depicted inanimate objects.

"Yours are better," Wade said from somewhere close to her ear, and Leigh shrugged. He meant what he said. The art that was being peddled in the Market Area paled in comparison to Leigh's paintings. It had been years since he'd seen any of her work, but he still remembered the feeling that emanated from them. They walked only a few feet farther before Wade turned them away from the shopping stalls and crossed the street to a less crowded and less noisy sidewalk.

"I can't understand why you stopped painting, Leigh. Don't you ever think of going back to it?" Leigh tugged at her hand to remove it from his grasp and crossed her arms over her chest, unconsciously shutting him out.

"It's not like a fork, Wade. You just can't pick it up and put it down," she said.

"Why not?" he asked. "It seems to me that you never gave yourself a chance. Where would I be if I had put away my typewriter? Where would Robert Redford be if he had quit after his first role? Where would Baryshnikov be if he had stuffed his ballet slippers in the back of a closet?"

"You've made your point. So let's change the subject," Leigh said dryly.

They passed an ice-cream parlor, and a shaft of cool air streamed over them as two noisy children stood in the open doorway begging their parents for two scoops instead of one. The popular Italian restaurant Leigh had earmarked for lunch was a few doors away, and they covered the distance in silence.

Neither spoke until they were seated inside the crowded, intimate dining room. Waiters dressed in crisp white shirts bustled from table to table, trying to make themselves heard above the din. The noise called attention to their silence instead of masking it, and Leigh shuffled nervously in her seat. Across the table, which was covered with a red-and-white-checked tablecloth, Wade looked dark, brooding and unfamiliar.

"What are we doing here, Leigh?" Wade said, and she had to strain to hear him. "The irony of all this hit me when you wouldn't talk about your art. But why should you? It's not like we're friends. Hell, I don't know what we are. I resented you for a long time. Sometimes I still resent you, but—"

"What can I get you?" The waiter's question put an abrupt end to what Wade had been going to say. Leigh's face was ashen, and she was glad of the interruption so she could compose herself. After the waiter had taken their orders, she looked at Wade levelly across the table and thought that the single red rose on the table seemed incongruous. It symbolized love, and the love between them had been lost for more than a decade.

"What are you trying to say, Wade?" she asked, dreading the answer. She had a terrible premonition that he was going to say the hell with Burt and announce plans to move back to New York and that watching him go the second time would be more painful than it had been the first time.

Wade released a heavy sigh and lowered his head. He looked at her from beneath his lashes, which were ridiculously long for a man's. "I honestly don't know. I guess part of it is I'm feeling bad about this trip. Poor Mrs. Culpepper. I keep seeing her sitting alone on the porch, mourning a loss she'll never get over. I keep thinking that it was wrong for us to come here and dredge it all up again. Maybe we should have let the past stay buried."

Leigh stared at her hands, which were kneading each other nervously in her lap. He seemed to be talking about more than Martha Culpepper. She bit her lip and fastened her violet eyes on him, noting that the strain made his handsome features appear pinched and drawn. Had Martha done that to him or had she?

"I don't agree, Wade," she said finally, putting aside her whimsical notion to enjoy a lunch unencumbered by the past. "We're talking about a crime we both played a part in. I know neither of us kidnapped Sarah, but maybe we were guilty by disassociation. We never even tried to solve the crime, and maybe we were the only ones who could have. Now another girl is missing, and I don't think we should ignore that. You may be right. This may all be just a wild-goose chase, but it's a chance."

Wade ran a hand through his thick black hair and rubbed his neck. "Listen, Leigh. You and I aren't Sherlock Holmes and Dr. Watson. All we're doing is stirring up dust. What purpose did it serve to grill Mrs. Culpepper? Everything's as much a puzzle now as it was twelve years ago."

"We found out some things," Leigh protested. "We didn't know about Sarah's cousin Joyce before today. Maybe if we paid Joyce a visit and talked to her, we could put together another piece of the puzzle."

When she finished, Wade stared at her for long moments as though he were seeing her for the first time. Finally his eyes hardened and his lips twisted slightly. "Ask yourself why this is so important, Leigh. Is it because you want to find out what happened to Sarah, or is it because you feel guilty as hell for what you did to me twelve years ago?"

The waiter's arrival with plates of steaming pasta forestalled Leigh's answer, but she doubted she could have given him one anyway. It seemed like a large hand had a grip on her throat and wouldn't allow her to speak. She ate a few forkfuls of pasta, which tasted more like glue than the Italian delicacy she had remembered from a previous visit. The silence lengthened, and Leigh realized Wade wasn't going to be the one to break it.

"I do feel guilty," she said finally, putting down her fork and giving up all pretense of eating. "I haven't been able to think of you even once in all these years without feeling guilty."

Wade took a swig of his ice water while he thought about what she had admitted. He wanted her to feel guilty for what she'd done, but a part of him didn't want that to be the motivation behind her offer of help. When he looked at her over the rim of his glass, his animosity was palpable.

"Would it help if I said I was sorry?" Leigh said, feeling as though she were talking to one of the trees in Kinley; he was about as responsive. "Because I am, you know. I can't turn back the clock, but I would if I could. I never wanted you to leave Kinley the way you did. I never wanted you to leave at all."

But he had left Kinley, and she had been the reason for that. Wade swallowed some more water and set his glass down with a thump. Only yesterday, he'd wished that she would apologize. Now that she had, he didn't want to accept it, didn't want to let down his defenses around her. If luck were on his side, Burt would solve Kinley's mysterious crimes and Wade would be free to go back to New York. He didn't need Leigh Hampton complicating his life.

"I already told you to drop it," he said, echoing the words he'd spoken at the cove the last time they had discussed her betrayal. "It's just not that important."

"Then why do you glare at me when you think I'm not watching?" Leigh asked and took a breath for courage. "If it's not important, why do you act like you hate me?"

Wade picked up a napkin and unconsciously crumpled it. He distrusted her, yes. But had he really been acting as though he hated her? He noticed Leigh bite her lower lip in an effort to keep it from quivering, and suddenly he felt like a heel. No matter what she had done in the past, she was trying to help him now and he wasn't making it easy for her.

"I don't hate you, Leigh," he said, releasing the crumpled napkin. When he spoke the words, he realized they were true. He felt a lot of things for Leigh Hampton, but hate was no longer one of them. "I don't even know you anymore. When I left Kinley, you weren't much more than a girl. But you're a woman now."

"I'm a woman who'd like to get to know you better. Can't we be friends?" Leigh asked hesitantly, and realized she didn't speak the entire truth. Friendship was a good place to begin, but she didn't want it to stop there.

Friends? Wade wished it could be as simple as that, but they once had a friendship that had blossomed into love. If he let her too close, he'd be in danger of falling for her again. Looking at her now, with her eyes all dewy and skin still rosy from their recent walk, he knew he couldn't make any promises.

"We're in this crime-solving business together, right?" Wade said, skirting around her question. "Before we're through, you'll probably know more about me than you want to know."

Leigh doubted she could ever know enough about him, but she wasn't going to admit that after he'd ignored her question.

When was she going to face that he wasn't interested in renewing any kind of meaningful relationship with her? But the more she was with him, the more she wanted to be.

"Does that mean you'll go with me to see Joyce?" she asked, pressing the only advantage she had. He may not want to get too close to her, but he had agreed to help her solve Sarah's kidnapping.

"Like I just said," he drawled, picking up his fork and winding some more pasta around it, "we're in this together."

Chapter Seven

"Here we are," Wade said as he pulled the Mustang into the driveway of Leigh's home late that afternoon. Their conversation had gone smoother after they'd aired their differences at lunch, but an uneasiness still prevailed. Leigh wanted to lift it, but she didn't know how.

"Would you like to come over tonight for dinner?" she asked, and Wade turned in the bucket seat so that he was directly facing her. He studied her for a few moments, realizing that she had been offering olive branches all day. She wanted to make amends; maybe she even wanted to finish what they'd started all those years ago. Her offer was tempting, but he couldn't accept. He might forgive her one day, but he wasn't going to reach out and get his hand singed a second time.

He was silent for so long that Leigh felt as though she had to explain herself. She didn't know why it was so important to keep seeing him; she just knew that it was. "We have things to talk about if we're going to find out what happened to Sarah, you know," she said. "We need to plan what we're going to do next. Dinner would be a good time for that."

"I'll take a rain check, Leigh," Wade said, and the words came out more gently than he'd intended. "And we already know what we're going to do next. We're going to talk to Joyce. Let me know what time's good with her, okay?''

"Sure," Leigh said and got out of the car, embarrassed and dejected. "No, don't bother walking me to the door. I'll call you when I set things up with Joyce."

Once she was inside, Leigh threw herself down on her secondhand Queen Anne sofa and covered her face with her hands. She shouldn't have set herself up for rejection by asking him to dinner. Before his return, she would have sworn that the passage of time had dulled what she had once felt for him. Now she knew that wasn't true. Something real and strong had survived the separation, and it had the power to hurt her. Leigh lay on the sofa for a long time until hunger pangs forced her to move into the kitchen.

She'd been home for almost two hours when the phone rang. Leigh's heart leapt, and she dropped the packet of frozen meat and vegetables she had been holding into a pot of boiling water. Before she picked up the receiver, she already regretted having started dinner. She and Wade could have had dinner together. They still could. She wouldn't even mention the frozen packet of food thawing in the bubbling water.

"Wade?" she said softly into the phone.

There was a short pause, and Leigh thought she heard someone breathing. Then there was a click and a dial tone. Strange, she thought. It was the third hang-up call she had received in as many days. Leigh replaced the receiver, resigned to a solitary instant meal.

Later, as she picked at her food, Leigh reflected on the day's events. She sat cross-legged in front of her television set as she ate, but paid so little attention to the screen that she couldn't have named the program that was on.

Wade had asked why she was so determined to clear his name, and it was time she examined her motives. Leigh shoved the plate of half-eaten food away and lay back on the Oriental rug she had spread over the wood floor.

The problem was that everything was so mixed-up in her mind that she didn't know the answer. She still saw Wade both as a wounded twenty-year-old and as a mature man who awakened feelings she had thought long dead. It was true that she had wronged him years ago and wanted to make amends, but there was more. When he reentered her life, it was like a lightning bolt had pierced her heart and recharged all the old feelings. She sat bolt upright as a thought thundered into her mind. Could she be falling in love with Wade Conner all over again?

When the doorbell rang, Leigh was so startled, she didn't recognize the sound. It rang again and she sprang to her feet, wondering if the object of her thoughts were on the other side of the door. Half hoping it was Wade and half praying it wasn't, she covered the distance to the door and pulled it open.

"Hi, Leigh. I hope you don't mind me stopping by," Everett said, looking unsure of his welcome. He pushed his glasses up on his nose. "Is this a bad time?"

Leigh's entire body sighed when she realized the identity of her visitor. "No, it's a fine time. Come on in," she said and turned away from the door, leaving Everett to close it and follow her.

He sat on the sofa, sinking into it in such a way that his bony knees were just about even with his chest. Everett had changed from his work clothes, but his faded short-sleeved blue dress shirt and dark slacks made him seem as though he was still on accountant duty.

He pushed the glasses up on his nose again and stared at her intently. Leigh was accustomed to his scrutiny, but she could never get used to the way he so obviously adored her.

"What's up, Everett? Is there any special reason you stopped by?" she asked, trying to put the visit on friendly terms. She had assumed her previous position on the floor, and tilted her head slightly to talk to him.

"I was worried about you," Everett said without preamble. "I stopped by the store this afternoon, but you weren't there."

Leigh wondered if Drew had told him where she'd gone, but she wasn't about to ask. The last thing she needed was Everett prying into her business and trying to be more than a friend.

"It was sweet of you to be concerned, but there was nothing to be worried about. I just had some business to take care of, that's all," Leigh said, choosing her words carefully. She guessed that Everett would be jealous if he knew she had been with Wade, and she didn't feel like dealing with his jealousy.

"I always worry about you, Leigh," Everett said, biting his lower lip and looking as if it wouldn't take much to make him burst into tears. "Don't you know how much I care about you?"

She knew, of course. She'd always known, but Everett never seemed to hear no matter how many times she tried to tell him she wasn't interested in him as a lover.

"Oh, Everett," Leigh said on a sigh, knowing she had to try again. "I care about you, too, but not in the way you mean. Don't look that way. We've known each other since we were children. Can't you accept that I think of you as a brother? Is that so awful? You must know that I love you as a friend, but just as a friend. Nothing more."

For a moment, the room was so silent that Leigh could hear the ticking of her grandfather clock. Everett's lower lip trembled, and his eyes watered as he struggled to gain control of himself. When he failed, the change in him was remarkable. His eyes dried up, and he regarded her icily.

"It's Wade Conner, isn't it?" he bit out, sounding unlike the Everett she knew. "He's the one you were with today. He's the reason you don't want to be more than friends."

Leigh rubbed a tired hand over her face. The day had drained her physically and emotionally, and she didn't feel up to assuaging the ego of a man who never listened to reason. But he was her friend, and she had to try.

"Wade has nothing to do with this," she said in a careful, controlled voice. "You've known for years that there can't be anything more than friendship between us. I wish you'd accept that, Everett. I don't want to lose you as a friend."

As rapidly as the anger and hurt had risen in Everett, it died. Once again he looked like a puppy eager to please his master. If Everett had a tail, it would have been between his legs.

"I don't want to lose you, either, Leigh," he said meekly. "I don't know what came over me or why I said those things. Will you forgive me?"

She nodded, thinking it had been ridiculously easy to quash Everett's attempt to deepen their relationship. It was probably because she had lots of practice at it, and he was such a mild, passive man.

"Of course I forgive you, Everett," she said and saw the look of gratitude on his face.

Maybe Leigh was right, Wade thought as he made the short walk to the house where the Coopers had moved to after Sarah Culpepper's kidnapping. Maybe it did make sense to dig up the past and find out what role, if any, they'd played in Sarah's disappearance. He'd been only half convinced until now, especially after their visit to Charleston. It had pained Martha Culpepper to talk about what had happened that night, but the truth would hurt if they were able to find it.

Another neighbor had ignored Wade's greeting that morning, and he had overheard yet another person imply that he was a criminal on the loose. It angered Wade, but it also made him realize that he needed to clear his name. For years, he'd been living in Manhattan while the people of Kinley made insinuating remarks about him. Now that he could hear them, he was struck at the unfairness of it all.

But that wasn't all. He liked children, and Sarah Culpepper had been one of his favorites; he'd probably like Lisa Farley, too. What if Leigh were right and they were the only people who could solve the crime against Sarah? He owed it to both girls to try.

Since the Coopers' residence was in the opposite direction of the general store, Leigh had arranged to meet him there at noon. He glanced at his watch and saw it was almost noon now. The house was in sight, and he strained for a glimpse of Leigh, admitting that he was looking forward to seeing her.

He had spent the previous night alone with a ponderous novel, wishing he had taken Leigh up on her offer to make him dinner. What would it have hurt anyhow? It was time he admitted to himself that he was still physically attracted to Leigh. He knew enough about her to not let that physical attraction turn into anything else, so why shouldn't he take whatever she offered? It wasn't as though he'd be stupid enough to fall in love with her again.

He got to the sidewalk leading to the Coopers' front porch before he saw her.

Leigh was rushing, and it occurred to her that she'd been doing a lot of that lately. She hated to hurry, but she didn't

want Wade to get to the Coopers before she did. After the way
Mary Cooper had sounded on the phone, Leigh suspected she
wouldn't even let a solitary Wade in the door. Besides, Leigh
had promised Drew she wouldn't take more than an hour for
her lunch break.

Mary Cooper had been suspicious when Leigh phoned to
arrange the visit. Yes, she had said, Joyce was home from college for the weekend. Yes, they did have some free time that
afternoon. And yes, they would see her. But when Leigh mentioned that Wade would be along, Mary had almost rescinded
her permission.

Leigh looked up then and tried to ignore the leap of joy her
heart gave at the sight of Wade. He looked tall, dark and lean,
and it simply wasn't fair that God had made him so handsome. She gave a slight wave that he acknowledged with a nod.
Leigh wore an unstructured sundress of blue and white with
white slip-on sandals, and he was dressed equally casually in a
loose-fitting short-sleeved white shirt and tan slacks. It was
such a hot day that she wouldn't have blamed him if he had
worn shorts, but Wade probably remembered enough about
Kinley to know that men didn't formally call on their neighbors with their bare legs exposed. And this was definitely more
than a friendly visit.

Minutes later, Leigh and Wade sipped tall glasses of lemonade in the Coopers' formal living room as they listened to Mary
Cooper express her disappointment. At her side, nineteen-year-
old Joyce Cooper twirled a long strand of blond hair around
her index finger.

"Really, Leigh, I can't understand you," she said, disapproval dripping from her voice. Aside from a polite hello, she
had yet to look at Wade. "Whatever can be going through your
head? Investigating the past? Martha phoned yesterday and
told me that you even showed up in Charleston to talk about my
niece." Mary Cooper pursed her lips and shook her head.

Leigh bit back the angry retort that threatened to spill from
her. *If I lose my temper,* she told herself sternly, *we'll never get
to the bottom of this mystery.* She needn't have worried, because it was Wade who answered Mary.

"I'm sorry you feel that way, Mrs. Cooper," he said. "Leigh
and I are just trying to get to the truth. We think the same per-

son kidnapped Sarah and Lisa. That's why we went to talk to Martha and that's why we want to talk to you and Joyce.''

"What if I think you did it?" Mrs. Cooper asked rudely, her eyes finally meeting his, her lips still pursed.

This time, it was Wade who had to control his temper. He took a deep breath and silently counted to five. "Then you'd be wrong," he said after he had exhaled.

"Oh, Mama, how can you possibly say such a thing?" Joyce broke in, unwinding the golden swirl of hair from her finger. "Look at him. A man like Wade—I can call you Wade, can't I?—doesn't have to kidnap girls. They probably want to kidnap him."

Joyce ignored her mother's shocked gasp and smiled broadly at Wade. "I'll help any way I can. What would you like to know?"

"Anything about the night your cousin was kidnapped," Leigh said quickly, unwilling to give Mrs. Cooper a chance to accuse Wade again.

Joyce pouted as she tried to remember, and Wade was struck by how pretty she was. If Sarah were alive, she'd look much the same way. Joyce's blond hair was a riot of curls, and her startling blue eyes peered out from a roundish face with a turned-up nose. The college boys were probably tripping over themselves to get a date with her. Leigh hadn't been much younger than Joyce when he'd fallen in love with her. He wondered what kind of effect she'd had on the male student body when she'd gone off to college.

"I don't think I'm going to be much help," Joyce said. "I was only seven, you know. I can remember the day I found out Sarah was gone, very clearly, but I can't remember hardly anything about the night before."

Leigh's spirits sank and she exchanged a baleful glance with Wade. "Tell us anything you remember, Joyce. Even if it doesn't seem like it has any connection, it could be important—"

"I can't see what you hope to gain from this, Leigh," Mrs. Cooper cut in, but Joyce ignored her. The younger girl screwed up her forehead and thought.

"I remember that she always carried that silly red blanket around with her," Joyce said finally and laughed softly. "She was sort of dreamy. She used to pretend that her blanket was a flying carpet and that it was going to take her to all sorts of exotic places."

A thought struck Wade. "Did she ever talk about running away?"

Joyce nodded. "All the time. She had these picture books she used to show me where she'd point out places she wanted to go. She wasn't unhappy at home or anything, she was just adventurous. They were places like Hawaii and New York City and Florida. But I don't think she would have ever run away. We were only seven years old."

"Do you remember if she talked about running away before she disappeared?" Wade asked.

"I can't remember. I can't even remember if she was supposed to sleep over that night. She slept over so many times that everything just blends together. All I can remember is getting up that morning, and Mama telling me she was gone. None of it's ever made any sense...." Joyce's voice trailed off, and then she was silent.

"How about you, Mrs. Cooper? Do you remember anything else?" Leigh asked, reluctantly accepting that Joyce wouldn't be able to provide any more information.

Mary was silent for so long that it seemed as though she might refuse to answer. "Nothing important," she said finally. "But I do remember checking in on Joyce that night and thinking it odd that Sarah wasn't spending the night. Nothing was ever prearranged, but they always seemed to find some way to be together. How I wish they would have tried that night."

Darkness had fallen on Kinley, and Leigh sat on her front porch gazing into the night. Their interview with the Coopers that afternoon had shed about as much light on Sarah Culpepper's disappearance as there was in the night sky. Was there an obvious clue that they were overlooking or was it possible for a little girl to disappear without a trace? The more people they talked to, the more puzzling the mystery became. Leigh frowned. If Wade had been framed, as she believed, that meant somebody—probably a trusted friend or neighbor—was insane. Could anyone be safe in Kinley?

At the sound of footsteps on her porch steps, Leigh's throat constricted and her heart seemed to stop. The form of a man was outlined against the darkness, but as it came closer she could see it was Wade. Her body relaxed, but her heart resumed its beat in double time. He moved closer, and she noticed that when he took a breath his white T-shirt expanded to reveal the outline of his hard chest.

"Mind telling me why you're sitting out here without a porch light? It's an awfully dark night. I don't think there are any stars in the sky," he said, and he had a nice voice, rich and low. But she'd liked it better years ago, when he still sounded as though he was from the South. Even though he'd now spent weeks in Kinley, no trace of an accent had returned. She wondered if he were consciously guarding against it, if everything from his Southern past was just a bad memory, if that included her.

Leigh slid over on the porch swing to make room for him. "I was thinking, that's all," she said quietly.

"About me?" he asked as he sat down, brushing Leigh's thigh with his and sending an uncontrollable shiver through her. She wrapped her arms around herself, suddenly chilled even though the night was warm. She wished she had worn more than a light cotton shirt and shorts.

Leigh nodded, trying not to let him know how much his nearness affected her. "About you. About Sarah. About how things don't add up. I keep thinking there's a clue that will yield all the answers, but that it's just out of grasp."

Wade was silent, and a little disappointed. When had it come to this? When had she become so serious, so introspective? When had she stopped telling him about her artwork and her dreams for the future and started talking about kidnappings and mysteries? When had he become such a daydreamer?

"Joyce did say that Sarah used to talk a lot about running away," Wade said, surrendering to the fact that things between them were never going to be as they once were. He had warred with himself before deciding to come here tonight, and he didn't want to talk about the case. But he didn't see how they were going to avoid it.

Leigh nodded. "She was just an adventurous little girl who thought there must be more to the world than Kinley. She wanted to go places and see things...." Leigh's voice trailed off. Sort of like me, she finished to herself. Only I never got to see them. She wondered if Sarah had.

"Maybe she wasn't kidnapped from in front of her house," Wade said, and Leigh focused her attention on him. His brow was knitted as he voiced his theory. "What if she did decide to run away that night? Maybe she even tricked her mother into thinking she was going to spend the night with her cousin. Then she waited until it got dark and sneaked away."

"Then what?" Leigh asked when he had finished. "A seven-year-old girl wouldn't get very far before she realized that running away isn't as easy as it seems. And, if she ran away, why didn't she take her bike?"

"Maybe she wanted to be inconspicuous," Wade ventured, but the conviction was gone from his voice.

"Okay. Let's say she did run away," Leigh said. "It doesn't change much. She couldn't have gotten far, so the kidnapper would still have to be someone in Kinley. And that brings us back to square one."

Wade pushed off the porch with one of his feet, and the swing rocked gently. "This is a nightmare, Leigh," he said after a long moment's silence. "For some reason I can't begin to understand, I'm the link between the kidnappings of two innocent little girls. Even though I had nothing to do with it directly, I feel responsible."

He took a deep breath, then continued. "I was going crazy today just sitting in my mother's house thinking about it, so I decided to join the search for Lisa Farley. I was looking through a patch of woods not far from town when I came across Ben and Gary Foster. All of a sudden I could tell they weren't looking for Lisa at all. They were watching me, wondering what I was doing there. I don't think it entered their minds that I was searching just like everybody else. They thought I was covering up clues."

"You can't know that for sure, Wade," Leigh protested even though he was probably right. The Foster brothers were about their age and were terrible snobs. Perfect marriage material, her mother had often called them, especially during the brief period when she had dated Gary Foster.

"Oh, yes I can," he answered softly. "The people of Kinley don't trust me, and I don't trust them. Hell, Leigh, I don't even completely trust you, and you're the only one who believes me."

"Martha Culpepper believes you," Leigh said, and her voice was sad because he still doubted her. "And Ena believed in you."

"Ah, Ena," Wade said, savoring the sound of his mother's name. "It's funny. I didn't see her more than a couple times a year, but I miss her constantly. I never realized before how much I relied on her just being there. Anytime I phoned, she gave the impression that talking to me was the most important thing she had to do that day. She was such a confident, strong woman."

"She raised a strong son," Leigh said, meaning it.

Wade laughed although she hadn't said anything funny. "Then why am I letting the gossip get to me? And why have I come close to slugging Burt and the Fosters?"

Leigh smiled. "Don't be so hard on yourself, Wade. When I knew you years ago, you would have gotten into both those fights. You've just grown up. You used to be so impulsive, you'd do what you wanted no matter what the consequences."

She was right and wrong at the same time, Wade thought. He had grown up, but the boy he'd been still lived somewhere inside him and there were some impulses he still wasn't able to control. Those impulses were fueled by the flashes of desire he thought he read in her eyes and in the softness of her body sitting so near his.

"You mean that years ago, if I felt like kissing you, I'd just do it?" Wade asked, covering her shoulder with one of his hands and turning her toward him. She stared at him wordlessly, and he saw nothing in her face to dissuade him from what he wanted to do.

"Because I'm feeling an impulse right now," he whispered.

They moved forward as if drawn by a magnet until they were in each other's arms. Their breath mingled, their mouths met and their tongues mated with a passionate urgency. His fingertips brushed her nipples as if by accident, and she gasped with pleasure. He touched her again, more purposefully, and Leigh closed her eyes as a white-hot desire seared through her, centering in the female core that already ached for fulfillment.

His large hands cupped her breasts, which were bare beneath her thin shirt, and she was on fire with need. He kissed the side of her neck, then her throat, then her full mouth. She felt like the teenager who hadn't been able to control herself on a grassy bank a dozen years ago. She felt like a woman who had never fallen out of love with her first love.

He'd wanted to touch her like this again from almost the moment he'd seen her at the graveyard, but Wade had never imagined it would be this way. Her skin was silkier, her curves more generous, her response more passionate. He had grown hard before he'd even touched her, and already he was skittering out of control. If he didn't stop right now, he didn't think he would be able to. But he didn't want this feeling to stop, not when he hadn't experienced it for such a long time.

"Invite me in," Wade rasped against her lips, and Leigh nodded without hesitation. Denying him was as impossible as denying the urge to blink. Why hadn't she admitted that before now? Wade reluctantly pulled his lips from hers and got to his feet, and she immediately felt bereft. But then he drew her to his side, and her entire body felt warm again.

They went through the door and, hand in hand, ascended the stairs to her bedroom, and Leigh felt as though she were floating to the second floor on a cloud. But when they reached her bedroom with its ridiculously feminine pink-and-white bedspread, Leigh tensed. No man had ever been inside her bedroom, and she considered it a sanctuary where she could daydream in private. She drew her eyes to Wade, and the tension suddenly eased. After all, most of her daydreams had been about him.

The walk up the stairs hadn't cooled Wade's passion, but when Leigh took a few steps toward the bed, he realized that her small, perfect body was his for the taking. He remembered the time at the cove and it gave him pause. He reached for her but held her at arm's length. In the glow of the moonlight, he could barely see her eyes. "Leigh, I want you to be sure," he breathed. "I don't want there to be any regrets this time."

"No regrets. Then or now," Leigh said and stood on her tiptoes to kiss him. His mouth was as soft and as warm as the downy comforter she used on chilly nights. It was also as familiar. She outlined his lips with her tongue, knowing the bottom one was slightly fuller than the top and that the corners of his mouth lifted slightly. Wade deepened the kiss with an urgency that took her breath away, and the room seemed to spin. Suddenly they were lying across her bed and she wasn't sure how they had gotten there.

Her hands, however, seemed to know exactly what to do. She ran them over his body, tracing the sinewy hardness of his back and the curve of his buttocks. Wade groaned and ran his hands over her bare belly until they reached her breasts. She arched toward him and felt the rosy tips harden in welcome.

When he nudged the garment over her breasts, she lifted her arms to help him remove it completely. Then he sat up and pulled off his own shirt, making Leigh draw in her breath at the sheer perfection of his bare chest. Wade Conner was no longer a boy, but a man, and the distinction didn't make her want him any less than she had all those years ago.

Never taking her eyes from his, Leigh removed her shorts and underwear so that she lay naked, trembling with desire. He hesitated and Leigh thought for an instant that he might change his mind, but then Wade shed the rest of his clothing, and she saw that his desire was as urgent as hers.

He joined her on the bed; their bodies met, and it seemed to Leigh that they had never been apart. He captured her mouth again and she moved her hips against his in blatant invitation. Later there would be time for slow, luxurious lovemaking, but they had been apart for too long and she was on fire for him.

Wade was usually a considerate lover, intent on giving as much pleasure as he took. He wanted to delay the moment when he entered her, but he felt as though he would burst if he did. The sensation of bare skin, soft lips and Leigh was too much for him to bear.

"Now, Wade," she begged as if she read his thoughts. "Let's not wait any longer—"

Before she could finish the sentence, he was inside of her and an incredible joy that had everything to do with sex and nothing to do with it filled her. She drew in her breath at the sheer pleasure he brought her, and he slipped his tongue inside her mouth at the same instant they moved in unison against each other. Their rhythm was perfectly in sync, as though they had been lovers for the past twelve years, as though they were meant for each other.

She had missed this man. The years had been empty because he was the only one who could fill them. Something rare and wonderful burst inside her on the heels of that thought at the same time Wade's body shuddered in fulfillment, and Leigh's eyes filled with tears before her own body came back to earth. In a moment, her face was wet with moisture and Wade felt the tears against his cheek.

"Leigh, what's wrong?" he asked when he could speak. "Did I hurt you?"

Leigh almost laughed at the absurdity of the question. Hurt her? He had transported her somewhere she had never been. But how could she tell him she was crying for all they had lost and all they had found? They had only just rediscovered each other, and she didn't want to jeopardize the start of their new relationship. "I'm just happy," she said instead, and he smiled.

After a moment, he rolled off her, but she snuggled against his side. "I've wanted to do that since I first saw you again," he confessed, and she loved the way tiny lines appeared around his eyes and mouth when he smiled. But it was a sad smile.

"Me, too," she said, happy that he had made the confession but sad because he said it as though the truth didn't please him. She was in his arms, but it was because he couldn't help himself, not because he consciously wanted her there. Be patient, she told herself. Maybe someday he would forgive her for the past and fall in love with her again. She already knew that she loved him; she always had and always would. But it was too soon to tell him that.

"Wade, I don't have any regrets," she said instead.

He was silent, because although he had no regrets at the moment he knew he might have some later. Keeping his feelings on a casual level while sleeping with Leigh was going to be harder than he'd imagined. Now that they'd made love once, he knew he had to have her again. But now wasn't the time to warn her against expecting too much from him.

He kissed her instead, and Leigh fell asleep in his arms, happier than she'd been since she was a teenager.

Chapter 8

They awakened once in the night to make slow, sweet love, and the mood was so dreamy that later Leigh couldn't be sure if it had really happened.

Leigh shut her eyes tight, trying to block out the insistent ringing in her ears, but it didn't work. The noise grew more penetrating until gentle hands shook her awake. Her eyes flew open, and Wade was looking at her. The ringing hadn't stopped.

"Your phone's ringing, sleepyhead," he said, and she looked at the clock and groaned. It was already nine-thirty, and she was late for work. She reached for the phone, sure that Drew was on the other end. She was miffed that she had to think up an excuse for being late when she only wanted to linger in bed with Wade.

While he watched her shake off the sleep, Wade deliberately put distance between their bodies until no part of him touched her. It had been a mistake to spend the night with her. He had meant to leave quietly in the middle of the night, but she had been curled up against him and he had felt cozy and content. He'd have to be more careful in the future if he wanted to keep their affair on a casual basis.

Leigh sensed his withdrawal and wanted to reach out to him to reassure herself that last night hadn't been a dream, but the phone wouldn't stop ringing. She reluctantly picked up the receiver. "Hello," she said, already wanting to hang up.

It was Ashley's voice and not Drew's that came over the line. "God, Leigh, why aren't you at the store?" Ashley said, and Leigh would have hung up if it hadn't been for the despair in her sister's voice. "Never mind. Something terrible has happened. Ben and Gary Foster were searching the marsh this morning, and they found a skeleton. Burt's almost sure it belongs to poor, little Sarah Culpepper."

"How can they be sure it's Sarah?" Leigh asked, suddenly wide-awake. In bed next to her, Wade sat up. Leigh's troubled eyes flew to his, and it seemed as though a dark curtain came down over his face.

"They're not positive, Leigh, but who else could it be?" Leigh's eyes widened in horror as Ashley talked and the reality of the situation sunk in. Sweet, pretty Sarah was dead. "The coroner was already there. The bones weren't intact, but he said it was the skeleton of a child. It's positively gruesome, Leigh. I don't know how Martha Culpepper is going to handle it."

"Was there any sign of Lisa Farley?" Leigh asked, hoping the answer would be negative. But, if the same person who kidnapped Sarah had snatched Lisa, wouldn't she meet the same fate?

"None," Ashley said and paused. "Leigh, Burt's been trying to get in touch with Wade to ask him some more questions—"

"Why?" Leigh cut in before Ashley could continue. She knew Wade wouldn't appreciate her interference, but she wanted to shield him from any more unpleasantness.

"You know the answer to that, honey. Wade's always been a suspect, and it's only natural that Burt should want to question him. Anyway, if you see him, could you tell him that Burt wants to talk to him? Burt can't seem to find him this morning."

"Okay," Leigh answered dryly, even as she realized her sister had probably guessed that Wade was with her and had actually been tactful. "I'll tell him."

Leigh replaced the receiver slowly and met Wade's haunted look. He had been spending time running shirtless in the Carolina sun, and the only part of him that was pale was his face, which was about as white as the sheet covering part of his body. It made his day-old stubble appear even more prominent. Leigh sat up, pulling the bed sheets over her breasts. It seemed wrong to be discussing something so awful while lying naked in bed after something so wonderful.

"They found Sarah Culpepper," Wade said stonily before she could tell him; he closed his gray eyes briefly when Leigh nodded.

"The Foster brothers found a skeleton early this morning while they were searching for Lisa. It was in the marsh somewhere. They can't be positive on the identification yet, but it's the skeleton of a small child. It doesn't seem likely that it's anyone other than Sarah." Leigh spoke in a monotone, as though the truth in her words hadn't yet been accepted by her mind.

Wade was very still and very quiet for a moment. He had been heartbroken when he found out about his mother's fatal heart attack, but it had been nothing like this. Ena had died naturally at an advanced age, but they were talking about a child who had been snatched in the dark of night. He shook his head back and forth, trying to deny the inevitable. When he spoke, his voice was unutterably sad.

"All this time I kept hoping that Sarah was alive somewhere, living the life of a teenager. I even imagined what that blond hair and those blue eyes would look like on a young woman. I wanted her to be alive, Leigh, but deep down I always knew she was dead. Why, then, is it so hard to accept?"

It was a question that didn't have an answer, and Leigh couldn't think of a single word that would make him feel better. If only the townspeople could see him now, she thought. They'd know that a man with a heart as good as Wade's couldn't hurt anyone, let alone a sweet little girl.

"What did you mean when you said you'd tell him?" Wade asked finally. His voice didn't crack, but it didn't have its usual authority, either.

Leigh lowered her head, unwilling to bring him any more pain but knowing she didn't have a choice. "Burt wants to talk to you, but I'm sure it's just a formality."

He was silent for a long time, and Leigh watched the shadows of yesterday play over his face. Last night, she had thought they had chased some of the shadows away with their love-making. But the sun was shining, the birds were singing and the shadows still lingered.

"I need to get dressed," Wade said stiffly and got out of bed. A single tear trickled down Leigh's face, and it was soon joined by another and then another.

"Tell me everything you know," Leigh demanded as she sipped a cup of perfectly brewed coffee and regarded her sister across a kitchen table. Ashley's kitchen was unremittingly cheerful, from the paisley tablecloth to the frilly matching curtains. Pots and pans hung artfully from hooks on a wall covered with bright yellow paint. The airy mood the kitchen created was in stark contrast to the seriousness in Leigh's face.

"Really, Leigh, I told you most everything over the phone," Ashley said, pouting prettily as she played with her coffee cup. Her fair hair was swept back in a chignon, and she looked cool and sophisticated. Leigh didn't. She had taken a quick shower after her sister's phone call that morning, and her long hair was partially wet. She wore an oversize T-shirt and old, blue shorts. On her feet were a pair of worn tennis shoes.

"I can't see why you had to rush over here looking like you do." Ashley's disapproving eyes swept Leigh up and down. "At least you could have taken the time to put on some makeup."

"Ashley, please tell me what happened," Leigh said again, ignoring her. If she persisted, Ashley would spill what she knew mostly because she was an incurable gossip. "Burt must have told you the whole story."

"Of course he did," Ashley said and leaned forward, as though she were confiding something of great importance. "You know that Ben and Gary Foster were part of the volunteer team hunting for Lisa? Everybody else was pretty much sticking to the high ground, so the Fosters decided to fetch their hip-high fishing boots and search some of the marsh."

"That sounds logical," Leigh said, and Ashley nodded.

"Apparently, there's a dirt road that branches off Old Kinley Road. You probably know the one. It's about two or three miles outside of town. Ben and Gary drove down the road and discovered there was sort of a beaten path at the end of it. They walked on it a little ways, veered off and started searching the marsh alongside it. They hadn't been there an hour when they came upon little Sarah's bones. Ben said they might not have seen them at all if we hadn't had so little rain lately. The marsh had drained in some places, and the skeleton was in plain view in the mud. Leigh? Leigh, honey, what's wrong?"

The color had ebbed from Leigh's face, and she was staring down at the linoleum table. A dirt road. A narrow path. A marsh. Sarah's skeleton had been discovered near the secret cove where she and Wade had first made love. It seemed too cruel to be true. Her hands started to shake. Did the killer know they met there? Had he or she deliberately dumped Sarah's body there in the hope that it would implicate Wade?

"Leigh?" Ashley's voice was louder this time, and she came quickly to her younger sister's side and took her trembling hands. "Leigh, are you all right?"

The panic in her tone jolted Leigh out of her private nightmare, and she willed her hands to stop shaking. She raised her eyes to her sister's, and saw that the concern in Ashley's was quite real. "I'm fine, Ashley. It's just . . . just that the picture you painted was so horrible. I can't see how anybody could do something like that."

"I know, dear," Ashley said and bit her lip. "I keep thinking how terrible it would be if somebody snatched Michael or Julie. I don't think I could stand it. Really, it was a fluke that Sarah was found at all. Burt said that somebody who knew the tides had to have dumped her, because her remains were covered even in low tide. It's only because we had record low rainfall this year that the site was exposed. Anybody who had searched the place years ago never would have seen her."

Ashley sat down again, and the sisters were silent, each lost in their own thoughts. "Leigh, please don't take this the wrong way," Ashley said with a tentativeness that wasn't characteristic. "But I'm worried about you and Wade Conner. Don't say anything yet. Just let me finish. It didn't take me long to figure out where Wade was when Burt couldn't find him this morning. I know you're seeing him."

Leigh crossed her arms over her chest and glared at Ashley, silently but clearly telling her sister she resented the big-sister-knows-best role she was playing. Ashley ignored her body language and kept on talking.

"You probably don't want to talk to me about this, either, but I feel I have to say a few things," Ashley said. "I know you think Wade didn't do these things, but most people think differently. I can't see how anything but bad can come out of your association with him. Why, you're even willing to tell a fib to protect him."

Leigh knew Ashley was referring to her claim that she was with Wade the night Sarah was kidnapped. She sighed audibly. If her own sister didn't believe her confession, who would? "Ashley, it's not a fib. Why won't you believe that I was with him that night?"

"I guess I don't want to believe it," Ashley said with such stark honesty that Leigh looked at her through new eyes; Ashley seemed genuinely concerned about her. "I don't want you to get messed up in all of this. I have a feeling things are going to get ugly, Leigh."

Leigh reached across the table and captured one of her sister's hands. "I have to get involved, Ashley. I was silent once, and nothing good came of it. I have to tell what I know."

Ashley nodded in understanding, and Leigh felt guilty for all the times she'd wanted to hang up on her or walk across the street to avoid her or tell her to mind her own business. Ashley was far from the perfect sister, but she had proved that she cared about Leigh.

"You don't really think Wade took those little girls, do you?" Leigh asked quietly after a moment. Ashley's blue eyes grew troubled, and the corners of her mouth twitched.

"That's what worries me, honey," Ashley answered just as quietly. "I don't know. I really don't know."

It was midday, and the sun was as hot as it was going to get. Wade walked along Kinley's main street, his temper even hotter than the weather. Burt Tucker had a lot of nerve summoning him to the police station and then casting veiled insinuations. Wade was sick and tired of being accused when the real criminal was probably laughing in enjoyment at the way his plan was working. Burt didn't have any evidence against him; how could he when Wade had nothing to do with the crimes?

Wade wiped his brow, which was damp with sweat, and silently cursed the heat. The temperature during South Carolina springs was usually ideal, but it felt hotter than hell today. Wade laughed aloud. That shouldn't be surprising. He was starting to think that Kinley was hell on earth.

Wade heard a sound behind him and turned to look. Instantly he wished he hadn't. The street was nearly deserted, but there in the middle of it was Abe Hooper. Wade hadn't seen Abe since he'd left town, but he hadn't changed. He must have been over sixty, but his clothes were still unkempt, he still needed a shave and he was well on his way to getting drunk.

"Repent," he yelled, and there was no one he could have been talking to except Wade. "Repent for your sins or face eternal damnation."

The last thing Wade needed was a confrontation with the town drunk. He spied Marshall's Hardware store a few doors down and decided to duck in to buy some paint. His bedroom looked as though it hadn't been painted in years, and physical labor might be a good way to work off some of his tension.

The whoosh of cold air was welcome after noon's oppressive heat, but Wade soon realized that Sam Marshall paid a price for keeping his place of business cool. A rickety window unit supplied the cooled air, and it made such a din that customers had to raise their voices to be heard. Wade nodded in Sam's direction, and made his way down one of the narrow aisles toward the paint. Within minutes, Sam was ringing up a couple of brushes and a gallon of paint.

"Hot enough for you?" Sam asked as Wade paid him. Sam wasn't smiling, but he wasn't peering at Wade suspiciously and that was an improvement over the way most of the townsfolk treated him. Wade barely remembered Sam from his youth, probably because the older man didn't have any children his age.

"Too hot," Wade answered, swinging the paint can off the counter. "But then the heat in this town's been a little too much for me since I arrived."

"Not everyone believes the stories," Sam said, barely loud enough to be heard above the air conditioner.

"Not everyone's as good a man as you," Wade said and left the store. Still, he felt a little better. There was no reason he should be subjected to suspicion everywhere he went, but he was glad when he found it absent.

There was no sign of Abe Hooper on the street, and Wade breathed a sigh of relief. But the relief was short-lived when he saw Gary Foster walking toward him. With his sandy hair and hazel eyes, Gary looked like the boy next door, but he and Wade had never been neighborly.

Gary, who had gone into business with his attorney father, was wearing a pair of muddy hip boots instead of a suit. Sarah Culpepper had been found, so that could only mean that the search for Lisa Farley continued. The look in Gary's eyes when he saw Wade made it seem as though their high school days were only yesterday instead of fifteen years ago. Wade had once thoroughly embarrassed Gary in a game of playground basketball that had disastrous consequences, and it was obvious Gary had neither forgiven nor forgotten.

"Well, well, if it isn't the prodigal son returned," Gary drawled sarcastically, and then he stopped in his tracks. "Why don't you just tell me where Lisa is so we don't have to go through the trouble of searching for her?"

Wade had every intention of ignoring Gary and his remark, and he actually passed him and put a few steps of distance between them before Gary's next words gave him pause.

"You're not going to get away with it, even with Leigh Hampton lying for you."

Wade's eyes were steely when he turned to regard Gary, but he felt at a disadvantage because he didn't understand his remark. "What are you talking about?"

Gary laughed. "Oh, so you're going to play dumb and say you don't know that Leigh is telling everyone in town who'll listen that she was with you when Sarah disappeared twelve years ago? Fortunately we have enough sense around these parts to know when something's not true."

Wade's world reeled. He knew that Leigh had told Burt she'd been with him that fated night, but he had no idea that she'd been spreading her story around town. Didn't she realize that a confession like that, one that had come years too late, only made him appear even guiltier? He'd had enough of Gary Foster and turned to leave, but Gary didn't intend to let him walk away so easily.

"You know, it's a good thing your mother's dead, Wade," he said cruelly. "A closed casket will stop her from seeing what a disgrace you are."

Wade didn't think; he just reacted. He laid the paint and brushes down on the sidewalk, closed the gap between himself and Gary and let his right fist fly. The punch connected with a thud somewhere between Gary's left eye and his cheekbone and knocked him off his feet.

Then Wade turned on his heel, picked up his purchases and walked away. All the while, Foster sat on the pavement cursing him and telling him that he was going to be sorry. The funny thing was, Wade was already sorry. Punching Gary and defending his mother's honor had felt good for a moment, but it wouldn't have pleased Ena and it wasn't going to put an end to his problems. It was probably going to add to them.

The day dragged once Leigh reached the general store. Every time the phone rang, she rushed to answer it in the hope that it was Wade. It never was. The suspense of what Burt had said to him was driving her crazy. Did the chief know that Sarah had been found close to Wade's secret cove? Would he ever be convinced of Wade's innocence if he did?

Leigh paced from the cash register to the display of paper napkins and back while the questions hammered at her. She picked up the phone and dialed Wade's number, but all she heard were the repeated rings that had greeted her the other dozen times she had called. Where was he? The shop was empty, and Leigh suddenly felt claustrophobic. She let herself out the front door and leaned against the cool brick wall that formed the front of the store.

On the surface, it was a beautiful spring day but an underlying chill had settled over the town. Everywhere Leigh looked, she saw posters of Lisa Farley emblazoned with the word *missing*. She stared across the street at the empty playground adjacent to the elementary school. School was in its last week before summer break, and the children were infused with spring fever. At this time of year, they usually chased each other around at recess and laughed in anticipation of a summer without classes.

Today had been different. The children had been almost solemn during recess, playing in an orderly fashion while a few of the teachers stood guard. Or at least that's what it looked like. Just before school let out, mothers started to gather on the school grounds. The children didn't walk, skip and jump home as they usually did. Instead, their mothers took them firmly by their hands and walked briskly away. It was a chilling commentary on what had happened in their town, and Leigh couldn't blame them for their actions. But she couldn't forgive them for blaming Wade, either.

"Business slow, Leigh?" drawled a voice near her ear, startling her. She had been so lost in thought that she hadn't heard anybody approach. Gary Foster gave her a half smile, and Leigh pulled herself together. He was a nice-looking man who came from what her mother termed a fine family. Leigh had dated him a few times, but his kiss had never ignited the spark that a mere look from Wade caused. She had rebuffed him gently, knowing she would have to listen to her mother scold her about what she had thrown away. Gary was one of the few eligible bachelors in Kinley her mother deemed suitable. Gary also had a black eye.

Leigh nodded to his question about the slow business day. "It's been a bad day all around, Gary," she said and preceded him into the store. "Judging from your eye, I'd say you aren't having a very good one, either."

Gary ignored her comment about his eye, and grabbed a couple of packages of batteries from the display near the front of the shop before following Leigh to the cash register. "My flashlight's running low on batteries, and I thought I'd replace them in case we went out looking for Lisa tonight," he explained.

"No luck, then?" Leigh asked, even though she knew the answer.

"None. Everybody seems a little more desperate since Ben and I found Sarah's skeleton, but we don't even have a clue as to where Lisa could be." Leigh rang up the batteries on the cash register as she digested the information, and Gary handed her a few bills.

"Are they sure it was Sarah?"

"Now they are," Gary said, and the answer wasn't unexpected. "Dr. Thomas still had her dental records, and they matched. Unfortunately the bones had been in the marsh too long to be able to tell what happened to her. Of course, it's pretty unlikely that she got all the way out there by herself, so we have to assume she was murdered."

Leigh's entire body tensed at the thought. "I'm sorry you had to be one of the ones to find her," she said. "It must have been pretty awful."

Gary nodded shortly, and Leigh saw a flash of what might have been pain pass through his eyes. "At least Martha Culpepper finally knows what became of her. Not knowing for sure could be even worse."

Leigh handed him his change, but he didn't move from the counter. "Leigh," he said and hesitated before rushing on. "I hear that you've been seeing Wade Conner."

"I hardly think that's any of your business, Gary," Leigh said smoothly, wondering if there was anybody in town who didn't know she had been keeping company with Wade.

"I know I'm out of line here, Leigh, but maybe you should think things out more carefully before seeing him again. You know they're saying he did it, don't you?" Gary's eyes shone with what looked like concern as he tried to gauge her reaction. The concern, more than anything, saved him from the full weight of Leigh's anger.

"You *are* out of line, Gary," Leigh said tightly. "You're also dead wrong about Wade. Open your eyes, for God's sake. He's a novelist with a successful career in New York who came back here for his mother's funeral. He didn't come back to snatch a sweet, little girl from her parents and do something unspeakable to her. The person who did this is sick. Do you hear me, Gary? Sick. And Wade is a warm, caring man who is the victim of a small town's ugly suspicion. No one's ever going to catch the real criminal while so much attention is focused on Wade."

When Leigh finished her tirade, her chest heaved beneath the thin fabric of her T-shirt. It didn't escape her notice that she was making a habit of defending Wade. Gary took a step back from the counter, almost as though he were trying to escape her anger.

"I'm sorry I made you angry, Leigh, but I've known you a long time and I'm worried about you," he said. "I know you're going to do what you want, but at least think about what I said. Mark my words, Leigh. You're going to be sorry you ever laid eyes on Wade Conner again."

He made his way to the door and paused, looking back at Leigh. "And, by the way, that warm, caring man is the one who gave me this shiner."

Gary turned and walked out of the door before Leigh could reply. She wouldn't have been able to say anything anyway, because she was in shock. Why had Gary and Wade fought? Did it have anything to do with the disappearances? And, if Gary had a black eye, did that mean that Wade was injured?

When six o'clock finally came, Leigh locked the front door and hurried down the main street of town, almost frantic with worry about Wade. Why hadn't he answered his phone all day? She quickened her step when a terrible thought struck her. What if the people of Kinley had decided to take justice into their own hands by punishing the man they held responsible for Sarah's death and Lisa's kidnapping?

Leigh started to run, uncaring that her hair had come loose from her ponytail or that the few people in the street were looking at her curiously. Of course she was being silly, she told herself. Lynchings had gone out of style, even in small towns like Kinley. She knew she was letting her imagination run away with her, but she kept running.

The midday sun had given way to cloud cover, but it was still a hot day and Leigh was winded and sweaty by the time she reached Wade's house. Uncaring of how it might look, she pounded loudly on the door and kept on pounding until it swung open.

Wade was splattered with paint, but otherwise unmarked and Leigh's knees buckled in relief. He wasn't surprised to see her, but he hadn't expected her to look quite like this. Her hair was coming loose from her ponytail, her face was bathed in sweat and she wore an old T-shirt and shorts. Only Leigh could show up on someone's doorstep dressed like that but still look beautiful.

"Are you going to make a habit of pounding on my front door?" Wade said while he opened the screen door to admit her. "Because if you are, I might as well just give you a key. It might save my hearing."

"You're not hurt," Leigh said instead of responding to his teasing, and Wade wondered what she was talking about. Instead of explaining the comment fueled by her runaway imagination, Leigh said the next thing that popped into her mind. "Why does Gary Foster have a black eye?"

Wade's earlier funk had vanished when he'd seen her, but it came back with a vengeance. Now he understood. The heavy pounding. The disheveled appearance. The frantic air. She, too, was going to stand in judgment of him.

"My, my," he said sarcastically. "Word sure does travel fast in two-bit towns. So now are you going to ask me what I did to provoke him?"

Leigh shook her head, wondering how he had come to that conclusion. "Of course not," she said, but he didn't pay any attention to her denial.

"But why should I expect anything else? You're from Kinley, aren't you? You're one of them. Something happens, you need a scapegoat and I'm available. A little girl disappears? Well, Wade must have done it. Gary Foster ends up with a black eye? It was big, bad Wade's fault."

He was ranting, and Leigh hardly knew why. "You're not making any sense, Wade. Everybody in Kinley isn't out to get you. I'm not," she said, backing away a step. He didn't look like the man she loved. His face was taut with barely contained rage, and it was directed at her.

"No, you're the one who doesn't make sense," Wade said, his voice a notch louder than usual. "Open your eyes and look around, Leigh. Why do you keep defending this godforsaken town where nothing is the way it seems? Sure, it's a beautiful place but the people who live here are ugly. Why do you even stay?"

"We're not talking about me, Wade," Leigh said, uncomfortable with the turn the conversation was taking. She couldn't even follow his train of thought.

"Sure we are," he said. "I thought you were different from the rest of them, but it seems like I was wrong. So tell me. I want to know. Why haven't you left?"

Leigh was still wary but thought her best course of action was to answer him. "I have to run the store, Wade. My mother and my brother depend on me."

"Do you even know how ridiculous that sounds?" Wade laughed. "How long have you been fooling yourself? Drew is a grown man capable of taking care of himself. And, if you're worried about your mother's security, you can just sell the damn store. Neither of them needs you."

"That's n-not true," Leigh stammered, but Wade didn't allow her to defend herself.

"It sure is," he said. "You know what I think? I think you need to feel like you're a martyr, like you have no choice but to stay in this awful town. Because if you didn't, you'd realize you never intended to leave at all. You gave up your dreams, you gave up your painting, you even gave me up. But you can't give up Kinley."

"How can you say that?" Leigh asked, wounded. "How can you say any of it after last night? Didn't that mean anything to you?"

"Maybe last night was for old times' sake, too," he said, using the same words she'd spoken before he'd kissed her in Ena's bedroom.

Leigh didn't need to hear anymore. Hot tears started to spill down her face and she only wanted to get away from him. She turned, pushed open the screen door and ran into the twilight.

Wade watched her go, and some of his anger left with her. He believed most of what he had said, but it hadn't improved his disposition any to reduce Leigh to tears. He was angry at the way Kinley had treated him, and he had taken it out on Leigh. He hadn't given her a chance to explain why she'd shown up on his doorstep disheveled and frantic, and he had even refused to admit to her that last night had meant something to him. But he refused to admit that to himself, too. All he knew was that he couldn't forgive her, but he couldn't forget her, either.

Sighing, Wade closed his front door and locked it behind him. He might not be sure why he'd slept with her, but he knew he owed her an apology. He started walking the three blocks to Leigh's house.

Leigh was too winded from her recent exertion to run more than a block, but her mind raced as she walked the rest of the way to her large antebellum home. How could he have said those things, she asked herself while she wiped away the tears that were still flowing down her cheeks. She had to admit that he was probably right about some of it. She had thrown away her dreams and her painting and resigned herself to a second-rate life in Kinley. And she had abandoned him in the process. But she wasn't the fool he made her out to be. And she certainly hadn't slept with him just for old times' sake.

When her house came into view in the next moment, she stopped dead in her tracks. Sweat trickled down her face from the exertion, but Leigh didn't notice anything except the front door standing wide open. Leigh walked slowly toward the house, unconsciously wiping damp palms on her shorts.

She entered the house, not bothering to close the door behind her. It was deathly quiet, but she knew instantly that something was wrong. Ever since Lisa's disappearance, Leigh had been careful to secure her locks when she left home. Why, then, was the door standing agape in flagrant invitation?

Her eyes swept the interior of the home, taking in the stack of newspapers on the floor and the pile of clean laundry that needed to be folded. Everything was just as she'd left it that morning. Leigh's breath was coming in shallow gasps as she climbed the stairs, but it was as much from uncertainty as to what she would find as from her recent workout.

She made her way down the upstairs hall, and the only sound she heard was the beating of her heart. She rounded the turn to her bedroom, and an icy terror filled her veins. The room looked as if a cyclone had touched down on it. The contents of her dresser drawers and closets had been dumped unceremoniously onto the floor. Her lamps were smashed as if they had been hurled against the walls, and her quilt and bed sheets had been slashed.

Leigh's hand came up to her mouth to stop the scream that was welling inside her, and she turned and ran down the stairs and toward the front door. She wanted only to be out in the fresh air, away from the evil that had invaded her home, but she collided with a man's hard, unyielding form. Mindlessly, wanting only to get away from her tormentor, Leigh started to pummel his chest.

"Leigh. Leigh. Stop it. It's me, Wade," a voice commanded, and Leigh raised her terrified violet eyes to his face. Their argument forgotten, she sagged against him in relief, her tears spilling onto his shirt.

"Thank God it's you," she murmured brokenly.

"Who did you think it was?" he asked as his arms came around her, wondering at her reaction. He'd expected anger, not affection. She clung to him, trying to catch her breath. When she did, she drew back slightly so she could look at him. His features were etched with concern, but he didn't press her for a response.

"When I got home, my door was wide open," Leigh explained briefly, her voice shaking. "I came inside and found that someone ransacked my bedroom."

Wade swore under his breath and gave her a little shake. "Don't you know better than to go inside a house when you suspect someone has broken in? He could have still been inside, for God's sake."

She was momentarily taken aback by his anger, but recovered sufficiently to disentangle herself from his arms. "Well, he wasn't," she said, rubbing the parts of her upper arms where he had gripped her.

She looked so small and defenseless standing before him that Wade could have kicked himself. He had been scolding her when she needed comfort, but he hadn't been able to help himself. There was something terribly wrong in Kinley, and it had spilled into Leigh's house. When he thought of what might have happened had she chanced upon the intruder, he shivered. Neither of them had said it yet, but it was possible the person who had broken into her home was the same person who had killed Sarah Culpepper.

"Promise me you'll be more careful if something like this happens again," Wade said forcefully. He would rather have gathered her into his arms and offered comfort, but the point he had to make was more important.

Leigh nodded mutely. "I guess I just wasn't thinking," she said. "Nothing like this has ever happened to me before."

Wade held out one of his hands. "C'mon, let's go look at your bedroom."

As Wade surveyed the damage moments later, his dark eyes narrowed in puzzlement. It didn't make sense. The room was in chaos, but he couldn't fathom why. There didn't seem to be any method to the destruction. It looked as though clothes had been dumped from drawers and then scattered, perhaps kicked, in various directions. The clothes that had been hanging in Leigh's closets were also strewn on the floor as though someone had hurled them without design or direction.

Stepping over the broken glass from the ruined lamps, Wade made his way to the bed he and Leigh had shared the night before and bent to trace the slashes in the sheets and the mattress with his fingers. He would have wagered the cuts had been made with a hunting knife, but the deduction didn't shed any light on the mystery. Just about every man in Kinley owned a hunting knife. And why would anyone have done this to Leigh's bedroom? Did it have anything to do with the two little girls who had been kidnapped?

"Is anything missing, Leigh?" Wade turned and saw that she was standing in the doorway, biting her lip as she surveyed the scene.

"I don't keep anything valuable in here except some jewelry. I guess I won't know if it's missing until I clean up this mess," Leigh said, and her voice cracked slightly.

Wade was instantly at her side, cradling her head against his shoulder as she wept. It was a sound borne of uncertainty and fear, a sound that was tearing at his heart. "I hate to admit this, but I think we should call Burt," he whispered into her hair.

Chapter 9

Twenty minutes later, Burt gazed upon the mess somebody had made of Leigh's bedroom. Wade and Leigh, her eyes still rimmed with red from her recent cry, stood beside him. Burt exhaled heavily and shook his head from side to side.

"I don't like the looks of this," he said. "No, siree, I don't like the looks of this at all."

He took a few steps deeper into the room and stopped at Leigh's bed, bending to finger the shredded sheets. "Looks like somebody used a hunting knife to do this," he said, repeating Wade's earlier assessment. "Now, tell me if I've got this right, Leigh. You got home from the store and the door was wide open. When you came upstairs, you found this. And Wade here just happened by a few minutes later."

"Not exactly," Leigh said and glanced at Wade. She still didn't know why he had followed her, but she was glad he had. "I stopped by to see Wade before coming home. We had a, uh, disagreement and he followed me home."

"I see," Burt said, although he clearly didn't see anything at all. "Anything missing?"

"Not as far as I can tell," Leigh said, and it amazed Wade that a woman who had broken down in his arms less than an hour ago could sound so strong. "Why do you think anyone would do this, Burt?"

The chief straightened and met his sister-in-law's questioning look with one of his own. "That's what I was going to ask you. Got any ideas?"

"If you don't mind me answering that one, I have a couple," Wade announced, and Burt nodded toward him. "But I think Leigh might be a little more comfortable if we talked about this downstairs."

Leigh nodded gratefully and preceded the two men out the door. Wade placed one of his hands at the small of her back, and the action didn't escape Leigh's notice; if he wanted to apologize for what he'd said earlier, she was ready to forgive him.

Moments later, they were sitting in Leigh's living room. Wade and Leigh were on the couch, and Burt sat in a chair facing them.

"What's your idea, Wade?" Burt asked when they had barely settled in.

"I think someone's trying to scare Leigh so we'll stop looking into the past," Wade said, and Leigh was silent as she digested his theory. "Leigh's hell-bent on discovering what happened to Sarah Culpepper twelve years ago, and I think maybe we're getting too close."

"What?" The word was an explosion of anger. "Are you trying to say you've been investigating Sarah's death?"

"Yes," Leigh said defiantly. "We want to find out what happened as much as you do. And arguing about it isn't going to change anything."

Burt put his hands on his hips and exhaled deeply. "So somebody tore up your bedroom as a warning?"

"Exactly," Wade answered, because that was the thought that had been forming since he'd first seen Leigh's bedroom.

"Do you think this somebody is the person who killed Sarah? Or the one who kidnapped Lisa Farley?"

"We think the same person committed both of those crimes," Wade said, and Leigh nodded.

"And what else do you think?" Burt asked with more patience than he usually displayed.

"I don't necessarily think the killer was here in Leigh's house," Wade said slowly, because he hadn't yet worked out all the details. "I'm not saying the killer wasn't here. But maybe it was just someone who doesn't want to see the mystery solved."

"Yes," Leigh said thoughtfully. "Maybe it's somebody who'd rather not see Wade's name cleared. Because that's what's going to happen whenever we get to the bottom of this."

Burt shifted in his seat and ran a hand over his thinning hair. Apparently his patience with Wade's theory had run short. "Will you two stop already?" he said irritably. "I'm sure you could go on indefinitely with your theories, but it's not getting us anywhere."

Burt's voice deepened with authority. "Now, before I say anything else, I want to get something cleared up. You're both going to have to answer to me if I hear tell of you playing amateur private investigator again. Now don't look at me like that, Leigh. I know you don't like being told what to do, but let's just say for one minute that Wade is right and somebody doesn't want you nosing around. If you keep on sticking your pretty face where it doesn't belong, you're going to get hurt."

"You're right, Burt," Leigh said, her chin thrust at a determined angle. "I don't like being told what to do."

The in-laws glared at each other like enemies, and a chill settled over the room. Neither was willing to give an inch, even though they should have been on the same side. Wade was starting to think that Burt might be right about their investigation, but he wasn't about to take the chief's side. There would be plenty of time to talk to Leigh about this in private. He cleared his throat to draw their attention.

"I thought you wanted to ask some questions, Burt," he said, and Burt turned his glare from Leigh to Wade.

"I do," he said gruffly, reluctantly dropping the argument against Leigh and the investigation. "Now, Leigh, you said the door was open when you got home. Was it locked when you left this morning?"

This morning Leigh had awakened happily in Wade's arms and then the light had gone out of her day when she'd been told Sarah's remains had been found. It seemed like such a long time ago. She had thrown on some clothes and hurried to find out what Ashley knew about the discovery. Leigh screwed up her forehead. She had been making a conscious effort to remember to lock her door. But had she locked it that morning?

"I don't know," Leigh said finally. "I was upset when I left this morning, and I may have forgotten."

"Okay, next question. Does anyone have a spare key?"

"Ashley does," Leigh answered.

"Anyone besides Ashley?"

Leigh shook her head. "I thought about giving Mother one, but I was afraid she'd take it as an open invitation to drop in whenever she pleased."

"Where do you keep the spare?"

"In an ashtray in the kitchen," Leigh said and rose. "Wait, I'll go see if it's there."

"Next you're going to ask her who could have taken the key, and maybe even put it back, without her noticing," Wade said levelly when Leigh went out of the room. "You're going to ask her if it could have been me. Isn't that right, Chief?"

Burt eyed the other man with open dislike. "I didn't think you were smart enough to figure that out, Wade."

"It's still there," Leigh said as she reentered the room. "So I guess that means nobody could have taken it."

"I guess you're right," Burt said, but he didn't take his eyes off Wade. Just then, the doorbell rang and it broke the uneasy spell between the two men. Leigh went to answer it, and Ashley stood on the doorstep.

"Oh, sugar, I came over as soon as I could," she said, embracing Leigh. "What an awful thing to have happen and especially with everything else going on."

Ashley stepped by her sister into the house and Leigh, shrugging slightly in resignation, closed the door. "Burt, I do hope you find the scoundrel who's responsible for this. Oh, hello, Wade."

"Ashley," Wade said, half rising from the couch, but Ashley had already returned her attention to Leigh. Aside from her greeting, she acted as though Wade were invisible.

"Darlin', if Burt hasn't already told you, I want you to stay at our house tonight. You can't possibly stay here after what happened." Ashley sounded as though the matter were already settled, and Leigh glanced helplessly at Wade, wishing he had made the offer first.

"Burt, are you through with Leigh? I'd like to take her home now," Ashley said, firmly in charge.

"Really, Ashley, I'm a grown woman. It's nice of you to ask me to stay the night with you and Burt, but I don't think that's necessary. I'll be fine right here."

"I don't think that's a good idea," Burt said at the same time Wade voiced his disapproval. "It would make us all feel a lot easier if you'd at least spend tonight with us. Why don't you pack a bag while I make out this report?"

"I'll come upstairs with you," Ashley said quickly, not giving her an opportunity to refuse. Leigh started to disagree, but in the end she followed Ashley up the stairs.

"You're wrong about me, Burt," Wade said when the women were out of earshot. "One day I'm going to prove that, and you're going to owe me a monster of an apology."

"Don't hold your breath waiting for it, Wade," Burt said as he pulled a pen from his pocket and headed to the table. "Or it won't only be a little girl who's dead."

Leigh paced Ashley's living room, feeling as caged as an inmate in a jail. In a way, that's exactly what she was. Not for the first time, she wished she had resisted Ashley and Burt's insistence that she stay with them. After today, she certainly didn't want to be alone, but she felt reasonably sure Wade wouldn't have allowed that. Right now, they could be resolving their earlier argument or brainstorming about what the trashing of her bedroom had to do with the kidnappings. Or they could be in each other's arms. Leigh's body warmed at the thought, before she deliberately thrust it aside to concentrate on her predicament.

Leigh didn't even know what Wade and Burt had discussed that afternoon. Did Burt know that their secret cove was along the same path as the place where Sarah's skeleton had been found? Did Wade know that she loved him? She could still see his face when she had left that evening with Burt and Ashley. On it was a mixture of concern and, she could have sworn, hurt. Did he think she was abandoning him again?

"Leigh, Burt and I have to talk to you." She had been so absorbed in thought that she started at the sound of Ashley's voice. Her sister entered the room with Burt close behind and they sat on Ashley's lovely leather sofa, a family heirloom. She indicated the matching leather chair adjacent to the sofa, and Leigh sat down, curious as to why Burt and Ashley looked so serious.

"Are the kids settled in?" Leigh asked politely, and Ashley nodded. "I know they were upset tonight because of Sarah," Leigh continued, and then stopped. "But that's not what you want to talk to me about, is it?"

"It's Wade, honey," Ashley said and glanced at her husband. "We don't know quite how to say this, but—"

"Wait a minute, let me guess," Leigh interrupted sarcastically, her eyes narrowing. "You want to warn me about how dangerous he is. You think he killed Sarah and kidnapped Lisa. Tell me if I've got this right—on the night Sarah was kidnapped, he somehow managed to be at two places at once since we all know I was with him and I didn't have anything to do with Sarah's disappearance. Then he came back to town for his mother's funeral and decided to risk his career as a successful novelist, not to mention his life, to kidnap a second little girl. It makes perfect sense to me."

Burt and Ashley exchanged another worried glance.

"Leigh," Ashley said calmly, ignoring her sister's tirade. "Do you know anything about Wade's father?"

The storm in Leigh's eyes abated slightly as she puzzled over the question. Wade's father? He had never talked about him, so she had assumed that the gossip was true. She thought Wade was an illegitimate child fathered by a man with Indian blood, a man Wade had never known. "I don't understand. What does that have to do with anything?" Leigh said.

This time it was Burt who spoke, and his low-timbred voice was serious. "Leigh, I shouldn't be telling you any of this, because it's a part of an ongoing investigation. But, seeing that you're spending so much time with Wade, me and Ashley thought you should know."

"Know what?" Leigh exploded. "What are you talking about?"

Burt sighed. "I guess you know Wade is a suspect." Burt ignored Leigh's snort of disgust. "As a matter of routine, I check into the background of suspects. I couldn't find any of Wade's public records here in Kinley, so I called that county in Texas where he and Ena came from and asked for his birth certificate.''

Burt paused, and Leigh was suddenly afraid. She could tell by the closed look on his face, which was normally so florid and open, that there was something terrible in Wade's past, maybe something even more terrible than her betrayal.

''Wade's father was a man named Willie Lovejoy. I was surprised as heck to see a father's name listed on the birth certificate, so I did some more checking and found out all I needed to know about Willie Lovejoy.''

Burt stopped to look at Ashley again, and Ashley leaned forward on the sofa, physically reaching out to her sister. ''Honey, Willie Lovejoy died last year in the county's mental hospital. He'd been there since he went mad twenty years ago.''

Leigh was silent as she tried to absorb that Wade's father had been insane. She wondered if the young Wade, growing up alone and misunderstood in Kinley, had known. It would be terrible at any age to deal with the knowledge that your father couldn't handle the pressures of the world. But why were Burt and Ashley telling her this? What did his father's sickness have to do with Wade and the dual tragedies in Kinley?

''Leigh,'' Ashley said gently. ''Did you hear me?''

''I heard, Ashley,'' Leigh said, still sympathizing with Wade. ''But I don't understand why you're telling me this.''

''I guess we're going to have to spell it out then,'' Ashley said and then paused significantly, giving her next words greater weight. ''What if Wade takes after his father?''

''Excuse me?'' Leigh said, barely believing she'd heard correctly.

''What if Wade did kidnap Sarah twelve years ago? Let's say you were with him that night. What if he hid Sarah someplace before he met you and then went back and finished what he started?'' Burt continued. ''What if he came back to the scene of the crime last month and the urge struck him again?''

''Of all the idiotic ramblings I've ever heard, that has to top the list,'' Leigh said, shaking her head in disbelief. ''I guess I'm supposed to assume he's mad, right?''

''It's possible,'' Burt said.

"So explain who broke into my house and ripped my bedroom to shreds. I'm helping Wade, remember. Even you couldn't find a motive for him to do that."

"What if he vandalized your bedroom so we'd think someone else was guilty of the real crimes? Or because he wants to scare you into stopping because he's afraid you'll find out he's guilty?" Burt said. "Just because you were with him right before you found the mess doesn't mean he couldn't have done it earlier in the day."

Leigh placed her hands on her head and closed her eyes. "I can't believe I'm hearing this."

"We only told you because we're worried about you, Leigh." Ashley's honey-laced tones reverberated in Leigh's head. "We thought you should know what you're getting into with Wade."

Leigh's eyes came wide open, and she fixed them on Ashley and Burt. "It doesn't make sense, you know. Just because Wade's father was mentally ill doesn't mean he is. Madmen don't write books and cry at their mother's funeral and agonize over missing children."

"They don't have horns on their heads, either," Ashley said. "Just think about what we've said, Leigh. And, for God's sake, be careful."

"Oh, don't worry," Leigh said. "I'm going to be careful. But I assure you, Wade's not the one I need to be careful of. Someone ripped my bedroom apart today, remember? Now, if you'll excuse me, I'm going to turn in."

Leigh rose and walked away, her back held regally straight and her head high. Ashley and Burt exchanged another worried look and shook their heads.

The fragrant bloom of azaleas filled the air the next day as Leigh walked up the sidewalk to Wade's house. The late-afternoon sun turned the blossoms in his flower boxes into a buttery yellow that made the flowers look as though they might melt. What had she told Everett the other day? That one of the pitfalls of living in the South was that it was easy to take beauty for granted because there was so much of it. Life was so short and their hold on it so tenuous that Leigh thought it was wrong to take anything for granted. She'd have to remember that the next time she saw Drew, because he'd offered to take care of the store for the next few days while she sorted out what had happened to her.

Leigh subconsciously smoothed the white skirt that she wore with a pink-and-white-striped cotton shirt. Flat, white sandals completed her ensemble. Leigh and Ashley had spent the better part of the day putting her bedroom back in order, and she had felt like dressing up a little when Wade called, inviting her to dinner. She didn't tell Ashley where she was going although she figured her older sister had guessed.

Leigh was almost at the front door when Wade appeared behind the screen, wearing a pair of faded cutoff jeans and a T-shirt and looking like a dream instead of a madman. Burt and Ashley were way off base. They had to be. Wade smiled when he saw her, and she liked the way the sun shone through the screen door and cast slivers of light through his black hair.

"You look great. You could knock me over with an ocean breeze," he said, and the words were echoes of the past. The young Wade had talked to her that way before fate had intervened and wrenched them apart. Wade opened the door, still smiling. "But did I miss something? I thought we were going to grill some burgers."

Leigh stepped through the door, hating to break his carefree mood but knowing she must. Since he had returned to Kinley, his smiles were so rare that they were like treasures to be stashed and taken out on lonely days. She'd remember this one. To soften her plan, she took his hands, callused from recent yard work, and reached up on tiptoe to kiss him lightly on the lips. He seemed surprised at the display of affection, and it reminded Leigh that their argument of a night ago still stood between them.

"I thought we could go to Mel's Diner," she said brightly, trying to make the outing sound as though it would be fun. Mel's was only one of two restaurants—if you could call it that—in Kinley. Its basic fare was hot dogs, hamburgers, French fries and milk shakes.

When they were kids, Mel's had been a drive-in restaurant and a hangout for young people. Leigh had even worked there as a carhop for one night before her father found out and forbade her from continuing because he thought it wasn't a suitable job for the mayor's daughter. She and Wade had never been there together. Back then, she wouldn't have dreamed of being seen there with him.

"Any special reason?" Wade asked. He was tired of being stared at, tired of being the object of a small-minded town's suspicion. He didn't want to go to Mel's Diner or anywhere else, even if it were with Leigh.

"A couple," she answered, watching him carefully for a reaction. "Number one—Kinley's a small town, and people talk. I thought we might find out something that would help us piece together the mystery of Sarah's disappearance. And number two—so many people suspect you that going out might be good for your image. It would show you have nothing to hide."

Wade started to shake his head even before she finished her explanation. She was going to add some more reasons, but he silenced her by placing two fingers against her lips. He thought that over dinner he'd have plenty of time to talk about her Nancy Drew impulses, but he wasn't going to have that luxury. She wasn't even thinking about slowing down their investigation.

"Shh, and listen to me, Leigh," he said. "I've done some thinking, too, and I don't want you to keep looking into the past if it's going to put you in danger. I don't want a repeat of what happened yesterday."

"There's nothing to worry about," Leigh protested, lightly pushing his fingers from her lips. "I had the locks changed today."

"You're wrong, Leigh," he said, irritated by her stubbornness. "If someone really feels threatened by what you're doing, locked doors won't stop him. He may try something else when you're alone at the store or when you're walking home."

"Well, I can't just lock myself in the house," Leigh said, touched by his concern but exasperated by his words.

"I'm not asking you to. I'm asking you to stop investigating. I'm not saying that your idea to look into the past wasn't a good one. It was. But I think I should handle it myself from here on out. Okay?"

She could tell he was serious from the way his gray eyes bore into hers, reminding her of unyielding granite. He wanted a promise from her, but she couldn't give one. Didn't he see that the only way they would be free to live in the present would be to exorcise the past? And didn't he see that he needed her help, that half the people in Kinley wouldn't want to talk to him about anything, let alone this?

"I don't see why that has to stop us from eating at Mel's," she said, evading his request. He stared at her for a moment longer, sensing that she wasn't going to make any promises, and then shrugged. His handsome face was so troubled that she wished Ashley and Burt, with their unspeakable suspicions, could have seen it.

"Mel's it is, then," he said finally. "I'll go change into some jeans."

A half hour later, they sat across a linoleum table perusing one of Mel's menus. It was still early, and the only other people in the restaurant were an elderly couple and a few high school kids. Wade wished he were at his mother's house getting the grill ready and was annoyed at himself that he wasn't. It seemed all Leigh had to do was smile at him, and it got him doing things that were against his better judgment. He'd slept with her, allowed her to put herself in jeopardy by looking into yesterday's mystery and now he was at Mel's, getting ready to eat with her. He wasn't usually so pliable, but then he wasn't usually living in Kinley amid memories and clouds of suspicion.

He glanced down at the menu again. The diner had changed over the years and no longer offered only basic hamburgers and cheeseburgers. Now the menu listed bacon burgers, mushroom burgers and blue-cheese burgers. He smiled at the unexpectedness of it all, and Leigh giggled.

"I see you got to Mel's Health Burger, made with soybean and garnished with sprouts," she said, her eyes dancing.

"Actually, I just noticed Mel's Vanishing Burger for the strict vegetarian," he said and read from the menu. "'A burger piled high with zucchini, sprouts, tomato, lettuce and sauce—sans burger.' This place has sure changed."

Leigh giggled again, and she looked almost as young as the teenager he'd loved. Wade sobered. He needed to remember that teenager as the girl who would never have eaten at Mel's with him. A dozen years ago, he had dreamed about buying her dinner here instead of at some fancy restaurant in a romantic city like Paris or New York. It would have meant that she accepted him and what they were to each other, but it never happened. He pulled his eyes from hers and looked down at the worn linoleum table. She was here now, but it wasn't quite the same.

The laugh died on Leigh's lips as she saw the play of emotions run across his face, and she wished she knew the reason for his sudden change of mood. He wasn't looking at her now, but even if he were, the lights were so dim at Mel's that she couldn't have read anything in his eyes.

Someone cleared his throat, and both of their heads snapped around to see Mel standing beside their table. He was a short man with a head so bald, even the poor lighting at Mel's cast a sheen on it. Leigh had seldom seen him smile, but he was smiling now and it wasn't at her.

"Well, I'll be," he said, sticking out his hand. "Wade Conner. I was wonderin' when you'd make it down here."

"Couldn't stay away, Mel," Wade said, shaking the restaurant owner's hand.

"Best burger flipper I ever had," Mel said, addressing Leigh before turning his attention back to Wade. "But that sure was a long time ago. I hear you live in New York and do some writing."

"You heard right. I'm a novelist in Manhattan. And the way things have been going for me in Kinley, I should have stayed there. But, of course, I needed to come back. You must have heard about my mother."

"Yes, I did," Mel said, absently rubbing his bald head. "I'm awful sorry about that. I'm awful sorry about how people in Kinley's been treatin' you, too. I want you to know I don't believe a word of it."

"I appreciate that, Mel," Wade said and glanced at Leigh. "It means a lot when people believe in you."

"Now, what can I get you?" Mel asked, reaching in his apron for a pad. He did it so awkwardly that Wade guessed he didn't take orders often.

"You never told me you flipped burgers," Leigh said when Mel had retreated from their table. She was relieved to see that the darkness that had fallen over him before the restaurant owner's appearance seemed to have lifted.

"I never told you a lot of things," Wade said. "I bet you didn't even know that I thought up the slogan on the advertisement Mel runs in the local paper. You know the one. It says, 'Eat at Mel's.'"

Leigh wrinkled her nose at him and laughed. "You missed your calling then. You could have had a brilliant career in advertising. What else have you never told me?"

He reached across the table and touched her nose. "That you have a little place on your nose that makes a kind of dimple when you laugh."

"Get out of here," Leigh said, brushing aside his finger.

"It's true," Wade said. "And I never told you that I have never seen a woman with better legs than yours. Longer, yes. But yours would definitely take first prize in any contest."

Leigh crossed her legs under the table. "You're making me blush."

"I like the way you blush, too." Wade put his elbows on the table, sparks of enjoyment dancing in his eyes. "I really wouldn't call the color red. It's more of a delicate pink."

Leigh's face flushed even more. "Make that a bright pink," Wade amended.

They both turned when the door of the restaurant opened, and Ben and Gary Foster walked in. Ben's eyes flickered toward their table and flickered away, but Gary stared from Leigh to Wade. His black eye was noticeable even from a distance.

"He looks like he thinks I'm the big, bad wolf and you're Little Red Riding Hood," Wade said dryly, and his silly mood of a moment ago was gone. The rush of red was also gone from Leigh's face, and she was as serious as she'd ever been.

"Do you think it would do any good if we talked about it?" she asked.

By "it," Wade assumed she meant his fracas with Gary Foster. He leaned back in his chair, distancing himself from her. He didn't particularly want to tell her what had happened, partly because he thought she'd come up with an excuse for Gary just like she came up with excuses for the rest of Kinley. But, then again, he was curious to see what she would say.

"Why don't you just ask me why I punched him?" he challenged.

"Okay," she replied. "Why'd you punch him?"

"A lot of reasons," Wade answered, "but the upshot was that he said something ugly about my mother."

Leigh bit her lip. She'd always heard that Gary had a mean streak, but he'd never shown her that side of his personality. Not for the first time, she tried to put herself in Wade's position. He'd shown remarkable restraint for an innocent man showered with accusations, and she didn't blame him for slugging Gary Foster. But she wasn't quite sure how to tell him that.

Wade misread her silence and tried to stem the disappointment that rose in his throat. "So you were wrong when you said I'd outgrown the damn-the-consequences way of life," he said flippantly. "I'm sure you think I should have just walked away from him."

Leigh thought it over for a moment and nodded. "You're right. I do think you should have walked away," she said, and he set his lips together even tighter. "But if I had been in your shoes, I probably would have punched him, too."

Her comment was so unexpected that Wade couldn't stop himself from adding a rejoinder instead of graciously accepting it. "What? And risk rocking the boat in your precious Kinley?"

She looked at him levelly. She knew his opinion on her decision to remain in Kinley, and she had done a lot of thinking about it.

"It's just a place, Wade," she said, meeting the challenge in his eyes with calm honesty. "Places aren't what's important. People are."

"If Kinley doesn't matter that much, then why haven't you left?" Wade asked, and he really wanted to know the answer. The Leigh he'd known years ago would never have been content in a town so isolated and self-centered that the rest of the world seemed as though it didn't exist.

"I guess I never had a strong enough reason to leave," she answered, and Wade immediately thought that he should have been that reason. Only she never even gave him the chance to ask her to come with him.

"How about your art?" he said instead. "That was a good reason to leave."

Leigh sighed. She hadn't talked about her art for so long that she wasn't sure she could explain her reasons for abandoning it. But if she shut Wade out again, he would never learn to trust her.

"No, it wasn't," she said, shaking her head. "I only painted one more picture after you left town. After that, I just lost the desire to paint. I'm not exactly sure why. It just seemed like, with you gone and Sarah missing, the life had drained out of the town. And I always got my inspiration from things that were alive, things that had a certain joy surrounding them. Am I making any sense?"

Wade nodded, and he thought he understood more than she would have liked him to. "You're saying you just gave up?"

Leigh winced, but then realized his statement was a blunt way of explaining what had happened. She had given up, not on him, but on herself.

"That's one way of putting it," she said thoughtfully. "Maybe you were right the other day when you said that I've deluded myself into thinking that my mother and Drew couldn't make it without me. Maybe I just used that as an excuse not to leave."

Wade ran a hand through his hair. She had brought up the other night, and it was his opportunity to apologize. But even though he felt badly for what he had said, so much of it had been true.

"I was too hard on you the other night. I shouldn't have said those things," Wade said finally, and it wasn't quite an apology. "And I shouldn't have told you I made love to you just for old times' sake."

"That's okay," Leigh said, her eyes filled with sadness. She loved this man, and it was plain that he still harbored resentment toward her. "We don't always know why we do what we do."

Their conversation was interrupted by the arrival of hamburgers, French fries and milk shakes. Mel set them down on the table with a flourish. "I flipped these burgers myself," he said proudly before he left them alone again.

Glad of the respite, Wade bit into his burger, which was smothered with blue-cheese dressing, and nodded in approval. He already regretted telling her that their lovemaking had meant more to him than a rehash of old times, and he didn't want her to start analyzing his feelings. He just wanted to change the subject. ''Junk food extraordinaire,'' he said when he had finished chewing.

Leigh barely heard him as she munched on her bacon burger and thought. It was obvious that Wade was uncomfortable talking about their new relationship, and she wasn't going to press the issue. Besides, they had other things to discuss. Maybe she couldn't make him love her, but she could help him.

A couple more people entered the restaurant and immediately cast suspicious looks at Wade. Although Leigh knew both of them, neither greeted her. She knew Wade had noticed their behavior by the way he stubbornly set his lips.

''It looks like you were wrong about eating here,'' Wade said, showing he had been thinking along the same lines as she had. ''There's no way we're going to hear anything that might lead us to Sarah's killer, because no one is even going to talk to us.''

''But we have to talk, Wade,'' Leigh said, ignoring his sarcasm. ''I know you have reservations about looking into the past, but we have to put our heads together and come up with some suspects. If we don't, maybe no one else will.''

For a minute, Leigh felt sure Wade would refuse. He stared down at the table and pursed his lips while he considered her proposal. Anticipating his refusal, Leigh was busily conjuring up new arguments that would make him see reason. Wade, on the other hand, was deciding that nothing he said was going to dissuade her. Finally Wade's eyes met hers. ''Okay, shoot. Who do you think kidnapped Sarah?''

''Somebody who doesn't like you,'' Leigh said hurriedly, and noticed that Gary Foster was watching them from across the room. ''The more I think about it, the more I think somebody wanted everyone to think you did it.''

''Why do you say that?'' Wade put one finger aside his face as he considered her answer.

''One reason in particular,'' Leigh said. ''Sarah's skeleton was found by your cove. Did you know that? I think somebody planted her body there on purpose, wanting it to be found,'' Leigh continued when he nodded. ''The fact that it took so long to discover may mean this person didn't have a very good knowledge of the tides.''

"That's pretty farfetched, Leigh. You could look at it another way that makes a lot more sense. Maybe someone who understood the tides put her there so she wouldn't be found."

"Maybe," Leigh conceded. "But then why was it your next-door neighbor who was kidnapped? Why not mine or Ashley's or anyone else's in town? Why Sarah?"

"You're saying she was kidnapped because she lived next door to me," Wade repeated. "Let's suppose you're right. Who would hate me so much that they would murder an innocent little girl just to pin a crime on me?"

"I was going to ask you that," Leigh countered and watched the way his brow knotted in consternation.

"Everett," he said after a moment.

"Everett?" Leigh was shocked. "Just how did you come up with that?"

Wade leaned toward her as his theory took shape. "It makes a lot of sense, Leigh. Just think about it. He lived across the street from me and from the Culpeppers. He could have seen me talking to Sarah that night and waited until I was gone to make his move."

"That's preposterous—" Leigh said.

Wade interrupted her to finish his train of thought. "Of all the people in Kinley, Everett's the one who would most like to see me out of the picture. He's in love with you, Leigh. What if he knew about us twelve years ago? What if it was driving him so crazy, he couldn't stand it? That would even explain Lisa's disappearance. I'm back in town, and we've been spending time together. If it worked once, maybe he thought it would work again."

"Brilliant," Leigh said when he paused for breath. "There's only one thing wrong with it."

"What?"

"Everett couldn't hurt anybody, let alone kill somebody." Leigh's voice was impassioned. "Everett can't even kill a fly. It's true, Wade. Once he was having dinner at my place, and a fly was bothering us. I was stirring something on the stove and told him where the fly swatter was, but he wouldn't use it. He said he'd never killed anything. I thought about it, and realized I'd never even seen him stomp on an ant."

Wade scratched his head and shrugged. She was right; he hadn't seen much of Everett since he returned to town, but the Everett he remembered was the epitome of mild mannered. "That does put a major hole in my theory, but it sure seemed to make sense. He is in love with you, you know."

"I know," Leigh said on a sigh. "And I love him, too, in a different sort of way. I just wish he'd accept that."

Leigh took another bite of burger and chewed absently. Her gaze caught Gary Foster's across the room, and he immediately looked away.

"Gary Foster doesn't like you," she said after a few minutes. "He dropped by the store the other day and told me I should steer clear of you, which I guess is why he keeps staring at us."

"What are you getting at?" Wade put down his hamburger to give her his full attention.

"Maybe he found Sarah's skeleton because he knew exactly where to look."

"Wait a minute," Wade said, shaking his head. "You're talking about the preppiest guy I've ever known. He was so perfect in high school that the worst thing he ever did was forget to have one of his shirts monogrammed."

"You're forgetting about his grudge against you," Leigh said, ignoring his sarcasm.

"I didn't think you knew about that," Wade said, twisting his mouth in acknowledgment. "You know, it's funny. It's been almost fifteen years since high school, and I think he remembers it like it happened yesterday. On the street the other day, he looked at me with pure hatred."

"I understand you embarrassed him pretty badly," Leigh said, forgetting her dinner.

"It was a dumb thing to do, but he always acted so superior," Wade said, remembering. "He was the school's basketball star back then and damn proud of it. I didn't even go out for the team. But I knew I could beat him one-on-one. When I challenged him to play me, I never imagined he'd let half the school know about it. I thought it would just be me and him and an empty court—"

"Instead, half the senior class showed up," Leigh interjected. "Even Ashley was there, because I can remember her telling me about it."

"It wasn't my fault he broke his leg. He was pressing too hard, because I was embarrassing him in front of his friends. I remember it being the best game of one-on-one I ever played. Every shot I took dropped, and somehow I kept getting a piece of his shots. Then, when I got around him and had an easy layup, he came from behind me and jumped over my back."

"Only you didn't fall, and he did," Leigh said.

"And then he couldn't get up, because he landed on the concrete and his leg was broken," Wade said. "So his senior season was shot, and he blamed me for it. I think he thought he was going to get a college basketball scholarship."

"He probably still holds a grudge."

"A grudge big enough to kill for?" Wade shook his head. "I don't think so."

Wade looked across the restaurant and caught Gary Foster staring at them. Foster didn't avert his eyes this time, but met Wade's gaze with a narrow-eyed one of his own. "He sure doesn't like you," Leigh said, and Wade broke the eye contact to turn to her.

"A lot of people in this town don't like me," Wade said, and picked up his hamburger again. "Your brother-in-law, Burt, is the perfect example, and you don't think he did it. Or do you?"

Leigh stared at him in disapproval while he took another bite of his food. "Of course I don't think Burt did it. He's the police chief, for goodness' sake."

"Then who?"

"Who else in this town has something against you?" Leigh countered. Wade picked up some French fries and ate them while he thought.

"Maybe you're wrong about it being someone with a grudge against me," he said finally. "Maybe it's just somebody who's crazy."

Somebody who's mad, Leigh amended silently. Somebody who seems perfectly normal on the surface, but who is evil on the inside. Somebody who might have a family history of insanity. Stop it, Leigh told herself before the suspicion could take root. Stop it right now.

"Leigh, what is it?" Wade's brows drew together in concern. "You got kind of white there for a second."

"It's nothing," Leigh said, forcing herself to smile. How could the thought have even entered her mind? How would he ever believe that she loved him if he knew what she had been thinking? "I'm fine."

"Old Abe Hooper's crazy," Wade said after a moment. "I saw him the other day at about noon, and he was already well on his way to getting plastered. He started yelling something at me about hell and damnation. He told me I had to repent for my sins."

Abe Hooper was a Kinley institution as old as the buck's head oak tree in the center of town. Leigh didn't know for sure, but she guessed he was in his early sixties. Abe lived with an elderly aunt and squandered most of his money on cheap wine and whiskey. Burt had locked him up in the town jail many nights for disorderly conduct, and he'd been through detoxification four or five times. It would help for a week or two, but Abe always adopted his old ways again.

"Do you think he could be behind all this?" Wade had finished his food and was sipping on his milk shake.

Leigh bit her thumb while she pictured Abe Hooper and what he might be capable of doing. Some of the crueler children in town taunted him because of his shoddy appearance and ever-present liquor bottle, so she gathered that he didn't particularly like children. "Possibly," she said. "I don't know why I didn't think of him before. Maybe we should find him and have a talk with him tomorrow."

Wade held up both his hands in protest. "No way," he said. "After what happened yesterday, I don't want you snooping around. It could be dangerous. I should talk to him."

Leigh took a sip of her own milk shake and regarded him from over the lip of the cup. It might not mean much, but Wade was concerned about her. And at least that was something. But it wasn't enough to keep her from talking to Abe.

Chapter 10

When they left Mel's Diner, the night air was so still that a fine sheen of perspiration formed above Leigh's upper lip as they walked. She wished the wind would whip up and blow away the ugliness that had invaded Kinley, but the leaves on the trees were completely still, dead still.

"It hasn't been much of a homecoming, has it, Wade?" Leigh asked, breathing deeply of the ever-present smell of the sea. "I bet you wish you'd never come back."

Their path was illuminated only by streetlights, and Leigh could make out their shadows, long and eerie, on the sidewalk. Wade moved a little closer to her as they walked, and the two shadows became one.

"I always knew I'd come back," Wade said, and somehow she understood what he meant. He knew he'd come back, because she was there.

They stopped walking, and they were bathed in light from a street lamp. She could see how his face had changed in the years since she'd seen him last. The handsome, half-Indian features were harder and his eyes had lost some of their innocence, but he was still the man she remembered, still the man she loved.

She looked so beautiful in the streetlight that for a moment Wade wondered why he was fighting the attraction he felt for her. He might as well admit that he was like the moths that surrounded the light above them; he couldn't resist her lure even though he might get too close and scorch himself.

She raised on tiptoe at the same time he bent his head, and their lips met. The kiss was feather-light, a mere meeting of souls, but then Leigh's mouth moved on his and Wade couldn't stem his response. He'd made love to a fair number of women in the years he'd been away from Kinley, but none of them had made him feel like this with a kiss. He wanted to find someplace, anyplace, and make love to her in the night air. He wanted to forget about the past and concentrate on the future.

Leigh wrapped her arms around him and wished she'd never have to let him go. She wanted this moment on this night to last forever. Wade's tongue darted inside Leigh's mouth and began a sensual duel that lifted her heart high above Kinley and its deadly secrets. He crushed her against him, and she could feel the evidence of his desire against her hip. Her own female core was already aching from unfulfilled desire. After a few moments of mindless kissing, he shakily put her away from him.

"Seeing that we're in a public place," Wade said when he had regained his equilibrium, "I don't think it would be wise to continue this."

Leigh blushed because he had been the one to call a halt to their lovemaking; it hadn't even occurred to her that anyone could have come across them. Sensing her embarrassment, Wade took her hand in his and they resumed their walk. The night was black, and it was impossible to see more than a few feet ahead, but Leigh felt safe and even slightly optimistic. In spite of all that had happened, maybe it was possible for her and Wade to rebuild their broken relationship. She wanted nothing more than to banish all the doubt and all the secrets between them. Now was a good time to start.

"Wade, will you tell me about your father?" Leigh asked, and felt his fingers tense. Instantly she knew it was the wrong thing to say. Just as quickly as it had been formed, the fragile bond between them was broken. He untangled his hand from hers and shoved it into one of his pockets.

"What hasn't Burt told you already?" he asked, already feeling defensive. The question had sounded so innocent, but he knew better. "Oh, don't deny that Burt's behind that question, because he's already talked to me about it."

"I wasn't going to deny it," Leigh said, hurt that he had made the assumption. "I did hear about your father from Burt, but I wanted to get the truth from you."

"What did he tell you?" Wade's voice had lost none of its edge, and Leigh was sorry she had brought up the subject. Every time she and Wade made a step forward in their relationship, something happened to push them backward. Would it always be that way?

"He told me that your father's name was Willie Lovejoy and that he died last year," Leigh said, leaving out the most pertinent fact.

Wade stopped walking and sat on one of the benches that lined Kinley's main road. After a moment, Leigh followed his example and sat next to him. Wade looked into the darkness, and his Indian heritage had never seemed more pronounced. His black hair seemed even blacker, and the streetlight shone on his long, straight nose.

He was no longer angry, just sad. His parentage had come as a shock to him, so he shouldn't expect Leigh to be unaffected by it. Her snobbish parents had been right when they whispered about his "questionable" background. Wade didn't judge others on who or what their parents were, but Leigh had been brought up in a society that valued lineage above all else. Telling his story would only prove to himself once more that she wasn't much different from the rest of the people in Kinley, and that's why he had to tell her.

"Did Burt tell you that he died in a mental hospital?" Wade asked, and Leigh confirmed that he had.

"It's true. The old man was crazy," he said and paused. "Now, let me see if I can figure out how Burt's mind works. I'm sure he thinks he's found my motive for supposedly snatching little girls. I'm mad, just like the old man."

Wade lapsed into silence, and Leigh waited quietly for him to go on. When he did, it was with a rash of words that seemed to have been bottled inside him. They were sad words, spoken slowly and softly.

"Willie Lovejoy was never a good man, which is a hell of a thing to say about your father. But I didn't consider him my father. See, I didn't even lay eyes on him until a few years ago in that mental hospital. I went into his room, and I was so nervous, my knees were shaking. But he was nobody to be nervous about. He sat on his bed wearing a green medical gown and staring straight ahead. I could have sworn nobody was home.

"Willie was my mother's secret. When I was growing up, she never talked about him. Never. I just figured I didn't have a father. Then a couple years ago, I needed a copy of my birth certificate. My mother said she didn't have one, so I wrote off to Texas. When it came, it had Willie Lovejoy's name listed under father."

He paused, and somewhere an owl hooted and a cricket sang. Leigh, however, could only hear Wade's soft words.

"I was surprised, to put it mildly, and I started wondering about the man. I knew my mother wouldn't tell me anything, so I paid a visit to my aunt in Texas and the story came tumbling out of her.

"Willie Lovejoy was a full-blooded Indian who lived on a reservation a couple of miles from my mother's house. He drank too much, he fought too much and he cussed too much. But for some reason the ladies liked him. When my mother was sixteen, she fell for him. Willie was nearly twenty-five, but that didn't matter to him. He got her pregnant, and then never wanted to see her again when she told him.

"A few years later, he started acting bizarre. He quit his job at a gas station and started living off the streets, begging for money and refusing to bathe. A few years after that, he exposed himself to a couple of young girls and got himself arrested. They diagnosed him as schizophrenic and locked him up. Great father figure, huh?"

"I'm sorry, Wade," Leigh muttered. "I didn't know."

"What gets me about all this is how people like Burt jump to conclusions. He probably doesn't know anything about schizophrenia. Well, I do. I did some reading and found out quite a bit. Their offspring don't necessarily go around kidnapping little girls and murdering them, for instance."

"Nobody's accused you, Wade."

"Not publicly, no. But they sure have condemned me silently," Wade said and rose, drained by the story. "Come on. I better get you home."

Leigh rose and they started to walk again, but they were farther apart than they had been before. Somehow, the revelations about Willie Lovejoy seemed to tear them apart instead of drawing them together. Leigh wasn't sure why and, when an owl cried in the distance, she felt like crying, too.

"What time should I pick you up for Sarah's memorial service?" Wade asked after they reached her front door and she unlocked it.

Leigh bit her lip. She had expected him to ask, but she hadn't figured out a way to respond without hurting his feelings. There probably wasn't a way.

"I don't think you should go, Wade," Leigh began and rushed on before he could interrupt. "Hear me out before you say anything. I think it would be upsetting to most of the people there. Attention would be focused on you instead of the ceremony. I know you were fond of Sarah, but I think your presence would be antagonistic."

Wade shook his head in disbelief. But after telling her his story, considering everything that he knew about her, what had he expected her to say? She was probably just like her father at heart, and her father was against their association even before he knew of Wade's parentage. "Antagonistic? Since when is it antagonistic to pay my respects to a little girl who didn't deserve to die? A little girl who may have died because someone holds a grudge against me?"

Leigh still wasn't familiar with the new Wade, but she knew enough to tell that he was fighting back anger. "It's unfair. I know it is," Leigh said gently, "but I still don't think Kinley's prepared to see you at the memorial service. I think you'll alienate some people it would be good to have as friends."

Wade lowered his eyes and rubbed his forehead, and Leigh wasn't sure whether she had persuaded him to avoid the service or not.

"Will I see you tomorrow?" he asked finally, although he wasn't sure why. It was entirely possible that he had a masochistic streak he hadn't known about until he returned to Kinley. Why else would he be asking for more punishment?

"I'm afraid not," Leigh said, genuine regret in her voice. "Since we're closing the store tomorrow in memory of Sarah, my mother invited the family over for an early dinner. I'm expected to be there."

"And I'm not invited." Wade filled in the unspoken blanks in her sentence. He didn't want to spend the afternoon with Leigh's family, but he was getting tired of being treated like an outcast. She was willing to make love to him in private, but she still wasn't willing to display any sort of affection in front of her family. He didn't know why he had expected anything different, but he had. "Don't bother to say anything. You don't think it would be proper for me to go to the memorial service, and you don't want me at the Hampton dinner table. I don't think things between us have changed at all."

He turned on his heel and strode down the sidewalk before Leigh could reply, but not before she saw the anger and the hurt in his gray eyes. And suddenly, all that had stood between them was back in place.

The small country church that was the site of Sarah Culpepper's memorial service was brimming with the townsfolk of Kinley. Leigh attended services every Sunday, but she had never seen so many people in the small, white church that sat on the edge of town. Everybody seemed to be present except Martha Culpepper and Wade. Martha had chosen to remain in Charleston with her memories, but Leigh had made Wade's choice for him. She bit her lip and wondered whether her advice had been correct. Or was it possible that his absence would be construed as an admission of guilt?

"Is Wade coming?" The question came from Ashley, who along with Burt and the children had spotted Leigh in a nearly empty pew and joined her before the church got crowded. For some reason, Ashley had dressed in a summery white dress that was in stark contrast to Leigh's black suit. But then, Leigh reasoned, Sarah's death hadn't hung a dark cloud over her sister's life.

Leigh shook her head in response to the question. "I told him not to," she whispered back. "I thought most people would be upset if they saw him here."

"I think that was wise," Ashley replied, still whispering. "Town sentiment is running pretty high against him."

A movement on the other end of the pew distracted Leigh, and she looked away from her sister to see Everett trying to squeeze by seated mourners. He went about it so clumsily that he had apologized to just about everyone in the pew before he sat down in the vacant space beside Leigh.

"Hi, Leigh," he grinned, pushing up his glasses.

"Hi, Everett," Leigh answered, but her attention was already wandering from Everett's haphazard entrance. Her friend had claimed one of the last empty spaces in the church, which gave Leigh a chilling thought. If just about everyone in Kinley were present, that meant Sarah's murderer was probably present, too. Her eyes swept the mass of humanity inside the church while she tried to fathom which one of her neighbors could be a killer. Her gaze stuck on Gary Foster, but she couldn't believe he could be guilty of such a heinous crime. But if he hadn't done it, who had?

In the next minute, a rasping cough filled the relative quiet of the church, and Leigh turned to see Abe Hooper at the entrance. He was dressed in a worn brown suit that was torn across one sleeve and a shirt that must have been white at one time. When he finished coughing, he thrust a lit cigar back into his mouth. Something bulged in one of his pockets, and Leigh could make out the edge of a brown paper bag. She knew without looking that Abe Hooper had a bottle of whiskey inside the bag. Abe didn't attempt to go any farther into the church, and Leigh wondered why he had come at all. At this time of the morning, Abe was usually sleeping off last night's drunk.

At the opposite end of the church, Reverend Manigault, wearing a black robe that looked suitable for mourning, had stepped onto the altar. The reverend, who was in his sixties, took his place behind a microphone on a raised platform.

"My friends, we are gathered here today to remember a little girl who never got the chance to grow into a young woman," he began, and his voice was filled with sadness. "A little girl whose life was snuffed out in a way that is unfathomable to anyone with a heart. We may never know the whys—"

"Why not?" A voice yelled from the back of the church, and it belonged to Abe Hooper. Just about every head in the church turned to discover the source of the words, but Reverend Manigault paused only slightly in his speech, clearing his throat before he continued.

"We may never know the whys of this heinous crime, but we must not focus on the negatives every time we think of Sarah Culpepper."

"Why?" Abe Hooper's yell interrupted the holy man's refrain another time, and this time Burt rose and headed for Abe and the back of the church.

"Although she only lived a short while, Sarah left her mark on this community with her sweet smile. Her time to go to the Lord came too soon—"

"Why?" Abe had time to bark one more inappropriate question before Burt reached him. Abe put up only a minor protest as Burt escorted him out of the church.

"Her time to go to the Lord came too soon, but not before she left her indelible mark on Kinley," Reverend Manigault continued, but Leigh was no longer listening. Now was her chance to talk to Abe Hooper, and she planned to seize the opportunity. She tapped her sister on the shoulder and half rose.

"Excuse me," Leigh whispered. "I have to go."

"Now?" Ashley's perfectly shaped eyebrows shot up. Everett was leaning across the space Leigh had vacated, trying to figure out what was happening.

"I think I left the stove on," Leigh lied, congratulating herself for conjuring up such a believable exit line. She threaded her way past her niece and nephew and hurried down the center aisle.

"We should remember her with a smile on our lips and warmth in our hearts, with gladness that she lived at all and thanks that she will be delivered to her final resting place...." The reverend's words faded as Leigh slipped out the door into the blinding sun, almost running into Burt in the process.

"The memorial service can't be over," Burt said skeptically. He was wearing a dark suit instead of his police clothes and seemed even larger than usual.

"Of course not. I don't know if I turned off my stove this morning, and I thought I better check." Leigh brushed past him and spotted Abe Hooper walking toward the center of town.

"Leigh," Burt called after her, and she turned to acknowledge him. "Watch out for Abe. He's crazier than usual today."

Leigh nodded and waited until Burt had reentered the church before she hurried after Abe. For a man in his sixties who was usually filled with cheap liquor, Abe Hooper walked swiftly. The sun had already chased away the relative coolness of the morning, and Leigh was overheated by the time she caught up with him.

"Mr. Hooper," she called when she was a few feet behind him, and Abe stopped so suddenly, Leigh almost careened into him. He regarded her with suspicion and narrowed eyes that had a faintly yellow cast.

"Why are you following me, girlie?" he growled, and his breath smelled of stale liquor.

"Uh, I just wanted to talk to you about Sarah Culpepper," Leigh answered, surprised at the snarl her reply elicited.

"What makes you think I want to talk back?"

They were standing on a sidewalk in the middle of a downtown block, and they were alone. The unfriendly expression on Abe's face brought that point crashing home to Leigh, and she belatedly remembered Wade's insistence that she not seek him out. Almost everybody in Kinley was at Sarah Culpepper's memorial service except her and Abe, and Abe could be the one responsible for Sarah's death. He could even be the one who ransacked her house scant days ago. But that was ridiculous, Leigh reasoned. She had always regarded Abe as a pitiful drunk, and there was no reason to be afraid of him. Besides, if she were, she might never get to the bottom of Sarah's murder and Lisa's disappearance.

"I'm just trying to find out what happened to Sarah. From your comments in the church, it seems like you might know something." A drop of sweat rolled down Leigh's forehead, and she wiped it away. Was it the sun or Abe who was making her nervous?

Abe's lip curled in a distorted version of a smile and then he threw back his head and laughed. When he did, traces of spittle dribbled from his mouth. "I tried to tell what I knew before, and no one listened," Abe said when he had stopped chortling, and now he was deadly serious. "Folks in Kinley don't want to believe someone like me. I'll tell you what, girlie. They all think I'm just a drunk. But I see things, and I know things other people don't."

"What things?" Leigh asked, and Abe laughed again.

"I know who murdered that little girl, because I seen it with my own eyes," Abe pronounced, and an eerie feeling of dread came over Leigh. She knew, even before he said it, what he was going to say. "I don't mean I seen her die, but I seen who did it. She was having trouble with her bicycle. And then he grabbed her, and he took her away. I seen it all, but he don't know it."

Wade. Abe Hooper was fingering Wade. A lump caught in Leigh's throat. It was ludicrous, and yet she couldn't just walk away. She had to press for more information.

"I don't understand. If you're telling the truth, why didn't Chief Cooper arrest him?"

"Oh, he questioned him all right. But that one, he's a sly one and he made it seem like it was me who needed to be arrested," Abe said, snorting derisively. "Just because a man has a little to drink don't mean he's not trustworthy. I wasn't hall... How do you say that word?"

"Hallucinating," Leigh supplied.

"Yeah, that. Anyway, the chief didn't put much stock in what I said, and after a while I quit saying it," Abe continued. "I can tell you don't believe me, either. But listen to this, girlie. You're keeping company with a dangerous man. If you don't believe anything else, believe that."

And then he was gone, leaving Leigh alone. She wasn't sure how long she stood there before it occurred to her that she needed a fresh change of clothes before heading to her mother's house. She walked home slowly, her mind on Abe Hooper and the terrible thing he had said.

By the time the Hampton family gathered around the dinner table, Leigh had convinced herself that Abe Hooper was either crazy or cunning. The most likely scenario was that his memory had been impaired by endless bottles of alcohol, so much so that he thought he witnessed the most famous crime ever committed in Kinley. Of course, it was still possible that Abe was the killer. After all, he'd been unstable for years before Sarah Culpepper vanished. It wasn't inconceivable that he'd committed the crime in a drunken fit and implicated Wade to divert suspicion from himself.

"Leigh," Ashley said loudly, and Leigh blinked. Had someone been talking to her?

"I swear, Leigh, lately it's like you're living in another world. I was just askin' you if you had left your stove on."

"My stove?" Leigh's mind was a blank.

Ashley shook her head, and her blond curls bounced. "Your stove. Wasn't that why you left the memorial service when you did?"

"Oh, of course, my stove. No, it wasn't on after all. Just a false alarm. But you know how those things can nag at you until you have to check to make sure," Leigh said and realized that everyone was looking at her suspiciously. She was sure that Burt, at least, didn't believe she'd left the service to check a household appliance.

"I'm glad Sarah can rest in peace now," Grace Hampton said, smoothing a few errant strands of gray hair back from her face. Grace was one of the few people in Kinley who had missed the service, claiming that she had felt under the weather that morning. Looking at her now, with her regal carriage and impeccable grooming, it was difficult to believe she had any frailties.

"'Fraid not," Burt said, his jaw jutting forward. "There won't truly be any peace until I make an arrest."

One of Grace's perfectly arched eyebrows rose, and she leaned forward with interest. "That sounds like you're closing in on a suspect. Would you care to enlighten us?"

"Hush now, Mother," Ashley said before her husband could reply. "You know Burt can't comment on his investigations. Why, it would be perfectly criminal. Especially this investigation, considering Leigh's in the room."

Leigh shut her eyes briefly in resignation and opened them to meet Drew's sympathetic gaze across the table. They had both been on the receiving end of Ashley's careless comments numerous times, and they knew what was coming.

"What do you mean, dear?" Grace picked up on Ashley's innuendo just as Leigh knew she would. When Ashley hesitated, Grace turned to Leigh. "What does she mean, Leigh?"

There was no getting around it, and Leigh supposed this was as good a time as any to break the news to her mother. "I'm sure you can figure it out for yourself, Mother," Leigh said. "But just in case you have any doubts, she means that Wade Conner is the chief suspect in the case and Burt shouldn't comment in front of me because I've been spending a lot of time with Wade. Isn't that right, Ashley?"

Ashley nodded, and Leigh had to admit she looked miserable. Maybe Ashley wasn't manipulative and mean spirited as she had often thought. Maybe she just had a big mouth.

"I must have misunderstood, Leigh," Grace spoke, and her voice was colder than the winter breeze that blew off the ocean into Kinley in January and February. "I thought you said you'd been seeing Wade Conner."

Leigh met her mother's stare and refused to look away. She had known, maybe even from the time she was seventeen, that she and one of her parents would have this conversation. She just hadn't foreseen that the parent would be Grace. "You didn't misunderstand, Mother. To be perfectly honest, I was even seeing him the night Sarah was kidnapped. Daddy told me to keep away from him, but I didn't listen."

"Well, I never . . . I thought that was just . . . just an ugly rumor," Grace sputtered, and her angry features were replaced by a cool mask of indifference. Leigh knew better. Grace wasn't indifferent about Wade. "You're a very foolish young lady. He was all wrong for you when you were seventeen, and he's all wrong for you now."

"How do you know, Mother?" Leigh challenged, raising the tip of her chin. "You can't possibly expect me to listen to you when you've never bothered to even try to find out what I see in him. All you and Daddy ever saw was a fatherless boy who didn't fit into your social strata. Well, he's a man now, and a fine one at that. It's too bad you're too close-minded to realize that."

Everybody at the table seemed to gasp at once, the effect being one, shockingly loud intake of breath. It wasn't that no one else realized that Grace was close-minded. It was just that nobody else had ever had the gall to say it before. Leigh looked down at her half-eaten plate of food and realized her hunger was gone. There was no point in staying around any longer, especially since everyone was looking at her as though she were in a circus side show. Leigh rose with all the grace and breeding that her mother had given to her.

"I'm sorry if I've insulted you, Mother, but I meant what I said." Leigh addressed Grace, but her mother averted her eyes. "Now, if you'll all excuse me, I think I've said quite enough for one afternoon."

So this is what it's like to be miserable, Leigh thought as she bit into a potato chip. When she finished, she automatically reached into the bag for another chip. After leaving the Hampton dinner table, Leigh had headed straight home and the hours had blurred together until it was early evening. She'd considered calling Wade to talk about what she had discovered, but the thought of his hurt the night before stopped her. What would she tell him anyway? That Abe Hooper thought he was a murderer?

The problem was that the trail was cold, and it was entirely possible that they'd waited too long to try to figure out the mystery. If they didn't crack the case, though, Leigh had an eerie feeling that it would never be solved. The more they looked into Sarah's disappearance, the more Leigh began to feel she was the missing piece of the puzzle. Her wrecked bedroom attested to that. But where did she fit in with a grieving aunt, a falsely accused man, a heartbroken cousin, a drunken witness and two kidnapped little girls? It just didn't make sense.

Leigh reached for another potato chip and realized that the bag, which she'd just opened, was half-empty. Instead of eating another of the treats, she crumpled the bag and thrust it away. Her stomach already felt queasy. Why had she eaten so many of those things anyway? Leigh headed for the kitchen to fetch a glass of water when the telephone sounded. She picked it up on the first ring, half expecting another hang-up call.

"Hello."

"Stay out of the past." The voice was muffled, as though someone were holding a handkerchief over the receiver, and

Leigh was suddenly angry. Someone in Kinley was trying awfully hard to scare her, and she wasn't going to stand for it.

"Who is this?" she demanded. "What do you want?"

"Stay out of the past," the voice repeated, "or you'll be sorry."

"Who are you?" Leigh demanded again, but whoever was on the other end of the line broke the connection. She stared at the phone for a moment before replacing it on its cradle. What kind of madness had seized Kinley and turned it into a town where little girls disappeared, suspicion turned regular folks ugly with mistrust and anonymous voices delivered threats? If she believed Abe Hooper, that meant the voice belonged to Wade. But that was as preposterous as a full moon on a stormy evening. Wade wasn't the Kinley killer any more than she was, and they must be getting close to proving it. She certainly wasn't going to let the real killer scare her into stopping the investigation.

"I'm not going to stay out of anything," Leigh said defiantly to the silent phone.

Chapter 11

Wade got up from the seat in front of his computer and stretched his back, which was cramped from sitting in one place for too long. It was nearly dinnertime, hours after he'd taken his daily run, and he didn't know how much longer he could sit still. A sense of satisfaction, however, more than made up for his physical discomfort. Finally, after nearly a month of living in Kinley, he was making progress on his new novel. He'd probably subconsciously decided that fiction was preferable to the facts of his life.

Deciding he'd written enough for one day, he switched off his computer and headed for the refrigerator and a well-deserved beer. Come to think of it, drinking himself into a memory-fogging stupor was probably also preferable to the facts of his life, but Wade didn't intend to do that. He had been acting strangely since he returned to Kinley, but deliberately getting drunk would be too far out of character.

Wade pushed open the screen door leading to the porch and lowered himself into the swing. It wasn't yet seven o'clock, and the sun was low in the sky, a hazy red glow that looked utterly harmless. But that was an illusion; get too close and it would burn not only your being but your heart. That was an apt analogy for the way he felt about Leigh, too, and Wade was almost certainly getting too close to her.

How had this happened, Wade thought as he took a healthy swig of his beer. He had vowed not to let Leigh Hampton get to him again, and it had happened anyway. The problem was that he resented the feeling, and he resented her. When this was all over, he firmly intended to pack up and put Kinley and Leigh behind him. She was no more the woman for him than Cleopatra had been for Antony. Attraction wasn't a strong enough antidote for betrayal.

Wade took another swallow of beer as he mulled over his situation. He had been like a black bear the past few days, growling at Leigh for every slight, real and imagined. He had to admit that she'd seemed concerned when she'd shown up at his door after his fight with Gary Foster. She hadn't even recoiled in horror when he'd told her about his father. So why had he treated her so poorly?

Because it's the only way to keep her at arm's length, came the answer. Because she's the type of woman who was raised in an environment where she's ashamed to ask a man, who was born out of wedlock, home to dinner. That truth had bothered him when he was a young man, and it rankled now. She was spreading the word around town about their long-ago affair, but even that didn't appease him. Nobody believed her anyway, and all her talk had served to do was to make the townspeople suspect him more.

If it weren't for Burt's threat, he would get his belongings together and leave in the morning. He wanted to find out what had happened to Sarah Culpepper and Lisa Farley every bit as much as Leigh but he wasn't safe in Kinley any more than they had been. Only it was his heart that wasn't safe. The awful paradox was that even though he knew it would be better to never see Leigh again, he wished she were here in his arms.

He looked out into the yard and, as though he had conjured her up out of the fading light, there she stood. She wore a powder-blue sundress that made it seem as if she could have walked out of the mist of a dream. But he wasn't dreaming, and heat and humidity were more common to Kinley than mist.

"Hi. Still mad at me?" Leigh had been plotting her opening line all day, but her smile was tremulous when she delivered it.

The setting sun cast a soft glow over Wade, and Leigh couldn't remember seeing a man who looked better in shorts and a T-shirt. Her attention was drawn to the length of his legs, and she blushed when she realized he must have known she was staring at them.

"Where did you come from?" Wade asked, deliberately ignoring her question.

"I knocked on the front door," she said, walking toward him, "but nobody answered, so I thought I'd take a chance that you'd be out back. And here you are."

He didn't respond, and Leigh stopped walking. He'd been angry and hurt the other night when she'd advised him against attending Sarah's memorial service, and it was entirely possible he didn't want her around. Leigh had considered the possibility before she'd come, but still hadn't been able to stop herself from coming.

"Well, are you?" she asked quietly, putting herself on the line.

"Am I what?" Wade had been staring at her, noticing that her arms and legs were bare and that her hair looked blond in this light.

"Still mad at me?"

That wasn't the word he'd use to describe the sudden aching in his loins, but Wade wasn't about to tell her that. Besides, if he let himself dwell on it, he probably could raise a healthy dose of anger. He just didn't feel like dwelling on it.

"That depends on whether you brought dinner," Wade said, standing and opening the screen door to admit her into the house. She readily took him up on his unspoken invitation and brushed by him into the house, watching him with her blue-violet eyes to gauge his mood. Pinpricks popped up on her bare arms at the incidental contact. The sundress had kept Leigh cool all day, but now she was shivering.

"Dinner?" Leigh snapped her fingers. "I knew I was forgetting something."

Wade smiled, and the sight of it warmed Leigh. She had inadvertently hurt him the other night, but he couldn't send her away any more than she could walk away. "Maybe you could help me whip up something," he said.

"Are you asking me to dinner?" Leigh batted her eyelashes, trying some obvious flirting.

"Actually, I'm asking you to make dinner. That is, if you haven't already eaten," Wade said, laughing, and Leigh shook her head to indicate that she hadn't. "I'm afraid the time got away from me. I've been working on a new book all day, and I needed to unwind. C'mon, let's go into the kitchen."

"A new book?" Leigh asked as she followed him. "That's wonderful, Wade. I want to hear all about it. How long you've been working on it, what it's about, where it's set."

"Whoa." Wade stopped in his bright kitchen and opened a cupboard. "An author doesn't give away all his secrets after one day of work."

He pulled out a box with a Mexican design. "Is a taco dinner okay? Good. Then I'll brown the ground beef and you start chopping the lettuce, tomato and cheese."

"Surely you can tell me a little about it. At least give me a hint," Leigh said as she gathered the ingredients. Her mood was upbeat, because he seemed to forgive her for suggesting he stay away from the memorial service and the Hampton family dinner. He still didn't trust her, but she could work on that.

"I'll tell you what it's not about." Wade was capable in the kitchen, locating the frying pan as though he'd done it before. "It's not about murder and mayhem in a sleepy, Southern town. That's a little too close to the truth. If you must know, it's partly based on Ena's life, but I don't have all the details mapped out yet. All I know is it's going to be about a woman feisty enough to leave everything behind to start a new life."

"She would have been so flattered, Wade. How I wish she were still alive." Leigh's voice was sincere, and although Wade didn't reply, she knew he echoed her thoughts.

They worked in companionable silence, and it struck Leigh that this meal was different than the first one they had shared in Ena's house. They had acted like enemies then, warily circling each other like natural adversaries. Had that really been only a month ago? It seemed much longer since Wade had come home for Ena's funeral to find a town unable to forgive and a woman unable to stop loving him.

Wade hadn't shaved, and the stubble on his lower face was visible in the harsh kitchen light. While he stirred the ground beef in the frying pan, he took periodic breaks to down some more beer. Unexpectedly, Leigh giggled.

"What's funny?" he asked, cocking an eyebrow.

She giggled again and put down the knife she was using to cut up the cheese. "Nothing, really. It's just that I can't believe I'm making tacos with the respected author of *A World Beyond*."

Wade's eyebrows shot up. *A World Beyond* was one of his early novels, and it explored the possibility of reincarnation through the life of a retarded youth who had flashes of insight so brilliant, they led others to believe he had lived before.

"You read that?" He seemed stunned. "I didn't think many bookstores carried it."

"I didn't get it at a bookstore," she said sheepishly. "I know I shouldn't have, but I saw Ena's copy in the house one day and I lifted it. I was still living with my parents back then, and I locked myself in my bedroom and read it in one sitting. I thought it was brilliant."

"I had no idea," Wade said. He didn't write for anyone in particular when he crafted his books, but it touched him that Leigh had thought them worth reading. "Have you read others?"

She nodded sheepishly. "I know you mailed them to Ena to read. She had a habit of just leaving them out after she was done, and I helped myself. When I look back on it, I know she must have done it because she knew I wanted to read them but that I would never have asked."

Wade went back to stirring the ground beef, not knowing what to make of her confession. Just when he thought he had her figured out, she proved that he didn't. Could it be possible that he was wrong about Leigh? He thrust the thought out of his mind, the meaning behind it too much to contemplate.

A short while later, after they had eaten the spicy tacos and tidied the kitchen, they sat on the porch swing at the back of the house. Wade had his arm lightly draped over the back of the swing but their bodies weren't touching. Still, Leigh imagined they were a married couple enjoying the evening now that the dinner dishes were done. Would her dream ever come true?

"I'm sorry I blew up at you the other night," Wade said, and he almost choked on the words. Apologies weren't his strong suit, and he still had a lot to be angry about. But she had offered to make peace by coming here tonight, and he couldn't remain at war. "Maybe you were right about the memorial service."

"I'm sorry, too, Wade," Leigh said, squeezing the hand that rested near one of her shoulders. "I really thought it was better that you didn't come. And I never thought you'd want to have dinner with my family. My mother and Burt aren't exactly members of your fan club."

She didn't see any reason to rub salt into his wound by telling him about the argument at the Hampton dinner table. He had enough problems without concerning himself with her relationship with her mother.

"I know," Wade murmured, and he couldn't stop himself from saying the next words. "But it would have been nice to know that you weren't ashamed to have me there."

"Oh, I wasn't, Wade. I wasn't. It's just that my family is . . . well, my family. They aren't exactly the most accepting people around," Leigh said, but he didn't give any indication that he believed her. When he spoke again, it was to change the subject.

"You're not still looking into Sarah's death, are you?"

Leigh sat up straighter and turned so that she was looking at Wade. She raised her chin a notch, bracing herself for his reaction to what she was going to say.

"As a matter of fact, I am." Wade was about to protest, so Leigh placed two fingers against his lips to silence him. "Shh, let me finish. I told you that I wanted to talk to Abe Hooper. Well, he was at the memorial service acting very strange. He was standing in back of the church and every time Reverend Manigault started talking, he'd yell something to interrupt him—"

"Leigh, after your house was broken into, you said you'd stop," Wade interrupted, and he sounded almost dangerous.

"I did not," Leigh stated, ignoring the fact that she had let him believe she was going to stop investigating. "You said I should stop. I never actually agreed to it. Now do you want me to tell you about the service or not?"

Wade was silent, and Leigh was grateful she had his interest even though she didn't have his approval.

"The reverend would say something like we may never know why Sarah died, and Abe would yell, 'Why not?' Or he'd say her time had come too soon, and Abe would yell, 'Why?' None of it made a whit of sense and finally Burt had to escort him out of the church."

"And naturally you had to follow him," Wade said wryly, admiring her spunk despite himself. Leigh nodded.

"At first, he didn't want to talk to me but then he changed his mind." Leigh drew in a breath to prepare for the difficult part of her narrative. "Then he claimed he was an eyewitness and saw you walk off with Sarah that night. I'm just trying to figure out why he would say something like that."

Wade stiffened and removed his arm from the back of the swing. The porch was partly in darkness, and it hid the shock that registered on Wade's face. The other day on the street when Abe Hooper had loudly ordered him to repent, Wade had dismissed it as the ravings of a lunatic. But was Abe telling him he should repent for murdering Sarah and kidnapping Lisa? And why would Abe claim he had seen him abduct Sarah twelve years ago when nothing like that had happened? His brain must be impaired by years of hard drinking. But would anyone believe that? Would Leigh? When Wade spoke, there was nothing in his voice to reveal what he was thinking. "What do you think?"

"I think someone is trying awfully hard to have all the clues point to you," Leigh said thoughtfully, and some of the tension ebbed out of Wade. Once again, he had thought she would believe the worst of him. Once again, she had fooled him. "Let's examine the evidence. You come to town, and another little girl disappears. They find the first girl's skeleton near the cove where you used to spend a lot of time. Then an old man says he saw you kidnap the first girl."

"You're forgetting the discovery that my old man was insane," Wade said dryly.

"I'm not forgetting anything, Wade. I'm merely stating facts," Leigh said. "Someone is trying to frame you, and I think we may be getting close to figuring out who it is. First there was the fiasco in my bedroom and then there was the telephone call last night."

"What telephone call?" Wade sat at attention, all his senses on alert. She hadn't said anything about a telephone call before now.

"Oh, it was nothing. I've been getting a lot of hang-up calls, but last night the caller didn't hang up. He just told me to stay out of the past," Leigh said, deliberately making light of the incident.

"Is that all he said?" Wade's voice was laced with concern.

"No," Leigh said, shaking her head. "He said, 'Stay out of the past, or you'll be sorry.'"

"Why didn't you tell me about this before?" Wade clutched her shoulders and his fingers bit into her soft skin. He didn't understand her. She was so small, yet so fierce and independent. He wanted to protect her from the evil that had descended upon Kinley, but she acted as though she didn't need his protection.

"I am telling you. And would you please let go of my shoulders? You're hurting me." He complied readily, and Leigh rubbed her sore flesh. He hadn't even realized he'd been gripping her so tightly.

"I'm sorry," he said, and meant it. The last thing he wanted was to add to her problems, but maybe he was part of them. After all, he was the one she was trying to defend. "I didn't know anyone was threatening you. You've told Burt, of course."

At the negative shake of her head, he swore under his breath. This time, she'd gone too far and his anger overflowed. "Damn it, Leigh, this is not a game. Somebody out there has killed once, and we have no way of knowing whether he'll kill again. You're in over your head."

"No, I'm not," Leigh said, looking like the spitfire she was with her flashing eyes and jutting chin. "I'm making somebody nervous."

"You're making me nervous. Don't you think Burt should be investigating instead of you?" Wade asked, still angry. "Something could happen to you."

The sun had set hours ago and only a sliver of a moon illuminated the sky. It cast enough light that Leigh could see the sincerity behind his anger. Maybe it was possible that Wade felt the same way about her as she did about him. But if they were to have any happiness together, they didn't have any choice but to go forward with what she had started.

"Something worse might happen to you if we don't get to the bottom of what's going on. Something like false arrest," Leigh said after a moment.

"You're too stubborn," Wade said, slumping back against the swing. He didn't want to admit defeat, but he couldn't make her change her mind. His brain worked feverishly trying to think of another way to dissuade her, and he settled on logic. "Anyway, it seems to me that we've talked to everybody there is to talk to. I think the investigation has reached an impasse."

Leigh was silent for a moment while she considered what he had said. Had she talked to everybody who had a part in that long-ago drama? "Everett," she said suddenly. "It's funny. I see him almost everyday and talk to him about everything imaginable, but I've never asked him directly about that night."

"We'll talk to him together then," Wade said, figuring it would be better to join forces with her since he wasn't going to win this battle.

"Don't be silly. That won't do any good at all. You know how he feels about you. I'll talk to him. Now don't look like that. It's not like I'm putting myself in any danger. I've known Everett for years."

"You've probably known the murderer for years, too," Wade said ominously, his anger replaced by resignation. "Come on, I'll walk you home."

He got to his feet and extended one of his hands to Leigh. She took it, and he couldn't stop himself from pulling her into his arms. Her sandals were flat so she had to rise on tiptoe to meet his lips. Their mouths molded together like two halves of a whole, and Leigh closed her eyes to savor the sensations of desire dancing within her. He was unshaven, but the rough texture of his skin added to her excitement. Wade kissed her like a man who was drowning and didn't want to come up for air, and she responded with all her being. Nothing mattered—not her mother's disapproval nor the town's suspicion—except being in his arms.

He shakily put her from him, as affected as she was by the kiss. He wanted to ask her to spend the night with him, had wanted to since he shared her bed for the first time. Instead he took her hand and led her out the front door and into the muggy night. They held hands as they covered the few blocks to Leigh's house, and Wade fought the impulse to lift her into his arms and carry her back to his bedroom. He was fairly certain that she'd be willing to come, but he wasn't ready to take from her what she had to give. Still, he wasn't ready for the night to end when they reached her doorstep. Neither, apparently, was she.

"Why don't you come in and let me fix you a cup of coffee?" Leigh said, hoping he'd agree to stay. Even after all that had happened, she didn't mind being alone in Kinley. She just didn't want to be lonely for him, and she would be as soon as he returned to his own house.

"I don't drink coffee," Wade said, and she couldn't tell whether he was refusing her offer to stay, or just being honest.

"I don't drink it, either," Leigh confessed. "How about some iced tea, then?"

"What self-respecting Southerner could refuse an offer like that?" Wade said, smiling at her alternate choice. Soda was the beverage of choice in the North, but Southerners always kept a large pitcher of iced tea in the refrigerator.

Leigh smiled back and unlocked the door. He followed her into the kitchen, which was surprisingly small considering the size of the house. Leigh liked it anyhow, mostly because it was cozy and decorated in a country-kitchen motif, with calico curtains and copper pots and pans suspended from hooks on the walls. She would have suggested that they drink their iced tea in the living room, but Wade had already sat down on one of the kitchen chairs. There was something incredibly intimate about the sight of Wade Conner sitting in her kitchen, something that made her stomach somersault. When she sat down beside him, however, she saw that he was wearing a slight scowl.

"What's wrong?" she said, dreading the answer. She didn't want to talk about kidnapping or murder or anonymous telephone calls anymore tonight.

"I just noticed that you don't have a painting in the house," Wade said. "For somebody who used to be crazy about art, that's a little strange."

"It's not so strange," said Leigh, relaxing and wondering why. Just weeks ago, she wouldn't have allowed anyone to bring up the subject of her painting but now she wanted to confide in Wade. "After I gave it up, I didn't want anything around to remind me of what I was missing."

"Then you do miss it," Wade said, and it was a statement rather than a question.

Leigh nodded. "I hadn't realized how much, until recently. I'm almost tempted to unlock my storage room and resurrect the old hobby."

Wade was on his feet almost before the words were out of her mouth. She looked up at him in surprise, wondering what he was up to.

"C'mon," he said, offering her an outstretched hand. "Let's go clear the cobwebs."

Leigh bit down on her lip and tried to come up with a reason to refuse, and of course there were a hundred. She hadn't even let herself think of painting in twelve years, but now she was considering starting again because Wade had encouraged her. She thrust the remaining doubts from her mind, and took his hand. The smile on his face was reason enough to believe she was doing the right thing.

Fifteen minutes later, they sat cross-legged on the floor in a small room down the hall from her bedroom. Around them were canvases in all shapes and sizes, and Leigh tried to look at them with a discriminating eye. Wade, however, couldn't. Once upon a time, Leigh had had a talent that couldn't be denied. Wade thought she probably still had it.

"You were very good," Wade murmured absently, and flipped through some of the canvases.

There was a large painting of the Blessing of the Fleet, which was an annual springtime event in Kinley; the rationale was that the shrimpers would have a fruitful season if they were sent off with the clergy's blessing. Another painting was of children playing on and around the large oak tree in the middle of town. Another was a landscape of the street where Wade had grown up, but it looked different, more melancholy.

"I painted that just after Sarah's kidnapping," Leigh said when she saw him studying the bleak panorama. The painting was marred by a curious dab of red, and Wade absently rubbed at the speck, but it wouldn't come off. "It just looked so sad that day. Maybe that's why I packed up my paints and never took them out again."

"You mean this was the last painting you ever did?" Wade asked, wondering if he had been too hard on her. Sarah's kidnapping had been the catalyst that had forced him to leave town, but he hadn't known it caused her to stop painting. "I never knew that."

"How could you?" she said, shrugging, and Wade continued to flip through the stack of canvases. When he came to a painting of himself, he stopped. Leigh remembered it instantly, only partly because it was one of her best works.

She had never used much imagination in her paintings, instead preferring to be as realistic as possible when recording an image, but this one was different. Wade hadn't posed for it, so she had painted him from memory.

He looked younger, of course. His black hair was darker and thicker, and the faint lines that had formed on his forehead and around his eyes were absent. His gray eyes were dancing in a way she hadn't seen them dance in a dozen years. She could see why she was so wildly attracted to him that she'd risked the wrath of her parents by sneaking out at night to meet him. Wade had represented danger and excitement, and that's what had drawn her to him. That wasn't what had kept her there, though. When Leigh looked at the young Wade, her heart had trouble separating him from the man he now was. She loved them both, and she always would.

"I don't remember sitting for this," Wade said after a moment. It was quite good, but he could hardly remember a time when he'd looked like that. His face didn't hold a trace of concern for the future or any hint of the cruel cards life would deal him. The young man in that painting had lived simply and loved simply, and it was Leigh whom he'd loved. He'd even imagined marrying her and envisioned what the children of their union would look like. And he hadn't thought about the future in those terms for a very long time.

"You didn't sit for it," Leigh said. "This is just how I saw you."

He looked at her for a long moment, thinking about what should have been until some of the old bitterness welled up inside him. He rose. "It's late, and I've got to get going," Wade said, and Leigh couldn't for the life of her figure out why his mood had changed. Maybe she'd never again know him as well as she had when she'd painted him years ago. It was a sobering thought.

Beads of sweat rolled down Burt Tucker's face and perspiration darkened the underarms of his khaki uniform when he walked into Hampton's General Store later in the week. Leigh sat behind the cash register flipping through a magazine, trying to get through a slow morning. She rose when she saw Burt.

"What can I help you with, Burt?" She hadn't talked to him since she'd belatedly told him about her anonymous phone call, and she expected him to issue another warning about staying out of the investigation. She needn't have worried, because the police chief had other things on his mind.

"How 'bout a package of cigarettes," Burt said, wiping the back of his brow with his hand.

"Cigarettes?" Leigh was surprised. "But, Burt, you stopped smoking months ago."

"I feel the urge to start again," Burt said, and he sounded weary. "It's not enough that we have Lisa Farley missing. Now Abe Hooper's dead. And I always thought being the police chief of Kinley would be a low-stress job. I don't know what's happening, whether there's something in the drinking water or something in the air."

"Abe Hooper's dead?" Leigh choked out the words, fighting off a feeling of dread. "How?"

"I'm going to have to wait for the autopsy, but it looks like he drowned," Burt said. "He was found floating facedown at the edge of Mason Creek."

"Was it an accident?" Leigh asked, trying not to sound frantic. "Was there anything suspicious about it?"

"What kind of questions are those, Leigh?" Burt sighed. "You know as well as I do that Abe was always drunk. My guess is that he drank too much, fell into the creek and couldn't get up."

Or maybe someone pushed him and held his head under the water until the life bubbled out of him, Leigh thought. Was it a bizarre coincidence or had somebody killed Abe because he'd talked too much? And if somebody had killed him, wouldn't the prime suspect be Wade?

"How 'bout those cigarettes, Leigh?" Burt's request broke her train of thought, and Leigh reached for his favorite brand. They completed the transaction in silence and then Burt tipped his hat and started for the door. He stopped before he got there.

"Oh, Leigh. Your mother's awfully upset about what happened the other day. Maybe you should give her a call." With that, he was gone. For the rest of the afternoon, Leigh thought about Abe Hooper instead of her mother. Ironically, she realized that if Abe Hooper had been murdered, yet another finger was pointing at Wade. She'd told him and nobody else about her conversation with the old man, a conversation that a guilty man wouldn't want repeated. But Wade was innocent. So why had Abe ended up dead in Mason Creek?

She couldn't come up with any explanation except coincidence. But she'd read in a detective novel years ago that a good investigator didn't believe in coincidence. She wasn't exactly a good investigator, but maybe this was a sign that she should keep digging. She hadn't yet questioned Everett, and she resolved at the moment to do so.

The phone rang, and Leigh was so distracted that she didn't pick it up until it had sounded six or seven times.

"Hampton's General Store," she said.

"Hello, Leigh. It's Wade," he said, identifying himself unnecessarily. She could distinguish his voice from thousands of others in milliseconds, maybe because she had yearned to hear it for days. But she was getting used to stretches without hearing from him. It was obvious that Wade hadn't yet decided what to do about her and the undeniable attraction they shared.

"Hello, Wade," Leigh said, trying not to sound too happy that he had called. For all she knew, he might want to know whether the store carried his brand of mustard. "What's up?"

"I was hoping you weren't busy tonight," Wade said. "I felt like having some company for dinner."

It obviously wasn't the kind of invitation that came with wine and roses, but Leigh was relieved that he had asked. She was starting to think that their new relationship was more one-sided than she wanted to admit, but a man didn't issue a dinner in-

vitation if he were completely disinterested. Unfortunately,
Leigh had other plans.

"Sorry. I'd love to, but Drew and his girlfriend already invited me to dinner," Leigh said. She didn't add that she planned
to call on Everett after the meal, because she didn't want Wade
to issue another warning about the danger of looking into the
past.

"Maybe another time, then," he said, and she couldn't hear
any disappointment in his voice. "I'll let you get back to
work."

"Wade, wait," Leigh said before he could ring off. "Something's happened. Abe Hooper was found dead in Mason
Creek. Burt thinks he fell in and drowned."

There was a significant pause at the other end of the line.
"That's entirely possible. He was a drunk, you know."

He didn't sound surprised to hear of Hooper's death, and
Leigh told herself there was nothing incriminating about that.
People died everyday.

"Don't you think it's a little unsettling?" Leigh asked what
was uppermost in her mind. "Abe Hooper being found dead
days after he told me he knew who killed Sarah?"

"No," Wade said without pausing. "He implied that I was
guilty, remember? And since we know I didn't drown him, I'd
say it was just coincidence. Wouldn't you?"

The last question sounded almost like a challenge, and maybe
it was one. If Leigh trusted Wade, she should trust him completely. And if she trusted him completely, then his conclusion
about Abe Hooper's death was probably on target.

"Yes," she said finally, and heard a customer enter the store.
"Look, Wade, I've got to go. I've got a customer. Do you want
to try for dinner tomorrow night?"

"Tomorrow," he repeated, and the line went dead.

Chapter 12

Later that evening, Leigh stood knocking on Everett's front door. Since the death of Everett's parents fifteen years ago, he had lived in the cavernous house alone. He didn't keep it up terribly well, but it was passably clean even though Leigh suspected he only dusted about once a year. The house was distinctive because it boasted a small tower, which was really an extra room. Leigh knocked again.

"Oh, it's you," Everett said when he opened the door, and his hair and clothes looked more disheveled than ever. He pushed his glasses farther up on his nose and peered at Leigh.

"Hello, Everett," Leigh said, thinking Everett was acting weirdly even for Everett. "Can I come in?"

"Come in? Oh, yes, of course," Everett said, and stepped aside. All the ceiling fans in the house were operating, creating a whoosh of warm air and a terrific din. Everett didn't believe in air conditioners and he obviously didn't believe in replacing household items that had run their course. The clattering fans made such a racket that Leigh could hardly hear herself think.

"Can we sit on your back porch?" Leigh asked in a louder-than-normal voice. Even if she could have tolerated the noise from the fans, Everett's house was uncomfortably warm. He nodded, and she led the way, crossing the living room, the dining room and then pulling open the heavy doors leading to the porch. The slight breeze was immediately refreshing, and the silence of the night welcoming. Leigh and Everett sat side by side on his porch swing, and it reminded Leigh of a moonlit night and Wade.

"Wasn't it terrible about Abe Hooper?" Leigh said without bothering to ask if Everett had heard about it. In Kinley, people heard about the happenings of the day soon after they happened.

Everett cleared his throat, and Leigh once again noticed how disheveled he looked. His blond hair was uncombed, and there was even a streak of dirt across his cheek. "I heard he got drunk, fell into Mason Creek and drowned."

"That's what I heard, too," Leigh said, noting that Everett didn't seem to find anything unusual about Abe's death, either. She realized that Everett was waiting for her to continue and figured she might as well get to the reason for her visit. "You're probably wondering why I dropped by. I realize this is going to seem a little odd, but I wanted to ask you about the night Sarah disappeared."

"Why?" Everett said after a moment of silence which he spent staring down at his hands. He obviously didn't approve of her investigation any more than Burt did.

"You're the only one I haven't asked," Leigh answered, keeping her voice businesslike, as though it were perfectly natural for her to question a friend. She'd adopted the tactic when they'd first started the investigation, and it hadn't failed her yet. "I heard what you said about that night, of course, but it was only hearsay. I wanted to ask you directly what happened."

"I thought Burt wanted you to stop looking into that," Everett said, and he sounded agitated. "I thought it was too dangerous."

"I'm not afraid, Everett," Leigh said with more bravado than she felt. She didn't remember telling him about her ransacked bedroom or the anonymous phone calls, but everyone in town probably knew about them by now. "I just want to get to the bottom of this. So, will you help?"

There was another long moment of silence before Everett started to talk. "It was a very dark night, but when I looked out the window there was still some light," Everett said almost tonelessly. "I saw Wade Conner and the little girl bent over her bicycle. I remember that she was dressed in pajamas."

"And?" Leigh prompted when he stopped talking.

"And that's all I saw. I didn't look out the window again so I didn't see what happened."

"Do you remember anything else about that night?"

"Just that it was cold."

Leigh sighed and leaned heavily against the porch swing, causing it to sway. "What do you think happened, Everett?"

"If I tell you, you'll just get mad again like you did the other day when we were walking to work." His voice was pinched, almost afraid. Leigh reached across the swing and cupped his cheek affectionately. He rested it against her hand.

"You know, you're probably right," Leigh said. "Thanks for telling me about that night. You're a good friend, and the next time I snap, you should snap right back."

"I could never snap at you, Leigh," Everett said, and she rose. "You always will be the woman for me."

Leigh smiled, letting the comment roll off her like water. After nearly thirty years, she was used to them. The pair traversed the interior of the noisy house to get to the front door.

"I'll walk you home," Everett offered, but Leigh shook her head.

"No, thanks, Everett. It's nice of you to offer, but I was looking forward to a little solitude. One of the nice things about Kinley is that a woman can still walk home alone after dark."

But was that still true, Leigh asked herself as she walked away from Everett's house. A muffled voice on the telephone had warned her to stay out of the past, and she hadn't listened. Did that mean she was in danger during a solitary walk of a couple of blocks? Leigh looked up at the sky and could see only a few stars, possibly the same number that had been shining when Sarah disappeared. Like this one, that had been a dark night.

Maybe she was being foolish for paying such reckless disregard to the voice on the phone that she would walk home alone on a pitch-dark night. Maybe she shouldn't have refused Everett's offer. She thought about stopping at Wade's home, but there were no lights on so she kept walking.

Leigh picked up her gait, dismayed that she was nervous in a town where she had always been so safe. She heard the first sound when she turned the corner at the end of the block. It sounded like a twig snapping, perhaps being broken in two by the weight of a human foot. Leigh whirled around but confronted only darkness and her own fear.

She walked faster, wondering why she had never before noticed how little light the street lamps cast. The second noise was the rapid beat of footsteps, or so Leigh thought. Frightened, she began walking even faster, allowing herself only one backward glance at the dark of the night.

The screech of a cat filled the air and Leigh gasped, but it was the sound of labored breathing that made her take off in a dead run. Like many people her age, Leigh had once thought the best way to stay in shape was through jogging, but it had been years since she'd so much as laced a pair of running shoes. The sandals she wore with her summer slacks and lightweight blouse weren't suitable for flight, but she ran anyway. One girl was dead, another was missing and a man had ended up drowned in Mason Creek. She didn't intend to be the next casualty.

Leigh didn't hear anything now except the sound of her own breathing and the clack of her sandals on the sidewalk, but still she ran. If she had been thinking straight, she could have stopped at any number of houses along the way, but Leigh only wanted the safety of her own living room.

Her home, large and welcoming, was in sight when Leigh's sandal caught on a crack in the sidewalk and she went sprawling. Her right knee caught the brunt of the fall, and Leigh reached down to feel something wet and sticky through her torn pants. Ignoring the blood, Leigh scrambled to her feet and started to run again. Tears streaked down her face, and her breath was coming in quick gasps when she approached her home. As usual, she hadn't left on a light and the porch was in shadows.

At the door, she cast about wildly in her purse for her keys, cursing herself for not having them ready to slip into the keyhole. Whoever was after her could be here at any minute. All he'd have to do was come upon her from behind, clamp his hand over her mouth and squeeze her throat until she could breathe no more.

"Leigh, is something wrong?"

Leigh gasped, certain her morbid fantasy was about to come true. Her fear rendered her motionless, and she turned toward the voice to see a shadowy figure rising from her porch swing. She tried to scream, but no sound came out, and all the while the man was closing in on her. She looked up expecting to meet her fate, but saw Wade instead. She cried out in relief, and took a few steps until she was in his arms.

Wade cradled her against his chest, and he could feel her rapid heartbeat through the thin material of her clothing. He had struggled against an overwhelming urge to see her tonight, and now he was glad he had surrendered to his feelings. He was sure that whatever it was that had her so upset was related to Kinley's thickening mystery.

"Honey, what is it?" Wade asked as he stroked her hair, which was disheveled from her mad dash. "I hope I didn't scare you. I was just sitting on the swing waiting for you to come home."

Tears streamed down Leigh's face, and she didn't bother to wipe them away. "Someone was following me, Wade. I heard footsteps and breathing and . . ."

"Calm down, love," Wade said when she faltered. The people of Kinley tended to retire early and rise with the sun, and nights were customarily quiet. He looked over her head and saw no activity on Leigh's street. If someone had been following her, he had turned around and given up. "There's no one here but me. Now give me your purse and let me find your keys so we can go in."

Once inside, Wade cleaned the wound on Leigh's injured knee as she related the events of the night, from her talk with Everett to her frightened trip home to her encounter with Wade on the porch. Her tears had dried but some of the fear remained, and it made Wade angry that someone had frightened her. They were in Leigh's bathroom, and she was perched on the edge of the tub with Wade on his haunches in front of her.

"Who could be doing this?" Leigh asked, wincing as he applied antiseptic to her wound. She looked down at her knee, which was reddened with blood. Wade had cut off her pant leg, and she had a moment's remorse that her slacks were ruined but it was tempered with the thought that the damage to herself could have been far worse.

Wade's aquiline features looked as though they had been chiseled from a block of ice. The long straight nose, narrow cheekbones and steely eyes belonged to a man who had had enough. They also belonged to a man who was more worried than he wanted to admit.

"I don't know, but this can't go on," he said, the anger slowly building within him. "It's one thing for someone to try to frame me, but it's another thing entirely when someone tries to hurt you."

"I think someone's trying to scare me more than hurt me," Leigh said, even though she didn't entirely believe it. "But why? We've talked to everybody there is to talk to about Sarah, and we're still no closer to finding out who killed her."

"Somebody must think we are," Wade said. He opened a box of bandages and applied one to Leigh's cut. Leigh's bathroom was decorated in black and white, and it occurred to her that this case wasn't as clearly delineated. If the guilty party were from Kinley, there had to be a sizable gray area. How else could one of her neighbors be a murderer so cunning, he had covered his tracks for a dozen years?

"But we're not, Wade. Our strongest suspect ended up dead in Mason Creek, and if he were guilty, the only way that makes any sense is if he drowned himself because he couldn't stand the guilt anymore."

"Maybe he couldn't."

"Then why did someone try to scare me tonight?" Leigh shook her head. "I don't believe in ghosts. If Abe Hooper had kidnapped those girls, there wouldn't be any more insanity."

Wade rose and extended a hand to Leigh. "I think you should call Burt and tell him what happened," he said as he helped her up. "With everything that's been happening, we can't be too careful."

Fifteen minutes later, Leigh sat curled up on her couch with a glass of milk in her hand. She would have preferred a comforting glass of hot chocolate, but the spring temperatures in Kinley were too warm for that. Besides, her head was leaning against Wade's shoulder and that was comfort enough.

"Burt seemed more annoyed than worried," Leigh mused. "He said I wouldn't have anything to fear if I'd just stop sticking my nose in his business."

Wade smiled, because he had expected the police chief to react that way. "Was that before or after he warned you to stop seeing me?"

Leigh laughed, and Wade was glad that she seemed to be shaking off the effects of her recent fright. "Actually, it was before and after," she said. "He hasn't been exactly close-mouthed on that subject."

She snuggled closer to him, and Wade liked the feel of her soft body against his. She had needed him tonight, maybe more than she ever had, and he wanted to comfort her. Actually, he wanted much more and had since even before they'd slept together again. And tonight he vowed not to come up with any reasons to deny himself the pleasure of making love to her.

"Why were you waiting for me tonight, Wade?" Leigh whispered, and Wade briefly wondered if he should tell her the truth, that he couldn't seem to get through the day without seeing her. But he wasn't ready to put himself on the line like that.

"An impulse," Wade said, stretching the truth; it had been more like an obsession. "Maybe a sixth sense told me something was wrong."

"Thanks for being here for me tonight," Leigh said softly.

He smoothed her hair back from her temple and kissed it. "Think nothing of it."

"I can't do that," Leigh said, savoring the feel of his lips against her skin. The events of the night and the warmth of his body against hers inspired confidences. "I think about you all the time."

"I think about you, too," Wade said, and his voice was almost a whisper. He'd rather kiss her than talk to her, but he could tell that she needed some reassurances. Only he wasn't sure that he could give them.

"Sometimes it's hard to tell. We made love days ago, but since then you've been either arguing with me or trying to find a reason to keep me at arm's length. I don't know how you feel about me or if we have a relationship." Leigh stopped talking and laughed shortly as something else occurred to her. "I don't even know if you have a girlfriend back in New York."

Wade was silent as he thought about how to respond to her concerns. He couldn't tell her where their relationship stood when he didn't know himself, but he could tell her about his life in New York. He usually didn't feel as though he owed a woman his romantic history because he had been to bed with her, but Leigh was different. Leigh was Leigh.

"I haven't been a saint, Leigh," Wade said, confirming her suspicions. "There have been more women than I care to admit, but I was never serious about any of them. Let me tell you a little about the women I usually date. They're usually attractive in an artificial kind of way. You know the way I mean? The best clothes. The best makeup. A fair share of them have been models. I've found that type of woman doesn't make any emotional demands on me.

"I guess at one point, I thought about marrying one of them. I figured why the hell not. I'm thirty-two and it would be nice to have children one day, and I'd like to have a wife before I do that. But then I came to my senses, because I've never dated the type of woman I'd marry."

The band that was constricting Leigh's heart eased a little. She believed him. She had a harder time believing he would remain in Kinley.

"Any more questions?"

"Just one," Leigh said, glad she didn't have to meet his eyes. She was still leaning against him, but she no longer felt quite as secure. Her future could be riding on his answer. "Are you going back to New York?"

Wade disentangled himself from her and rose. He walked over to a large window that gave a view of Leigh's backyard and looked out into the night. Then he looked back at Leigh, but she couldn't read his eyes from where she was sitting. But, even before he said the next words, Leigh knew what they would be.

"Everywhere I go in Kinley, people look at me like I'm some kind of monster," Wade said, his voice barely audible. "Even if they do find out what happened to those girls, I'll always remember those looks. And this town will always carry bad memories for me."

Even though Leigh had suspected how Wade felt about Kinley, she hadn't prepared herself for it. Her eyes filled with tears, and she wiped them away impatiently before Wade could spot them. The hold she and Wade had on each other was tenuous, and she didn't have the right to flood him with demands. She hadn't even told him that she loved him, but she could show him.

She placed her glass of milk on the coffee table and covered the distance between herself and Wade. When she was standing next to him, she put her hands on his chest and felt the steady beat of his heart. She raised her eyes to his face and saw a man who had changed a lot over the years. But he could still look at her and make her feel she was the most important person in his universe.

"Stay with me tonight," she said, smiling. "I want to make some good memories for both of us."

Leigh offered her lips, and Wade took her up on her invitation. His mouth closed over hers, and the events of the night and the horrors of the past disappeared in their kisses. He kissed her softly at first, then more urgently. He wrapped both arms around her, and ran his strong hands down her back toward the curve of her bottom. He kissed under her ear, then along her jawline to her throat. Her breath came harshly and the warmth of desire spread within her. He kissed the base of her neck, and she gasped.

He took her face in his hands and looked into her smoldering eyes and kissed her mouth again, gently. It was as sweet as a baby's breath and as soft as a kitten's fur, and Leigh knew that the night ahead would be filled with promise and hope. Now was not the time to unravel a mystery with deep, dark secrets. Now was the time for a love that, for Leigh, had survived over the miles and the years. She smiled against his lips before he picked her up and carried her into the bedroom.

Wade switched on an overhead light, intending to enjoy their interlude visually as well as physically, before depositing Leigh gently on the bed. He didn't give her time to miss his closeness, because he kicked off his shoes and instantly joined her. He wanted her even more than he wanted to breathe, and his maleness was already straining against his blue jeans.

Their mouths met in a kiss that was desperate and tender at once, and Leigh closed her eyes to savor the feel of him pressed against her. She held on to him with all her might, never wanting to let go but knowing someday she might have to. No wonder she'd never been serious about another man. Her heart had always belonged to Wade.

When he moved his mouth from her lips to her throat, Leigh pulled back slightly and saw the confusion in his eyes at her withdrawal. She smiled, sat up on the bed and started to unzip her ruined slacks when Wade stopped her with his own smile.

"Let me," he said, his eyes shining with what Leigh hoped was more than desire. One of his large hands covered hers and together they worked the zipper down her pants. His hand left hers and traced the outline of her hips before he gently pushed Leigh back onto the bed and slipped her pants down, caressing her slim legs.

Leigh's stomach clenched at the sensuous feel of his palms on her smooth skin, and she closed her eyes to better enjoy the experience. Once he had discarded her slacks, Wade unbuttoned her shirt, raining feather-light kisses on her stomach. When she was wearing only a bra and panties, he shrugged out of his own clothes and then slipped off her underclothes so there was nothing between them.

I love you, Leigh thought, but she didn't say the words aloud and soon his kisses rendered her unable to even think.

His mouth covered hers, and her mouth answered. He bit her lower lip gently, then kissed her harder, his tongue teasing hers. The fingertips of one hand traveled from her shoulder to her waist, then traced the outline of her hip. He kissed her neck, her collarbone, her breasts. She drew in her breath sharply, and her nipples grew stiff with desire as his tongue teased them. His hand moved from her hip to the curve of her bottom, and he drew her to him, his mouth moving up to meet hers yet again.

She ran her hands down the length of his spine and felt him shudder when she reached his rounded buttocks. Her hand moved from behind him as his did the same. He clasped her fingers for a moment, and when she opened her eyes, she saw he was looking at her, smiling. He kissed her again, closing his eyes as he guided her hand to his manhood. He was alive with desire. His hand left hers, and she stroked him for a moment, then sighed as his fingers found the warm, moist center of her.

She didn't want to wait another moment for their ultimate joining. He pulled back slightly and she guided him inside her, a sensation so exquisite she caught her breath.

For Wade nothing could ever compare with the sensation of being enveloped by Leigh's femininity. How had he lived all those years without her, without this feeling? Determined to make their lovemaking last as long as possible, Wade paused within her before starting the rocking motion of love. Again and again he came to a pinnacle, but stopped to prolong her pleasure.

And then their world exploded in bursts of passion so intense, it felt to Leigh as though the bed were quaking along with her body. And then the world was still, and all was right because she was in Wade's arms.

"That was wonderful," Wade said, planting a kiss on her moist brow. He hugged her to him, enjoying the way her smooth legs felt next to his. She was even more desirable than she'd been in her teens, although the young Wade wouldn't have thought that was possible.

It wasn't until Leigh awakened in the middle of the night and tried to make out the profile of Wade's face in the darkness that it occurred to her that he hadn't told her if he planned to move back to New York. She loved him, but she knew that he still hadn't entirely forgiven her for the past. Maybe love wasn't enough. Their relationship was somehow linked to the murder of one little girl and the kidnapping of another. The memories Wade associated with Kinley would make it difficult for him to stay. Did he associate Leigh with those same memories?

Restless, Leigh stepped out of bed and pulled on a robe. She turned to see if Wade had stirred, but he was motionless, as though sleeping the sleep of the innocent. She walked to her bedroom window and pulled back the drapes. The streetlight in front of her house had blown out, and she couldn't see anything but the black night. Somewhere out there, a murderer slept, a murderer who might have stalked her this very night. Leigh shuddered, suddenly afraid for the town and for herself. Did she and Wade have a chance to make things work? Or was their relationship too tenuous to survive the awful truth lurking in Kinley?

Working at Hampton's General Store seldom brought a smile to Leigh's face, but she couldn't stop grinning the next morning. Her dark thoughts of the night before had vanished when she'd awakened with Wade at her side. She didn't even mind the menial chores of opening the store, brewing the coffee and doing the sweeping that Drew was supposed to have done the night before. She really had to have a talk with him about responsibility, but not today. She didn't want anything to spoil today.

The door chimes sounded, and Drew walked in wearing a sheepish look. It soon turned into one of confusion. Leigh was straightening a row of paper towels, and she turned to wave gaily at her brother.

"Do you realize you're humming, 'Oh, What a Beautiful Morning?'" Drew asked after a few moments. Finished with her task, Leigh headed for the front of the store and the coffeepot.

"Well, it is," she said, smiling. "Want to join me in a cup?"

Drew nodded and walked slowly to where Leigh stood. His features, so like her own, were etched with worry and reminded her of the way Wade had looked the night before. She was getting used to that look.

"You're not making much sense," Drew said. "I stopped by to see Ashley this morning and she told me someone followed you home last night from Everett's after our dinner."

"Someone did," Leigh said, handing Drew a cup of coffee and sipping her own.

Drew threw up the hand that wasn't holding his coffee cup. "I give up. Since when is being followed on a dark night something to sing about? Aren't you upset?"

"I'm too happy to be upset," Leigh said, and she smiled at her brother to cement her words. She wanted to share the news that threatened to burst from her, and Drew was the perfect sounding board. Unlike Ashley, he could keep a secret so for the past few years he'd been her confidant. Drew waited expectantly, and Leigh smiled again.

"I'm in love."

"You're what?"

"I'm in love with Wade," Leigh said and put down her coffee cup. She leaned across the counter and tried not to notice Drew's troubled frown. "For the first time in years I feel really alive. I hadn't realized how stagnant I'd let my life become until Wade came back. I didn't know it until recently, Drew, but I've always loved him."

"What does this mean, Leigh?" Drew asked, betraying nothing by his tone of voice. "Are you going to marry him?"

For an instant, Leigh pictured herself married to Wade and giving birth to his children. She was honest enough to admit to herself that was what she wanted, but saying it aloud was a different matter.

"We haven't talked about marriage," she said and laughed nervously. "To tell you the truth, we haven't even talked about love."

"Do you think he loves you?" Drew asked.

Did he love her? There were so many words they'd left unsaid, so many things they didn't know about the person the other had become. It was possible that all he felt for her was a physical passion he'd waited years to quench. Maybe loving Wade was Leigh's sentence for betraying him when he needed her most. Maybe asking him to forgive her was asking too much.

"I don't know," Leigh said honestly, "but I do know that I intend to stick around and find out."

Drew put down his coffee cup next to hers and captured her hands. His eyes, almost the same shade of violet as Leigh's, locked with hers.

"Don't you think you're taking things too fast?" he asked, and Leigh got the feeling he was trying to be diplomatic. "Wade's only been in town for a couple of weeks."

"You're forgetting that I've known Wade for years," Leigh said, refusing to flinch from her brother's gaze.

"I'm not forgetting anything, Leigh," Drew said, and he was as serious as he had ever been. "I don't know what went on between you and Wade when you were kids, but I do know that you've never been able to think straight about him."

Angry, Leigh pulled her hands away from his. "What's that supposed to mean?"

Drew sighed and rubbed his forehead. "I'm handling this badly, I know. But I'm just trying to tell you to put on the brakes. Crazy things are happening in Kinley, and you're listening to your heart instead of your head."

"Maybe it's about time I did," Leigh snapped. "I've always been Little Miss Obedient, listening to what Daddy said and listening to what Mother said. Somewhere along the line, I forgot to listen to myself.

"Look at me, Drew. I'm almost thirty years old, and I've never followed my heart. I fell in love with Wade when I was seventeen, and I let him go. I fell in love with painting, and I put down my paintbrushes to run a general store."

Drew winced, and she knew he was thinking of the sacrifice their parents had insisted she make for him. She'd never been able to pursue art because the Hamptons wanted Drew to pursue a military career. Leigh had followed through on her part of the bargain, but Drew hadn't.

"I've always felt guilty about that, sis," he said. "I thought you had some real talent, and I was sorry you gave it up."

"Me, too," Leigh said. "But remember how I told you I felt really alive? On the walk here this morning, I actually thought about painting again. Wade and I opened my storage room the other day, and he's been urging me to give it another try. Maybe it's not too late, Drew. Maybe I can still do something with my art."

"Maybe you should take the rest of the day off and do something about it before the urge passes," Drew said, and Leigh's anger faded as quickly as it had flared up. Drew was only worried because he cared about her.

"Thanks. I think I will, and I'm going to leave before you change your mind," Leigh said, surprising herself. She stopped briefly on her way toward the door to give her brother a kiss on the cheek. "Don't worry about me, Drew. Wade's a good man, and he doesn't have anything to do with what's been going on around here."

Drew bit his lip, and all of the worry that he'd exhibited earlier was written on his face. "You're probably right, Leigh. But think about this. What if Burt never solves Sarah's murder or Lisa's disappearance? Could you live with Wade for the rest of your life with that suspicion hanging over him?"

For an answer, Leigh squeezed Drew's hand and walked out the door. She didn't have a better one, because she'd never considered the question. Threats aside, she still intended to clear Wade's name. She refused to think about what would happen if she didn't.

Leigh headed straight for her house and the storage room, the door of which she had left open. Had that been by design? Had she been afraid that if she shut the door, she'd shut out any hope of painting again? She searched the room for paints, a blank canvas and an old easel. Drew had given her the day off to paint, and that's what she intended to do. There was a spot a few blocks from her house that afforded a view of some of the loveliest homes in Kinley, and it was time to capture that view in something other than just her thoughts.

Chapter 13

Leigh hummed as she walked down the wide sidewalk to Wade's house. She had painted until the light was no longer suitable, and her neck and shoulders ached from the unaccustomed work of leaning over an easel. She was so glad to be painting again, she'd hardly noticed the discomfort. Leigh let her exuberance overflow and skipped for a few steps, laughing aloud as she did. She was only half finished with her work, but the painting of Kinley's stately old homes showed she hadn't lost her touch. She was rusty and could benefit from a few lessons, but her talent hadn't diminished. She felt like celebrating, and wanted to share her joy with Wade.

Minutes later, Leigh held back disappointment and chastised herself for not phoning ahead. Grace Hampton had taught her never to show up at anyone's door uninvited, but Leigh didn't always listen to her mother. Besides, she had been so happy about the day's events that she didn't feel like telling him the news over the telephone. She knocked on Wade's front door just in case the doorbell wasn't working, but there was still no answer.

* * *

A couple of blocks from home, Wade picked up a pace that was already too fast. He had thought he could run off some of the anger that had sprung from Burt's visit earlier that day, but all he had run into was near exhaustion. He could still see the burly police chief's self-satisfied sneer and hear his taunting words.

"You might as well confess, Wade, because the evidence is mounting faster than I can collect it. How come you never told me you used to hang out at that cove where Sarah's remains were found?"

It was obvious why Wade hadn't told him, but what was less obvious was who had. And the answer, inevitably, kept coming back to Leigh. After all, she was the woman he used to sneak away to meet. And she was Burt's sister-in-law. Wade knew that, with Leigh's track record, he should have expected something like this. But he hadn't, and it hurt him to the quick. Last night, he had almost allowed himself to forgive her for what she had done. He had almost started to think of a future that included her. Wade laughed through the pain of his run, and increased the tempo another notch.

Leigh turned from Wade's front door, not bothering to mask her disappointment, and walked to the street. That's when she saw him. Wade, dressed only in a pair of shorts, socks and running shoes, came around the corner at a dead run. His arms moved in concert with his long strides as he ate up the ground between them. But Wade, intent on his jog, was looking at the sidewalk rather than at her. A few houses from his own, he slowed as though he had just crossed a finish line, and he tapered to a walk. His hands on his hips and his breath coming hard, Wade finally looked up and spotted her.

"Hi," Leigh said, smiling. "You weren't home, and I was just thinking that I should have called ahead."

"You should have," Wade said through his gasps. He wanted to confront Leigh with his knowledge, but he had wanted to pick the time and place. As it was, she had caught him at a disadvantage. He was upset and exhausted, and with her red-and-white shorts set and French braid she looked as though she could have starred in a soft-drink commercial featuring the beautiful people of summer.

"I thought I might be able to persuade you to feed me some dinner," Leigh said, attributing his slightly terse comment to the aftereffects of his recent exercise. Sweat glistened on his chest and drops of moisture dripped from his face. His hair was tousled from the run, but somehow he managed to look sexy. "But maybe I should make something and feed you."

Wade screwed up his face and shook his head. Food was the farthest thing from his mind. "I'm not exactly famished."

"You will be soon," Leigh said, laughing and trying not to stare at his chest. He had a light sprinkling of mostly dark hair, but a few of them had already turned gray. That made Leigh sad, because she and Wade had let too much time pass.

A loud barking startled Leigh and she turned to see a large, black dog staring at them from a few yards away. The dog, which Leigh didn't recognize, had its teeth bared.

"Where'd he come from?" Leigh asked, unconsciously backing away from the animal.

Wade gave the dog a cursory look and shrugged, deciding he might as well seize the opportunity and have it out with Leigh now. "I don't know who he belongs to, but he likes to torment me when I run. Usually he chases me for a block or two, but he missed me today. C'mon inside."

Leigh hazarded one more look at the dog, which was still barking but hadn't moved. "I have some wonderful news," she said when she felt sure the dog wasn't going to attack, "but it can wait until after your shower."

"Why wait?" Wade asked as they walked to his house. "I could use some good news."

Something about the way he said it made Leigh look at him more closely, but all she saw was a man still trying to catch his breath after a strenuous workout.

"I've started painting again," Leigh said, the happiness that she couldn't wait to share creeping into her voice.

"That's wonderful," Wade said, but his voice was flat. It was then that his strange mood finally registered on Leigh. Strenuous run or not, this wasn't the way a lover was supposed to act the day after a night of passion.

"What's wrong, Wade?" Leigh asked without preamble.

Wade cut a path through the house until he was in the breakfast nook, and Leigh followed. He indicated that she should sit down, but remained standing himself.

"Burt came to see me today," Wade said and looked at her expectantly, waiting for a telltale sign of guilt. None came. She stared at him blankly. A curtain closed over Wade's face, and he folded his arms across his chest. His features looked as though they'd been chiseled from rock.

"And?" she prodded, wondering what he was getting at.

"And he knew that I used to spend a lot of time in the cove next to where they found Sarah's skeleton," he said flatly, and again searched her face for signs of guilt. Instead he saw a quick flash of something that looked like anger and then an emotion he couldn't identify.

"So, naturally you assumed that I had told him that." His comments proved one thing, Leigh thought sadly; he didn't trust her. They had shared their bodies, but not their souls. It was difficult enough getting to know someone over again; it was nearly impossible when nothing mattered as much as being in their arms.

"Didn't you?" Wade said, but it was more of a challenge than a question. He had been so ready to believe the worst of her that he hadn't allowed the seed of doubt to be planted let alone grow.

"Of course not," Leigh said. Her face was pinched and drawn, conveying her dismay. "Why would I do something like that? What possible motive would I have?"

Wade shrugged. He hadn't thought it out that far, because Leigh made it so very difficult to think. Leigh with her shining hair and violet eyes, Leigh with her lies and her betrayal.

"Are you so blind that you can't see how I feel about you?" Leigh asked, and her heart was nearly breaking. He didn't trust her, and without trust their relationship was little more than the ashes of yesterday's fire.

"Save it, Leigh," Wade said cruelly, wanting her to hurt as much as he hurt, "because I won't believe anything you say."

"Of course not," said Leigh bitterly. "You don't believe in second chances."

The effects of Wade's run had worn off, but the argument was taking its toll. He paced to the kitchen sink while he tried to control his anger, but it got the better of him and he whirled on her. "A second chance," he bit out. "So that's what you wanted, Leigh. I thought as much."

"What's that supposed to mean?" Leigh asked.

"I've said it before, Leigh. You're with me not because you want to be, but because you feel too guilty not to be," Wade replied, almost shouting.

"That's not fair," Leigh said, angry now. "You're the one who doesn't trust me. Don't try to twist it around and make it my fault."

"Not fair? Don't try to say that your campaign to find Sarah's murderer isn't inspired by guilt."

"You sound so angry," Leigh said, sounding just as angry. "Don't you realize people can have more than one motive for doing things? So what if I feel guilty about all that happened years ago? I admit it. I do. So what if I want to right an old wrong? That doesn't have anything to do with the way I feel about you now."

"It has everything to do with it," Wade countered, his voice rising. He wasn't going to be taken in by her again. "If you had spoken up for me when we were kids, we wouldn't even be in this situation. Everything would have been out in the open, and we would have had a chance to make our relationship work."

"You're so blind, Wade," Leigh bit back. "Nothing's ever that simple. Yes, I loved you, but I was only seventeen. Can't you get that through your head? I was a kid who wasn't ready to feel the way I felt. Even if I would have spoken up, things wouldn't have worked out between us."

It wasn't until that moment that Leigh realized the truth. Oh, she still knew she should have gone to Chief Cooper with the information she had. But, for the first time, the stars in her eyes were gone. The teenage Leigh had been scared to death of her father, and she hadn't been ready to stand up for the man she loved.

"And now," Leigh finished, "you're not even giving things a chance to work out. You waltzed into town after all these years with a gigantic chip on your shoulder and you've been expecting me to hack away at it. I'm tired of it, Wade. I've admitted over and over again that I made a mistake, a big mistake, but you can't forget it. If I could turn back the clock, I would. But I can't."

"Neither can I," Wade said, and he had lowered his voice. He looked miserable, which was the way she felt. Their relationship was like a seesaw, and he was about to get off and send her plummeting into despair. Before he could say the words to cement the deed, Leigh rose from the chair and walked through the entrance rooms and out of the house. Wade stared after her, but he didn't even try to stop her.

Wade frowned the next morning as he made his way back to his house after his early morning walk. He hadn't been able to sleep, and it seemed that a walk might clear his head. He'd always liked the mornings best as a boy growing up in Kinley. The temperature hadn't yet soared into the nineties, and everything was so peaceful. This morning, Kinley was as serene as he remembered it, but his thoughts were far from soothing.

He may have been wrong to accuse Leigh of revealing damaging information to Burt, but he didn't think he was going to apologize. The argument had driven a wedge between them and it would keep her at a safe distance, in turn keeping him from wanting her too much. Who was he kidding, Wade thought as he kicked at a large pebble in the middle of the sidewalk and watched it skitter down the path. He'd wanted her twelve years ago, he wanted her now and he'd probably still want her twelve years from now.

He remembered the way Leigh had looked the morning after they had made love, her hair tousled, her face dewy from sleep. He had awakened her with a slow kiss and then made the mistake of permitting her a glance at the alarm clock. Leigh had come instantly awake and scrambled out of bed, telling him she was going to be late for work and berating him for distracting her so much, she had forgotten to set her alarm. Wade had laughed, aware of the underlying message that she would like to be distracted every evening.

The memory was like a dagger piercing Wade's heart, because he couldn't make love to her again. Otherwise, he would forgive her all her sins and abandon all his pride. And when she dumped him a second time, he might not be able to survive the repeat blow.

Wade rounded the corner to his street, and his already poor mood took a dive when his house came into view. Parked in front of it was a black-and-white police cruiser, and Chief Burt Tucker was ringing his doorbell. When Burt didn't get an answer, he turned and spotted Wade. It was already a warm day, and Burt had his hat pulled low to shield his face from the Carolina sun. He was unsmiling. In one of his hands, he held a document.

"Wade Conner," he said when Wade was within hearing range, and Wade's brows rose at the formality. "I have here a warrant to search these premises."

"What you looking for, Burt?" Wade said as he walked up his sidewalk, cutting to the quick of the issue while he fought back annoyance. Still, he didn't intend to play cat-and-mouse with Burt.

Burt had a wad of gum in his mouth, and he chewed it slowly as he regarded Wade from narrowed eyes. "I don't choose to answer that at this time," he said. "I don't want to take a chance that you might destroy the evidence."

Wade shook his head, his lips curling wryly. When was somebody other than Leigh going to believe that he was incapable of hurting a little girl? "What evidence, Burt? You have to commit a crime before there can be any evidence, and I haven't done that."

For an answer, Burt shook the search warrant. "If you do not willingly cooperate, I'll have to arrest you for impeding an investigation."

Wade removed his house key from his pocket and brushed by Burt. His lips were set in a straight line as he considered his predicament. He didn't think Burt was a crooked cop, but the chief was so desperate to make an arrest, Wade vowed to watch him closely so he didn't plant any bogus evidence. "I didn't say I wasn't going to cooperate," he said as he unlocked the door. "I just said I don't have any evidence to hide."

"We'll see about that," Burt said, and Wade thought he sounded like a detective in a bad movie. Only, this movie wasn't on a television that had an off switch. When Wade opened the door, Burt immediately stepped into the house and headed for the staircase.

"Which one's your bedroom, Wade?" he asked, and his voice sounded unnaturally loud in the quiet house.

"Second door on the right," Wade answered and followed Burt up the stairs, wondering when all the blind accusations were going to end.

Wade leaned against the bedroom doorframe as Burt began opening and closing closet doors, muttering to himself unintelligibly as he did so. When he came to the closet where Wade kept his shoes, he got down on his hands and knees and rifled through them. The chief looked so intent that Wade felt as though he were caught in an episode of *The Twilight Zone*. It would be one in which an innocent man is wrongly accused of a crime and spends the rest of his life in prison paying for something someone else did.

"Are you sure I can't help you find something?" Wade asked after a couple of minutes, and the color was high on Burt's face when he looked up.

"Your running shoes," he spit out, and Wade was surprised. What could the chief possibly want with his running shoes?

Wordlessly, Wade entered the room. He bent, retrieved the shoes from under his bed and extended them to Burt. The chief immediately turned them over and examined the soles. He pulled out a large plastic bag from his pocket and deposited the shoes, sealing the bag carefully. Then he turned to Wade, and his expression grew even more serious.

"You're under arrest for the kidnapping of Lisa Farley," he said, the barest smirk creasing the corners of his mouth. "You have the right to remain silent. Anything you say can and will be used against you in a court of law. You have the right—"

"Wait a minute," Wade interrupted, not believing his ears. "What possible grounds do you have to arrest me? A pair of running shoes?"

"Footprints were found at the scene of the crime," Burt said. "I'm certain that when we get back to the station, these shoes will match those prints exactly."

"I don't doubt it," Wade said, dumbfounded. "I run in this neighborhood. It doesn't stretch the imagination to believe that I might have left a footprint in someone's yard."

"You might have left it there when you kidnapped Lisa, too," Burt said, and brought out a pair of handcuffs. "I suggest you don't say anything more until you get a lawyer, because you're in a heap of trouble. Now, am I going to have to handcuff you or will you come willingly?"

"I'll come willingly," Wade answered, making a supreme effort to remain calm while his mind reeled. Burt finished reading him his rights, and he felt as though he was stepping deeper and deeper into the Twilight Zone. It was fast becoming clear that he should never have come back to Kinley.

The Kinley jail wasn't much more than a holding cell attached to the police chief's office, but when it was built a few years before, the townsfolk had insisted it be situated on the outskirts of Kinley to keep the criminal element as far away as possible. Aside from the departed Abe Hooper and now Wade, the only so-called criminals who had spent time in the jail were a couple of Georgetown boys who had come to town to rob the gas station.

Leigh stormed into the building, and her eyes were blazing when she spotted Burt sitting behind his desk. After getting word that her brother-in-law had arrested Wade, she had closed Hampton's General Store and rushed to the jail. She hadn't forgotten her earlier argument with Wade, but she was willing to set it aside for now.

"Are you crazy?" She yelled at Burt, ignoring the answering anger that filled his face. "What can you possibly be thinking of, arresting Wade? Don't you know there is a murderer out there? Do you actually think you're making anything better by arresting an innocent man?"

Leigh's chest heaved in anger, and she looked as though she might strike something. Her hair had come loose from her chignon, and her anger made her look bigger than she was. Burt stood up and unconsciously drew himself to his full height to gain an advantage.

"Now you quiet down," he said, almost matching the pitch of her voice. "I don't tell you how to run Hampton's General Store. You don't tell me how to run this town."

"Like hell I won't," Leigh bit back, not even noticing the curse word that left her lips. Her mother had taught her that

Southern women never swore, and she usually abided by that edict. "I'm not going to watch you make points with the townspeople at the expense of an innocent man. I want to know what grounds you have for charging Wade with kidnapping."

Burt's eyes narrowed. "You know I don't have to tell you a thing, but seeing you're my sister-in-law and seeing you're so upset, I will. We found a couple of footprints in the Farleys' front yard. It matches the print of Wade's running shoe."

"And?" Leigh asked, expecting him to embellish the story.

"And we arrested Wade for kidnapping," Burt finished, clearly disliking answering to Leigh.

"That's ridiculous," Leigh said, coming a few steps closer to Burt and making an effort to control her anger. She wasn't succeeding. "That's the weakest piece of evidence I've ever heard. I thought Lisa disappeared on the walk home from a friend's house. And there are a hundred reasons his print could be in their yard. Why, a big dog chases him sometimes when he jogs. Maybe it chased him off the sidewalk and into the Farleys' yard. Or maybe the wind blew something there and he went to retrieve it."

Leigh expected Burt to say something—anything—but he was silent. If anything, that made her even angrier.

"Arresting him is crazy, Burt. It's been weeks since Lisa disappeared. If the footprints were made the day of the crime, don't you think the rain would have washed it away by now? Don't you know how dumb it is to arrest him?"

Like most men who don't count intelligence as their greatest asset, Burt Tucker disliked being called dumb. He glared at Leigh, his eyes appearing as little more than slits in his heavy face.

"If we weren't related, I'd throw you out of here on account of insubordination," Burt said.

"Only because you know I'm right," Leigh retorted, refusing to be intimidated by his size or his anger. "I think you feel so much pressure to arrest Wade that it doesn't even matter anymore if he's guilty."

"I'm warning you to hush," Burt said and then laughed mirthlessly. "Not that I expect you to listen. You didn't listen when me and Ashley told you to steer clear of him. Ashley called you last night at almost midnight, and when you didn't answer, it didn't take much imagination to figure out where you were."

"That's none of your business, Burt," Leigh said, actually managing to look down her nose at him although he was almost a foot taller than she was. Burt obviously thought she had spent the night at Wade's house; she wondered what he would say if he knew she didn't answer the phone because she was upset over her argument with Wade. He'd probably call her an even bigger fool.

"Maybe not," Burt said, "but it's blinding your judgment. Maybe you can't see what's in front of your face because you're too close to it."

"Spare me your psychoanalysis, Burt," Leigh said, realizing that her tirade wasn't going to get Wade released. "I'm going to hire the best lawyer I can find, and there's no way your charges are going to stick. They wouldn't stick even if I hired a bad lawyer."

"I'm warning you not to cross me, Leigh," Burt said, and he sounded menacing. Leigh didn't back down. If he wanted to declare war, war it was.

"Tell me how much bail is so I can get Wade out of here," she said forcefully. That would show him what she thought of his threat.

"Not possible," Burt said, and sat down behind his desk, looking smug. "I have to take him to Charleston so a judge can set bail, and I don't have time to do that until tomorrow morning."

"What?" Leigh was outraged. "It's only ten o'clock now. Why can't you do it today?"

"Police business," Burt said, looking down at his papers. "I just can't. He's going to have to spend the night here whether you like it or not."

"I don't like it," Leigh said, "and if I can think of anything to do about it between now and this afternoon, I will. In the meantime, I want to see Wade."

For a moment, she thought Burt was going to argue some more, but then he nodded toward the closed door that adjoined his office with the two small cells in the other part of the building. "He's through there."

Leigh was almost through the door when a thought struck her. She turned to regard her brother-in-law once more. "Why did Ashley call me last night?" she asked.

He was silent for a moment, obviously debating whether he should answer. "I reckon it was to tell you the results of the coroner's inquest into Sarah's death," he said finally.

"And what were they?" Leigh prompted, annoyed that he had made her ask.

He cleared his throat. "I wouldn't tell you this if the *Register* wasn't going to print it tomorrow," he said, referring to the town's weekly newspaper, "but it looks like Sarah died from a blow to the head."

Leigh turned the piece of information over in her mind, not sure what to make of it. Obviously, someone could have administered the blow, but there was another possibility.

"Could it have been an accident?" she asked, and thought she saw a flash of uncertainty cross Burt's face.

"In your dreams, Leigh," he answered curtly. "Remember this. If you're going to stick by Wade, you better get used to talking through bars."

Leigh ignored him and turned on her heel with more bravado than she felt. Wade was on the other side of the door, and she didn't think he was going to be happy to see her.

Because of their relative newness, Kinley's cells were cleaner than most but they weren't any cheerier. Each cell was dimly lit and had a single bunk. Wade sat in the middle of his, appearing agitated and out of place. He looked up when Leigh approached his cell, but there wasn't any welcome in his face.

"Hi," she said, but he didn't return the greeting.

"I never would have dreamed that one day you'd be visiting me in a prison cell," Wade said, shaking his head. He had had a lot of dreams about her, but in none of them were they separated by bars. But the entire scenario seemed otherworldly: the murder, the kidnapping, the cell, even Leigh. "In fact, I'm surprised you're visiting at all."

Leigh found a stool and pulled it up to his cell. How could she make him understand that she wasn't the girl he once knew, that as long as he wanted her around she wouldn't abandon him no matter how tough the going? "I don't hold a grudge, Wade," she said.

Wade wasn't sure whether she intended the words to strike a blow, but they did. She was gently chastising him for being unable to forgive her, and he was starting to see her point. She had ignored her neighbors and stuck by him since his return to Kinley, but he still held her accountable for something in the dim, dark past. She couldn't understand why he wouldn't forgive her, but he was beginning to. Forgiving Leigh Hampton would make him free to love her again, and he couldn't allow himself to love a woman whose every deed was motivated by guilt.

"Then you're the only one who doesn't," Wade said. "This town sure holds a grudge. Your brother-in-law sure holds a grudge."

"You need a lawyer," Leigh stated flatly, trying not to show that it was tearing her apart to see him behind bars. Wade hadn't moved from his cot, and Leigh hoped he had more fight in him than was visible. "I know a good one. Arthur Riley is the best lawyer in Charleston, and he also happens to be a family friend. I can call him as soon as I leave here."

Wade rubbed a hand over his mouth, wondering how to tactfully reject her offer. "Look, Leigh, I appreciate it, but I'd rather you didn't. Riley may be a fine lawyer, but I'd rather have someone I trust working for me. And the fact that he's a friend of your family's doesn't inspire much of that."

"Do you have someone else in mind?" Leigh asked, trying not to feel hurt that he didn't want her help. But why should he? He made it clear that he hadn't forgiven her for the past, and she'd been chasing shadows for months and was no closer to solving the crime than she'd been before he came to town.

"His name's Spencer Cunningham. He's a friend of mine who just happens to be a damn good lawyer."

Wade didn't tell Leigh that Spencer was his best friend, the man who knew more about him than any other man alive. Except Spencer didn't know anything about Leigh. Wade had never told anybody in New York anything about Leigh.

"You sound worried," Leigh said, picking up the strain in his voice. "You sound like you think this is going to go to trial."

"I do think so," Wade answered after a moment. "Whoever kidnapped Lisa and murdered Sarah, if it is the same person, has been clever enough to get away with it until now. I don't see why he'd slip up now. Let's face it. I'm the fall guy. I just want to see I don't fall so hard I can't be mended.''

Leigh wanted to rail against the injustice of it all, but that wouldn't serve any purpose. However, telling him what Burt had just revealed about Sarah's death might.

''There's a new piece of evidence about Sarah,'' Leigh said and briefly told him Burt's theory that the girl had been killed by a blow to the head. ''What do you make of it?''

''That whoever kidnapped Sarah murdered her deliberately,'' he said, trying not to picture the scene.

''That's the logical explanation,'' Leigh said while her idea took root. ''But what if we were all wrong about what happened to Sarah? What if nobody kidnapped her and she just ran away? Isn't it possible, then, that she could have slipped and hit her head on a rock?''

''In the marsh? All the way out Old Kinley Road?'' Wade said, shooting holes in her theory. ''Even if she did manage to walk the three or four miles to where her remains were found, wouldn't that have been the end of it? Wouldn't Lisa Farley be at home with her parents right now instead of missing?''

Leigh sighed heavily. ''You're probably right, but it was a thought. I guess it doesn't seem likely that Lisa just happened to run away from home, too.''

Wade shook his head, and Leigh felt as though her entire body were weighted with lead. Her amateur investigation was at an impasse, and she was reduced to making wild guesses at what could have happened. None of it was helping Wade.

''Maybe you were right to hire Spencer Cunningham, then,'' Leigh said. She peered at Wade through the bars. ''Is there anything I can do?''

''Nothing,'' Wade said flatly, and Leigh felt as though she had been dismissed.

She rose from her stool and walked to the door, pausing before she opened it to look at him through solemn eyes. ''You know that it might be tomorrow before you get out of here?''

''I know. Your benevolent brother-in-law already told me,'' Wade said and tried to smile, but all he managed was a poor semblance. She left him standing there like that, and her heart was more twisted than his smile.

Chapter 14

Spencer Cunningham looked levelly at his friend, and shook his head. He was tall, blond and good-looking in much the same way as the stereotypical California surfer boy, but Spencer had an added dimension. He was as sharp as they came. He was also as loyal. Wade knew his friend had a busy law practice, but Spencer had taken the next flight to Charleston after Wade's telephone call, rented a car and arrived at the Kinley jail in the late afternoon.

The two men were sitting in the breakfast nook in Ena's house drinking beer, but the brew wasn't relaxing either of them. "You better tell me how you got into this mess," Spencer said in a voice that was surprisingly soft. "And, believe me, it is a colossal mess."

"Don't I know it," Wade said, thinking even *that* was an understatement. He was starting to wonder if he'd ever be free of the web Kinley had cast over him. "But first I want to thank you. I didn't relish the thought of spending a night in jail. Come to think of it, you still didn't tell me how you persuaded Burt to let me go."

Spencer dismissed Wade's thanks with a flick of his wrist, as though it was the least he could do. "It wasn't exactly persuasion. I'd call it more of a threat. His evidence was way too flimsy to hold up in court. I told him I'd file a lawsuit for false arrest and imprisonment if he didn't find someone who could set bail real fast. An hour later, you were free."

"But not clear?" Wade asked, although he already knew the answer. They hadn't talked much on the drive from the jail, but Wade knew Spencer well enough to sense that he was holding something back.

"He may have more than a footprint," Spencer said after a moment and pressed his fingers together as though he were contemplating a particularly troubling problem. "The good chief says he has an eyewitness."

"An eyewitness?" Not many things had shocked Wade since his return to Kinley, but this was one of them. Even though he had begun to expect bad luck, he hadn't expected someone to come forth with a concocted story. "That's impossible. How can he have an eyewitness to a crime I didn't commit?"

"It's not an eyewitness to the crime. It's somebody who will testify that he saw you with the little girl before she was snatched," Spencer said, sounding like a lawyer making a very important distinction.

"Wait a minute. Are we talking about Sarah Culpepper or Lisa Farley?" Wade had already admitted that he'd been helping Sarah fix her bicycle tire shortly before her kidnapping, but he had never even seen the other little girl.

"Lisa Farley," Spencer answered and sighed. He suddenly sounded drained, as though Kinley and the evil that lurked within it was trying to suck the life out of him. "You mean there's more than one."

Wade nodded, becoming more certain by the minute that he was being set up. He briefly considered how to tell his friend about the mystery that had shrouded his past, and decided on a condensed version of the story. "She was murdered years ago, but at the time we just thought of it as a disappearance. I was blamed, but never charged, and then I left town. They found Sarah's skeleton a few days ago."

"The muck gets thicker," Spencer said, and for once Wade didn't appreciate his dry wit. Even in casual conversation, Spencer thought and sounded like a lawyer. "I guess you don't have an alibi for that one, either."

"Actually, I do," Wade said after a moment. He didn't want to elaborate, but now wasn't the time to keep the secrets he had guarded so closely over the years. If Spencer were going to mount a successful defense, he needed facts. "Her name's Leigh Hampton. I was with her the night of the first kidnapping."

"Ah, the one who got away," Spencer said with a flash of insight, and Wade silently cursed good friends. Even though he'd never mentioned Leigh to Spencer, his friend had picked up something in his voice and made his own deductions. "Is she a central player in this mystery?"

"You could say that," Wade said slowly. "We've been looking into the past, trying to figure out what happened twelve years ago."

Spencer finished off the last of his beer, set down his glass and stood up. Wade blinked once to make sure he wasn't hallucinating. A minute ago, Spencer had looked as though he needed a good night's sleep. Now he was energized. "Well, what are we waiting for?"

"What do you mean?" Wade asked suspiciously, guessing at the source of Spencer's change in moods.

"I want to know everything there is to know about these abductions, and three heads are better than two," Spencer said, sounding like a detective who was ready to chase a tip. "Let's pay a visit to this Leigh Hampton."

"It's not as easy as that," Wade said, staring down at the table. When he didn't elaborate, Spencer once again folded his long length into the booth, placed his elbows on the table, his chin in his hands and raised his eyebrows.

"Why not?" Spencer asked, and Wade could tell that his curiosity was piqued. "Isn't she on our side?"

"It's not that," Wade said, thinking that Leigh had been in his corner since he saw her standing at Ena's grave site. Then she had offered him sympathy. Later she had given him herself. And now Spencer wanted to ask her for support. "It's just that . . ."

"What?" Spencer asked when Wade's voice trailed off, but Wade couldn't finish his train of thought. How do you tell your best friend that you want a woman to stand beside you because she loves you, not because she feels guilty that she failed you once before?

"Nothing," Wade said, and rose abruptly. He glanced at his watch and saw that it was almost six o'clock. "She runs a general store a short walk from here. Let's go."

Closing time at Hampton's General Store was often an exercise in frustration. Kinley's residents were aware that the store closed at six o'clock, but many of them had developed the irritating habit of showing up at five minutes before the hour. By the time they picked up the items they needed, chatted about what was new in their lives and checked out, it was well past six.

Leigh normally took it in stride as a quirk of doing business in a small town, but today wasn't one of those days. Leigh had jumped every time the phone rang. Every time she picked up the receiver, she expected to hear news of Wade's predicament. Every time, she was wrong.

Now all she wanted to do was get out of the store and head over to the jail to make one last plea for Wade's release. But she had been so busy ringing up purchases that she hadn't locked the door and at a quarter past six she heard yet another customer arrive.

"We're closed," Leigh called, but she knew she'd allow the customer to pick up whatever he needed. She glanced up from her work and found herself looking at Wade and a man she was sure must be Spencer Cunningham.

"Mind if we wait?" Wade said, and the three people at the cash register turned in unison to stare at him. All three were elderly, and none seemed pleased to see him. Mrs. Guerard, a woman in her seventies who lived in the same block as Leigh, even emitted an audible cluck.

"Hi," Leigh said, ignoring the unspoken disapproval in the room and biting back the question of how Spencer had arranged bail. "I'll be just a few minutes."

Leigh rang up purchases for the next ten minutes, but the easy chatter was gone. The moment Wade and Spencer had entered the store, her customers and neighbors lapsed into silence. The two men stood unobtrusively against a far wall and talked quietly as they waited, but her customers' suspicion filled every corner of the store.

Leigh shrugged apologetically when they were alone and her day's work was finally done.

"Please tell me this isn't a jail break," Leigh said, only half kidding. Wade tried to smile, but didn't quite manage it. He looked as though the day in jail had taken its toll.

"No such thing. It's just the work of the best lawyer this side of the Mississippi," Wade said and indicated the man at his side with a nod. "Leigh Hampton, I'd like you to meet Spencer Cunningham."

Although Spencer was casually dressed in dark slacks and a short-sleeved knit shirt, Leigh would have pegged him as Wade's out-of-town lawyer even without the introduction. Not many strangers passed through Kinley, unless they had taken a wrong turn at the main highway. Spencer Cunningham didn't look like the kind of man who ever did anything that wasn't deliberate.

"I thought you were a lawyer, not a miracle worker. How ever did you get Burt to let Wade out of jail?" Leigh had slept in that morning and had been in such a hurry that she had yanked on the first thing that caught her eye, which happened to be a pale purple sundress that made her eyes appear startlingly violet. Her hair had long since worked its way out of its chignon, and it hung long and straight past her shoulders.

"Let's just say I used a little lawyerly persuasion," Spencer said modestly as he shook her hand.

Wade smiled at his friend, and Leigh could see the warmth between them. Both men were unusually handsome, but she far preferred Wade's dark look to Spencer's fair one.

"But it's not over?" Leigh asked, and Spencer shook his head.

Leigh was so frustrated, she stamped her small foot. "It's so maddening. I can hardly believe Burt filed charges on such a trumped-up piece of evidence. A footprint in a yard found days after the kidnapping. What kind of evidence is that? Why, they don't even know for sure that Lisa was kidnapped. It's outrageous."

"He may have more than a footprint," Wade said after a moment. He ran a hand through his dark hair. "Burt says he has an eyewitness."

"A what?" Leigh was shocked. "That's impossible."

Spencer cleared his throat, and Leigh's frantic gaze darted from Wade to the lawyer. "We're not going to solve anything in the middle of this store. I'd like for both of you to fill me in on the case, but there must be somewhere more comfortable for that.''

"My place," Leigh said immediately.

"I was hoping you'd say that," Spencer said. Leigh turned away from the two men, busying herself with closing the store and trying to swallow the helplessness that threatened to overwhelm her.

Twenty minutes later, the three of them were comfortably ensconced in Leigh's living room while a homemade pizza baked in her oven. The night before, after her argument with Wade, Leigh had busied herself with whipping up a stash of pizzas from an old family recipe. She hadn't anticipated one would come in handy so soon.

Leigh and Wade were seated on opposite sides of the room, and Leigh wished they weren't separated by so much distance. She wanted to slip her hand into his and comfort him. She wanted him to know she believed in him. Leigh's heart felt heavy. The way things were going, Wade might never believe that.

"Start talking," Spencer said once they were settled in, and they talked. They started with the fateful night Sarah was abducted a dozen years ago and ended with Wade's arrest earlier that day, with Leigh taking a break only to fetch the pizza and some drinks.

Because Spencer needed every morsel of information possible to prepare his defense, they left out only the most personal details. By the time they had spun the tale, a few hours had passed and they had long since finished eating. Spencer had mostly listened, occasionally interrupting to ask a question.

"Is that everything?" Spencer asked when they finally grew silent, and Leigh nodded.

"Everything except what a lousy detective I am," Leigh said. "Maybe we were kidding ourselves when we thought we could pick up the trail after all these years. The only new things we learned were that Sarah used to carry around a tattered red blanket and crazy Abe Hooper thought he witnessed the crime. But Abe's dead, and his word didn't have much credibility anyway."

"Don't be so hard on yourself," Spencer said. "None of this is your fault."

"Don't be so sure about that. You still don't know the whole story. It wasn't your future I put in jeopardy," Leigh said dejectedly and looked at Wade, but something about him was different. He no longer looked wary and distrustful.

"It wasn't your fault, Leigh," Wade said clearly, and found with a start that he believed his words. It had taken twelve years and a hellish return to Kinley to realize it, but Leigh hadn't been the cause of his problems after all; she was just a symptom of them.

Leigh stared at Wade as though he were the only person in the room. She had been waiting to hear those very words for years, but now that they were spoken, she couldn't accept them. "But if I would have spoken up in the first place, maybe none of this would have happened. Maybe Sarah would not have died, Lisa wouldn't have been kidnapped and you wouldn't have been blamed."

"I don't think that," Wade said, surprising himself as much as Leigh. When had he come to this conclusion and why was he able to state it so calmly after all this time? "I believe in fate. I think that no matter what you or I had done, this would have happened anyway."

"Do you really think that?" Leigh breathed, hardly daring to believe him. Before either of them could say anything more, Spencer cleared his throat.

"I hate to interrupt," Spencer said, forcing their attention away from each other and back to him, "but Wade's freedom could depend on what you tell me. Now think. Has anyone in town been acting strangely since Wade returned? Or nervously?"

Leigh rested her chin in her hands and thought. She glanced at Wade, but he shrugged. "Nobody except Abe Hooper, and he's dead," Leigh said finally. "He must have been crazy. If he wasn't, I can't for the life of me figure out why he warned me to stay away from Wade. But he said it, plain as day."

"He said to keep away from Wade?" Spencer asked.

Leigh paused. He had said something like that, but she couldn't remember his exact words. She screwed up her forehead, and her eyes narrowed. What exactly had Abe Hooper said? She remembered that spittle dripped down the side of Abe's mouth when he laughed at her plea for help. She remembered him saying that he knew who the murderer was.

Sarah was having trouble with her bicycle, he said, when the man grabbed her and took her away. But what had he said about Wade?

You're keeping company with a dangerous man.

The sentence thudded against Leigh's brain. That was it! That's what Abe had said. He hadn't named Wade after all. She had just assumed he had been referring to Wade.

"Leigh, Leigh." Her head snapped up at Spencer's worried words. "What is it?"

Leigh chewed on her lower lip. "I'm not sure if it matters. Abe told me I was keeping company with a dangerous man. He didn't refer to Wade by name, but he couldn't have meant anybody else."

Wade raised an eyebrow in doubt. "Surely I'm not the only man you've kept company with in the last twelve years."

He wasn't, of course, but she had already eliminated the other men in her life as suspects. "Well, no, but it's ludicrous to suspect Drew. Burt is pigheaded and maddening, but he isn't a murderer. And Everett, well, Everett is just Everett. Abe must have been crazy. He couldn't possibly have been talking about anyone except you."

"What about Gary Foster?" Wade asked, forcing Leigh to consider the possibility.

She shook her head, because it was too farfetched to believe that Abe Hooper had been referring to Gary Foster. "The only time I've kept company with Gary lately was when he was a customer in the store," Leigh said. "It's hopeless. I doubt if we'll ever find out who the murderer is. I'm starting to think we should just concentrate on clearing Wade, because this is one of those cases that may never be solved."

"You don't believe that," Wade said, and Leigh turned to regard him. He had changed shirts since she'd seen him in jail, and the soft blue he wore made his features seem darker and his gray eyes lighter. They were sparkling with insight. Maybe she'd been wrong earlier that week when she'd thought they didn't know each other very well; his insight was right on the mark.

"Of course I don't," Leigh admitted. "I'm not the kind of woman who believes that people can get away with murder. I think we all have to pay for our sins."

She'd paid. A dozen years ago, she'd kept her mouth shut and let the best thing that ever happened to her get away. Now he was back, but it seemed as though he was paying for some-one else's sins.

Spencer regarded her for a moment, obviously deep in thought. "You said something about a red blanket, Leigh. Maybe that could mean something."

Leigh shook her head helplessly. Spencer leaned back against the sofa and rubbed his eyes, and Leigh realized that both Wade and his lawyer friend had had a long day. She glanced at her watch and saw that it was nearing midnight, which was past the time she usually turned in for the night.

"Look, we're not getting anywhere," Leigh said reluctantly. "Why don't we just call it a night and talk some more in the morning?"

"That might not be a bad idea," Spencer said, yawning, but Wade suddenly was rigid with tension. He stood up and stared at Leigh while his mind reeled. He closed his eyes, and his whole world was red. There was the red blanket, the red flash of anger and the red speck in Leigh's painting.

"What is it, Wade?" Leigh asked frantically, causing Wade's eyes to snap open.

"Your painting," he said, willing her to understand. "The one of Calhoun Street the day after Sarah was kidnapped. The one with the speck of red."

When they had looked at the picture in the attic a few days before, Leigh had believed the splash of red to be an acciden-tal spot on the canvas. But what if it weren't accidental? What if she had deliberately depicted something red in the painting because it was in contrast to the bleak scene? Leigh's eyes wid-ened as a greater possibility occurred to her. What if the speck of red paint could pinpoint the murderer?

"Oh, no," Leigh said, and her face turned ashen.

"What is it?" Spencer said, looking from Wade to Leigh. "Have you two thought of something?"

It was the ugliest thought that had ever crossed her mind. It was so ugly, so preposterous, that she couldn't voice it until she knew if it were true. She got up from the sofa, and her eyes al-ready looked haunted. Then she took off in a dead run for the steps to her second floor with Wade and Spencer not far be-hind.

It wasn't possible, Leigh kept telling herself. He couldn't have done it. Again, she heard Abe Hooper's words: *You're keep-*

ing company with a dangerous man. But it couldn't be true. She knew him. He wasn't the sort of man who would do such a thing.

The door to her studio was unlocked, as it had been since she decided to resurrect her painting career. Leigh got down on her hands and knees and flipped through a stack of paintings, so nervous she could barely focus on what she was doing.

"Please, God," she whispered. "Please let us be wrong."

The painting she was searching for was the third one in the stack, and Leigh yanked it free from the others. She held it at arm's length and stared. It was as she had remembered it, a depiction of Calhoun Street on its darkest day. It had been overcast, and everything was painted in muted shades of color, as though the street were in shadows. But near the top of the painting was the spot of red, exactly where she had feared it might be. Sarah must have tried to use her red blanket as a beacon to attract attention, but it hadn't worked.

Twelve years too late, they had finally spotted the clue and understood what it meant. The red blanket, stuffed in the window of the alcove atop Everett's home, had finally done its job.

Leigh was kneeling on the floor, and when she turned to look at Wade, tears streamed down her face. Wordlessly, he stooped down beside her and gathered her into his arms. Over her shoulder, he saw the telltale spot of red in the painting. He stroked her hair while she sobbed. In the doorway, Spencer looked upon them in confusion.

After a few minutes, Leigh drew back from Wade and wiped the moisture from her face with the back of a hand. Her eyes, still brimming with tears, were the color of a rain puddle reflecting the sun. She sniffed and laid her head against his shoulder so that he couldn't see her face.

"The clue was in the painting all these years," she said, and she was so sad, it felt as though her chest were constricting. "It's funny, I don't even remember noticing the spot of red in Everett's alcove, but it must have made an impression on me. Such a cheerful color on such a bleak day. That's probably why I painted it."

Mild-mannered Everett, Wade thought. Leigh said he had never even hurt a fly, but he had done worse, far worse. He had killed one little girl, kidnapped another and nearly wrecked two other lives.

"That's who Abe Hooper meant when he told you that you were keeping company with a dangerous man," Wade said, and Leigh nodded against his shoulder. It occurred to him that Everett had probably murdered Abe, too. Anger, pure and unbridled, rose within him.

Leigh felt as though the knowledge had drained the strength from her body, but she managed to extract herself from Wade's arms and rise. She couldn't remember when she had felt worse.

"But why would he do it?" Wade asked as he followed her example and rose. The outrage in his voice was tightly reined, but Leigh was so miserable she didn't pick up on it.

"You were right when you said he's always loved me. I knew, of course, but I didn't know how much," Leigh said and sighed. "He must have known about us twelve years ago. All I can figure is that he kidnapped Sarah to frame you."

"And he kidnapped Lisa because the plan worked so well the first time," Wade finished for her, and there was regret and despair in his voice. "I left town—and you—once. It made sense that I would leave again."

"We played right into his hands," Leigh said sadly. "We were so busy blaming each other for what happened that we never took the time to see that someone else was to blame."

Leigh walked away from him, much as she had done on a dark night in front of her house years before. But how could she have known then that she was obeying the twisted plan of a man gone insane?

"I'm going to call Burt," she said, but Wade was already edging his way past her and the silent Spencer.

"Where are you going?" Leigh and Spencer asked at nearly the same time, but Wade didn't even pause.

"I'm going to Everett's," he said over his shoulder, not once pausing to reconsider his action. "One little girl is dead, and I'm afraid another might be if we waste any more time."

"At least let me phone Burt before we leave," Leigh called after him, but he was already halfway down the stairs.

"This isn't a good idea, Wade," Spencer added his objection, but Wade didn't hear either of them. He was thinking about Everett, the man who had terrorized a town, the man who had jeopardized his future.

"He's not acting rationally," Spencer said, and Leigh silently agreed. But she couldn't follow him until she made her call to Burt. Suddenly, chillingly, Everett represented danger, and she wanted all the help she could get.

Wade looked unseeingly at the sidewalk as he quickly covered the distance to Everett's house, and he didn't notice the smell of honeysuckle in the air or the incessant cries of the crickets. Their theory sounded logical, but it was insane. Everett had always seemed like the gentlest of men, but had he slipped into madness without anyone noticing? Because who else but a madman could murder a defenseless little girl? Wade only hoped Everett hadn't done it twice, that he wasn't too late to save Lisa.

Only a few lights shone in the windows of Everett's large home. The alcove was dark. Wade knew that Everett's parents had died fifteen years ago, and since Wade returned to Kinley, the house had looked sad and unkempt. Tonight, with clouds obscuring any light from the moon, it looked almost eerie, as though it could have been the setting for a horror movie.

Wade had known he was coming to Everett's home ever since he recognized the red speck in the painting for what it was, but he hadn't planned a course of action. Still, he was more determined than nervous. And why shouldn't he be? Everett had shoved him and Leigh into a dark hole from which they finally had a chance to emerge. The culmination of twelve years of tears, misunderstandings and sorrow was just behind the door.

Wade ignored the heavy knocker, realizing he shouldn't alert Everett to his presence. He couldn't underestimate what Everett was capable of doing. Everett had even tried to scare Leigh, ransacking her bedroom, threatening her with phone calls, following her home that night.

Wade reached for the doorknob and slowly turned the knob, but it wouldn't budge. He should have figured that a man with as much to hide as Everett would lock the door. Wade rested his forehead against the cool door as he thought about what to do next. He hadn't come this far to let a locked door stop him. The corner of his eye caught sight of a window immediately to the right of the door, and Wade figured out his course of action. It was going to be noisy, but he didn't have a choice.

He searched the yard until he found a large rock and heaved it against the glass. The sound of the window shattering was deafening against the stillness of the night, and Wade quickly reached through the gaping hole until his hand found the dead bolt on the door and unlocked it. Moments later, Wade was inside the house, letting his eyes adjust to the darkness. The house was still and much too warm. His eyes flicked to the fans suspended from the ceiling, but they were idle.

He expected Everett to appear out of the darkness to investigate the noise the crashing window had made, but nobody came. Swiftly, because he knew it was only a matter of time before Everett appeared, he made his way up a staircase he assumed led to the alcove. Instead, it led to another floor of rooms.

Wade hesitated, and then headed down the hall, trying to step as gingerly as possible. Just when he thought he should have gone in the other direction, there was another staircase. This one was dark and winding, and at the top of it was a door. Wade tried to turn the doorknob, but it was locked. Disappointment flooded him, but then he noticed a key dangling on a nail a few inches from the door. Holding his breath, he inserted it into the lock and heard the click that gave him entry.

The door creaked noisily as it came open, but the sound barely registered on Wade. His eyes scanned the room and there, in the corner atop a mound of blankets, was a little girl. Wade could just make out her blond hair, much the same color as Sarah's had been, in the darkness. The girl didn't move, and Wade steeled himself for the worst.

He switched on the light, and heard a wonderful sound, a whimper barely louder than a kitten's meow. The girl slowly turned her head to where Wade was standing, and the path of tears on a dirt-streaked face was visible.

"Lisa?" Wade asked softly, and the girl cowered against the wall. "Don't be afraid. I'm here to take you home."

The girl was crying by the time Wade gathered her in his arms, and her small body was shaking with sobs. "I want my mommy," Lisa said over and over again. "I want to go home."

"Don't worry," Wade said while his anger at Everett rose like a balloon within him. "I'm here to take you home. You don't have to stay here a minute longer."

"You shouldn't have come." Everett's voice sounded from the doorway, but it didn't startle Wade. Lisa sobbed louder, and Wade gathered the little girl closer to him. The balloon of anger inside him burst.

"And you shouldn't have a little girl in your attic," Wade lashed out. "What kind of a monster are you?"

Everett took a few steps into the room, and the situation seemed bizarre. He was dressed in the same dark slacks and short-sleeved shirt he always favored, his hair was tousled, and his glasses were inching down his nose. But there was something wild in his eyes that erased the picture of a small-town Southern accountant, something that glinted when he looked at Wade.

"I take good care of her. I feed her and give her books to read. I never even touch her," Everett said defensively, but then something in his voice changed. "This is all your fault. I never would have had to bring her up here if it wasn't for you. You ruined everything."

Wade saw the danger in Everett's eyes and thought better of making a reply. He stood and lifted the sobbing little girl with him. "I'm taking you home, Lisa."

"No one's going anywhere," Everett said, and his voice was shaking. He reached behind his back and pulled out a pistol. It was long, black, sleek and pointed toward them. "You walk out that door, and you might as well sign my death warrant."

"You should have thought of that before you kidnapped Sarah and Lisa," Wade said evenly. Lisa's sobs were more regular now, but she was holding onto Wade's neck so tightly that he thought they'd probably have to pry her off later. If they had a later.

Wade's comment made Everett angry, and he waved the gun. A sound at the door drew their attention, and they both turned. Leigh stood there, her mouth slightly agape and her heart heavy. After phoning Burt and informing Spencer he would be more of a hindrance than a help, she had covered the few blocks to Everett's house on a run. All the while, she had prayed that they were wrong about Everett. All the while, she had known they were right.

"Everett, how could you?" Leigh said, sadness and anger intertwined in her voice.

Everett paled at the sight of Leigh, but he didn't lower his gun. Instead, he waved her over to where Wade and Lisa stood. Leigh covered the short distance effortlessly, but her heart was hammering. She wasn't afraid of Everett, but this wasn't Everett; this was a madman.

"I had to take them, don't you see that?" Everett shouted, directing his tirade at Leigh. "He was like poison for you. All wrong. He would have ruined your life. Don't you see it was the only way to keep him away from you?"

Leigh's stomach heaved and sank at Everett's admission. Her theory had been true. A dozen years ago, she had loved Wade with the pureness of a child while something evil brewed in her best friend's heart, something so evil that another child had paid for it with her life. The pizza she had eaten for dinner churned uneasily in her stomach.

"No, I don't see. I don't see why you had to kill Sarah," she said softly, revulsion in her voice. Everett heard it and looked wounded, but he kept the gun pointed at them.

"I didn't kill her," he denied, sounding like a little boy who had just been scolded. "I saw her stupid red blanket in the window, and I yanked it out and yelled at her. She started crying. I told her to stop, but she just kept on and on. I came toward her to try to scare her into stopping, and she kept backing away, backing away. And then, then, she lost her balance and hit her head on the windowsill. I tried to wake her up, but she just lay there. And then I realized she wasn't breathing."

The horror of the story was reflected in Everett's voice, and she and Wade both turned and looked at the windowsill, which was fashioned of marble and as high as a seven-year-old girl was tall. Sarah would have had to stand on her tiptoes to manage to stuff the red blanket on the ledge, but her plea for help had come to naught.

"So instead of calling a doctor, instead of trying to help her, you took her to the marsh," Leigh accused, and there were tears streaming down her face for the little girl who'd died and for the fool she'd been.

Everett took a step closer, and his gun was pointed only at Leigh. "You're not listening to me," he said, and his voice rose in pitch until it sounded like the desperate cry of some wild bird. "She was already gone. I couldn't do anything for her, but I loved you. It was your life I was trying to save."

"What about Abe Hooper's life? Did you kill him, too?"

Everett's hand was shaking so hard that the weapon moved from side to side. "Don't you understand? He had to die. I followed you out of church that day, and I heard him telling you that he'd seen me take Sarah. You didn't understand that he meant me, but it was just a matter of time. I had to follow him to the creek and hold his head under water. Don't you see? None of this is like you make it sound. I only did it for you.''

"Oh, no," Leigh said while it registered that the Everett she had known and loved was gone forever. "You made threatening phone calls to me. You ransacked my bedroom. You followed me home that night and scared me half to death."

"I couldn't stand the thought of you sleeping with him in your bed. I only did what I did because I love you," Everett said, and the last sentence was almost a scream.

"Was driving away the only man I could ever be happy with, love?" Leigh asked recklessly, a mixture of anger, shame and revulsion overcoming her fear of the weapon in Everett's shaking hand. "Is pointing a gun at me and threatening my life, love?"

"You don't understand," Everett screamed, but then his shoulders sagged and he started to cry. "I only wanted you to love me."

Everett let the gun dangle loosely from his hand, and Wade knew that this could be the only chance they had to get out of this alive. He had been silent for minutes, sensing that anything he said might further enrage Everett. He caught Leigh's eye and nodded toward the open door. The only sounds in the room were the sobs coming from Everett and the ones from the little girl in his arms. Leigh was closer to the door so she preceded Wade as they started moving toward safety.

"Don't move," Everett cried out, pointing the gun at them again and trying to focus through his tears. "I'll shoot if you do."

Wade glanced from Everett to Leigh and Lisa and knew what they had to do. They had to call Everett's bluff and keep walking. "Don't stop," he whispered to Leigh, hoping that she had been correct when she told him weeks ago that Everett was basically nonviolent. If she were wrong, he would feel a bullet rip through him in the next instant.

"Stop," Everett said again, but still they walked. The door was closer, only steps away, but Wade braced himself for the explosion of pain that would come with the bullet. But instead of a bullet, he felt a flood of relief when first Leigh and then Lisa and himself passed through the attic door in time to see Burt climb the last two steps with his gun drawn.

"Everett's in there with a gun," Wade said tonelessly. "He just confessed to everything."

Burt nodded curtly. Everett had been yelling so loudly that his voice had carried through the house. "I heard him," he said and nodded toward the girl in Wade's arms. "Is she okay?"

"As well as can be expected," Wade answered, and Burt brushed past them into the attic room.

"Let's get out of here," Leigh told Wade, her voice trembling. As they walked down the flights of stairs and out the heavy front door, Leigh felt only sadness. Lisa was still crying loudly, but Leigh was only crying on the inside.

The night was quieter than either of them had ever known it. Even the crickets had stopped their chattering. When they were inside the house the moon had peeked from behind the clouds, but as they exited the crescent slipped back into place and turned the sky black.

On another night, they might not have heard the noise. But even though the gun was fired from inside the house, the sound of a single shot blasted through the night air. A moment later, Burt walked slowly out of the house with his head downcast. He looked at the trio and shook his head.

And then there was no more quiet, because Leigh was crying every bit as hard as the little girl who had found herself in the middle of a triangle Leigh hadn't known existed until that night.

Chapter 15

Leigh awoke the next morning with a throbbing headache and eyes that were red and puffy from crying. The first thing she saw was the frilly pink canopy over the bed, and she abruptly sat up and glanced around at the finery that made up the quintessential little girl's room. And then she remembered.

She was upstairs in Ashley and Burt's home sleeping in her niece's bedroom, only she hadn't spent much of the night asleep. Leigh glanced at the bedside clock and saw that it wasn't yet nine. Considering that she had gone to bed well past two and tossed and turned for hours, she couldn't have gotten more than a couple hours of sleep. She was surprised she hadn't had nightmares, but last night had been enough of a nightmare.

She brought her knees to her chest and rested her forehead on them. She'd like to believe last night hadn't happened, but she knew that it had. Everett was really dead. Everett, who had seen her through childhood and loved her past the point of reason. Everett, who had caused two deaths to keep Leigh from the man she loved.

After Everett had turned the gun on himself and Burt had come out of the house, Ashley and Spencer had arrived on the scene. If Leigh hadn't been crying and Lisa hadn't been clinging to Wade as though her life depended on it, Leigh felt sure

Burt would have scolded them for entering the house without him. But even Burt wasn't that tactless. Leigh had taken her comfort in Ashley's arms, and thankfully for once, her talkative sister had nothing to say.

Leigh missed the only happy time of the night—the tearful reunion of Lisa Farley and her parents.

The rest was a blur of sadness. She remembered an ambulance, Wade's arm around her shoulders, their joint statement at the police office. And then, in the wee hours of the morning, it was finally time to go home. Since she didn't want to be alone, it seemed logical to accept Ashley's invitation. So here she was alone and miserable.

The door was partly ajar, and Ashley's blond head peeked through the opening. Even her sister's appearance showed the effects of last night. Ashley was one of those women who always looked immaculate, even first thing in the morning. But her makeup couldn't hide the dark smudges under her eyes or the concern in them. "Leigh, are you all right?" she asked, hesitantly coming in the room.

Leigh looked up and tried to smile, but failed. "That's not one of the words I'd choose. Try sad, betrayed, foolish. Why couldn't I see it, Ashley? Why couldn't I see that Everett was behind everything . . . ?"

Her voice trailed off at the end of the sentence, and Ashley sat beside her sister on the bed. She reached for Leigh's hand and squeezed it.

"Oh, honey, don't blame yourself," Ashley said, her voice rich with feeling. "You couldn't have known. You were the only one who was on the right track. Do you know that Everett even came to Burt a few days ago and told him Wade used to hang out near the marsh? He even told him he had seen Wade with Lisa before she disappeared. It wasn't true, of course. Maybe something should have clicked then, but we were so ready to blame Wade that we never even considered anyone else."

Leigh sniffed, determinedly holding back her tears. She'd cried enough; now was the time for healing. "I never did understand why everyone used Wade as a scapegoat."

"I don't entirely understand, either, honey," Ashley said, regret on her face. "I guess because it's easier to feel safe if you know who the enemy is. Who would have dreamed it was Everett?"

"I should have," Leigh said, self-disgust in her voice.

"Oh, stop that, Leigh," Ashley said sternly, dismissing the thought. "If you hadn't started looking into this, maybe Lisa never would have been found. And maybe Wade would have gone to jail."

"And maybe you never would have admitted you were wrong about him," Leigh said, conscious that Ashley hadn't yet done so.

"Oh, I was wrong, all right," Ashley said without pausing, "about the only man who was ever right for you."

Leigh smiled then, and even though the smile didn't quite reach her eyes, it was more than she would have dreamed she could manage the morning after misery. Impulsively, she moved forward and met Ashley halfway in a hug that was as warm as the sun that shone on Kinley on a summer day. They had spent so much of their adult lives bickering that the embrace was all the more special for it. When they drew back, they both had tears in their eyes.

"You should try to get more sleep," Ashley said, and Leigh appreciated her concern even though she was going to disregard it.

"I can't," she said and wiped at a tear that was trickling down her face. "I need to go home and sort things out for myself before I can get any rest."

For a moment, Ashley didn't say anything and Leigh thought her sister would order her to explain what she meant. And what could Leigh say? That she needed to prepare herself for a future that didn't include Wade Conner? But instead of arguing, Ashley gave Leigh's arm a little squeeze. "If you need me, Leigh, I'm here," she said simply.

Wade leaned over and placed his hands on either side of the driver's window of Spencer Cunningham's rental car. Genuine affection filled his face as he looked at his friend.

"I can't thank you enough for coming, Spence," he said. "Are you sure you don't want to stay for a couple more days?"

Spencer shook his head, reached for a pair of sunglasses to negate the effects of the bright, Carolina sky and smiled. "What for? I got you off the hook, didn't I? What more do you want me to do?"

Wade laughed at that, although he wasn't in the best spirits. The night before had been filled with a horror it would take a long time to shake. And, now that it was over, it meant he was free to leave Kinley. And Leigh.

"Keep a beer cold for me in Manhattan," Wade answered, and Spencer's smile disappeared.

"You're coming back then?"

"Just as soon as I pack and put the house up for sale," Wade said, and there was a catch in his voice that Spencer immediately picked up.

"What about Leigh?" Spencer asked. The color ebbed from Wade's face, because his friend had struck a nerve.

"What about her?" Wade replied, interjecting a false nonchalance into his voice.

"You told me once that you left your heart in Kinley. It wasn't until I saw Leigh that I realized you'd left it with a woman," Spencer said. "Isn't it about time you told her that you still love her?"

Wade smiled, but there was no mirth in his eyes. "And have her laugh in my face? No, Spence, some things are better left unsaid."

"She loves you, too," Spencer added softly.

Wade patted his friend on the shoulder and straightened to his full height. "Once upon a time, I believed in fairy tales, too. But not anymore. All Leigh ever wanted from me was absolution, and she's got it. Now she's free to live the rest of her life without feeling guilty about what she did to me, and I'm free to go. See you in New York."

With that, Wade turned and strode away. He was already on his porch when Spencer turned on the ignition and drove away. But, before he'd gone, Wade had looked into his friend's eyes and realized that Spencer thought that he was leaving an even greater tragedy than the one that had unfolded the night before.

It was nearly six o'clock when Leigh finally sat down on the sofa in her living room and put up her feet. She had told Ashley that she was going to spend the day sorting things out, and she hadn't lied. Her closets and dresser drawers were tidier than they'd been since she moved into the house. Keeping busy was a way to avoid sorting out her personal problems, but Leigh couldn't put off thinking about them forever.

Wade was going to leave town; she was even more sure of that than she'd been that morning. That morning, there was the glimmer of hope that he still cared. But he hadn't even phoned to see how she was, and that slim hope had faded with the day's light. She didn't blame him, not really. Last night he had all but said he'd forgiven her, that what had happened years ago had been "fate." But forgiving her was not tantamount to loving her. And she'd known, right from the moment she saw him again at Ena's grave site, how he felt about her. It wasn't his fault she had fallen hopelessly, irreversibly in love with him. Again.

Leigh's eyes welled with tears, and she wiped them away. Wade was going to leave, and she'd have to get used to it. She'd done it once; she could do it again. But this time, she didn't have to get over him in Kinley. This time, she could sell the store, enroll in art school and hope that her new life was enough to blot out the pain of her lost love. She looked around at the house that she loved and saw beyond it to the town where she'd been born.

Kinley wasn't an evil place because it had harbored an evil man, but it was just a place. And it was time that she stopped paying penance for another man's sins by working in a general store that brought her only drudgery. Her guilt had prevented her from leaving Kinley, but she had nothing to feel guilty about anymore. Everett had kidnapped those little girls, not her. He had paid for his crimes with his life, and it was time for her to get on with hers. It was time to leave Kinley.

The doorbell chimed, and Leigh reluctantly rose to answer the door. It was probably Ashley with a home-cooked casserole or her mother offering even more apologies. They hadn't spoken since the fiasco at Grace's dinner table so Leigh had been a little surprised to hear her mother's voice at the other end of the telephone line earlier that day. Grace hadn't wasted words.

"I hate to admit I was wrong about Wade, but I was," she had said. "I don't want to lose you, Leigh. And if it's Wade Conner you want, I'm not going to try to stop you from having him. Your father and I never made things easy on you two. Maybe it's time I started."

Leigh was so taken aback by Grace's words that she hadn't said much in reply, but the irony of the conversation struck her as she went to answer the door. Grace assumed she and Wade had a future together while Leigh was preparing to relegate him to the past. They'd never once spoken words of love, and Leigh had to admit that their renewed relationship had revolved around solving Sarah's murder and Lisa's kidnapping. Now that it was over, it was possible that Wade didn't want to see her again. Maybe he'd even left town with Spencer Cunningham.

Of course, there was an off chance that her visitor could be Wade. Leigh started to smooth her hair, but abandoned the effort. She looked like a woman who had spent the day cleaning, and that's who she was. A barefoot woman in shorts and a T-shirt who had never been glamorous and never would be.

She yanked open the door, and there Wade stood. His dark hair was tousled, as though he'd taken a shower and let it dry without combing it, and he wore shorts, a T-shirt and tennis shoes. But he still looked handsome and dear and...unattainable.

"Hi," he said, but she didn't reply and Wade wondered why he had come. Was it to torture himself with the image of a woman he couldn't have, a woman who was desirable even when she wasn't at her best? But he wasn't the kind of man who left town without saying goodbye.

"Can I come in?" he asked. Leigh nodded, belatedly regaining control of herself and her manners. Wade looked her up and down, noticing the smudge of dirt on her chin and the streaks of dust on her clothing.

"Have you been cleaning?" he asked, finding the idea more than a little preposterous. Her world had shattered the night before, and she had spent the day dusting?

Leigh nodded, shrugged and decided to tell him part of the truth. "Yes. I just didn't feel like sitting around thinking about how one of my best friends was a murderer."

"People aren't always what they seem. Something snapped in Everett a long time ago," Wade said, and Leigh noticed that there wasn't a trace of bitterness in his voice despite all that Everett had done to harm him. To harm *them,* she amended. Everett was gone and she wanted to forgive him because he had been sick, but she couldn't. He had killed an old man and a little girl, kidnapped another and in the process almost wrecked her and Wade's lives.

"I wish I would have heard him snap," Leigh said softly, and Wade wanted to reach out to her. But he didn't have the right. Not when their relationship was about to come to yet another end.

"I ran into Burt today," Wade said after a stretch of silence. "He said that Lisa was doing much better. A doctor examined her and found no evidence of physical harm. Apparently Everett was telling the truth when he said he'd barely touched her."

"What about you? Did Burt say you were free to go?" Leigh asked, almost choking on the last question. She knew he had come to tell her he was leaving, but she didn't want to hear the words. They would make everything so final.

Wade nodded, picking up the distress in her voice and wondering why the prospect of him leaving Kinley upset her. It wasn't as though she loved him. "Burt dropped all charges against me."

Leigh tried to say she was happy for him, but she couldn't. Not when the prospect of never seeing him again overwhelmed her. It suddenly dawned on her that they were still standing in the foyer. She hadn't even asked if he wanted to sit down.

"Forgive my manners," she said, and her voice sounded stilted and unnatural. Had she really spent a night of uninhibited passion with this man just days ago? "Do you want to come into the living room? And can I get you anything? A glass of lemonade, perhaps?"

"I didn't come here for a glass of lemonade, Leigh," Wade said, and took a deep breath. Now was the time to say goodbye, and he wasn't ready for it. He didn't think he'd ever be ready for it. "I came to tell you I'm moving back to New York."

Leigh had expected the declaration, but she didn't think she could breathe, let alone move. Yesterday's nightmare was carrying over into today. Wade was really leaving. He was leaving Kinley, and he was leaving her. After all these years of aching for him, Wade was leaving. And, already, the ache was worse than it had ever been.

She stood staring at him, noticing how his T-shirt hugged his upper body and drew attention to his long arms. She wondered if those arms would ever hold her again. The twelve years they had lost seemed like nothing compared to the greater loss that was about to come. She looked as devastated as she had the night before when they had uncovered the truth about Everett.

Wade was perplexed by her reaction and sought to fill the silence. "I put the house up for sale today and packed some of Mother's things to donate to charity. It hasn't been an easy day."

Leigh finally found her voice. "It's hard to let go," she said, talking about his feelings for his mother and her feelings for him at the same time. And then she asked the question uppermost in her mind.

"When are you leaving?"

"Tomorrow," he said, and her heart felt as though it had been sliced open with a rapier. Averting her eyes, Leigh turned and walked to her living room. A large picture window afforded a view of the backyard she kept lovingly tended.

Everywhere in sight were azalea bushes that bloomed with beautiful showy flowers for a short time each spring. But they were already starting to look plain and slightly barren. Her love with Wade was like that. They had only enjoyed a few short bursts of happiness and in between had been a dozen years of emptiness. And now she had to prepare herself for an even more barren season, a season that would stretch a lifetime.

She sensed rather than heard Wade come up behind her. He put a hand on her shoulder, and she didn't shrug it off. She'd spent so long building up her defenses against him that she didn't have the strength to erect them again after they'd come crumbling down.

"Before I go, Leigh, I want you to know that I don't blame you for what happened when we were kids," Wade said, and it felt good to finally admit it. "I did blame you, but I finally realized it was just one of those things that happen on your way to growing up. You were right. I can't forever hold you accountable for something that happened when you were only seventeen."

"So you're saying you forgive me?" Leigh said, and her voice would have sounded harsh if it hadn't started to quiver.

Wade nodded, still confused by her reaction. Why was she acting so strangely when all she'd ever wanted from him was forgiveness? That was all she wanted, wasn't it? "Yes, I guess that is what I'm saying. I forgive you. Isn't that what you wanted?"

Leigh laughed, a shrill and unnatural sound, and then the tears streamed down her face. Wade forgot about not having the right to comfort her and put his arms around her. She rested her head on his solid chest, thankful for the comfort he offered even though she couldn't count on it past this moment.

"Of course I wanted you to forgive me," Leigh said through her tears. "And I understand why you couldn't be happy living here after all that's happened. I know you can't stay in a town whose people don't believe in you."

"Then why are you crying?" he whispered against her hair, and Leigh was silent for a long time. She debated briefly about lying to save her pride, but then decided against it. When she hadn't been completely honest years ago, she had unwittingly prolonged a tragedy. It was time for the truth.

"It's never been easy to let you go," Leigh said, talking into his shoulder. "It wasn't easy when I was a girl, and it'll be even harder now that I'm a woman. But I learned to live without you once, so I guess I can do it again."

A flare of hope ignited in Wade, and he gently pushed her back from his chest. Her violet eyes were glistening and her delicate features had never been more beautiful. He took her hands in his, and she made no move to remove them. She couldn't have moved anyway, because she was held captive by the look in his gray eyes. They looked starkly honest and a little desperate.

He smiled to himself. For twelve long years, every thought of Leigh had been ripe with resentment and hurt. He had kept his anger alive, because his true feelings would have been harder to live with. There was something about this small woman with the long, dark hair that had captured him years ago and never let go. He wasn't sure what it was, but he knew that he loved her, pure and simple.

He traced the curve of her cheek and settled his fingers on her lips. Spencer had been right. It was about time he told her how he felt.

"I've been fighting this feeling from the moment I saw you again," he whispered. "Even after we slept together, I kept telling myself it couldn't be love. And all the time, that's exactly what it was."

Leigh's eyes widened and some of the moisture spilled from them. "You love me?" she asked, sounding awed.

"I don't think I ever stopped loving you," he answered and put his fingers on her lips to quiet what she had been about to say next. "I don't expect you to love me back, not right away anyway. It's enough for now that you care. You do, don't you?"

Leigh smiled at him, her heart in her eyes, and removed his fingers from her lips. "What makes you think I don't love you? What do you think I've been trying to tell you for the last ten minutes? Of course I love you. You don't think I go to bed with every old lover who comes to town, do you?"

"You better not," Wade said, and their mouths met in a kiss that was urgent and tender at once. Leigh closed her eyes to savor the feel of him pressed against her. He wound his fingers in her long hair the way that he once had, and Leigh's memories of how she used to feel about him mingled with her present feelings until they were indistinguishable.

"Then come with me," he said when they broke off the kiss. The rays from the setting sun shone through the window and glinted off his dark hair and olive complexion, and he looked as young and carefree as he had years ago. "I have this great place in New York that's right around the corner from an art school."

"What would I do with the store?" Leigh asked, enjoying the way his mood brightened as his idea took hold. His gray eyes danced, reminding her of the lighthearted boy he'd been, the one for whom she'd fallen hard.

"You could sell it," he said, sounding like a salesman himself. "The profit could go toward a retirement fund for your mother. And Drew would be free to pursue any career he wanted. Didn't you tell me he disliked the business?"

Leigh nodded and pretended to consider his proposal. "That's an idea."

"It would solve everything," Wade pointed out quickly, not giving her a chance to disagree. "Your family would be happy, and you'd be free to marry me and come to New York."

"Marry you?" Leigh said and experienced a bolt of pure joy. "You're asking me to marry you?"

Wade Conner, whom she'd always loved and whom she'd been on the verge of losing an hour ago, wanted to know if she'd marry him. And this wasn't just for old times' sake. She felt like dancing to Cotton-eyed Joe.

"Of course I'm asking you to marry me. After all, I do love you," Wade said, smiling indulgently. "But I know you'll need time to think about selling the store and leaving Kinley. Just don't take too long. And think about this, too."

Wade brought his head down to hers. His lips were incredibly soft, and he had barely touched them to hers when she snaked her arms around his neck. He pulled her closer and there wasn't even room to slip a sheet of paper between the length of their bodies. Leigh closed her eyes and let her feelings for him wash over her until there was no room in her thoughts for anyone but this man and this kiss. His tongue played with hers, and his hand tantalizingly caressed the soft skin near her breasts. And then, maddeningly, he drew back and she felt emptiness where his arms had been.

She opened her eyes in surprise, and he was smiling down at her. He was so close that she could see a little spot he had missed while shaving, so close that she could smell the fresh scent that was uniquely his, so close that she could barely tolerate that he wasn't closer. His gray eyes were dancing with hope, and his aquiline features were dear in his handsome face. She couldn't string him along any longer.

"Wade, I have a confession to make," she said. "I decided to sell the store and leave Kinley before you came over today."

Wade smiled at her admission, glad that she had finally forgiven herself, too. The time had come to put the past behind them where it belonged. "Then all you have to think about is whether you'll marry me. Will you?"

Leigh closed her eyes and saw Wade in a myriad of ways: as a reckless young man, as her first lover, as a man betrayed, as a grieving son, as the man she couldn't live without.

When she opened her eyes, everything seemed strangely bright. It was nearly seven, but the sun hadn't yet set and it bathed Kinley in light. It was as though, with the mystery solved, all the shadows had disappeared. Her heart felt light, too, when she looked at the man she would always love.

"Yes," she said simply and knew from the love shining in his eyes that the shadows were forever gone from their lives.

*   *   *   *   *

▼ SILHOUETTE
Sensation

COMING NEXT MONTH

DRAGONSLAYER Emilie Richards

He Who Dares

Thomas Stonehill had lost his faith in God and in himself, but he was doing the best he could and so was Garnet Anthony. But Garnet had made some enemies and Thomas knew he couldn't protect her unless she came to live with him. Trouble was, a preacher couldn't live in sin...

FINALLY A FATHER Marilyn Pappano

He had a daughter and he had a right to know. But it had been ten long years, once the secret was out would anyone forgive her? Would she find herself at the heart of a family...or on the outside looking in?

TWO FOR THE ROAD Mary Anne Wilson

Sister, Sister Duet

Jackson Graham had better things to do than baby–sit some mobster's mistress until she could testify and he let his beautiful witness know it. Ali didn't want to be around when he found out he had the wrong twin in his protective custody—Jack was just as dangerous as the bad guys!

SHADES OF WYOMING Ann Williams

When Julia Southern's car conked out in rural Wyoming, she didn't expect to be rescued by a suspicious cowboy right out of the wild west! After all, it was the 1990's...wasn't it? And why was Ryder McCall so suspicious and secretive?

COMING NEXT MONTH FROM

 **SILHOUETTE**

Intrigue

*Danger, deception and desire—
new from Silhouette...*

FOR LOVE OR MONEY M. J. Rodgers
DOMINOES Laura Gordon
LOST INNOCENCE Tina Vasilos
THE MASTER DETECTIVE Heather McCann

Special Edition

Satisfying romances packed with emotion

FOR THE BABY'S SAKE Christine Rimmer
C IS FOR COWBOY Lisa Jackson
ONE STEP AWAY Sherryl Woods
A DAD FOR BILLIE Susan Mallery
JAKE RYKER'S BACK IN TOWN Jennifer Mikels
THAT SPECIAL SUNDAY Maggi Charles

Desire

*Provocative, sensual love stories for the
woman of today*

AN OBSOLETE MAN Lass Small
THE HEADSTRONG BRIDE Joan Johnston
HOMETOWN WEDDING Pamela Macaluso
MURDOCK'S FAMILY Paula Detmer Riggs
A LAWLESS MAN Elizabeth Bevarly
SEDUCED Metsy Hingle

SLOW BURN
Heather Graham Pozzessere

Faced with the brutal murder of her husband, Spencer Huntington demands answers from the one man who should have them—David Delgado—ex-cop, her husband's former partner and best friend…and her former lover.

Bound by a reluctant partnership, Spencer and David find their loyalties tested by desires they can't deny. Their search for the truth takes them from the glittering world of Miami high society to the dark and dangerous underbelly of the city—while around them swirl the tortured secrets and desperate schemes of a killer driven to commit his final act of violence.

"Suspenseful…Sensual…Captivating…"

Romantic Times (USA)

MIRA